Catching Hell

Part 2: Destination
A Novel by Marc Watson

I hope you love
the Destination!
Marc Watson

Double Dragon Press

An Imprint of
Double Dragon Publishing
PO Box 54016
1-5762 Highway 7 East
Markham, Ontario L3P 7Y4 Canada
http://www.double-dragon-ebooks.com
http://www.double-dragon-publishing.com

ISBN-13: 9781790375585

A DDP First Edition November 26th, 2018

*

For River: As long as you're with me, I know I'll reach the destination better off than when I started. Also, you'll likely have built a death ray somewhere along the line…

Prologue:
Cutting Away a Piece of a Hole

There was once a beautiful tower here. It rose from the flowery meadow and stretched so high into the sky some swore that it had no end; a creation of the ancient, powerful ones.

They were wrong, of course. It had an end, and at that precarious top was a room of solitude where the sprightly entity known as Crystal Kokuou had sequestered herself for more than eight hundred years, seeking a place of peace and zen in order to find an answer to the question her beloved father had given to her: how can mankind maintain and serve the balance?

After her lover Ryu had finally passed away by playing chicken with Death and actually winning, she had seen the true extent that humans were capable of reaching. She had seen Embracers reach unimaginable levels of power, be it for evil or good, and all the time she had been assured that in the end, everyone still dies. Death had been the great equalizer. It was the balance keeper in all the universes.

But then Ryu had played the game against the Dark Stranger, and Death miscalculated both her lover's power, and his resolve to end things, regardless of the consequences. Yes, Ryu was still dead after all was said and done, but it was on his terms. Reason didn't matter to someone so determined.

She remembered that day so well. She had been in her Haven at the time, not in the tower that existed in the real world. Her Haven was her most perfect place in the world. It was so close to where she had been raised and loved so purely by her mother and father, where she had been taught to be a warrior in service of the balance.

Her Haven was also an unwitting protective shield against the horror Ryu had created with that gross and destructive wave of power that erupted from his mind.

The wave of unbridled Power swept the world, and suddenly the rules didn't apply. A man, a human man, had become more powerful than the governing forces of the universe. He had battled Death, and Death had flinched in a most spectacular way. The lives it cost were immeasurable. If not for the dumb luck of being in her Haven at the time, she had no doubt that she, his oldest friend and most trusted confidant through all the ages, would have been one of them.

After that point, when her period of mourning was over and every tear she'd ever cried was multiplied a thousand times, she returned to the tower to feel the real world for what it was, hide herself and her feelings, and shield everyone from her Power. After all, with the death of the original Ryuujin, wasn't she now the most powerful Embracer that there was? Although Ryu's son may argue that point, she knew that she could very well become a threat to everything she loved. Eventually, she was simply alone in the sky.

For centuries she sat; wondering about life, love, and everything in the universe. She never feigned herself smart enough to figure it out on her own, but she knew she was the best candidate left alive in the whole world to try.

She focused the Power more and more. She listened frequently to the Omnis, determining the waves Ryu had made and how far they stretched. She was shocked to learn just how much damage he'd done.

With the Omnis came the Est Vacuus. That was a truth no Embracer could escape when they reached her level. At first she fought it. She tried to shield herself from its awesome nothingness, but she failed, damaging her psyche to the point where it took days of agony to recover.

Then she attempted to understand it, but willingly accepting it into her mind and spirit was incredibly costly. At times it felt as if it was trying to consume her from the inside out, which it likely was. She was so full of the Power and the glory of the Omnis that she was particularly susceptible to the pain the Est Vacuus caused.

And then the epiphany struck her like a kick to the gut: she was being ravaged by the Est Vacuus, and yet she was still whole. Her voyages into trying to understand and balance the Est Vacuus in her life were a failure, but she was still successful in dancing close to it and coming out on the other side.

Slowly, methodically, the plan formed. The way to find the balance she needed. Within her was the strength to make it happen. It wasn't going to be easy, and it may kill her in the attempt, but she could no longer sit in the tower and await another force like Ryu to arise. She would either stop it, or she would be dead and leave the fate of the world on its path.

With more focus and strengthening, she began the journey into the depths of the warring factions of the universe. Using what she had learned with the countless years studying them, she became powerful enough to graze just enough of both the Omnis and the Est Vacuus to get what she needed: an encapsulated microscopic hint of the Nothing, bent to her will by her strength with the Omnis and the Power. Within her hand the war was fought, and so long as this fraction of a particle was warring with the Omnis around it, it didn't dissipate, or worse, react with the real world and suck a piece of it away.

Bit by bit, it came together. Soon, it was almost visible to the naked eye. A shimmering, translucent pocket of non-reality.

Eventually, after years and years of work and personal sacrifice, she felt it happen: the thin, imperceptible slice of the Est Vacuus she had stabilized in the world coalesced and became encapsulated. She no longer had to fight to keep it from imploding. It had balanced itself enough against the Omnis that naturally occurred in the world that she could finally breathe. She dreaded to think what she looked like after all of this work, or what would happen to her if she didn't have the Power in such large amounts to shut out the maddening feeling this hint of Est Vacuus would cause if she was to look at it.

Buoyed by her unprecedented success at a task that she doubted even Ryu could have completed (not that he would have ever been stupid enough to try), she used her new skills with the Power to mold the Omnis at war around this infinitesimal Est Vacuus into the only logical shape she could. The universe was cyclical, and she had her plan.

The long, thin blade of shimmering nothing took shape. From the sacrifice of an ancient item of focus, she was able to craft a handle that could manipulate the Est Vacuus like the weapon it was.

When it sliced, the outer Everything forced aside whatever it came in contact with, exposing the Nothing inside. When it met something real, it would eliminate it. In essence, she had created a hand-held portal into the worst kind of Hell anyone could ever imagine. Doing something like this willingly was almost certainly a sign of madness, but she still felt sane in her resolve. Her father's voice echoed over and over: we serve the balance.

So with the tower gone save for a few reminders of her time there in aged bricks in a circle on the ground, she set out with the weapon she'd made. She knew full well who was going to get it. There was never a doubt. All things were cyclical. That wasn't important.

What was important was not the enemy she needed to find, but

the champion she needed to make.

Chapter 1: A Damn Good Reason

The things that he'd witnessed over the last few weeks had turned the young man named Aryu O'Lung'Singh into something resembling a wrecked shell of a human with wings. When the massive battle station called HOME that had been launching the army he was so hell-bent on destroying was lost and his escape in the small boat was firmly in motion, Aryu let the truth of all that had just occurred sink in. He didn't have a reason why it had happened yet, but apparently it had, and had done so quickly.

In a short time Crystal Kokuou, the once-immortal Keeper of the Dragon Spirit, had affected his life like few others. She didn't care about his leathery, dragon-like wings in the slightest. She had helped him get past the fear of his youth and accept the strength of his manhood in the form of the Power, in a way that his year away with his blood-brother Johan never could have come close to. She had showed him that not all who had command of the Power, the fearsome ability mankind had embraced to take control of natural forces in a way many would have called madness, were to be feared (at least, not until she had betrayed them, it seemed). She had put him instantly at ease and comfortable with the task at hand, as intimidating as it seemed, and had done so with just the right amount of ego-boosting flirtatiousness.

Now it appeared she was never what she seemed, leading Aryu to wonder if it was her plan all along to help him tap the Power only to leave when it was at its most dangerous: different and uncontrolled. He knew now what had to be done to reach that point. He had all the faith in the world that he could do it again. The question now was, would he? Did he want to pursue this course any further while knowing that she was the enemy all along? If it was a tactic she was using to help further her ends, it may have been a part of her future plans as well. She may need to use what she taught Aryu for some other dark purpose.

It was a conglomeration of distinct possibilities that he considered here, chopping through the waves on the long trip back to shore in the small boat he and his companions had secured before HOME sank. Thus far, it seemed most of the awaiting attack ships in the area had no idea what they were doing, or that they were too small to worry about, and were either sitting idle or beginning to travel northwest, likely to the mouth of the Vein River. This battle Aryu found himself in the middle of, a battle with machines long thought destroyed, seemed to have found a brief moment of respite.

In his weaker moments, he considered asking Nixon of the Great Fire and Ash what to do, but always ended up thinking better of it. The inhumanly massive phoenix warrior had been sent to kill Aryu, but now he sat as his friend, teacher, and ally (though at this moment Nixon was nearly unrecognizable in his rage). On the deck of HOME they had each feared that Nixon might lose control in his rage and unleash his considerable magic, which would have tipped off Izuku to the non-dormant powers still possessed by the phoenix, but Nixon had maintained his head and only the ground-shaking scream from the top of the gigantic sinking ship had shown his anger at the way things had played out.

Crystal's son, the quiet and calm Sho, piloted the craft as the other two sulked in their own way. If Sho was horribly distraught at what his bizarrely younger-looking mother had apparently done, he never gave a sign of it. He simply carried on as if it was just another bump in the road, letting the other two have their silence.

Aryu and Nixon sat in the front of the boat facing each other but not speaking. Aryu had a million questions, mostly why it was so obvious that it was Crystal who had betrayed them (or honestly, exactly what that betrayal was) because that was a piece of information he simply didn't have (the reoccurring theme of these adventures of the last few weeks once again rearing its ugly head. How many times had he been stymied by a lack of information and a myriad of new questions?)Nixon locked himself into his own glowering head behind his long flame-shimmering hair and did nothing but emanate heat and anger.

It was his obvious foul mood that did an excellent job of stopping Aryu from telling him about what Crystal had done with him; the abilities she had nurtured and helped him tap in such a short time. If Aryu even hinted at the possibility that he had touched upon the awesome strength of the Power, Nixon was liable to simply swing his mighty sword once and be done with this whole debacle, especially once he discovered that it was Crystal Kokuou that had helped him do it.

Perhaps Sho might be a touch more inclined to help him, but as of yet the opportunity to ask him had not occurred.

Why Nixon had even held back now was another thing Aryu didn't understand. If he was so certain that Crystal had betrayed them to the enemy, why hide behind this lie anymore? She would have told Izuku, Sho's older half-brother and apparent commander of the abhorrent army, long ago that Nixon was still fully imbued with his abilities. Izuku had injected a drug into Sho and Crystal, making them both powerless and mortal, but Nixon was a different creature all together: a being made up entirely of the Power. He was created by the hands of a God thousands upon thousands of years before the Power was even a known thing.

So why hold back? Why not step into the masses of the enemy and destroy them all with the flames of divinity he was comprised of?

Hours passed in the little escape skiff, and soon night came. A small light on the hull of the boat was all they had to navigate by, but Sho was no slouch at this and simply carried on unaffected. Aryu was very hungry and was waiting for some sign of what was ahead, but only the rush of air through his wings and the whine of the electric engine as they went were around him.

Aryu, despite his hunger and now growing thirst, had begun to drift in and out of sleep. The length and events of the long day were catching up to him at last, coupled with the hypnotic sway of the ocean. He was almost fully out when Sho said, in his now-infuriatingly casual way, "Land-ho boys. Looks like we'll be on solid ground in the hour."

Aryu looked to the horizon they were heading towards, and through the rise and fall of the sea swells he could faintly make out a smattering of lights in the distance. He supposed they could be ships just as easily as they could be land, but he trusted Sho's thousands of years of experience. He tended not to question immortals (though perhaps he should revise that policy in the wake of recent events). If he said they were about to make landfall, then it was likely so.

Nixon didn't acknowledge the statement, or even move an inch. He just sat, black/red eyes glowing in the dark, a soft glow creeping its way to the surface of his onyx armor and pale, freckled skin in small waves. It was as if the great auroras of the North were locked inside of him.

"I'll make for a large patch of black that I saw between lights," Sho declared. "It's the best I can do to assume that it won't be inhabited by anyone we don't want to know of our arrival. Still, I'd be prepared, just in case I'm wrong." Aryu questioned if he still had an ounce of fight left in him if it came to that, his body saying *no* and his mind leaning towards agreeing, but he supposed there was little to do about it now. They couldn't just float around until a plan came, fly away without giving themselves up, or head up the Vein River, as it would be the most likely place to be crawling with more of the army of the Old.

Or were they the army of the New now?

Izuku had taken his mechanical monstrosity of an army and injected fresh terror in the form of Team Yosuru, a collection of Embracers of the Power who had turned to his twisted side and were to be spearheading the assault into the north. A combination of horrors from the past set loose on an unsuspecting world. Aryu was rushing to confront an unholy union between the two things he'd been raised since birth to fear. The machine, and the Power. Everything fell into place so perfectly. Aryu knew that if he had his way, neither one of them would survive this mission.

Aryu had spent much of the sea voyage thinking of his friend Johan. It was likely that he was still in the heart of the Paieleh Valley, but for how much longer was something he didn't know. How long was he in the mountain village of Huan where the two had originally said they'd meet? How fast was he traveling? Was he alone or in a group? Was he alright, waiting for Aryu's return anxiously? How was he getting along with Esgona, if he was even still with him? Was he forcing himself to endure the company of their childhood tormentor simply because as far as they knew, they were the last three remaining survivors of the village of Tan Torna Qu-ay? Izuku's army had seen to that with a senseless and brutal attack by a High-Yield bomb.

When the once-distant lights came closer, Sho killed the throttle and slowed the craft down to a crawl. Aryu looked at him wonderingly in the dark. Nixon frowned on relentlessly.

"Aryu, I think we'll need your assistance before we arrive," Sho said, searching the dark shore in the distance for something unseen. "Would you be alright flying high above and seeing what you can, if there's something waiting for us or not?"

Aryu hadn't considered this, but whether landing by sea or taking to the air, they were just as easily detectable. So if they were going to be found out, they may as well risk getting a better look at what was going on. Aryu agreed. Nixon said nothing and gave no indication if he approved or not. He continued to sit, brooding wordlessly at the waves around them.

Aryu fastened the powerful sword Shi Kaze firmly between his wings and stood shakily on the bow of the boat. Aryu couldn't fly like a bird due to his weight; however, with the ample wind of the sea and with the gliding help Nixon had been giving him during their adventure so far, he knew it would be easy to get high enough to do as Sho asked. He spread his wings, faced the wind, and was easily whisked off of his feet like a kite without a string.

At first as he climbed he feared his ability to find them in the vast water once more, but as he left he heard the electric whine of the boat motor come alive again, heading along with him. The light on the hull was also visible.

That, and the soft red hue of one of its surlier passengers.

Satisfied he could find them again, he began using the Nixon-improved methods of speedier flight and headed for shore, thankful for the rush of the wind in his ears. No matter how much he loathed these abominations that had labeled him an outsider all of his life, the feeling of flight was always a welcome one.

The moonlight above made things slightly clearer as he went. He was reminded of flying above the Valley of Smoke so many days before, after he'd parted company with Johan the first time. The colors were eerily familiar, despite being so far from home. Only now the desert landscapes were replaced with that of the ocean waves.

Aryu could see the lights off to either side of him where the land met the water, though there were much less than he thought there'd be, likely because there was no one left except what may remain of the army of the Old. Aryu had hoped they'd have all moved north but knew that wasn't likely. It didn't make sense to leave nothing at all behind, just in case some foolish and weakened force decided to attack from the rear.

It was a fairly consistent row of lights until the dark patch he was rapidly approaching now. Once he'd reached the center of the dark spot and beyond, the reason for its existence was much clearer, and the thought made Aryu sick.

He could see it in the dark far below him now. A deep feeling of uneasiness consumed him as his eyes followed the darkness in a circular fashion that stretched out into the distance ahead and all around him.

It was a blast sight. Once, at the epicenter of the dark circle, there was likely a town or village just like his. A place that had simply been erased, along with every living thing in it. When Izuku's metallic minions had first arrived, they'd begun by peppering the coast with the bombs like the one used to destroy Tan Torna Qu-ay, his own home far off in the distance that looked just like this. Dark. Empty. Lifeless. His home had known it was coming. They at least had a warning. A moment to pray and hopefully make peace. What about this place, where the enemy had first arrived? Had they known what was happening? Did they have a warning at all?

Enough! he thought to himself. *This doesn't help. I know what I needed to know.* He turned and went back the way he'd came and soon was back out to sea, searching for his friends.

He found them with little effort and landed back on the small deck. Nixon would be no help now, so he simply focused on Sho. "It's a bomb site," Aryu told him. "Leftover from the blast of one of the weapons that destroyed my home. It's nothing but a huge black circle, wiped out and polished clean of anything. If there were any enemies there, I didn't see them."

"Well, I supposed that works in our favor. Better to land there and trudge across the wasteland than into something were we know they'll be. I'd be inclined to say we go there."

The thought of hiking across a huge and dark void where once there had been children playing and mothers calling after them made Aryu's blood run cold, but he saw the truth in Sho's reasoning. If there were any of the Old there, they likely would be easy to spot and easier to fight. Aryu agreed and Sho pointed the nose of the hull to the center of the space and continued on. Nixon simply continued being Nixon, lost in whatever a being of a God's creation gets lost in.

Shortly after, they came to a stop a short distance from shore where they could now see the waves crash on the black, hard surface in the faint light of the moon and stars. No beaches were left; the sand was either blasted away or melted to small shards of glass. They could see nothing good or bad coming to greet them.

Sho took the lead. "We get off here. If we reach land and set off some kind of trip wire or alarm, at least we won't all be sitting ducks in a boat. We'll spread out and see what we see when we get there. Can you swim?"

Aryu nodded. The truth was that his wings worked just as well in the water as they did in the air, only slower. "The better question is can you two? How do you plan on getting there dressed in full armor?"

The scene in the doomed plane that they had managed to crash into HOME played out again. Sho and Nixon had leapt from the craft as it fell like a missile and headed into the ocean. Aryu had been paired with the petite Crystal, and had shown fear when Sho hurdled out into space covered in heavy battle armor and carrying his massive bladed shield. At the time Crystal had told him not to worry about it but offered no explanation as to why. Sure enough, when they'd met up with each other once again, after the short but memorable battle through the burning superstructure, Sho was wearing his armor as if it hadn't just gone swimming in a warm salt water sea. He hadn't really thought about it, even in the hours before they'd reached shore, but since the topic was on them again, now maybe he'd at least get an answer.

Sho came around from behind the controls and looked down at Aryu. "Well, I admit that the shield is a bit of a pain, but the armor itself won't be an issue."

With a wry smile, Sho set the shield down on the deck of the cresting boat and clasped his hands together.

It was difficult to tell what precisely he was doing in the poor light of the night, but soon Aryu could faintly make out the dark tones of the armor slowly disappearing, almost as if it was melting off of Sho's body and into nothingness. After a minute, Sho stood before the two of them wearing nothing but canvas pants and a knit shirt with wooden toggle buttons. The armor was completely gone.

Aryu didn't know what to say. Even after everything, something like what he'd just witnessed was still hard to believe, and that went double for someone who had supposedly lost any kind of mystical power he may have had.

Naturally, Sho expected this reaction and took no time in explaining it. "That, my young friend, is what they call Makashi armor, and as you can see, it's a very handy thing to have right now."

Aryu was still speechless, waiting for the answer to the question that didn't need to be asked. "It's not a product of the Power. Well, not really anyway," Sho explained, picking up the great shield once more and prepping to leave. "Once, thousands of years ago, in the time of my father, there was a clan of warriors called the Makashi, famous for their prowess in battle and their light and nearly indestructible armor.

"The armor is closer to being called a living thing than it is anything else, although even that makes it seem like more than it is." He turned his back to Aryu and lifted his shirt slightly. Even in the dark Aryu could see a thin dark line running the length of Sho's spine. It even reflected what light there was from the moon and stars. Aryu had no doubt that if seen a little clearer it would have that same deep shade of red as the full set of armor was. "It's forged from metals and the Power in unison, but the Power of another, not one's own, which is likely why I can still control it. The Makashi never made it for just anyone. Only the most elite samurai of the Shoguns of what was once called Japan. You know of it?"

Aryu did. The birthplace of Sho and Izuku's father, the legendary 'God' and immortal warrior Ryu Tokugawa, and the source of most of the stories regarding him. In the years since it existed, however, the actual location of what was once had been lost or confused. Soon, it was nothing but a place of myth. "The Shoguns ruled Japan and commanded their own personal warriors, the samurai. The Makashi armor was forged for them, and in return the Makashi family was made very powerful and wealthy.

"However, by the time of my father, there was only one or two Makashi left. The armor itself is eternal, and to that end, perfect for those of us who tend to last a little longer than others.It can be passed on to someone else, just like a real suit of armor. The armor lives in its natural, passive state until called upon. Then, it molds and forms itself to the user like a shell, growing and adapting as the user does.

"The armor I have was passed to my father from the last known Makashi. When I defeated Ryu, it went on to me. Not that he really needed it anymore, anyway. He'd long since outgrown need of it, and I believe he held onto it for sentimental reasons."

"So there's no way I could get my hands on some, then?"Aryu asked, intrigued by the possibilities a retractable armor would afford him. "Other than someone passing it on to me."

Sho shook his head. "Not anymore. That last Makashi died before teaching another the secrets. Handed down is the only way, and there's not many others left in the world with it. Me, and one other I know of…" Sho drifted off into silence, as if the answer was obvious, though Aryu didn't catch on.

"He made some for Crystal," Nixon said suddenly, startling Aryu. Nixon was on his feet and standing by the gunnels of the boat. Aryu hadn't even heard him move. "A gift years ago, when Ryu was in the midst of his insanity to die.

"I knew the lone Makashi from his father's time. A quiet, strong man. He helped me learn the limits and weaknesses of the armor. He explained the intricacies of it. Helped me get to know it. And from that, I can say one thing unequivocally: Crystal's armor is easily the strongest, lightest and most well-crafted Makashi armor I've ever seen, making her that much harder for me to kill."

With that revelation, Nixon took one step into the sea with a splash followed by a sharp hiss of steam.

Aryu watched wide eyed and frightened as he never resurfaced. Soon, Sho took his place, shield in hand."Don't worry. He'll be fine. His armor is a part of him, as much as an arm or leg.He could just as easily swim to shore, but I think he wanted a few more minutes of privacy. I supposed he's just enigmatic like that. I suspect he'll be closer to his usual self once we reach land."

Then Sho was in after him, side stroking his way to shore. Aryu, tired and beaten from the day that was, soon joined them.

The water was cool and refreshing, and instantly transported his mind to the pools below the towering Tortria Den where he'd grown up swimming and relaxing with his friend. He briefly wondered if Tortria Den still stood, or if the valley walls had collapsed once the bomb shockwave hit.

The memory of home wandered to how Tan Torna Qu-ay had ended, and his part in it. His role led into Nixon's, and he tried to picture the phoenix picking the limp and lifeless Aryu and Esgona up and winging them away; a decision that flew into the face of all that Nixon was created to do. A cold chill that had nothing to do with the water ran up Aryu's spine. A lingering question about Nixon still needed to be asked, and before things got too much deeper, now was the time. The events on the plane and HOME had passed, and now the next chapter was about to begin. Aryu respected Nixon too much to let it slide anymore. Even if this time it could mean Aryu's death. Nixon had to know, and had things to answer for before Aryu would take another step.

Ahead, even with just one arm, Sho was surprisingly fast and was already near shore; a testament to his strength. Aryu carried on, swearing to himself to one day see if the Den still stood.

Chapter 2: A Question of Faith

Once on shore, Sho and Aryu began looking around quickly for the first sign of trouble. Although they remained on edge, they saw none.

The ground around them was horrible. It was sharp and black, a collection of glass shards and broken fissures. The image of families at play on a picturesque beach in this same spot came and went into his head in an instant, but that instant was enough to sink his heart unfathomably low.

After a few minutes of waiting, the first plumes of steam rose up from the waves. Sho looked out into the dark, looking for the enemy as Aryu watched the glowing monster emerge from the ocean. At first it was only a bobbing head, followed by the massive body, and soon Nixon stepped comfortably to the shore. Stream was rising like smoke all around him and engulfed him like a cloud. Aryu noted that although he'd just taken a leisurely walk on the ocean floor, he was as dry as a bone by the time he made it to where they were standing in the black wasteland.

"Anythin', Sho?" he asked. Sho shook his head. It appeared they were in the clear for the moment.

"What took you so long?" Sho asked, likely testing the phoenix to see if he was closer to normal than he was when he had gone into the drink.

"I had t'take a few detours, talk t'old friends, clear my head. Sorry t'keepya' waiting," was the reply, followed by a shared smile between the two. Once the relaxing smile was on his face, Aryu was instantly at greater ease. He may not be in the best of moods, but at least he was closer to the man Aryu liked so much. That was enough for now.

Sho continued, "So, how are the fish?"

Aryu caught a glimpse of something pass between the two old

friends before Nixon replied, "Fine. Passive as always. They warn of dark times ahead and t'tread lightly."

Sho smirked but said nothing more. Whatever it was they were talking about, it wasn't for Aryu.

"What's the plan?" Aryu asked, eager to get into the conversation to attempt to steer it the way he wanted. Sho looked to Nixon, wondering the same thing.

"We cross this wasteland t'the far side tonight. We see wha' we see when we get there. I'd not risk goin' t'one side o're the other yet. If it is as vacant as I hope it is when we get there, we hunker down and let ourselves get some much-needed rest. Tomorrow, we start the hunt up this valley. Do ya' know where we are, Sho?"

"I do. It's the mouth of a great river called the Vein. It goes on for hundreds of miles until it reaches the Blood Sea." Aryu perked up instantly at the mention of the familiar name. The Blood Sea! That meant that, although he'd taken the long way, he might still be able to meet up with Johan.

"The river valley is very wide. Almost imperceptible as a valley, really. When I was young it was a huge inlet that nearly split this part of the world in half.

"To the far west is the beginning of the Westlands. To the east is the bottom of the Great Range all the way back to my home. North beyond the Blood Sea, I can't tell you. It's been too long to trust what was is still what is, if that makes sense."

"Tha's fine. That's more than enough t'get started. So, this river valley is a corridor t'all points north?" Nixon asked, gears clearly turning as something began coming together in his mind.

Sho agreed with the statement. "One could go through the Westlands if needs be, but if we're talking about moving an army, even one as advanced as this, it would have been a hassle to move through the mountains found there, and there was no way anything, no matter how advanced, was getting through the Great Range and the Hymleahs."

"So they're heading north. That's for certain." Nixon began, mostly talking to himself. "How far is the Blood Sea, Sho? And do ya' know anything about it tha' could help?"

"It's not a short hike, that's for sure. A week on foot.Perhaps more.Hard to say. I don't know what lies between here and there. If we could get a ride out somehow, or perhaps you two could fly out and leave me…"

"Tha's not goin' t'happen right now," Nixon said, cutting him off. "My feet are stayin' planted firmly on the ground."

Sho looked at him questioningly, the same thought going through his head as it was Aryu's, but Sho didn't press the matter. Yet.

"Anyway," he continued, "the path from here is lush and green. This was a large agricultural area all the way up to the Sea. Towns once lined the river to the west, and there were a few large settlements on the Sea itself. Given enough time, I wouldn't doubt that there is a city there by now."

He looked at Aryu for the next part. "Provided they haven't reached that far yet, that would likely be where your friend will be, Aryu. Fingers crossed they aren't walking into Izuku-occupied land when they come out of the Paieleh Valley." Aryu noted and appreciated the fact that he said *when* and not *if*. There was enough *if* in his head already to hear it spoken by another.

"Alright, here's the plan fellas'. We're goin' north, and we'll stay t'the east side along the base of the larger mountains. The trek'll be harder, but it's less likely tha' we'll come across any major interference. When we catch up t'the army, we'll work out the next step at tha' time. We go by foot. No machines or carts. We've seen tha' no one 'ere is any more honorable than another, and if they've got people on their side now like the ones we saw on HOME, no one can be trusted to be on ours." A jab at Crystal? Aryu wasn't sure, but considering his blunt personality and the recent events, he had to assume it was."With luck, we'll meet those bastards again and get what we need before we finish'em and their leader."

Nixon, his point clear and his stride strong, led the way out of the rubble with a head of steam driving him north. Sho looked at Aryu with his passive glance and shrugged, following after the beast with long sure steps.

Aryu didn't move. He watched them leave, growing farther away. He knew they'd turn around and notice him. Nixon, for one, was drawn to Aryu like a magnet, thanks to his need to kill him.

After a moment they stopped, looking back to see Aryu staring out to sea, clearly not following or caring. "Oy!" Nixon called back. "Ya' comin'?"

Aryu didn't respond. He knew what time it was. He feared it, but he knew.

Nixon came back, passing Sho as he did so. "Aryu! We rest after the blast site! Now we walk!"

"No," was all Aryu replied.

Nixon came back now, only a step or two from the young man and his defiance. "No?"

Aryu turned to meet him. "No."

Aryu feared Nixon as much as he liked and respected him. He respected the drive and the honor this man-thing had. He respected and also feared his strength. He didn't, however, enjoy defying Nixon now. Before, when they first met, it was simply instinct. Now, weeks later, they were friends. They'd fought and suffered together. They were on the cusp of the bond between two people built through joy and hardships. The same bond Aryu had with Johan. Now, Aryu knew it was time to test that fragile new connection, and the loss of it almost certainly meant his death.

"And why 'no'?" Nixon asked. His eyes weren't angry, even while glowing fiercely. They were, however looking for a quick and concise answer to justify the delay.

"Because you're wrong, Nixon, and I don't want to follow you into a war with no more of a reason than you telling me to."

"This is a war ya' wanted to fight, Aryu," was the steady reply. "Whether I'm here or not, ye' would be in it still, wouldn't ya'?"

"Why are you here, Nixon?"

"Pardon?"

"Why are you here? Why are you chasing Izuku and his army? You are a weapon of your God. You have a task to fulfill, a task-I'd like to add—that I thank you whole—heartedly for not finishing, but a task clear and written none-the-less. Why fight this war? For me?For the people here? Why are you suddenly wrapped up in this?You told me a lot of stories while we went east to find Crystal. You never once told me one like this; one where you abandoned your purpose to defend anyone against an unrelated obstacle. Each time, amidst the chaos around you, you did your job and then rested.

"Now, the person you pinned all your hope on answering your multitudes of questions has apparently betrayed us which, by the way, I want a clear reason as to *why* you two seem to think that so readily, since it seems to be something I'm not in on. Now, what do you do? Where are your answers? Why are you chasing an enemy and fighting a war when all you have to do is cut me in half and call it a day?"

Aryu's wings spread in the darkness and his chest heaved as he spit out the words. Nixon had made it perfectly clear what his task was from the start: kill Aryu, or get answers. The answer part of that equation was seemingly lost until Aryu was told otherwise. Why keep going? That 'why' was what bothered Aryu. Why defy his God? Why keep this up?

"You're right, Aryu," he said in a calm tone. "I've not been in a situation like this before. I've not been so conflicted about my purpose or creation before. But, I am now, and I'll tell'ye why, and if it's enough for 'ya, indeed, for us both, then we keep goin'.If it's not, on my God's honor I'll strike ya' down right now and be done with this whole damn thing."

Aryu didn't waver. He simply nodded firmly in agreement. He was surprised to find that he wanted a good answer more for his own validation in continuing than he did for staying alive. The revelation, although sobering, wasn't entirely surprising to him now.

"I'mma weapon of God, Aryu. My task each time I've awakened has been clear. My faith is absolute and my cause is just.

"I admit though, that in the past I've often questioned my task as I saw it. Not everyone I've set out t'find has been outright evil. Barely any of'em, if you'll recall. They were mostly good people doin' bad things 'ferthe sake of righteousness. Their reasonin' was compellin'. They didn't just set out to be conquerors and destroyers. The *believed*tha' their course was the right one. Straight t'their core. When I met those people and my task was clear in their eyes, I was the evil one to 'em. I was the bad guy. I was the enemy t'thecause they'd taken.

"I've been that enemy often. I've questioned if it was true on more'n one occasion. I've fought 'em and won each time, watching 'em die clingin' on 'their belief that they died in the cause of goodness tha' they believed.

"Here though, in this place, face t'face with Aryu O'Lung'Singh and his pain and confusion, I'll'ne question it again.

"God granted me free will, Aryu, just as he did all His children. It is His infinite and merciful gift t'everyone, even now long after he's been gone. Now, as I watch ya' defy me and my idea, even though it's exactly wha' you'd be doin' whether I was here or not, I've chosen t'exercise that free will and I choose to use it for 'ya, not against 'ya.

"I don't believe God is wrong, but why grant me, a weapon of 'is own creation, free will unless I was meant t'use it? I know 'ya. I've seen yer' honor and yer' heart.I can't in good conscience, in the shadow of my free will, ignore those things. I see ya' standin' there, ready t'die by m'hand, and although my creator demanded of me I do just tha' and take yer' life, we both know you've done nothin' to deserve it. You're not my enemy, Aryu. Our paths are the same, and until you and only you prove me otherwise, I'll raise no hand against ya.'"

Nixon knelt before Aryu, dirt and glass cracking beneath his large knee as he did so, and at this height he could meet Aryu in the eye. "I have not and will never do what I was made for based on what *may* happen. Free will gives everyone the option."I am here because I see innocents like ye' and yer' friends sufferin', good people like yer' family dyin' needlessly, and an enemy that is far too powerful attemptin' to dominate everythin' he sees. I can'na get the answers I seek now, or possibly ever, but in my time 'ere, I can make a difference. Until I know for certain by Divine proclamation that I'm not supposed t'be doing this, I will continue on this course. Your course. I serve the balance, and now the balance is shifting too far one way for me t'ignore."

Nixon knelt there looking into Aryu's eyes, looking for what may come next. At first, there was still silence.

"Crystal taught me to use the Power."

The words were out before Aryu could stop them, but in this instance of heartfelt honesty, the truth had to be known. He wanted to know why she had betrayed them, but he also wanted them to know that he had a very close tie with her as well. He had also decided that if he was to die here as he suspected he would, better it be because of the truth.

Nixon showed no outward reaction, but Sho could be heard making a passing sigh. Then, Nixon was up to his feet and full height once more, and a moment later the broadsword was out, tip inches from Aryu's face once more. "I know," he said in response. "I could feel it buildin' every time ya' wer' alone with 'er. She might've thought I couldn't or wouldn't, but I did. I knew. I know abou' the moment on the plane. I know it all. And here ya' still stand."

"With a sword in my face."

"Yes, but not through it." Nixon relaxed a bit, but the blade never moved. "Listen Aryu, just because I know ya' and like ya', doesn't mean I won't do what I must if needed. At the first sign of you doin' anythin' even close to goin' against my mission, ya' would have been dead. All yer' tellin' me now will result in is lettin' ya' know wha' will happen if ya' do let it get the best of ya'. Once ya' tap into the Power, it is very hard t'shuttha' tap off.

"Your life, indeed the lives of many, rest on the fact that ya' don't go one step further. It'll be hard. It will test ya'. Ya' will be tempted in the days and weeks t'come. But ya' also have the Shi Kaze. It can still be all you'll e'er need on its own. Remember wha' I've shown ya'. Wha' I have yet to teach ya'. There is a world of things to be learned in a regular lifetime, without the Power to aid yer' direction. A mountain of good ya' can do with yer' bare hands. You don't need the Power t'get what ya' want. Ya' just need a good heart and a strong will, two things I know ye' have in abundance.

"I don't wanna kill ya', Aryu, but I'll not hesitate for a moment if I have to. I asked ya' when we first met, and I'll ask ya' again now, in the midst of these newfound understandins'; do ya' believe me?"

"I do, Nixon of the Great Fire and Ash. I believe every word you say."

Aryu extended his hand to the fire-man, knowing it was likely going to hurt. Nixon smirked, reminded of the old man in the bar not so long ago, and reached out to clasp the young man's hand in return after lowering his sword. It was hot, no doubt about that, but not crippling. Maybe after a bit, but for now Aryu just thought of it as a passing pain to mark a lasting bond. Nothing great, especially friendship, was ever obtained without sacrifice.

Hands released and meager equipment secured, the three headed off north, chasing an enemy none of them thought they could defeat. Even with HOME destroyed, there were still countless mechanical soldiers already ahead of them, as well as the mysterious Team Yasuku; the enigmatic and powerful Izuku, and now possibly Crystal Kokuou; knower of all the truths and tricks they'd be likely to employ.

Still, like those in the Paieleh Valley, they walked on despite the exhaustion and taxing day that was now behind them. They saw no enemy and when they reached the far end of the horrific blast zone, a large grove of trees of a kind Aryu had never seen before acted as their shelter, with Nixon promising to watch over them as they rested up for the hunt to come.

Sho and Aryu settled in and prepared to get some rest. Not, however, before Aryu finished this day with all the answers. "So fellas," he said, drawing Nixon's attention and Sho's ire at not being allowed to sleep yet. "Who wants to tell me about Crystal?"

A sad look on Nixon's face and a look of passive non-interest from Sho. "He does," Sho spit out at last, tossing his hand at Nixon before falling asleep.

Chapter 3: Unification

"I've come across Crystal many times in my life, and I've always been amazed at 'er ability t'soldier through everythin' she's seen," began Nixon as Sho fell asleep instantly, not wanting to hear this tale.

"Her father, as I've said, was an amazin' and honorable man. I can't say I've e'er been completely behind 'is mission in life t'spread the word of the Power t'alltha' would hear it, but if he'd lived long, like his daughter 'as, he may 'ave succeeded in bringin' bout his vision peacefully, instead of the twisted wreck of abuse it became in certain times afterwards.

"The good Lord had other plans for'im, though. He died saving 'er life, and in doin' so saved millions, but the seed was sewn then and there; Crystal would'nah completely connect n'truste'eryone she met 'fer fear of losin'em.

"The following years of 'er life didn't help at all as she became more powerful with the help of Ryu and 'is still-young command o'the Power. 'Er mother, aunt and cousin were lost along the way t'one horrible encounter after another. They died, all powerful Embracers in ther' own right, and she lived on, now the last of 'er family. As 'er bond with Ryu grew, so did 'er hint of mistrust at the man he became. Over the decades, they were apart and together like a young datin' couple, and when they stayed together, having their son and then daughter, Emerald, Ryu did what she always feared he would; he left 'er forever in 'is ridiculous quest to find a meaningful end to 'is life.

"Then, of course, he found it at the hands of tha' man there," Nixon indicated the deep-in-sleep (so it seemed) Sho, "and it all went to Hell.

"At first she thought her son 'ad actually killed 'im, until she realized it wasn't true, learnin' that Death had denied 'im 'is earned rest. That, of course, created the perfect storm of rage and blindness tha' Ryu unleashed on the world, and the rest is 'istory.

"I met with Crystal after I was awakened by Ryu's action, and although she was clearly in a tragic amount of pain, she put on 'er strong face and tried t'deal with the truth like the warrior she is, but it came at a price.

"She is a good person, but given enough time, the will of good in someone can break down. It's a 'orrible thing t'say, but it's true. The number of Adragons I've met and heard the story of is testament t'that. For Crystal, I'd say it took longer than anyone could 'ave thought, but it seems tha'er will is finally broken.

"I know she's betrayed us 'cause I've been expectin' it from 'er since the day I met 'er. She'll follow the path she deems correct."

"Why?" Aryu asked, exhaustion at bay for the time. "What makes you so sure? What is she doing that could possibly make you think this?"

"'Cause the most logical place for 'er to be is at 'er son's side, and mine, to get wha' she wants. She says she wants t'end this fight after they took her power, but I doubt she'd 'ave even given a moment's thought to joinin' us if that hadn't happened. She is mentally beyond this world, happy in 'er cocoon of 'er own makin', poking 'er head out t'make sure the world hasn't fallen away from the sun or somethin' else she likely coulda' stopped but chose not to.

"I've been suspicious of 'er intentions the whole time, but my need for answers, which I'd like to point out she knows I'm after but 'as conveniently avoided answerin', blinded me. Every day is new territory t'me, a weakness she's exposed t'the world now."

"But what makes you think she's *betrayed* us? Not just left to find her own path? Maybe she thinks she can find a cure and stop Izuku another way?"

"Because Aryu, you've seen proof of 'er betrayal. If t'were I who was with 'er when ya' encountered Izuku, I'd 'ave known right away what 'appened. His sword told me the truth the moment ya' mentioned it."

Nixon didn't wait for the question and simply launched into it. "It's 'ardt'explaint'someone who 'asn't tasted it, but the Omnis and Est Vacuus are states of reality so far above and beyond what ye' see around ya' now it's unimaginable. As 'ard as infinity is to grasp as a measurement of distance, absolute nothingness 'n absolute everythin' are 'ard to grasp as states of bein'. They are awesome in scope, 'n terrifyin' in nature." Aryu agreed, twitching in place at the thought of that kind of otherworldly power.

"That said, t'not only graze these things, but t'actually grasp them, manipulate'em somehow and mold 'emt'yer' needs is so frightenin' tha' I doubt Ryu Tokugawa or any before 'imcould'ave done so." Nixon didn't mention his creator God directly, but the implication was clearly there.

"So somehow, in ways unfathomable to me, a sword was made tha' taps into the Est Vacuus and made its 'orrific existence into a weapon. I can tell ya' the truth as I see it, Aryu: tha' fact puts a fear into me I didna' know was possible."

Anything powerful enough to make Nixon say those words was more than Aryu needed to ever know existed, and he'd faced it so recklessly, thinking it as something less than it was. "And you know it was her that made it?"

"Aye. The Est Vacuus isn't somethin' one can reach with enough time and patience. I'd say tha' maybe two or three people e'er could do it on this bafflin' level. There is not, 'owever, a doubt in my mind tha' she'd be one of'em, and I can guarantee tha' all the others foolish enough t'do so are dead." Nixon didn't illustrate how he knew this, but Aryu took him at his word.

"And no one else could have lived this long and done it? A person who's stayed the course and eluded your knowing?" Aryu knew the answer, but wanted to hear the words.

"There are no others tha' would do this, Aryu. I'm terrified of it, Aryu. And ya' should be, too. No one else would dare. Nah Ryu. Nah others tha'ave come and gone. Nah others like me.No one. If ya' get anythin' from this, make it tha'."

"Others like you?" Aryu asked. Nixon briefly looked disappointed in himself, like he let a secret slip, but only a small one.

"Oh aye. Dinna' think I'm an only child, Aryu. There 'ave been others, but none tha' serve the same purpose as I do. I am the avenger. The balance keeper of this living world. There are, or were, other aspects of the Lord's will that walked the earth just as I do. But they're either long gone, or so far removed from this place tha' I wouldn't 'ave a clue where t'lookfor'em.

"But out there or not, I swear to 'yatha' it wasn't them. Their purpose is different. It was Crystal, and t'tha' I'll swear a thousand lifetimes of huntin'."

Aryu believed him. As promised, he believed every word Nixon said. Nixon had nothing to gain from lying or hiding something. Then why did doubt still exist in Aryu's head? Something about Crystal, something so beyond anything he'd ever felt before, told him there was something else to this, something about her and what she was doing that wasn't so easily written off as a broken, overly-powerful woman causing havoc for havoc's sake. He decided, though, to keep this belief to himself.

"Why Izuku?" Aryu asked. "Where does he fit in?"

"Izuku is the oldest 'n arguably the most powerful person alive, after maybe her 'n Sho in their fully equipped state. He would be the best option t'show how t'use the weapon without losin' himself t'the madness it radiates. I'll wager it takes almost every ounce of ability he 'as t'use it, but I know tha' with her instruction, it would be possible.

"I also know tha' given time, it will consume 'im just as it does everyone else, even Crystal. There isn't much love lost between those two, so I'd guess she's set things in motion with 'is assistance, or perhaps the other way 'round, knowing tha' no matter how it ends, Izuku will either lose to us, or the sword."

"This madness, I'm safe from that?" Aryu had seen what it could do to a person, even one as powerful as Crystal.

"As long as ya' keep tha' thing close at 'and," he pointed a strong, hot finger at the Shi Kaze beside Aryu, "it will shield ya' from its power. Not forever, but long enough."

"What about you two? When it was unsheathed only a bit, it drove Crystal crazy like when she had lost her grasp of the Power. Would it do the same to you?"

"T'me? No. I know of the Omnis and Est Vacuus. I'm not a person like you or 'er. The Omnis was wha' I and mine were raised from. I know of 'em and can protect m'self accordingly. Plus, I've nah' lost any of my abilities. Sho, however, is just as vulnerable as anyone else unless he gets 'is power back."

A sobering thought. Now all that was left was the obvious question. "Nixon? One last thing." The phoenix raised his shimmering red eyebrow, unsure this time of what was to come. "Why are we walking? If she's working against us, why continue the charade?"

The large man let out a heavy sigh and any sign of peace and joy he might have had to offer was lost in deep thought and depression. "'Cause, Aryu, we've seen Izuku. He's known I was near, though I did miss 'im face t'face. If 'e knew, he would 'ave *had* t'do somethin' more 'an he did t'stop me. If he really wanted t'win this fight, and I was so close at 'and, he'd 'ave done anythin' t'not allow someone or somethin' with my power t'get so close.

"Basically, Aryu, given what I've seen, I'm quite certain he doesn't know and tha' it's something Crystal hasn't informed 'im of yet, either because she didn't 'ave the chance, or didn't want to. Until I see proof tha' I'm wrong, it 'as t'be an advantage we try t'keep t'ourselves. Whether we meet 'im now or a week from now, we need more t'win than wha' we 'ave. That little secret could be a very large difference maker in time. We need t'see if tha's true. I can limit wha' I can do t'small, simple things like shieldin' us from being mechanically observed like Sho did back east withou' raisin' anyone's interest, but other 'an tha', I will do nothin'.

"So, unless you 'ear otherwise from me, we walk."

As placated as he thought he was going to be, Aryu thanked Nixon once more for everything. Nixon nodded but said nothing more than, "G'night," when the time came.

The day was over at last, and tomorrow would bring the start of the trek north, hopefully to his friend and maybe, if the Gods were still feeling generous, to the revenge they both deserved. Somehow, with all the weapons they had at their disposal, and even with Crystal seemingly plotting against them, there had to be a way. Then, Aryu slept.

***

"I'm open t'suggestions," Nixon said at last as they looked down at this seemingly peaceful evening fire below them. These were the first living people they'd seen up close since making landfall. It had been over a week since the fall of HOME and the mission up the Vein Valley had begun. Although there were no clear indications of any H.Y. bomb sites as they went, there were plenty of destroyed towns and villages; many with the bodies of the dead still scattered around, looks of panic and fear on many faces, frozen for all time as horrible reminders of the deaths they'd suffered.

Below them now was a sprawling forest which had become progressively thicker as they'd traveled north. The fire burned peacefully in a small clearing.

Nixon's meaning was clear. If they skirted around the fire, one that was obviously behind enemy lines and likely surrounded by some agents of the enemy, they risked being found out and reported. Nixon could block invisible waves of energy with ease, but to influence a human eye or ear was simply more then he dared risk now that they were so close to Izuku.

Aryu looked at Sho to get some kind of indication which way this could be going. Aryu had grown to like Sho very much since their trek began. Where Nixon was strong, forceful and at times brutal in his instructions to Aryu in regards to his training, Sho was far more patient, giving Aryu advice, but also letting Aryu devise many of the options available to him on his own. When he had first met Sho he'd thought him a passive. Almost a timid and uncaring person, only thinking about the task he'd given himself years ago, although his fighting prowess was clear. That, Aryu thought, was to be expected given that he was thousands of years old and from a line of famous and powerful martial artists. It was unreasonable to assume that he wasn't as good as he was.

Sho had done a wonderful job of explaining the mentality required to do the things one needed to do in the heat of combat. Although Aryu had seen Sho don an intimidating face during combat, Sho's thought process from the day he was born until now was largely unchanged. Patience and reasoning were needed always, and Sho spoke to Aryu in a way that didn't make it sound daunting. Aryu suspected that Sho wasn't so much aloof as he was constantly thinking things out and paying attention to how the world around him unraveled. Nixon could use his history to teach Aryu everything he needed to know about using the Shi Kaze as an effective weapon in the short time they had been together, but Sho was invaluable in helping him guide his mind to keep control of a situation. Aryu respected Sho's methods very much. They were tactics and thoughts he found in himself. Sho simply gave him an outlet to express them.

Also, Aryu could easily recognize that bit by bit, he was amassing quite an arsenal of weapons to use against his enemy.

The drive for revenge from the Army of the Old.

The desperation to stay alive to see Johan again.

The weapon skills gifted by Nixon.

The mental toughness of battle guided by Sho.

And, in dire situations, the Power still licked at his fingertips thanks to Crystal.

Sometimes, when the combat training was particularly fierce, Aryu noted extra attention paid to him by Nixon, whether he was the one training him or on the sides doing something else. "He's watching you to make sure you don't slip up," Sho explained to him once while Nixon was off scouting the surrounding area of a camp they'd made. "He wants to make sure you don't suddenly revert to what my mother taught you in the heat of the moment."

Not likely, Aryu thought. *Not with what he'd do to me if I did.* Still, the action worried him. Nixon clearly thought that the possibility of Aryu doing that just might happen, to the point that he was watching Aryu closer now. The specter of the real Nixon Ash, the weapon of a long-dead God, was now much larger to Aryu than it had ever been.

"How far do you think we'd have to travel to get around them?" Sho asked, ideas and plans turning in his head.

"Too far, I'd guess," Nixon answered. "Any closer t'the army's main route of travel is likely t'get us close enough t'be spotted, even with my minimal assistance on the matter. Ya' don't happen t'have any other ideas, do ya', Aryu?"

The question startled Aryu at first, until he remembered that he had already come up with at least one plan they'd used, and to great effect, when he'd suggested singing back when Sho and Crystal had just lost their Power and the enemy was approaching in order to hide their intentions from listening ears. Aryu's spirits were brightened to know that Nixon valued his opinion, at least on a simple level like this.

And, as luck would have it, Aryu did have an idea.

"What if we sent in Sho?"

Nixon and Sho didn't write it off immediately. A good sign to Aryu at least. They were both clearly attempting to come up with as many counter-arguments as possible. Aryu tried to head off as many of those as possible.

"No one is looking for Sho, at least not as much as a giant fire-beast and a boy with wings." Aryu hated using the word boy, especially now considering all the past few weeks had done to him, but to the untrained eye, he had to accept how he'd look. And although dirty and battered, he looked like a boy... with wings.

"Also, if he goes in and finds out that these people aren't necessarily the enemy, perhaps only people who've made a foolish deal just like the ones from Tan Torna Qu-ay, we may be able to help them, and in turn gain some much needed assistance."

"And if it's nothing more than some scouts who have betrayed their own people?"

"Then we'd at least know. What then though, I haven't got a clue."

Nixon thought it over and looked at Sho, more so to look him over and appraise if he was inconspicuous enough to pass as an average person. He'd have to retract the Makashi armor, and maybe even leave the shield behind, but otherwise he couldn't see why it wouldn't work. "Wha' do ya' say, Sho? I'd prefer ye'd go now while the cover of night aides you. It's as good a plan as any."

Aryu beamed at the comment. Once more, he'd out-thought the thinkers. Perhaps they simply thought too much? Sho nodded. "Agreed, but I'm not too keen on leaving myself so vulnerable."

No one was, but in the end the common thought was that an unarmed, Power-less Sho Tokugawa was still likely more than a town full of marauders and cut throats could handle, and if they were found out by taking some other means to get around, they'd likely have a town of human enemies as well as an army of soldiers to deal with. In the end, they all agreed that this was the best course to take.

Sho retracted the mythical armor to its resting place and handed the shield to Aryu, who was reluctant to take it, insisting Nixon would be the better candidate to wield it. "No," Sho disagreed at once, "Nixon has his own armor and his own power to help him, and although the sword you carry is what it is, it wouldn't hurt to have another powerful weapon in your possession, at least while I go off and have a friendly chat with those folks. If the chat becomes less-friendly than I hope, you'll be thankful for it." With that, Sho thrust the shield into Aryu's hand, followed by a quick tutorial on how the spinning blade mechanism worked. "Just place your fingers into the loops and squeeze your fist repeatedly. The rest is self-explanatory. Keep it away from your legs, head and free arm or you won't have any left." With a deep swallow, Aryu took the God-killing devise and stepped away, amazed at the lightness of the large metal weapon.

"How do I look?" Sho asked them, turning to show no outward signs of his true person or abilities. He simply looked like a tall, dirty traveler in a woven canvas outfit.

"Like a man who needs t'eat more, I'd say," chided Nixon with a huff. A nod of recognition coupled with a wink and salute, and Sho was off into the forest, heading down the hill to the base of the rise and the town below. Nixon and Aryu watched him until he disappeared, followed by setting up their camp for the night.

Sho circled the clearing, learning all that he could. There were three, a woman and two men, deep in conversation. Nearby, on the old dirt road, was what looked like a car of some kind. Not terribly advanced, but clearly more technological than what many in this area would possess. Near it was a pile of discarded gear. They sat laughing, seeming to be at ease. It was practically impossible to tell if they were the enemy without getting closer, but by then he'd likely be found out. In the end, he opted to simply go for broke.

"Hello there!" Sho called out. If they were the enemy, they likely had weapons that would very easily go off a little too quickly if the user were jumpy. The three stopped abruptly and looked around, but none produced any weapon Sho could see. "Hey! You three! Over here!"

They each got up cautiously, looking all through the darkened trees to find the one who had called out. *Let the fun begin,* Sho thought sarcastically as he took another few steps towards them. "Thank the Gods! I've been wandering for days looking for someone. I can't believe I found you!"

"Stay where you are!" the smaller one shouted. "Who are you?"

Sho stopped stepping forward and half smiled. "My name is Shinza," he answered, pulling a name of an old friend out like it was his own. "I'm a farmer from south of here. My family was taken from me when the robots arrived. I was on my way back from a trading trip and heard what had happened."

"What part of the south?" the taller one asked in a very broken and gruff voice, almost as if the words were giving him trouble as he spoke them. "What was the closest town?"

A standard line of questioning, Sho reasoned. An encouraging sign at least. These were suspicious questions, not forceful ones. "The Northlands, near Pikiana. I had a large folme herd and dairy farm there."

"Who was the mayor of Pikiana when you left?" More questions of suspicion. Sho's encouragement rose again, especially with the obvious trap question. He tried his best to stifle the smile he felt coming. "Mayor? Pikiana, like all of the other towns and villages in the Northlands, was run by revolving council, but Houghton Price was the head of the council, if that's close enough for you."

"And what did Mr. Houghton Price look like?" Another trap. Sho was now convinced that these people weren't the enemy, so he continued to play the game simply to earn their trust.

"Well, MRS. Houghton Price was an old bat of a woman with a crooked walk, evil eye and a terrible sense of humor." A laugh from the three and Sho knew he'd made it in.

The farms, towns and villages of all the lands near his own, right up to almost the Vein Valley, were well known to Sho. Indeed, he'd helped build many of them once upon a time. As such, he had a vested interest in them and their peoples. Pikiana was one of many places he could have chosen to speak so educated about.

"Indeed, my farming friend," said the small one. "And, I'd like to add, she stank to the good high heavens."

Sho stepped forward, arm out in greeting, which was met by each in turn. "That she did. That she certainly did." It wasn't a trap statement this time. Mrs. Houghton Price reeked of dead fish.

"Well now, Mr. Shinza is it? Tell me," the tall man began. Thus far the woman had said nothing, only appraising Sho as he joined them all at the fire. "What brings you so far north? Most would have gone into the mountains, or somewhere more readily available for protection."

"You haven't," Sho replied, sure to show the man the same level of suspicion he was being shown. "This place seems to be moving along without any interference."

"Oh, there is interference," the man answered, "but for the time being it's held at bay."

"Well," Sho began, "I came north because I knew of the large numbers of villages and people here. I was hoping to find some form of resistance to the threat I might take on with." The taller, mumbling man raised an eyebrow at this, but said nothing. "I'd rather fight than fly."

"Ha, and die foolishly. I'd rethink your course of action, friend," the smaller man replied.

Sho stood fast and the man let it slide. "Well," the stranger continued, "that said, what do you plan on doing now that you've found us? We have some food if you would care for some. I'll wager you're hungry after that trek."

"No, thank you. Perhaps if I just rested for a time, that would be enough, then I'd like to continue on my way to search out allies to stand against them." Sho met the dark eyes of the man again. "Unless I already have?"

The man suddenly became uncomfortable, waving off the statement like a fly in his face. "Bah, not here. Not here by far. No, we aren't about to take up your fool's errand, that's for certain. Rest all you like, but don't go getting any ideas about anything else."

Sho took on a look of mock-disappointment, and settled back into his seat. "Well, I'll thank you for what you offer and be on my way before I am more trouble than I'm worth."

A nod returned to him, and he concluded that these folks, although gruff and odd, likely weren't a threat. He stood and looked into the forest, trying to act as casual as possible.

Even those who are thousands of years old are prone to mistakes.

Sho, even in his 'weakened' state, was as nimble and talented a warrior as the world had ever known, but even so he couldn't dodge the first blow that was struck from the darkness, catching him in the back and throwing him over in pain, followed by another fast and skilled strike to the side of his face from the other side, causing his eyes to flash and twinkle as he was sent to the ground.

Sho knew instantly that these were no mere mortals making these strikes. There wasn't a mortal human alive that had the skill to take Sho Tokugawa by such surprise. Still, he wasn't without skill even against an enemy so devious, and he was up on his feet like a shot before the strangers could stop him. Soon, he was stable and trying to run, needing more time to give himself the focus needed to enwrap himself in the Makashi armor he always carried with him, but a bright flash and a lifting sensation ceased that thought at once as Sho was tossed back through the trees like a rag doll.

Another bright flash followed, causing Sho's head to snap back against a rock, dazing him instantly and sending him to his knees.

Footsteps then, as his vision faded. Although he couldn't believe it, he knew he was about to pass out from the blows. Blows that certainly weren't made by normal human hands. As he fell to all fours, he looked up in time to see three sets of feet step into the light of the fire. Blood trickled from his mouth and down the back of his head as he forced himself to look up.Unfortunately, his vision was almost useless as he began fading to black. What he could see was blurry and diluted.

He saw what he needed to at last: the woman stood before him.

Sho saw her hand and knew at once what he was seeing. Weapons that sing into the mind of Sho loud and clear. Then, the blackness consumed him, and for the first time in memory, Sho Tokugawa was knocked out.

Chapter 4: Meeting With The Devil

Three weary travelers from Inja via Huan were awoken. Somewhat prematurely, as the festivities and weariness had created three extremely tired young souls. Though still late in the morning, they easily could have slept the whole day through.

Chief Rider Caspar didn't have that kind of time, and after he'd let them rest for what he deemed a sufficient amount, he entered their room located in a civilian inn beside the barracks and got them up. The War and Glory Council, and specifically Mr. Auron Bree, would not be kept waiting any longer.

Johan Otan'co, Seraphina Langley, and reluctant companion (and once bullying tormentor of Johan) Esgona dragged themselves out of bed, gruff and still completely road-weary. The dark-skinned sons of Tan Torna Qu-ay never looked at each other once. The animosity between them still more than palpable, despite the adventure they'd endured in the Paieleh River Valley. Even having saved each other's live more than once, it was clear that these two were destined to forever be at odds.

The valley had forged them all into stronger souls. From the deadly river to the attack by the massive stalkers, which Johan had saved them from, they always were on edge. Having a night in the relative (though still unsettling) safety of the city of Bankoor was welcome, as well as the revelry they were treated to. A hero's welcome was given to the man who had saved them from the monsters with his quick thinking (and dumb luck, a fact not lost on Johan), and now they faced the morning-after consequences.

They each cleaned themselves up as best they could and joined Caspar outside where he stood beside an awaiting transport vehicle. All three of them went white at the sight of it. They'd all seen powered carts and similar things in their lives, but this was far more advanced than anything they'd ever been asked to ride on. They'd even seen similar things ripping up and down the road coming into town, but never before had any of them been asked to *ride* in one, and the inherent fear they each had for it was obvious.

"Well, lady and gentlemen, this is how we ride when not on horseback around here. I think you need to resign yourselves to the fact that the world beyond your borders is a little more frightening than you'd care to realize." Caspar took them in one at a time as he spoke, but the apprehension remained. "Look, my friends, it's too far to walk, and I haven't got the horses to spare. Please, I assure you it's harmless."

Johan, the most comfortable with both the current situation and the technology of the ride, was the first to board the small transport, followed by Seraphina, who had taken to not being more than two steps away from Johan at any point in time now. Esgona remained perfectly still.

"Not coming?" Johan mocked at him, seeming to forget his own reluctance not thirty seconds prior. Esgona simply glared at him, but said nothing.

"Look, sir," Caspar said, beginning to lose patience with each of them and their irrational fears, "they said they'd like to see each of you, and I can tell you this; when the War and Glory Council call you to them, you go. Even if the invitation is as polite as this one."

Esgona didn't move. "I'm not getting on that thing," he said at last, the defiance clear. His eyes told Merrik Caspar that this wasn't a fight the Chief Rider was going to win. With a shrug, he told Esgona to please wait at the inn and closed the door of the transport.

The two blossoming lovers rode in silence to the glass spire. Up close it was even more beautiful and awe-inspiring than they could believe. The top of the spire was shrouded in low-level morning clouds and the image appeared to each of them as if it was attempting to rip open a hole in the sky.

The ride stopped and the door opened, allowing Caspar to slide out first, followed by the other two. He led them up a staircase and into a set of doors in the side of the tower's base. Being who they were and what they feared, this place was easily as bad as whatever the army of the Old could throw at them. A lobby was massive. It was easily the largest room either had ever been inside of. At the far end was a set of large closed doors.

As soon as they approached, a chime echoed in the halls and a man's voice was heard from above them. "How may I help you?"

"Chief Rider Merrik Caspar of the Inja Army. I am here with the travelers from the Paieleh Valley at the request of Auron Bree."

The words were no sooner spoken then the doors opened to reveal an even *larger* room than the one they had come from. Huge pillars rose up from the floor to the exceptionally high ceiling and windows stretching in every direction above them. The windows were tinted and kept most of the glaring morning sunlight at bay.

At the center of the mammoth room was a long table. Caspar indicated they follow him to the head of the table closest to them, footsteps ricocheting around the room as they did so. Johan appraised the members at the table as they moved.

It was a mix of both men and women, each different from the last. Some had dark skin like the West Landers, others were pale as ghosts. Some tall, some short, some a perfect mix of each. No two faces were similar.

At the other end of the table was Auron Bree.

He was an average man with average build. Easily in his late sixties with hair cut short and a mix of whites and grays. He wore glasses on his face and had on clothes of a nature they didn't recognize, such as a fine-woven shirt with no buttons and elbow-length sleeves and rugged, dark pants. On his feet were boots, but so finely sewn and flawless that Johan had a serious doubt that human hands had crafted them.Johan knew at once that this was the one who had beckoned them here. Johan also knew that these people were the people of power for Bankoor and beyond. He had heard Caspar refer to them as the War and Glory Council, and by looking at them, he'd say that description was perfectly apt.

Bree came to them along the table, passing the other personnel. The smile on his face as he did so was either terribly cheery or terribly forced. Johan suspected that either way, that was a smile that wanted something.

"Friends, welcome to Bankoor!" he said as he clasped each of their hands in a passive shake. He introduced himself, followed by each member of the WGC sitting around the table, names as quickly spoken as they were forgotten. Johan knew it didn't matter. Auron Bree ("Please, simply Auron to my friends, which you certainly are!") was the power behind this place, and he was likely the one calling any shots that had to do with them.

He asked them to sit on the far end by him where four chairs had been placed. It was then that Johan remembered Stroan was supposed to join them. "He's been indisposed for the moment. I hear the same could be said about your other friend?" Johan wondered how he'd found out about Aryu, until he realized that Auron was speaking of Esgona. Caspar took a chair on the far end of the table when indicated and the other three joined Auron in the empty chairs, still captivated by the room and its eerie wonder.

After turning down drinks and food, Johan met Auron's eyes in a manner that indicated he was serious. "We thank you for your hospitality, but why are we here, Auron?" The reasoning had worried him ever since he was told it was going to happen the day before.

"Straight to the point, eh?" Auron said uneasily, but no less pleasant. "Well, first and foremost was to congratulate you on your successful traverse of the Thunder Run and the Paieleh Valley. Not many had done so in as good of condition as your party, let me tell you."

Johan almost scoffed at the sentiment, but held his tongue. Considering all they had lost and everyone who had died, he would hardly call anything about is a success.

"The second is naturally to thank you for how you helped save so many lives of both the Inja Riders and civilian travelers. I've been told your resourcefulness and quick thinking helped pull them all through some very tough spots.

"I've asked you here to answer any questions you may have and to aid you in any way possible with the tasks you've set for yourselves. I understand your home was destroyed by these invaders. Is that true?"

"It is, sir," Johan said. "At least, it is for me and the other who didn't join us. The lady and her family were travelers we'd met along the way." Seraphina acknowledged it as the truth, but said nothing more.

"My condolences. Know that here you are not alone. Many in our city have similar stories. For many like you, it's why they came here in the first place. To have a chance to get their revenge on them. I believe you are in that same boat?"

"We are," replied Johan, waiting for the other shoe to drop.

"And would it be a safe assumption that you aren't interested in joining one of our glorious fighting forces to that end?"

"It is. That's not the path we wish to follow. Aid, but not follow."

"I see. And why is that, may I ask?"

"Well, frankly sir," spoke Johan with firmness, "we don't trust your methods or the technology you wield. We would prefer to travel our own path to our revenge, not yours."

Auron seemed nonplussed at the response. He'd likely anticipated it all along. "I'm saddened to here that, I must admit. Know that the offer stands, and will continue to." Auron Bree took a mental note that these ones weren't so easily persuaded (a fact he had already heard from Merrik Caspar but hadn't taken the time to consider it was actually true).

"Well, in the meantime, is there anything else I can do for you three, your non-attendee included? After such a trip, I refuse to believe we can't make you more comfortable while here in Bankoor."

"Auron," continued Johan, sensing the unknown weight in the air in regard to what exactly Auron Bree wanted, like waiting for someone to give you bad news you know is coming and wanting them to just get it out so you can deal with it, "we're not entirely comfortable with your city and way of life. You likely know our people shunned it as evil. As it is, we'd like the opportunity to carry on as we were."

Bree smirked. "I assure you that your words don't fall on deaf ears, but if I may tell you something to perhaps help sway you?" Johan nodded skeptically while Seraphina remained still. "I come from a land far north of here. A land where the technological advances you see around you are practically ancient. The world you've had the honor of living in, without these advancements and responsibilities to use it properly, is not normal throughout the world. Up until we came together all those years ago, my people had no idea such a large and isolated land still existed.

"You and your people are in the minority, my friends. It would seem that with the arrival of this new enemy, your blissful, self-imposed ignorance to the outside world beyond your borders is now and forever a thing of the past.

"I tell you this because I want you to understand that from this point on, things will progress very quickly for you. Indeed, for us all. If you wish to hide from the truth, that is your choice. In telling you this, I only hope to aid you in a speedier transition. Please don't think me rude because of it."

"Not at all," Johan grinned. He desperately wanted to get Auron out of this obvious act and to the point. "We thank you for your candor. All the same, I think we'd prefer to take our own time letting it all sink in." It was obvious to him that this was less a conversation about making them comfortable and more about trying to bend them to whatever will it was that Auron and the War and Glory Council was trying to force on them.

Auron shrugged. "As you wish. The offer, same as the one before it, stands." Awkward silence followed when no one in the room offered anything new. Johan could almost feel the pressure of the impending conversation, as well as the battle starting to rage in Auron's mind between being a politician and being himself, which was becoming clearer was far more ruthless. Johan knew the look of a man who was tempering himself.

"Tell me," Auron began again, "in your trek through the cursed valley, I'd like to hear the story of how you made it through from your own mouths. I think the tale loses something in translation."

The first hints of the true purpose reared its head. Johan and Seraphina did as they were asked and told the abbreviated version of all that had happened from the time they'd left Huan. Each member of the WGC listened intently to the riveting story, and when it ended, more than one began applauding them quietly, Auron Bree included.

In his parts of the story, Johan had naturally avoided the knife specifically, saying only that a deal had been reached with the stalkers, and it was a deal he intended to honor when the time came. The rest of the story played out for all to hear, and like a moth to a flame, once the applause died away, Auron Bree went right back to the topic of the deal Johan had with Skerd.

It was all a ruse, of course. He knew what it was he wanted to talk about. He knew Auron and the WGC wanted his knife for some purpose, but they also wanted to see how easily this group could be manipulated. Johan was more than content to play this game out all of the way. If they couldn't just come out and tell them what they wanted, he certainly wasn't going to help matters along.

"So, you say you agreed to return to them once your task here was complete?" Auron asked, the cat-and-mouse beginning in earnest.

"I did. I didn't want to, but they left me little choice. It was that or we all would have died."

"Indeed. A terrible choice to make, but you did you admirably. Tell me, though, why you?"

"Because I was the one that halted them. I stopped their attack."

"And how did you do that?"

Johan paused for a moment before responding. "Skillfully." Johan drew it out as best he could without outright acknowledging the knife, but also not denying its existence.

"Clearly," Auron replied, the cheer in his voice slipping. "Would you care to share with us the details?"

"I believe I just did," Johan answered. He caught the small smirk on Seraphina's face to his side.

"So, they just let you all go in exchange for a meeting with you and you alone?"

"Well, I think I had something they wanted." Johan baited him on, loving it all.

"And what was that? What did they want from you?"

"They wanted my knife," Johan said at last, teasing them with the tastiest of crumbs yet.

"Your knife, you say? What's so special about your knife?"

"I'm not sure, Auron. Perhaps you could tell me?"

The gauntlet was thrown down before Johan could stop himself, but in this brief, childish exchange, he'd learned all he needed to about Auron Bree. It was time to find out what these people wanted from him.

"How do you mean?" Auron asked, all signs of cheer now gone. He was clearly realizing what this whole thing had been about now, and he didn't enjoy being made a fool of.

"I mean," Johan said, leaning on the table towards the head of the WGC, "that you wanted us here for the purpose of asking me about my knife. I don't know why, and I don't care. What's so special about the knife that you'd bring us here under all the disingenuous bullshit?"

A sneer came to Auron's face, and it seemed much more at home then the strained smile he'd had up to this point. "Well, now, that seems a little presumptuous, doesn't it?"

"Not really. The only presumptuous thing was assuming we didn't know why we were brought here, wouldn't you agree?"

The sneer faded and the true Auron Bree-the cold, calculating head of the War and Glory Council,emerged. This kid had been playing him, and he was not happy about it. The fact that he was doing the same to them meant nothing. "Very well, my new friends. May I see this infamous knife?"

"No, you may not," Johan replied, settling back into his comfortable chair, indeed the most comfortable he'd likely ever sat in.

"And why is that?"

"Because, Auron, I don't have it with me, as anyone with your technology likely knows. How were we scanned? X-rays?Metal detectors? I'm not completely ignorant of these kinds of things, you know."

"So it would seem. No, I assure you our methods are more advanced than those old tactics. Still, I had to ask."

"And I thank you for doing so. No, I've taken the liberty of putting it somewhere neither your machines here nor the ones you've currently got scanning our room looking for it can find."

It was a guess, but not much of one. Johan had suspected underhanded tactics since he first saw Bankoor and its technology.

Evil in one form or another simply seemed to follow it around.

Although he never acknowledged it as the truth, Auron didn't outright deny it either. "I suppose simply asking for it would do us no good?" he asked.

"Ah, not true, but you'll have to forgive me if I wanted to know why?"

"And if I didn't want to tell you?"

"Then I don't want to show you," Johan said.

"I'm not sure if that's a wise option."

"Perhaps, but if you know as much as I'm sure you do about our recent trip down the Paieleh Valley, you'll know full well tough choices are the norm for us now."

The smirk returned to Auron's face, followed by him rising and waving his hand in the direction of a door opposite the one they'd come in. "If you please. I may as well indulge your little power trip, so if you'll come with me, I'll answer your questions, as promised."

Johan hesitated at first, but eventually agreed, taking Seraphina's hand and helping her up. It looked like someone would at last have an answer.

Auron led them through the door and down a set of stairs into a hallway much darker and danker than the room above had been. Clearly that was a room for show. This looked to Johan like the real Bankoor.

"Not many people other than the members of the WGC get to come down here, but as our relationship is new and special, I'm willing to make this exception." The underlying meaning was clear. Auron either didn't think knowing about whatever it was that was down here was important to two kids who could clearly do nothing about it, or he wasn't planning on keeping them around long.

Soon the hallway opened and a large set of doors stood before them. Auron pressed a button and they waited.

"I suppose this will be a new experience for you both," he said, indicating the door. "I'll bet neither of you have ever been on an elevator." He was right about that. Seraphina barely knew of them, Johan had only heard bits and pieces in books and stories of the people of the Old and their high buildings.

"Well, I hope none of you are afraid of heights," he said reading their faces, waiting for the telltale *ding* of the doors, which opened and let them each inside.

The sudden movement upwards once the doors closed sent each of the two young guests' stomachs lurching. The elevator, which was devoid of windows or any indicators of how far and fast they were going, sped upwards.

Once the door opened and the daylight flooded in, the feelings of illness only intensified.

The elevator opened into a round room with windows everywhere in a perfect floor-to-ceiling circle, the elevator sitting in the design's lone break: a box in the middle of the floor. Above them, a glass ceiling showed what remained of the spire stretching out even higher above them; wires running from the panels located there. Below them were finely crafted black tiles that glimmered in the sun, echoing their footsteps as they walked out of the closing elevator.

Johan had spent many summer days climbing to the top of Tortria Den, and although nowhere near as tall as this, the premise prepared him somewhat for what they were witness to now, not to mention the high mountain passes and cliff faces he'd seen while on their Journey for the past year.

Seraphina, though strong and well braced against the sight, still clung to Johan's side tightly, and was not likely to let go by the feel of it.

"This is the one and only observation deck of the spire. The rest below and above us is nothing but dedicated electrical systems used to harness the sun's light and power the city around you."

They looked out at the sprawling city below, facing south, with the expanse of the Blood Sea to their right and the massive Hymleah Mountains to the left. The day was clear now, the morning fogs and mists burned off. In the direction they were looking was the head waster of the Vein River and the beginning of the massive valley that would eventually drain the Blood Sea into the great southern ocean.

Having spent a great deal of time at this dizzying height, Auron strode over to the window before them, pointing south along the valley. "Down there, by our best reports two days travel from here by foot, as I assume that's the measurement of speed you are most familiar with, is the front-line defense against the insurgent army of what you call the 'Old'. For the past two weeks we have held firm, and even began pushing back against them. There are well-substantiated reports that their main base of operations, a massive battleship called HOME, was destroyed, causing a loss of replacement troops and a central networking hub for them to coordinate attacks. Although obviously very advanced, they lack the ability to devise elaborate plans of attack on their own. Somewhere, in the distance, someone living and intelligent had to be pulling their strings. We had hoped that person, or persons perhaps, had been lost at the time of the destruction of HOME. Early this morning, we learned that this was not the case.

"Just after sun up today, the chief field officer of the largest brigades sent word of a new weapon of the Army of the Old. A weapon we never expected, but knew could be a possibility. Enemies we attempted to prepare for, but lacked a certain instrument to fully protect us.

Bree crossed his hands in front of him, as if he was about to preach, or say something solemn. "We are now certain that your knife, Johan Otan'co, is that instrument."

"And what could possibly make you think that, Auron?" Johan asked stepping forward, looking not at the man but the panorama behind him. "You don't know who I am or what it is. You're putting a lot of faith in someone you've just met."

Bree's hands relaxed now. He was oozing back into his comfort zone: the confident, silver-tongued politician. "I am, but I don't believe it's misplaced. Once word came back from the Riders about how you'd dealt with the Stalkers and their leader, no doubt remained. For reasons left to another time, Stalkers fear and respect the so called 'focus' items that Embracers of the Power once held, and after hearing about your meeting, I'm certain that one of those is what you carry."

Johan had considered that possibility the moment he'd come to terms with what he had seen at Thunder Head while saving Seraphina after she'd fallen into the tumultuous waters and he had used the weapon to save both of their lives. He'd all but convinced himself it was true after he'd seen what it could do against the Stalkers and the way Skerd had feared it.

"You can't know that for sure," he answered, meeting the look of confidence on Auron's face.

"True, but according to my sources, it's almost a sure thing. True, it'd be better to see it in person, but for now I'm content in knowing that you've got it safe somewhere and that in time you will realize that you need to give it to us."

"Why?" asked Seraphina, not as comfortable as Johan with the scene around them, but no longer in shock of the height. "What is this new weapon of the Old you can't defeat without a simple knife?"

"The knife is just one of many such items still scattered over the world, but as it's the only one we have access to, it will have to do."

"That seems like a terrible act of faith, but fine," she answered, irritated at the deflection. "What is the weapon they're using now?"

"I believe 'who' is the weapon is a better question." With the cryptic answer, he produced a small, hand-held device from a pocket and held it before them. "'I, acting Field Commander Shan Dio, on the orders of currently M.I.A. Field Commander Edgar Taft, officially send word to headquarters and all within range of this message, that we have called an immediate retreat to regroup in the face of a new enemy appearing among the ranks of the opposition's front lines.

"'The enemy, although we are lacking concrete evidence at this time, appears to be a force of almost twenty living humans, generally referred to as Embracers of the Power. They fight for the robotic army and were last seen advancing towards our front-line field command post and the waiting, aforementioned M.I.A. Field Commander Edgar Taft. Fall back will continue until ordered otherwise. Yours in faith, and with the blessings of the Gods to us all, Shan Dio, acting Field Commander of the United Peoples Military.'"

With looks of disbelief, Auron Bree was certain that his point was made. "We received this communication approximately three days ago. No word from Mr. Dio or anyone else from his divisions has been heard since. Long range viewing devices and some video recordings seem to confirm it as the truth. Embracers, commanded by what has been described as a man with wings, possibly another of their kind and one who carries a powerful and dangerous sword, but we can't confirm this as of yet."

There were no words from Johan. The scope of this information was monumental.

Auron reveled slightly at getting the cocky Johan on his heels like this. "As best we can tell, these Embracers have completely decimated our forces, striking like an arrowhead and eliminating all they come across as they push north, followed by what appears to be the remainder of the mechanical forces of Old. Although they could likely be here much quicker, we believe they are deliberately taking their time, either for their own dark purposes or simply to strike fear into our hearts. At their current pace, they will arrive here sometime tomorrow afternoon.

"Any attempt by our drone aircraft to follow them or attack is quickly met with baffling, and frankly otherworldly, force. All tactics we've employed on the enemy up to this point have utterly failed in every conceivable way in the last five hours, all at the hands of these few people."

Silence from the two. Their eyes glistened as they contemplated everything they were hearing. It boarded on being too much.

"While I allow you all to let that sink in, I'd like for you to come with me once more," Auron said, passing the frozen and horrified faces as he walked back to the elevator door, which opened immediately once he pressed the chiming button. "If you please."

At first, nothing.Neither moved. "You can do no one any good simply gawking, my friends, so if you please." Auron waved them into the waiting elevator and soon they were inside, feet almost shuffling as they went. In the back of his mind, Johan thanked all of the good, sweet Gods that Esgona wasn't here to hear any of this. His smug *I told you so* look would have been enough for Johan to toss him out of the window, even in the midst of their uneasy truce.

The elevator began its descent. Auron, a master of political manipulation, basked in the glory of the state he'd put the smart-assed boy and his tart in. If he was concerned about this impending doom, he showed no sign of it. Instead he stood stoically, reveling in his verbal success.

The elevator came to a stop, and the doors opened to reveal not the hallway they'd started from but a darker, narrower space; one that instantly filled the small elevator with the odor of damp, salty earth and haunting, perfect silence.

Once more Auron led the way. "My friends," he began, his voice echoless in the hall, as if the words were muted the moment he spoke them. Even their footsteps were soft and soundless. "You are now deep below Bankoor and the spire above, in the depths of the War and Glory Council's strategic headquarters. Here, although you wouldn't know it now, we command our field forces, relay our orders and generally make everything having to do with our defenses tick. The most advanced technology from all the lands and peoples who make up this post are here, ensuring we live to fight another day."

He led them through a series of twists and turns, ending in a dark room full of mostly blank computer screens, though some still glowed with pictures and small words. "Most times in the last few weeks, it's been a hive of activity. Today, in the wake of this new enemy, only the people above us in the main Council hall remain. All others have been sent home to their families. No weapon we have or strategy we use, save one, can stop a force of Embracers, so we opted to not even try after the last of our tactics failed.

"There is that one option we have yet to employ, and that option is the purpose of my asking you here." He walked over to the largest screen, now blank, and with the press of a few buttons at its base, soft light filled the room, slowly highlighting a space to their far right occupied by what Johan knew instantly was the infamous High Yield bomb.

Seraphina turned away at once, burying her face into Johan's shoulder. Johan simply stared at it transfixed, humbled and angered just by being in its presence.

Auron stepped over to it, almost caressing it as he walked by; his hand gliding along its slender, oblong shape. It was a mix of both rounded and angular edges in a near perfect oval sitting on a steel base that supported it off the ground. It was matte gunmetal with a rectangular display set directly in the middle, more towards the top. For the moment, blissfully, the display was blank and silent.

"Judging by your reactions, I assume you know what this is?" Auron asked as the games began again.

"We do, and you know why," Johan answered, not wanting to play games but drawn in all the same. Just being in the presence of this thing drained him of all his guile.

"I do. Not much happens now that we of the WGC don't know about. I am sorry about your home. Truly. You and your people were thrust into this rather harshly, abruptly, and unfairly. I can only imagine…"

"No, you can't," Johan cut him off, not wanting any more false sympathy. "You can't *imagine* a damn thing."

"Yes, well, regardless, I think a bit of history is in order. I hope that once the story ends, you'll agree with our point of view and turn over your knife…"

"Not fucking likely," Johan interjected again.

"Tell me, with all you've learned since this unpleasantness began, or perhaps from before that, as you seem to be a sharp couple, what can you tell me about the land that lay north of the Hymleah Mountains?"

Not wanting to ignore the huge bomb in the room, but also not wanting to miss this chance to find out what this whole damn experience was all about, Johan released Seraphina reluctantly and stepped to the devil before him. "Not much. Most assume the mountains carry on all the way to a northern sea, but as there is no way for our people to know for sure, no one really knows. Except you and your people, I assume? Why don't you enlighten us? The faster you do, the faster you get to the point."

"Well, first of all, there are ways. Ways you and yours haven't found or have simply forgotten about. There are valley roads traversable by men. But I assure you, if you thought the Paieleh Valley was a harsh trip, it would be a casual jaunt in the kinds of places these roads go.

"There is a sea to the north. A vast frozen and lifeless sea. Nearly impossible for man to travel to, even ones with the technology you see around you. The winds are too strong, the temperatures too cold, and the journey too harsh.

"After the great wars of man and machine that led to the Fourth Fall of Man, most of the technology of the time wasn't wiped out. Military powers that had built large numbers of mechanical men were toppled, but many of those soulless soldiers were left behind, waiting for their time to be useful.And not just soldiers, but vehicles, planes, huge ships and battle cruisers as well, all abandoned before they had the chance to be activated and used in combat. Sound familiar?" They all caught the drift, but said nothing.

"One such reserve was located in a large underground series of bunkers and shipping yards on the coasts of the northern sea, though long covered with ice and snow and buried under massive glaciers.By the time we had developed the technology to get to these things, they had already been found and activated by someone else. Someone with much more power than we have.

"Although many parts of the world are still dark and lost to us, we do know most of it is in a state of maturity somewhere between us and, not to put too fine a point on it, you. No one we were aware of could have gone there, dug it all out, melted it all from its resting place, and got it all battle ready in the kind of time they did. This left us with one logical answer: an Embracer, or possibly multiple Embracers. Though mostly dormant ever since their own famous cataclysmic infighting, we knew that there were still some about, but it was information we kept to ourselves, not allowing the general populace to know about it.

"Now, as I said, that desolate land to the far north held the largest contingent of these things, that's true, but not the *only* collection. Although nothing was found large enough to counter the army that landed, pockets and bunkers of some of them have been found on and off for hundreds of years, including their pride and joy, the beast you see before you known as the High Yield bomb, capable of unfathomable destruction in a controlled area.

"Now, I'll try to make this next, most important part as understandable as possible. Everything, even the awesome abilities of the Embracers, is at its very core based in science and the natural laws of the universe. Although magic in appearance, I want you to know that nothing we've ever encountered can't be explained, given enough time and resources.

"This weapon was created to stop any enemy, and I mean *any*. At the time this was made, the abilities of Embracers were simple science to its creators. Weapons like this were built to contain Embracers if they ever get out of hand again.So, with technologies and abilities I admit are still beyond us, not to mention the assumed assistance of more than one Embracer, they made these, and they made plenty of them.They are a very sophisticated collection of high-intensity lasers, microscopic particles and computing power so far ahead of what we have now it's frightening. Place something in the sensor area, no matter if it's solid, liquid or gas, and that matter is broken down and turned into energy, which is released as the blast we know and fear. If you control the matter broken down and the amounts you use, you control the size and ferocity of the blast.

"Now, at last, we reach the point you are so eager to hear, my young friends. If the thing at the center of this device is that of a Focus weapon of an Embracer, the energy created channels the unique and mysterious, naturally embedded sub-atomic signature of that item into the blast itself, essentially creating a blast zone with the same properties as the matter of the item at its core."

Johan was with Auron, or at least he assumed he was.

The weapon was designed to be an Embracer-killer.

Seraphina looked to Johan with trepid curiosity. "What Auron is saying is that if they put my knife at the core of the bomb and detonate it while in range of the advancing army and the Embracers which seem to have crept up to lead them, the blast will destroy them all, Embracers included."

"Well," interrupted Auron, "that we can't know for sure. What we *do* know for certain is that it will stop them. These ARE Embracers, after all. It may not outright kill them, but it will make them hurt like they never have, and likely obliterate them into nothing more than particles of themselves. Whether or not they return from that is a question we can't answer, though we suspect it may have something to do with the power of the item at the bomb's core."

Seraphina stared at Johan incredulously, seeing that the

expression on Johan's face wasn't one of fear and terror, but one of understanding.

Johan was considering it.

Seraphina raced to him, taking his hand forcefully. "You can't even think about it, Johan!" she raged. "Let's go! Let's take your knife and leave this place! All I see are the weapons of the Old being used all around me and I can't stand by and let you take part in this! Even if the city is evacuated and the enemy destroyed, now we'd have *people* with that kind of power! We know what happens then! It's happened twice before, and I don't think the Gods are going to let us slip away a third time! We have to go. We have to find another way to fight this battle, a way that doesn't involve selling our souls to the Devil."

Johan was torn between the moral right and the need for retribution. Here, only inched from him, was the revenge he sought. Quick.Painful.Remorseless. Just the kind he wanted, awaiting his knife to make it that much more powerful. "Why leave it in the city?" he asked Auron. "Why not take it and drop it on the battlefield, in the heart of their ranks?"

"That was the first plan, but as I told you, we can't get close enough to them to make it work now, not with the Embracers cutting down all of our attempts.We can rebuild this city, and a million more like it if we have to. As long as we get the people out in time, we have no compunction about setting this as a going away gift as we turn over the city."

"And you can evacuate the city in that time?" Johan asked.

"My friend, it's being done as we speak. We'd have preferred more time, but this new enemy came out of nowhere. Honestly, we just wanted to lure in the Army of the Old and let the bomb do its thing, but since they have Embracers, now we need something at its core that can handle their kind of power."

"How lucky you are that we happened into town when we did," Johan answered. A smirk came to Auron's face that sent chills down each of their spines.

"Indeed."

Johan looked at Seraphina and read her face. "I think we'd like to leave now, Auron. The last little while has been pretty horrible and today is so far the limit of what I can take at one time, and it's only the morning. I'll tell you my decision tonight. I give you my word. No running. No hiding. However, my decision is my own, and like it or not, you *will* honor it. Agreed?"

He extended his hand symbolically over the top of the H.Y. bomb. Auron took the hand in a hardy and vigorous shake. "I agree, Johan Otan'co. I know you will do the right thing." With that, Auron led them back out to the waiting elevator and the streets of Bankoor above.

After the two had left, Auron returned to the council and informed them of the irritating and frankly baffling decision of Johan. Couldn't he see it was the most logical course of action? Couldn't he see that there was no other way to defeat these enemies? Damn it, why did the young have to be so defiant!

Merrik Caspar wasn't surprised in the slightest at the news. Not just the news of their decision, but also that he didn't have the knife on him and had hidden it somewhere away from prying eyes. It was more than true that there had been a search squad sent out to their room to find it, and that they'd all been thoroughly scanned once they entered the spire, but both tactics had yielded no returns, and those infuriating newcomers still held the upper hand on the WGC. As promised, Auron Bree had tried to fuck with Johan Otan'co, and he didn't like the results. Merrik seriously hoped Auron's next tactic was a little more open-minded when it came to those from Tan Torna Qu'ay.

Once the council was informed, the room was cleared and the final preparations on the H.Y. bomb were put in place by Auron, with the two final solutions programmed in. The first was the agreed upon 1-hour countdown, which wasn't to be activated until the city was evacuated and the enemy was confirmed to be within its borders.

The second, less-desirable option was the 30-second clock; the last hope against anything the enemy tried, should things not go as planned. With one press of a button, the emergency clock was activated with no stopping it.

The commands entered and the bomb prepared, Auron gave a

heavy sigh, took the manual remote that would activate the 1-hour clock (the last-ditch 30-second clock could only be activated on the weapon itself) and left the now silent spire to do its vigilant, city-powering duties. The WGC and anyone else who was involved with the military operations from here likely would not return. No military might or coordinated strike could stop Embracers, and if they needed to command field troops for any other reason, they could do so from home or any other computer terminal in Bankoor. Auron doubted it would come to that. Something about this turn of events told him that Bankoor wasn't likely to be here in the next few days. He hoped he was wrong, but something inside him laughed at any option that wasn't using the H.Y. bomb.

Embracers. Of all the things to add to this enemy, why that?

In the darkened spire, only the soft hum of the power generators and electrical equipment could be heard. Without the knowledge of security (the system had been easily deactivated) and with the grace of a cat, a dark and ominous figure oozed out of the shadows, hidden away for hours in perfect stillness until just such an opportunity as this arose: a chance to infiltrate the enemy headquarters and see just what power and abilities they possessed. The fools were so far behind the times it was a wonder they stood firm as long as they had. The task ahead of it was a simple one.

The shadow moved to the far doors, through the blackened hallways, down the elevator shaft to the awaiting, silent base of operations below. There it began uploading anything and everything useful that it found. Troop sizes, positions and armaments were first, followed by senior ranking officials, their standard battle tactics and the general overview of anything the enemy could use against them at any point. Simple stuff, really, but something might be important, should it ever get called back into the fray.

It was almost ready to take off again when it saw in the darkness an outline it was very familiar with. That of the oblong gray object sitting on the other side of the room. *That* wasn't mentioned in any report. No mention of it was made in any official channel, which meant it wasn't supposed to be known by anyone but the top brass.

It walked over to it and ran its black, metallic fingers along its edges, much the same as Auron Bree had done. This was not their weapon. It was too far advanced for that. It was even more advanced than the similar weapons used by its own forces. This one was special. This one was more than a killing machine. This was made to stop a war.

Perhaps they were smarter than it had assumed? To have something like this around meant they had the means to use it, and if that was the case, perhaps this invasion wasn't going to go as smoothly as its superiors intended.

It prodded the controls but wasn't surprised to find it couldn't access it like it had the low-security systems they employed on their other computers. The technology rivaled its own, and that was enough to stop it from checking its setting or altering them in any way. Disappointing, but not a complete loss. Somewhere there was a remote, likely with one of the important people that had just left the spire. It just had to figure out who had it.

For now, it knew all it had to. It didn't have the ability to hope, but it did have a need for self-preservation, and that need propelled it to think that it had better get some word from its forces soon. Not only did it have all the technical specs needed to crush these weak people, but it also knew about the active and waiting weapon they held in secrecy.

However, its orders were to wait, and wait it would. Until then, it simply turned and left, exiting the spire and eventually returning back to the city shadows that it had emerged from.

Chapter 5: A Deal is a Deal

After another silent, nerve-wracking ride back to their accommodations, the two returning from the spire met up with Esgona, who looked as though he hadn't moved an inch from the time they'd left. He still stood on the side of the road with his slight lean, a look of constant discomfort. The expression on his face was more determined than his general look of shame and disinterest. The expression told Johan two things: something happened while they were gone to draw him back out here, and he now had a very strong interest in what they had been told. Johan hated the coming confrontation already, especially in the wake of the news about the supposed leader of the coming Embracers and the army of Old behind them.

They got out of the transport, approached their glowering companion and proceeded to promptly walk right past him, back to the rooms they'd been given (free of charge, of course). Esgona never missed a beat and was right on their heels instantly.

"Nothing's missing, as near as I can tell," Esgona told them as they reached their rooms and began looking around. "They came with handheld equipment that beeped and seemed to do the looking for them. They never had to move a thing. Now, can you tell me what they're looking for?"

Johan said nothing, not wanting to engage in this conversation just yet. "Johan's knife," Seraphina eventually answered, perturbed by the childishness of the two in the face of the things they'd seen. "They suspect it's an Embracer's item of Focus, one that they have a use for. A use we certainly *will not* be turning it over to them for."

Johan looked at her but said nothing, continuing to look around his room, knowing full well he wasn't going to find anything out of place since the knife wasn't here. That part of what he'd told Auron was the truth. There was now the issue, however, of *where* it was that began to worry him slightly.

With prompting from Seraphina, Esgona began telling them of the strangely dressed men and women who had entered their rooms, never telling him any more than that it was a 'standard security matter', an obvious lie.Once they were done, they asked Esgona to return to his room and await his 'friends' once more. He instead and retuned outside to wait for them to finish their business.

"Now," he said, his part of the tale over, "who would like to tell me about your morning?"

Irritation on Johan's face, but reluctance as well. He began telling him of the initial meeting with the War and Glory Council and Auron Bree, followed by the exposure of some grander plan on their behalf and eventually to the ascension to the top of the spire (a trip Esgona was glad he never made) and the information learned there (save for the part about the man with wings). Esgona wasn't as shocked to hear about the involvement of the Embracers as they were, but that was likely because nothing was likely to shock any of them now, least of all the one who's been thrust into this whole war from the beginning.

Then followed the trip into the depths of the spire and all that went on there, right down to the H.Y. bomb and the plan to use it.It was then that Esgona, the one who feared (and had the most to fear from) the technology they spoke of, surprised them each with an actual smile, which remained on his face as he sat in a chair by a window.

"What?" Johan asked, curious and more than a little upset. "What's so damn funny?"

Esgona shrugged. "What isn't?" he asked playfully. "We've gone straight from the frying pan to the fire here, don't you see that? We've run directly into the arms of people that aren't any better than the enemy we face, an enemy we hate and fear. They just have a human face, so we accept it.

"What's funny is that you're shocked and frightened at what

these people have locked in their basement. You're shocked because you found exactly what you wanted to find and it scares the hell out of you."

"What do you mean we 'wanted' to find it?" Johan asked. What point was Esgona trying to make?"

Esgona's hard eyes glinted. "You wanted to and you know it. Or maybe you don't? Maybe your bravado was nothing but masked stupidity?" The old Esgona, the bane of the other's youthful existence, was creeping in.

"Think about it. Why did you run? To fight and win. How were you going to do that? With your knife? With guns? With lasers? With an army of outgunned Riders and whomever else had joined their cause? Of course not. "Now you tell me these people have a weapon that can not only stop our enemy, but the Embracers who've apparently taken up with them to lead the charge, all for the cost of your precious knife? Sounds to me that you're a fool if you don't make that deal, Johan, and make it fast. Give them the knife and let them destroy whatever the hell they want!"

They each knew of Esgona's history with the army of the Old and his overwhelming fear of technology, so it was shocking for them to hear him speak so boldly and openly about doing what Johan had feared so much.

Esgona read the expressions on their faces. "Seriously, Johan? You don't get it yet? We can't go home again, and I don't just mean because my mother foolishly got it blown up, either. I mean that we are now locked into a world of mechanical soldiers, laser pistols and devastating bombs. They have completely overrun our homeland by now. No one there can live in that blissful ignorance about the outside world.

"And look at this city! It's a collection of people and technology from lands far away. We were fools to ever doubt it was out there. We seem so shocked because we were so ass-backwards that we'd riot and go insane."

Johan and Seraphina sat on a bed across from Esgona now. For the moment, Johan was speechless at the audacity and truth in Esgona's words. Just what *was* their plan, anyway?

"I *hate* being here with you. I *hate* that I saved your life from that monster, and I *hate* the fact that if I want to make it to see two days from now I'm going to need you. But I hate that army coming at us a hundred times more than a disgraced bastard."

Johan was up at once, but Esgona and his defiance held him back. The points weren't finished being made. "Oh yeah, you're not high on my wish list of people I hoped I'd be in this situation with, and Gods help me if that winged freak friend of yours ever comes back, because I don't care what he said; something about him and what I saw doesn't add up, but I'll cross that bridge when I come to it.

"The bottom line is, I'm here, and so are you, so what are we going to do? Throw rocks at them as they march over the city? You wanted a weapon and a plan to beat them, and it's delivered to you on a platter! You said yourself that parts of the city are being evacuated right now. Let them take the city! Let our hosts burn this one to the ground! Let them do it a thousand times if it destroys them and we win and live to gloat about it!Back in Huan, I came to you because I knew that you, Johan, had some kind of plan to defeat that army based strictly on what minuscule amount of information I'd given you about my capture and torture at their hands. Tell me, right now, what was that plan?"

Johan flustered. So much had happened since then that he had to think back on it. "You told me about how they never spoke, how they communicated by some other means."

Esgona remained silent, waiting to hear what he had in mind.

"Well, that means they used some kind of unheard system to talk to each other, likely some kind of wireless communication.Any form of that kind of communication I've ever heard of is disrupted by sufficient amounts of electrical or magnetic interference. I assumed that whomever we met up with out here would have those means, at least according to how Stroan described them. The means to do something like that. There's even a possibility that a large and powerful enough shock would shut them down entirely."

Esgona shouted, jarring each of them, "That's fucking *brilliant*! With the Embracer's involved, it may not work now, but at the time I told you shit-all and you came up with a plan like that! That's why

I came with you two, and it's why I'm still here. Once this is done and this city is destroyed and crumbles around our enemies, I'll be the first one to shake your hand, and then I'll hobble off into the sunset and you'll never see me again. I'll go get a farm somewhere and never set my eyes on a piece of this damned technology. I've had enough for a lifetime.

"But I'll never, ever forget that it's out there, and you had better believe it's everywhere. Why else do you think they landed where they did? Because our lands are fertile, our position in the world was tactically sound, and our people were weak and easy to overrun. It was the smartest place to go, because everywhere else would have put up more of a fight."

Esgona exhaled heavily. The look of disinterest returned, likely because he could see on the faces before him that his point was made. They each understood, and that was all he wanted: to snap them out of their irrational fear and get Johan's brilliant gears turning again.

And you had better believe that turning they certainly were.

"We need to find Stroan."

It didn't take long to find the barracks where Stroan's company had been stationed, but the building was empty and only a security guard was left.

"All military forces have been pulled to the battlefront on the south end of the city in preparation to fight in case they get this far," they were told. This was likely Auron's doing. Telling the city's residence that an army and Embracers were coming at them now was almost certain to start a mass panic. It seemed that little tidbit had been kept from the populace by the WGC. Johan simply hoped they were pulled back before this meaningless posturing led to the empty and useless deaths of thousands of brave soldiers, their friend August Stroan included.

Stroan's whereabouts acquired, Johan pushed the guard to allow him access to the barracks, a request that was shot down at once. "We can't let civilians in without clearance, and the people who give that clearance are with the rest of the forces outside the city."

Johan had already formulated another plan, in case this was

an issue. "Do you know who we are?" he asked the guard, before explaining they were the brave and heroic fighting souls from the Paieleh Valley, the ones who the party the previous night thrown in these very barracks was for. He also explained that one of the Riders was a good friend of theirs and that in the good times at that party, Johan had given an item of value to this Rider friend. An item he needed to retrieve right now, whether the guards let them in or not.

Johan knew someone was looking for it, so he'd given it to Stroan to hold until he needed it. It was a great plan, except for the sudden and unexpected deployment of the Riders at the crack of dawn today. Johan had covered that as well, setting up a default hiding place among Stroan's personal things in case something like this came up. Esgona thought once more to himself that he'd done the right thing trusting the mind of Johan, despite his dislike of the rest of him.

After a couple of arbitrary questions to confirm their identity, the guard escorted them inside the building and led them to what his records indicated was Stroan's room. Johan began looking through nooks and crannies before finding what he was searching for, an old blanket used for campouts.

Inside, its firmness felt long before it was seen, was Johan's knife, along with a folded piece of paper tucked into the sheath beside it. Johan strapped on the knife and thanked the guard for his help. "Just a knife? I thought it'd be money or jewelry, something a little more valuable for you to want it so bad."

Johan smiled, "I'll remember you said that when it saves your life."

"It's only a matter of time until that guard calls in what just happened as a matter of protocol. Then, Auron and the WGC will know what happened. They may try something to get their hands on it, despite my promise not to run. This will at least give us a moment before they try."

"Do you expect them to?" Seraphina asked, her dark eyes looking at him with apprehension.

"I don't know, but what I do know is that they're convinced that this thing is the only course of action, so they may not be as honorable to our deal as I am."

They found a place to sit among a cluster of strange trees and flowers. Beautiful, but also a reminder that they were each very far from home. The sun was up in full force, and other than their impending doom, it looked like it was going to be a beautiful day.

Once comfortable, Esgona was the first to speak. "So what's your plan now, Johan? Tell me it's giving them the knife and being done with this stupidity." Johan took the knife from its sheath and looked closely at it. The echo it whispered in his head was much louder now, as it was for all of them who looked at it right. All that had happened in the last few weeks had made them older and wiser. It had begun to speak to him and whisper its history. The feeling was unsettling. He set it on the ground in front of him.

"No, Esgona," Johan said at last, "I don't think I am."

Esgona tore his eyes away from the knife. He looked at Johan and without a word.

"At least, not yet," Johan continued. "We fought very hard to get to this point. Many died by our side to get us here, and I'm not willing to forget them all so easily. Even if I give it to them, I never promised I'd give it to them today. I'll give it to them when I'm ready to. I only promised to give him an answer by the end of the day, not the knife itself."

"Cute," Esgona replied, "and your reasoning is?"

"My reasoning, Esgona, is that I want all the time in the world I can get."

"You have got to be kidding me, Johan. I thought you were so much smarter than that." Esgona looked disgusted with this idea and the man who had thought it up. Then, realization dawned on Esgona's face.

"You're waiting for Aryu, aren't you?"

Johan smirked. "Yes I am. Aryu, and with any luck, his big friend."

It was a gamble, but Johan thought it was one that was worth it, if for nothing else than the sake of honor. Aryu was still out there somewhere, and although he still didn't believe he'd make it in time, and he knew that the odds of him arriving and finding them in this city in the next day was extremely unlikely, the love and honor he had for his friend would allow nothing less. If Bankoor was lost to the coming army, what then? Where would they find Aryu? The chances of them being lost to each other for the rest of their lives became that much higher if the agreed meeting place was overrun or destroyed. But Johan knew it was deeper than that as well.

Aryu clearly had found a weapon of focus, that much was obvious to him by now, and if he returned with the one named Nixon, who was also a lock for being an Embracer of the Power, then that gave them a considerable increase in options about what to do next. Embracers were notorious for their lack of defense against one more powerful than themselves (the third fall of man being proof enough of that). If this Nixon person was more powerful, he would give them a strong leg up, and if he wasn't, well, this plan was already pretty thin as it was. What was one more long shot?

Johan had no illusions about any of this happening, and he told them that right away (with Esgona burning holes in him with his eyes as he talked). However, he had one more day to wait before he had to turn over the knife to the WGC, and that was one more day he had to give Aryu to return to them. As a man of honor, and a man who missed his good friend and brother, it was something he had to do. There was no reasoning him out of it. Seraphina understood, while Esgona shot daggers at the foolishness of this ludicrous hope. He knew that Johan would make the right choice in the end, and if not, well, perhaps he'd just have to make it for him.

They spent the rest of the day in the public eye; never straying too far. Johan never thought that Auron would try something if they remained in plain sight. He was a powerful man, but he was also a politician, and that position had many limitations. It was also simply an act of faith. If they chose to corner them and take the knife, there wasn't much they could do about it. Still, best to keep all options open.

They wandered through stores and shops, marveling as they went at the advancement of the toys and trinkets they saw there.

They'd been given some spending money in the form of strange coins the night before at the party, mostly as gifts of thanks, but they didn't really know what they were worth. When the time came to eat and they paid for their meals, Seraphina was convinced they'd been swindled after so many of their coins were taken.

Johan never cared, thinking only of the fact that the city would be empty and possibly not even there by the end of the next day. The odds were good that they wouldn't be coming back this way again, so let the dishonest ones take what they like.

They ate in a park near the spire in the heart of it all. They'd opted to meander to the impressive tower by the evening, not wanting another ride if they could help it, and the walk gave Johan the chance to mull over his decisions and plot his next move.He had the start of a plan. It was just a question of whether or not Auron would agree to it. If not, he still had other great options at his disposal, but nothing that made him feel as confident as the one he'd already concocted. Of course, life would be instantly easier if Aryu would just show up already. Then he'd be inundated with fantastic ideas. For now, he stuck with his simple solution.

As the evening darkened to night, they all couldn't help but notice the lack of lights in the buildings and stores around them. The city was almost empty.They made it to the base of the deep black spire, not a soul in sight except themselves.Esgona lagged behind as they climbed the stairs.

Johan opened the door he'd been through earlier that day and they entered the Counsel's main meeting room, devoid of anyone but Merrik Caspar and Auron Bree, both of which were seated at the far end of the table waiting patiently for the evening to get underway. Auron was on his feet at once, striding over to them in a rush. A hurried introduction with Esgona later, he was then indicating they take seats opposite Caspar on their end of the table.

"Pardon my rush," he said, though his voice was smooth and calm even if his body was rushed and shaky, "but the day has been eventful since you left here."

"Really?" Esgona spoke up at once. "Something other than searching our rooms for Johan's knife?"Johan shot him a look, but Esgona ignored it. He had been fairly silent since his eye-opening tirade earlier.

Auron smiled at the accusation. "Guilty, I admit, but we covered that base earlier, hadn't we folks?I won't deny attempting to do anything that increases my chances of defeating our enemies and that includes such backhanded tactics. We're not strangers to one another anymore, are we. Let's not pretend you're here of your own free will, because we all know you are here because of mine."

"You're not making much of a case for us to help you," Seraphina said, showing the fire she held under her skin. It's appearance always surprised Johan.

"Because, my dear, we need each other and although I don't always take the path of righteousness, I still prefer it given the options. If you can see that I'm right, you will do what I wish you to do. If you don't..."

Seraphina looked uncomfortable. Johan looked half-impressed at being confronted so boldly. "If we don't, you'll just take it by force and be done with us," Johan finished.

"We all know the facts, friends, so let's let that be that and continue with why you're here." Auron extended his hand to Johan, not in a handshake of trust, but as a clear sign that he was to hand over the knife now. Johan drew away.

"Not yet, Auron. I agreed to come to a decision by tonight and I've done that, but I never promised to give you anything." Johan watched Auron's face for some sign of anger or a movement that might indicate he intended to take it now.

Auron gave neither though, and simply retracted his hand and crossed his arms as he leaned back into his chair at the head of the table. "I'm listening," was all he said.

Johan took the knife out and set it on the table, not to be taunting, but to give a clear indication of the prize they both wanted. A trophy for the victor. Auron and Merrik took in the knife, and the expression on each of their faces told them all the truth: that they had seen the knife, and it was what they were seeking. A Focus item of the Embracers, and a very powerful one judging by the smile that came to Auron's face.

"I want you to tell me something, Auron," Johan began, "before you drop everything and destroy this city, are you open to other options, or is your mind set on this one?"

Auron grinned at the prospect of what Johan could possibly ask of him. "I'll listen, but you fight a very uphill battle."

"The story of my life, Auron," Johan acknowledged. "Tell me, what if I gave you to option of defeating the army of the Old in one move while saving Bankoor? Would you listen?"

"I would, but only as long as the story isn't a long one. Time is very valuable right now."

"Time is always valuable, Auron," Johan responded before he continued. "Now listen, because I don't want to repeat myself."

The others sat back and began to listen as Johan laid out the plan. It was makeshift and thrown together, but it could save the city.

"How tight can you make the blast zone on the bomb?" Johan asked.

"We're not sure. It's all fairly new to us, remember, but very small, a few city blocks, perhaps? However, a blast that small would likely tear a hole in the sky with the force contained to such a small area."

"Alright. Once the enemy enters the city we can likely stop them all, as well as those around Bankoor, with a minimum amount of damage to the city itself."

"And how do you propose that?" Auron asked. He honestly did want to know.

"With the glorious spire above us," answered Johan. "You've said yourself, it's a giant power collector. Enough power to keep this whole city glowing."

"And likely two or three more like it," Merrik piped in. "It was made to support far more than the drain the city puts on it."

"Perfect," smiled Johan. Like the knife to Auron, the spire was even better than he'd anticipated. "Auron, I believe you should overload the spire to the point of a total system collapse, possibly explosion."

"And I'd do that because…?"

"Because that much power when released into the city in a magnetic wave will fry anything electronic within the blast radius. Even things like this army that are likely protected against that kind of attack would be susceptible to the kinds of power we're talking about, even if it just cuts out all of their ability to communicate.

"I say you charge it up, let it pop, watch the enemy fall all around you and then use your precious bomb, full to its core with all the power my knife can give it, on the remaining position of the Embracers. I'm betting good money they won't be in the city at all."

"Intriguing. What makes you think that? They're leading the way now, why not open the doors and walk right in?"

"Because they are Embracers. They're immortals with unimaginable power and even more unimaginable pride. They fight to get to the city, but once here, they would let the massive army behind them do the dirty work. Then they come in and finish the job. Also, they're not stupid; they'd see a trap set up in the city from days away, likely from the moment you pulled back your forces all the way to its borders. You're a fool to think they'd walk right in, Auron. They're not so long lived because they're stupid."

Auron was no longer smiling. This boy had done something Auron didn't want or expect: he had created doubt in the master plan, and that doubt started eating away at Auron Bree's confidence. "And if they enter?" he asked, curious for more reasons than simply amusement now.

"Then you have the bomb ready to go already, don't you. Keep it buried, away from the pulse. Keep it separate and deep in the ground, and it won't be affected. Get it out and move it right under their feet if you have to. You can't tell me you don't have the means to get it to them quickly."

"Perhaps, but what's to stop them from catching it and destroying it, or worse, taking it before then? Our other attempts to even come close to them were all total failures."

"I can't think of everything, Auron, but it's a safe bet they'll scramble when that blast from the spire gets to them. You have a better chance getting them in the confusion afterwards than you do getting them any other way, no matter where they are. Last resort, take out the city and as much around it as you can, just as you planned, Embracers and all."

Auron was still out of sorts, but a glimmer in his eye told Johan he'd come through the worst of it and was making his own plans yet again. "Why save the city? You've only been here a day. Why try so hard to keep it intact?"

"Because I won't sit back and just allow you to kill countless innocents, Auron."

"Innocents?"

"Please, you all know we've been walking around the city all day. A lot of people are gone, but not all of them, and I doubt all of them will be. Tell me, in your calculations, what's your number of people who refuse to leave or haven't the means to survive on their own, like the sick and dying? How many innocents would die in your master plan."

Auron's amazement and respect for this young man grew with every discussion he had with him. Johan was correct, of course. "By our best guess, two thousand people will likely remain. It was the best we could do."

"I believe you," Johan said truthfully, "but that's two thousand too many to me. Not if I can help it."

Auron leaned forward, hands clasped in front of him. Auron was in charge, and he was more than a little egotistical, but that didn't mean he was completely unmoving when faced with someone like Johan. Indeed, it was his acceptance of others that helped keep him in power.

"Johan, you are a credit to your people and your home. Tonight I will have what little people I can spare look into your idea. If it is possible, I am willing to entertain it. I'd say I have nothing to lose by doing so, really, as I expect the end result to be the same. If and when my plan of action needs to be put in place, I want your word you will let us use your knife and allow us to do as we planned, knowing you at least tried to save the ones who remained."

"You have it Auron," Johan answered.

"Good, I've entertained you enough now and I have many other issues to attend. Merrik will see you to new quarters on the premises, I insist. What little you have has already been brought here. Forgive me for my rudeness, but until such a time as I deem it unnecessary, I'd prefer if you all remained close at hand."

"I expected no less," Johan answered.

With that, Auron left back through the far door that led to the basement or wherever it was he was going, and soon after he was gone.

Seraphina looked into Johan's eyes. "You did great, even though I still think you're giving him too much trust. I don't understand everything, but you certainly took control of the situation."

"Congratulate us in two days," Johan replied quietly.

Chapter 6: Dawn in the Forest

As the sun rose over Bankoor, so too did it rise up the hillside to the site of Aryu and Nixon's camp. It was a morning that didn't see the return of their friend.

"Do you think something's gone wrong?" Aryu asked Nixon after the big man had returned from a scouting mission to see what had happened.

"I know it has," Nixon answered, looking dejected.

Aryu was heartbroken at the thought of Sho being lost to some yet-unseen trouble, especially after the valiant battles on the plane or at HOME.

"There are Embracers. Two, possibly three, I canna' say for certain from where I was lookin'. Over by the road next t'some run-down vehicles."

Aryu went white. One Embracer far from home with little to lose was all they'd come up against when they first faced down the Army of the Old. Now they possibly had three to deal with. Aryu looked to Nixon for reassurance but found none. "I fear the time 'as come t' let the secret out, Aryu."

Nixon was referring to the fact that he still had his considerable power to use at any time, and possibly the fact that it was Nixon of the Great Fire and Ash and the wielder of the Shi Kaze that they faced. "Is there no other way?" Aryu asked. "Nothing we can do to hide?"

"Not without riskin' Sho's life," Nixon answered. "We've made it farther then I'd e'er hoped. Savin' Sho 'n keepin' our enemy off guard so close t' their lines seems t' be a good enough reason t' me.

"Don't get me wrong, I'm not sayin' I unleash everythin' I've got 'ere and now, but I doubt we can get through this without me usin' enough to alert Izuku 'n 'is other Embracers t'the fact tha' I'm so close and still in command of my faculties. This trip may get considerably more dangerous from 'ere on out."

That was an understatement. If Izuku knew Nixon was still powerful, there was no telling what fury he'd unleash on them just to keep the phoenix from interfering.

"I'm ready for whatever they try so long as it means we get Sho back alive," Aryu said, getting to his feet and tensing his wings in a sign of readiness. Nixon smiled at the bravado.

"Good, Aryu, because from 'ere on out, ye'ad better be ready for anythin."

They made their way to a road was likely used for logging or a distant mine in the mountains. They stayed to the tree line, weapons out and ready. Soon, as the road dipped away, they found a rocky outcropping that overlooked the hill below as it fell away into a series of switchbacks, weaving back and forth to the position of the Embracers.

"There," the phoenix pointed, "the three're still by those old transports. The road straightens beyond 'emto'ard the city." Nixon could see the city clearly now, spire and all. "I'd guess Izuku's front lines're getting' close t' it. Do'ya think tha's where yer' friend is?"

Aryu couldn't see the city, but he almost felt as though he could feel it now. "I hope so. It matches the description we gave each other about where to meet."

"Theodds're fairly small tha' he's even there, ya' know," Nixon said. It wasn't meant to be rude or reassuring; just a statement of fact. "The distances traveled, lands and the sheer scale of the places you've each traveled make it very unlikely."

"I know, but there's still a chance, and that's enough."

"Well focus. If yer too wrapped up in anything other than the moment at hand, you're of little use t' me."

Aryu's eyes went cold. "Don't worry. Sho is just as important to me. I've been through just as much in a few weeks with him as I did a year with Johan. Besides, I want to see him get his power back and inflict some real damage on Izuku."

Silence for a moment as Nixon seemed to be contemplating

every variable. "So what now? We go in swords blazing?" Aryu asked, hoping for a better plan that didn't rely on such quick and dirty methods.

"We do. Remember, the sword 'n shield, coupled with wha' little of my power I chose t' use, will only distract 'em 'fer so long. After tha', they'll come at us with everythin' they've got. I've no idea wha' that is; each Embracer's power shows itself in different ways, but be ready 'feranythin', even things ya' ne'er believed were possible."

A wry smirk appeared on Aryu's young face. "Ha, there's not much of that left, I promise you."

Aryu stretched his wings, ready for the dive into a maelstrom of the Power, something he had feared all of his life. He crouched, sweaty but ready for liftoff, when Nixon grabbed him again. "Wait, I'll lead the charge. If possible, stay behind me. Also, there's somethin' else ya' should know 'bout Embracers."

"Fantastic. And that would be?"

"Tha' they contain and control vast amounts of the Power while alive, but in death they lose tha' control 'n the Power they've drawn from the world around 'em. The fireworks when they're killed may be… distractin', as the Power is released 'n returned t' the world."

"And is that release dangerous?" Aryu asked, intrigued by this new information.

"Well," replied Nixon, a reassuring-yet-sinister smile on his face, "one time it saved the world, 'n one time it destroyed it. Remember tha'."

With that sobering thought, Nixon set alight his impressive wings of fire, and with a push of heat and wind he was off the outcrop and heading for the Embracers, broadsword in hand.

"For Tan Torna Qu'ay," he Aryu softly, the battle cry of he and Johan during their year away. The words that meant more to Aryu now than any others these days. With shield and Shi Kaze at the ready, Aryu followed into the heart of battle.

Fortunately for this rescue party of two, the three Embracers they currently rushed towards were not so far in tune with their powers to recognize what they felt: a tickle in the back of their subconscious that was more of an irritation than a warning. Luck favored the bold once more.

The woman appeared to lead this group. She was tall and strong, with ragged dirty hair and a nasty smile to go with her disposition. Although not the oldest of Izuku's Embracers, she was one of the most ruthless. She was one of the few Embracers who went the way of deception and destruction of their own accord, not because of some tragic back story. She was simply a horrible person, and she reveled in it. Her focus item, a long, curved two-handed scimitar, hung at her side.

"How long do we have to wait?" one of the men asked.

She growled fiercely at him like an animal and let that be her only response. How could Embracers be so impatient? They'd loaded the one named Sho onto an automated transport and sent him back to Izuku as requested. Now, they simply had to wait for the other two. Even one as unstable as her wasn't keen on fighting Embracers, fully powered or not, but they each agreed to go when Izuku assured them their targets were powerless. When they were captured, these three could return to the front line with the others.

They'd found the trio a few days before, set up camp here, and simply waited.

Suddenly, that prick of irritation in the back of her subconscious mind flared up enough for her to notice, but the source was still unknown, until the sound of a *thud* behind the three alerted them to the coming of something large and very dangerous.

The three turned, hands on their respective weapons, and each was dumbstruck at what they saw.

Even newer ranks of Embracers such as these knew of Nixon Ash, and more importantly, the power he possessed and the weapon he carried. The kind of power Nixon would have had to use to strike from afar was too much for him to risk, but it wasn't anything he concerned himself with. These three weren't more than children as far as Embracers go. Izuku's pickings had likely been slim thanks to Ryu and his temper culling their ranks thousands of years ago.

As they had been under the impression that Nixon was powerless, his sudden, Power-aided arrival was terrifying. They were three against one, and they weren't going down without a fight. They'd lived too long to stop now, but even still there was doubt.

One of the others, a small man with two short knives, was the first to strike. He dove at the beast with lightning speed, an aura of yellow encasing him as he did so. The blur of movement that came next was dizzying as Nixon parried away, thrusting a massive hand behind him and striking the attacker with his fist like a club, tossing him aside and through a nearby bramble like nothing.

The other man, a dark-skinned Embracer with a full suit of armor and a broadsword similar to Nixon's, leapt not to the phoenix but away, razors of white light streaking from his hands as he did so, crashing into the ground. Nixon dodged them each or let them glance off his mighty sword, which seemed to swallow them up as if they were ethereal snacks. None of them came close to getting through.

That is, until the first attacker was back on his feet and charged the distracted enemy again, once more incased in his yellow glow. He caught Nixon full-on in the back and drove him into one of the derelict machines behind them. With Nixon down, the woman grasped her weapon and headed towards the fight.

She allowed the Power to rise up inside her, a dark and unformed mass of fear and unpredictability she had taken years to master. The feeling of chaos and disorder poured into the long, curved weapon, filling both it and its user with strength and confidence. She raised her hand, channeling the energy from the weapon, and unleashed it all in a striking dart of smoky black and green.

The empowered and ethereal dart shot out from her hand towards the phoenix as he fought. The ecstasy of the use of the Power encompassed her as she watched her pride and joy surge forward, about to cripple the beast and allow his capture for Izuku.

Unexpectedly, she watched as another figure appeared from the sky, aided not by the Power but by wings.

The young man landed between her and Nixon with amazing speed and grace, a shield in hand. She had a split-second thought that he was a fool to believe he could stop the attack, but once the vapor dart hit the shield and it shattered away into nothing, her temporary amusement ceased.It was Sho's legendary shield! She'd thought it lost or simply left behind when the fool stumbled out of the woods at them unarmed. Sho was very powerful and likely had no use for in anymore, as elder Embracers like himself often didn't. Now, here it was.

The anger she felt fueled her Power even more. The build of it within her was almost too much for her to take as she looked at the young man with seething with rage for what he'd done. She wouldn't be denied again.She rushed at him, a cloud of black/green smoke engulfing her as she moved, her weapon striding out before her, covered in the same dark essence. She was on him in an instant, slashing at him with unbelievable speed, but he was amazingly able to counter. Not by use of the Power, but by skill and a need to survive. He was afraid, and the taste drove her forward madly.

Shockwaves of dark power rolled off her with each strike as the scimitar struck blow after blow onto the shield, all while keeping her a good distance away from it. She feared death, but it was possible she feared failure more. Soon he was matching her and her abilities, and in no time at all had forced her back a step or two.

The anger at the offensive was that much more fuel added to what she already felt, and soon the Power surged inside her. At last she'd reached a point where she couldn't take it any longer. The outburst was going to take this fool and half the forest with it, but she would not fall to a Powerless mortal.

With a hard swipe that forced him back a half-step, she poured what she could spare into the weapon she held and began swinging at him, eager to get him to a point where he couldn't stop the Power she was about to unleash.The swing missed, as he used his wings to force himself away from it with inhuman speed, causing her to lose her balance and stutter-step to the side. In that instance, he produced something else so quickly that she missed seeing what it was. Once she regained her balance and struck at him again, he countered by deflecting the blow. The sudden force of Power that surged through the clash of weapons and into her hand tossed the scimitar away like a toy.

With shock and surprise, she was instantly defenseless, though not without the aid of the Power. She turned her hands to him, prepared to strike with the force she had stored. He stepped back, shield in hand, ready for whatever she was preparing, and from his right side came the other item from hiding.

The Power left her at once, as did any control she thought she had. In her momentary hesitation, he struck forward, driving his sword, *the* sword, into her heart. She was felled instantly, and by the Shi Kaze no less!

The feeling an Embracer encounters when they are killed is more like falling asleep than an outright blackout. They gradually drift off, which is the feeling one gets when the Power leaves them. As they drift into the blackness of death, the Power surges out of them with great force, glad to be free from its entrapment, and into the world around it once more.

To Aryu, she looked as though she'd caught fire and exploded as the force of energy tossed him away almost as powerfully as the shockwave from the bomb blast that destroyed Tan Torna Qu-ay had, only this was more on a spiritual level than a physical one.

Once he was on his feet and in his guard again, she was gone. For one such as her, the world was better for it.

Pulling himself out of the shock of what he'd just witnessed, Aryu turned to the fight Nixon was engaged in and found the phoenix battling with one man while the other was cast aside, though not yet dead.

In a flurry of movement, the fire beast spun about, expertly countering every move his opponent threw at him. The skill of his swordsmanship was unbelievable to Aryu. He was truly a master warrior.

As he ran, Aryu began the strange and powerful motion of clenching his fists and the inner gears of the shield came to life, spinning the armored disk with a sharp whine just as Sho had instructed. Soon it was at full speed and spinning freely on its well-oiled bearings. At first Aryu had to fight to move it, its own g-forces threatening to make him lose control, but by the time he reached the battle the motion of the weapon was familiar to him and he had no fear of its misuse.

The man on the ground was moving, rising up in a way that made Aryu shiver. It wasn't a natural motion at all; more like levitation. He spun around, eyes a fiery yellow as he began to build whatever inherent Power he had stored, ready to hit Nixon. In an instant, Aryu was between them, spinning blades of Sho's shield protecting him as the Shi Kaze lay hidden behind.The man hesitated briefly at the sight of the shield, but soon he was rushing at them both, floating towards them as the yellow aura that encompassed him trailed behind like a comet's tail.

Aryu didn't have much time to think as the man was on them instantly. With the speed he was approaching, moving was impossible, and it was only a second for Aryu to go from hero to fool in his own head. Desperation kicked in at last and Aryu lunged forward with the blades of the shield, attempting to strike the empowered attack. The man saw it in time to move, and with no aid of wings or rockets, changed direction and launched into the sky, yellow flames following him the whole way.

Aryu never hesitated and was running uphill to get a better position, giving chase as best he could, careful not to allow the man a run at Nixon, who was still expertly weaving between attacks but wasn't as of yet getting an upper hand.

As the hovering man stopped, assessing his next move, Aryu could feel the small part of him that knew what the Power was beginning to vibrate, a sign that a large amount of it was nearby.The feeling of it reminded Aryu of just how easily he could embrace that same power if he needed to. Was it so wrong if he used it to save both himself and Nixon? Would it be an action Nixon would forgive?

Aryu wrestled with the possibilities as the man succumbed to the yellow around him, becoming nothing but a ball of flame and vapor. Then, he was at them, charging Nixon like a meteor from the sky, ignoring Aryu as he tried to climb higher. Nixon was powerful, but attacks from Embracers could still do damage to him, especially in a state that was trying to limit his own powers.Aryu, with a lack of options, wisely avoided use of the Power and instead put his faith in the weapons he carried and skills he'd learned. He squeezed the brakes on the spinning blades and allowed the weapon to halt, bringing it around to guide himself.

With some of his most powerful pushes he'd ever mustered from his wings, he drove outward towards the path of the diving man, Shi Kaze out and ready to pierce his enemy. He couldn't be sure he'd even hit him, but it didn't matter much now. The need outweighed the risks.

The gap closed in a heartbeat as the man and his otherworldly power saw Aryu coming and redirected himself, striking the shield and Aryu almost head on, seemingly intent to push them out of the way if possible. As the force struck Aryu, he allowed the shield to take the brunt of it and glance the blow off to the side as he brought the Ski Kaze through the center of the fireball.

At first he thought he'd missed, the effort of the blow being so minimal. Then, out of the falling star, the image of a man who had apparently cut cleanly in two appeared.

The fire surrounding him died away, and soon the shockwave burst out of the halves as they fell. The sudden pulse hit the ground, startling the last of the three enough for Nixon to break his defenses, and with a swift motion he brought down the great flaming sword. Moments later his opponent was no more, another sudden expulsion of the Power pouring out, leaving only a space where a man had just been.

Aryu landed next to Nixon as he sheathed the broadsword. "Are you alright?" he asked the beast, himself putting away the Shi Kaze.

"Aye. These weren't the oldest or most powerful I've seen, but they weren't slouches either. If it's indicative of the Embracers Izuku 'as with 'im, we're in for a 'ell of a fight from 'ere on out."

"That much I expected," Aryu replied. "That's some lightshow when they go down, isn't it."

"Tha' was nothin'. Tha' tells me these ones were relatively young so the boom was a'ight. Get an older one in tha' same spot 'n ya' may destroy a city."

"Well, let's hope we only have one of those to deal with."

"Huh. Let's hope." The veiled reference to Crystal and whom she sided with wasn't lost on Aryu.

Nixon inspected the remaining vehicles as Aryu looked over the places the fight had occurred with the memory of dying Embracers fresh in his memory. "As I thought," called Nixon, bringing Aryu over to him. Nixon pointed to the road. "Fresh tracks.Looks like they've sent our friend off t'wards the city. It'll only be a matter of time before Izuku knows wha's happened. We need t' leave right now. We may be able t' head off the thing tha' took him, but if not, we need t' be right behind 'im 'n ready t' save him from 'is brother. Should we win, hopefully we can get his command of the Power back."

"Should we win?" Aryu asked with a smirk.

"Aryu, I doubt ya' need t' be told the odds we face from 'ere on out, but after seein' you handle those two as expertly as ya' did, 'n without use of the Power, I like our chances much more. Ya' fought fantastically, with bravery 'n intelligence, and fertha' ya' should be proud. Ya' helped save many lives today, at nothin' more than the cost of three misguided souls. The decisions ahead may nah' be so easy."

"Killing them wasn't easy," Aryu answered honestly. After they had been beaten, Aryu was filled with a tremendous sense of shame at what he'd done. Given time, would they have treaded the proper path of the Power once more? No one could say, but Aryu hoped so, even if they had died. He hated to think that no one was beyond redemption. However, this was war, and they had struck first.

"And killin' shouldna' been easy, Aryu, but it was necessary. We 'ave no time t' argue or reason with'em. All we can do is punish 'emfer their weakness 'n be done with 'em."

"You make it sound so easy."

"After killing so many like 'em, it is." The phoenix suddenly looked sullen, as if he had just become very tired. "I wonder, if there were two of me, would I hunt myself? Is my cause so just? I believe it is, but outside eyes lookin' in may see it differently, 'n sometimes I wonder if tha' makes me any better than'em."

"I'm still alive, despite your mission. I'd say that's a good sign."

"Indeed, Aryu. 'N after tha' little skirmish, I'd agree. Now let's see if we can track down our friend." As the forest around them came to life with animal calls, Nixon headed down the road and prepared to give chase again, Aryu right behind him.

***

Izuku was beside himself with confusion and rage. He'd sensed the Power from the battle in the distance, but with so many Embracers nearby it almost muddled the signal like radio interference. Was it Nixon, his powers reawakened? Or was it the young Aryu? Had Nixon found one that was so talented with the Power? Well, not 'found' per-se, but that was a matter of semantics by this point. Either way, he either had a reinvigorated phoenix to deal with or an unstable young Power user with the Shi Kaze. What measure of response was needed?

He was so close to the clinching moment of his plans: the complete takeover of this large and tactically advanced land. It was a perfect launching point north and beyond, and so easy to march over. So, did he divert more Embracers or military might towards this possible threat from the south?Embracers had already failed, that much was known as soon as the S.P.O.T. that had accompanied his three hapless protégés had sent back word of what had gone on. They had been utterly beaten in just moments. Unbelievable.But would a tactical military force prove any stronger? Not likely, given the ease with which they had already destroyed three Embracers. There could be enough power in their hands to wipe out legions of the forces Izuku commanded.There was always the silent ruthlessness of Elutherios Duo, but that was Izuku's ultimate ace. Did he play it so soon?

The transport carrying his beleaguered half-brother would arrive shortly, and once it did he would have yet another delicious matter to deal with. Time was growing short. The space between his forces and the city of Bankoor farther north was closing more and more all the time. His Embracers were leading the way and were expected to be there in a day. Already the shine of Bankoor's famous spire could be seen from hilltops. The climax of his plan was so close.

Rational thought prevailed in the end, as it always did with Izuku. *Let them come,* he thought. He would spare no more of his masses to stop them. The remaining Embracers, although leery about dealing with the likes of Nixon Ash or the Shi Kaze, would surly find strength in numbers. Izuku had hid nothing from them where it concerned the enemy they faced, but had also assured them that Sho, Crystal and Nixon were all powerless and could be killed very easily. Crystal's questionable allegiance was not mentioned. Izuku never trusted her fully, and as such had kept her on the 'enemy' list until he chose to take her off.

Once his Embracers reached the front line and decimated the enemy, it was the army that would take the city and spring the traps likely hidden there. His minions would have nothing else to do but twiddle their thumbs until that objective was cleared. They may as well deal with the two stragglers, if they even made it in time.It will take Aryu and Nixon some time to arrive. And even if they found transportation from somewhere, the S.P.O.T. following them would keep Izuku up to date on all the needed information.

Yes. Izuku was still in control. The command of the situation was still his. The angles were covered and unfortunate eventualities were expected and prepared for. The days ahead would still belong to him.

His rage subsided, and Izuku exited his monstrous moving base of operations and prepared himself for the further glee of Sho's arrival.

Chapter 7: Collective Mentality

<u>Aryu and Nixon</u>

With many jostles and stutters from an old, beaten engine, the transport drove on. It had only been an hour from the place of the battle that they had found it. Nixon knew it for what it was and saw that it was still functional. They were atop it and speeding off to help their friend shortly thereafter. Aryu, steadied by his recent battle and first real kills, no longer feared the machines like this. However, that wouldn't stop him from destroying everything like it should he ever be given the chance. The luck that came into finding it (guided by the Omnis in its own, peculiar way) never entered into his head once.

Nixon couldn't guess at the time needed to cover the distance to the city, nor did he know how far along Izuku's army was, but he did know that they were being watched, their arrival hotly anticipated. No one was taking anyone else by surprise today, and that was fine with him. If Nixon and Aryu had to slice through every mechanical monster of that army and the Embracers that commanded it to get to Izuku or save Sho (hopefully both), then by God that's what they were going to do.

Aryu joined Nixon in the cramped and open-air driver's compartment of the transport, his face resolute. "Any thoughts on how far we have to go?"

"None," replied Nixon. "But ya' had better be ready t' bring all the fight ye' can muster when we get there, because Izuku isn't goin' t' let us walk up t' 'im again."

"You don't have to worry about me mustering anything, Nixon. I'll bring enough for both of us. You'll just have to keep up."

He grinned at the bravado. Where once it was simply the gall of youth speaking, now he could see it was the resolve of a man.

Nixon knew he was telling the truth. With that shield coupled with the sword, not many alive could stand against Aryu, even though he was still so young.

"I'll do my best, I'll guarantee tha'."

"Your absolute best?"

Nixon questioned the remark at first, then understood, "Oh yes, no more tinkerin' around. I'll unleash the wrath of God 'Imself with all the fury I can muster once we make it. I doubt Izuku could stop me when I'm on 'is doorstep, so I think I'm done pretendin' I'm weak 'n feeble."

"Good, I've wanted to see what kind of things you can do for some time."

"Oh, don't worry, ya' will. I may wait until I'm in range of the coward Embracers, but it'll come."

Aryu was ready for it. He'd only seen bits and pieces of the Power since embarking on this painful journey. It was time to see what it could really do, even though that meant never reaching that point himself. Wielding two weapons of unbelievable power (at least until he had to return one) would be more than enough for him.

Aryu was a changed man. The loss of his home village filled him with anger and the need for revenge. Being witness to the enemy that destroyed it so easily and for so little purpose made him swell with rage.Meeting that enemy and dispatching it, at least in small doses, was unimaginably satisfying. A feeling he desperately wanted again. Strength and stubborn resolve was what he felt now, and had he removed it from its sheath, he knew that the Shi Kaze would speak loud and clear to him, as would any weapon of the Embracers if he looked at it. The year in the mountains 'finding' his manhood was nothing but a vacation to him now. This was real life. This was the way it had to be.

Mist filled the Vein Valley in patches. Eventually they would break apart and scatter away with the afternoon sun.

Crystal

She stayed crouched and hidden in the trees. The going was

simple enough for one as skilled as her. Her ninpo skills, an art of silence and patience long since dead and gone, were unrivaled. Even the sharp ears of the mechanical army wouldn't be able to make out her approach. There was the possibility of them spotting her with thermal imaging or infrared, but that wasn't as likely. Izuku didn't trust her, but he didn't hunt her, either. His forces would be preparing the final assault on the city beyond and concentrated on the front lines. The odd eye may look behind them, but even then, they'd be looking for something much larger or more threatening than her, a small and powerless girl.

At least for now she was. Soon however...

She had followed the tail end of the monstrous caravan as it pressed north, waiting for the right time and place to find her prize. At last she discovered an extremely large, multi-floored cargo stopped in the midst of the crowd. She had no doubt that it would take her to the massive rolling fort, and what was likely inside, that was far ahead once the army reached its destination.

The inoculation to regain her considerable powers was what she sought. Then, there would be hell to pay for anyone who stepped in her way. Izuku included. True, she had made a deal with him, but it was populated with many shades of gray. First she needed to determine if what Izuku had said was true. How much of the antidote was available? Was it just the one vile? The time to find the answer to all of these questions was at hand.

The marching forces ahead of her were at a stop, likely preparing for the assault she assumed would come later in the day. The forces bringing up the rear were soon to be redistributed, and that meant a stop for the time being while the orders were being sorted out.

As the troops stopped, she watched carefully from her cover of darkness. Although she was ghostly pale, she still could slip from plain sight when needed, taking in all she saw.

Her time came and she was on the move, dodging watching eyes deftly, slipping from cover to cover with the expertise of a master, soon finding her way to the underside of the massive cargo transport.

Cloud cover had rolled in during the night, and the darkness was broken only by the noise of her surroundings, the peek of the sun in the distance, and the inhuman glow of the eyes of the soldiers around her.

She scanned the base of the machine and soon found what she was seeking. With a soft and effortless movement, she slid open a hatch and slipped inside, closing the doorway behind her. The inside was even darker than the outside, and her eyes did her no favors here. She closed them and listened to her surroundings, her ears making a perfect mental picture of where she was. It was a corridor. Narrow, with an opening to what sounded like a loading bay to the rear. Ahead was a corner, beyond that she couldn't tell. The soft throb of the engine both aided and hindered her here, and she would have to be very careful.

When she was satisfied that nothing was coming, she moved to the corner and listened again. Her mind painted the image of what lay beyond: another short hall and a set of stairs that carried on farther up. Like a formless wraith she was off, sitting at the top of the stairs and planning her next move.

The patience required was tremendous, but after a time she had successfully navigated the transport to its top level. Or at least, she assumed she had. Nothing could be found that went farther up. At first she'd had considered searching for the antidote once she was comfortable with the blackness around her, but then thought better of it. She didn't know it to feel it, which was her only option right now.

She felt her way through the small rooms and halls until she found a small cubby she could crawl into safely. It was likely an empty storage locker or a place for a container that was now in use. She was satisfied it was out of the way and had more than one means to escape if needs be. Once she was comfortable, she rested, letting the drone of the motors and the reverberations of the hull plates carry her off to sleep.

She was awoken once when the vibrations increased, and the pitch and yaw of her ride told her that she was in motion again. She remained awake for a time, ensuring she wasn't going to be discovered, and then she went back to sleep. Or at least, what passed for sleep. Her father had told something to her, something he'd learned from his master: *The wise dragon sleeps with one eye always open, the dragon with nothing to fear sleeps peacefully in total darkness.*

Crystal Kokuou had been in darkness for a long time having nothing to fear, and although physically she was encased in an absence of light, mentally she'd never been more on edge. She was resting, but was ready to move at a moment's notice, all the while longing for the days when her sleep had been peaceful and she had nothing to fear.

Patience was the key now. E-Force was breaking the trail, but when the time came to get dirty, they'd fall back and let the army invade the city. When that happened, the cargo vehicles like the one she currently found herself in would be moved up to the battlefront, ready to assist in the restocking of the masses. That was her time to emerge and search the tank, or find Izuku if she couldn't find what she was looking for here. She had to find a way to get to the antidote. The need for it consumed her. And she had to do it all while not being killed by Embracers or the giant and powerful robotic army surrounding her on all sides.

It was a better plan than nothing. Plus, at some point she needed to get to Aryu. He was the key to everything, whether he knew it or not. With him rested the future of all mankind, a future she had tried to orchestrate from the beginning. Success or failure was all on his head.

She smirked at the irony. She'd berated Izuku for being so much like his father, with his multitudes of outcomes possibilities to be planned for. Although she had only one final goal, she'd spun and woven multiple threads just to get there. Was she really so different? Just how close was she to the madness her lost love had been driven to?

Was it really madness at all?

The coming day would answer everything. For now she slept, always with one eye open.

Sho

By the time he had awoken, Sho's head told him everything he needed to know about the situation, and his mind told him a full night had passed.

He was beaten, captured and in a lot of pain. It had been ages since he'd felt so ragged. Although it wasn't a feeling he'd missed, it did remind him of pleasant times and places long gone, before the Power had taken hold in him and he'd chosen to live past his promised expiry date, the one given to Nixon during their last meeting.

He had never forgiven himself for his role in his father's ultimate madness, a fact punctuated by his constant need to preserve his homeland. Even now, bound in the back of what felt like an extremely fast and bumpy means of transport, heading to an end he'd suspected was coming for some time (ever since the phoenix and the winged boy entered his forest), his thoughts were on his beloved home and the state of decay it was likely in the throes of now. It would still take time to undo the good he'd done, but from the moment he'd stopped, when he'd led the Herald into his mother's haven, the process had already begun to reverse itself, and the land he'd loved had started to revert into lifeless chaos once more.

Still, given the choices to do over again, he'd still be in the same position. He knew what he was doing was for the greatest good of all, and he would change nothing.

Except, perhaps, for letting his guard down that last time.

He knew the Power the instant it had hit him. Although he had lost his own command of it, the Power itself was instantly recognizable as it sent him careening into the trees. Once he'd seen the weapons in their hands, he'd known everything, and then he was out. So keen was he on keeping up his act he never recognized three Embracers for what they were. His damned over-confidence in his abilities had been his downfall again.Izuku would revel in the defeat and capture of his younger brother, likely followed shortly thereafter by Sho's instant and torturous banishing into the heartless nothingness of the Est Vacuus. Not a welcoming thought.

As a bright side, however, there was still a fully empowered and angry phoenix on his tail, so long as the Embracers weren't slowing him down. Unlikely, but so was the great Sho Tokugawa being beaten and tossed helplessly into a utility trailer and hauled away in defeat. Anything can happen.

He tested his bonds, what felt like clamps around his ankles and wrists. He could stand and hop about if he wanted, but there wasn't much good in that. The chair he was seated on was old and rotted, no help to him even if he found a way to smash it. The walls were dirty pockmarked, and light streamed in through the roof as he moved. The jostling and bumping caused the gray light to waver and strobe just enough for Sho to see that there was nothing around him that was of any use. If he could break his bonds he may have had a chance, but a few more twists of the clamps and he knew that wasn't going to happen. It seemed that whoever had designed these shackles had done so with extremely strong and resourceful prisoners in mind. Prisoners who could possibly even possess Makashi armor, as Sho seemed unable to let the mystic protection flow over him freely in any useful way, the bonds too tight to allow it to fully form.

Izuku had what he had wanted: he'd beaten Sho, and he'd done it with his brains and not his fists. The youngest of the Tokugawa clan had been beaten and was now likely to pay the price with his life, just as his father had. His first defeat (at least on a grand scale, his youth was somewhat unaccounted for) may be his only defeat.

Like father, like son.

And where was his mother in all of this? Sho had never fully been trusting of her in the first place, but a son's love was blinding. He also believed none of what Nixon believed. She was up to something, something that didn't necessarily make her the enemy. Despite her flippancy in her use of the Omnis and the Est Vacuus, she wasn't an idiot, and if she tapped the Est Vacuus for Izuku's sword, she did it for a more noble purpose than simply switching sides. Still, Sho hated the thought of Izuku with a weapon like that, and he wondered if his mother knew entirely what she was doing.

He sat there, beaten physically but not mentally. He was resourceful, and also very patient. Izuku would have Sho brought before him, either for amusement or simply to kill him. Then, Sho would fall at last, miles from his homeland and embedded in a battle to save what was left of the world, a cause he'd have thought pointless until meeting Aryu and seeing that the Power of the world still held sway in young minds, even if those minds were forbidden to use it.

He sat, passing into various forms of meditation, pondering everything and nothing in turn. The thought of the Est Vacuus admittedly frightened him, but there was nothing to be done about it now. He would let Izuku gloat. Let him savor his ill-gotten victory. Sho didn't care. Soon, he'd either help save the world or die as he'd always wished.

These thoughts gave him peace, and his makeshift prison sped on. Let Izuku see him like this. He did know for certain that no son of Ryu Tokugawa was going to go down without a fight today, but one of them, if not both of them, were still going down.

<u>August Stroan</u>

The calm in the air before the battle was as thick as smog and every man around him seemed to feel it. Riders such as him were told to wait in the rear of the troops; their speed, mobility, and relentless training was needed more than the heavy ground forces that protected them. The Riders were simply the best.

They'd received word that all electronic communication may be terminated, at which point the Riders of the Inja Army were to be nothing more than well-trained go-betweens for different units, sending all standing orders down the ranks. Stroan never thought it was a job that was below them. They serve however best they can, because in the end, they always got a fist in the fight.

For the moment, while good men milled about tirelessly, August Stroan was simply ordered to eat, rest, and prepare for the days to come. It was the hardest order he'd ever had to follow: sit still.

His new brigade had been woken at dawn, a morning that came far too soon after the night of celebration. It was a celebration in which he'd been a guest of honor for his part in helping get everyone they could through the Paieleh Valley. He'd taken care not to imbibe too much, but he wasn't completely without symptoms of a long night, when the call came to get ready, mount up and join the waiting troops on the battle lines they'd drawn on the outskirts of the south boundary or Bankoor.

There was no rest for the wicked, and even less for the heroes.

Frankly, the last few weeks of his life had flown by so quickly and changed him so much that he barely registered anything anymore. From robotic invasions to winged young men, angry Dragon Stalkers to the city of Bankoor itself, Stroan was essentially on auto-pilot now, rolling with the punches as best he could.

He was upset that he'd missed letting his new friends know where he was and what he was doing, as well as ensuring the safe return of the knife to Johan, but he suspected they already had a good idea about those things by now. Still, it would have been nice all the same. They'd been through so much together that it seemed the right thing to do. He hoped he'd get the chance under better circumstances.

There were no secrets now about whom and what they faced: an army of the Old, with Embracers of the Power leading the way straight for them, due any time in the next day. The general order was to fend the enemy off, just as the amassed army had been before the Embracers had arrived. Their technology was inferior to these machines, but their numbers were just as great, and their strategizing was even better. Still, the enemy had a troop of Embracers and the H.Y. bombs they'd thus far opted not to use in their march up the valley. Would their restraint hold out if the collective might of the northern army began showing signs of palpable resistance? For the moment, given their orders, no one really knew for certain, and that simply added to the nervousness in the air. If the H.Y. bombs were used, even spread so far out along their lines as they were, the U.P.M. was certainly no match against that kind of power.

The added fact that one of those demon devises was now *behind* them in the city somewhere added no relief either. It gave a sense of not having any place to run. There were human hands on that trigger, and as much as he hated to admit it, Stroan knew human hands could be less trustworthy than robotic ones in situations such as this. Especially the hands of politicians.

His fellow riders seemed to have that same sense of unrest in their eyes. They would all fight when the time came. Many of them would die for the cause willingly, but each and every one of them still looked like they'd been backed into a corner with no place to run. That kind of mental game never resulted in happy endings and tip-top troops.

Rest was hard and Stroan found what sleep he could. No point worrying about it now. One young, fresh-faced Rider can't make that much of a difference in the grand scheme of things. A sad realization, but one August Stroan had resolved himself to when he decided this was what he wanted to do with his life.

There were no dreams for Stroan. There was no need. Every nightmare or glory he could conjure in his head paled in comparison to what was coming his way with murderous intentions. The brain of a mortal man simply couldn't compete.

E2-0901

Forged of unbreakable materials and full of the most advanced technology, Elutherios Duo 0901 seemed to be terribly wasted just sitting atop the buildings of this city. Izuku had told Elutherios Duo to wait in the city and compile information, which it had done to perfection. It was to continue until Izuku called it. Even the powerful weapon the enemy possessed, a weapon that could be a game changer if things were not handled properly, was currently just another line on a checklist while it awaited its next orders. It was cold and heartless. A device. A tool, not a person. It followed its orders.

In a move that seemed terribly uncharacteristic for an unfeeling, heartless object, while it sat in the darkness of the morning on a quite roof, it drew out its weapon. It simply wished to examine it closer, an action it had partaken of four times in the last few weeks. This was time number five, and it was still no closer to understanding the kind of energy it was said to possess. Something about this item was ridiculously powerful, and it had no idea the source of its perfection. It was not admiration it had in its too-human eyes as it looked at it, but more a computer's need to understand the unexplainable. It had a weapon that very powerful humans feared utterly. Humans who could (no less mysteriously) summon vast amounts of energy and wield it like a toy.

Its eyes could still not see the things these people seemed to see, and a part of it thought it was foolish to try, but it would persist until it had a better understanding.It was a learning machine. This was simply what it did.

Since discovering the hiding place of the human command hub and all the information stored there, it had attempted to find some kind of external control device that may have been in the possession of one of the higher-ups, but as of yet had found nothing. Searches and scans of their homes and offices had brought no luck. It was an assumption that the H.Y. it had found even needed such a thing, but a safe one.

By its own terribly accurate predictions, the first of its companions to the south would be arriving very shortly, likely the next eighteen to twenty hours assuming there were no major obstacles encountered.

Just before the sun had set, its seismic sensors detected the approaching robotic army, and it had monitored them ever since. It knew things were going to plan. It also hoped, at least in a mechanical way, that it would be called soon. It wanted back in the fight. It almost enjoyed testing itself against new and more powerful enemies. Especially if its prime target was found. That would be a battle it would never forget, if it ever got the chance.

Sword sheathed, it waited again, remaining perfectly motionless in the dark. E2-0901 was ready and waiting.

Esgona

They tried their best to sleep, but the WGC accommodations at the base of the spire were sparse, cold, and generally uncomfortable. Although they had at least had a window, it was one that looked out into the shadow of another building, effectively blocking out all sense of time until it was too late and darkness had set in.

They had been given cots as bunks to sleep in, set in a row along the wall opposite the window. Although their door was unlocked, there were cameras everywhere, and it was quite clear that leaving under their own recognizance wasn't likely.It was a moot point since they had made the deal to stay (on Johan's request), so stay they would. Where would they go? Where could they run off in the city that would help anyone but themselves? They couldn't, and that was enough to ensure they all stayed put, not the measures of security Auron Bree had set 'for' them (making it clear it was not intended to be 'against' them).

They were brought filling meals and each hungrily ate. Stuffed and bored, they had taken the seats scattered around a small table in what appeared to be a separate meeting room and fidgeted with their own fingers and talked about nothing of importance.

Johan thought of Aryu a lot, a part him knowing that this was it. If Aryu wasn't coming in the next day, he wasn't coming at all. Johan certainly never suspected in the least that Aryu's quest had been even farther and more traumatizing than their own (save perhaps for Esgona, should one include his misadventure to the south, where he was crippled and tortured by the machines when he should have been on his personal quest in the northern mountains like Aryu and Johan were).

The night carried on and soon the exhaustion of the days preceding this one took them each in turn. The day that was coming would likely change them all in innumerable ways. Some things you simply can't prepare yourself for properly.

Sleep took them one at a time. It was poor sleep that was rife with vivid dreams that had them awake in fits and starts. It was still better than the rest Nixon and Aryu would have as they kept racing forward on their transport, or the night of pain Izuku was inflicting on his own brother with the sword from the Est Vacuus in his hand, taking pleasure in the innumerable ways he could drive Sho insane; something he'd been doing to him since hours before when Sho had first arrived at his feet.

They certainly slept better than August Stroan, whose battalion was mobilized at the peak of night on advanced word that a legion of mechanical troops and battle-ready vehicles had broken from the protection of the Embracers and had been sent on forward at top speed as a way of upsetting the night and the all-too-human people they faced, a tactic used not to strike the first victory as much as it was to deny strong men and women of the proper rest they needed for the coming day. Just diversions and battle plans set in motion as it was meant to be.

But sleep they did. On and off, each in turn, at the base of a spire every one of them knew was being rigged into a time bomb. The monster below them, although it had been prepared to be moved hours previous, remained where they had seen it, ready for its ultimate purpose of destruction.

The evening jitters kept Esgona awake more than the others. He hated these people. He hated this place. He hated everything about this situation and where it had led him. He stayed along for the ride in the hope that he'd get his revenge, but he was starting to suspect that Johan wasn't the brilliant strategist he'd thought. A giant electric pulse?Seriously? These people came from this world. They were raised in it. Let the people of the city worry about the power of technology. Tan Torna Qu-ay was too far behind for one of its people to catch up and start forming plans with something so unknown to them.

He got up from his small bed, wincing as he did so, and looked out the window at the night beyond. The next day would see the return of the monsters that had done this to him, and he had no intentions of letting them get to him again. Just give the man the damn knife and be done with it!Esgona was sick of this unnecessary dealing. Johan thought he was so brilliant coming up with a new, safer plan. He'd do anything to save a couple of lives, even at risk of losing it all.

Then Esgona realized that something was up. Johan had more than one plan, didn't he? He had to. If one of these plans risked losing to the advancing army, then where would they be? Just lambs to the slaughter, running uselessly away from an unstoppable force.

He'd had enough of this. Fellow villager or not, it simply wasn't worth risking so many lives, or possibly the rest of mankind. Johan was weak. They all were. Pretty words had led to Esgona being here, a belief that despite their differences they'd come through this united.

No. Tomorrow, Esgona was finished with this foolishness. He'd find his own way, and his way was going to work. The thought gave him peace enough to go back to sleep.

Chapter 8: The Nightmare Begins

His head was fuzzy with mental white noise. It was a haze of quick and disheveled images, sounds, smells, and feelings that had no form other than chaos. He wasn't even sure if he was sitting, standing, or was flat on his back. Each sense he possessed told him something that conflicted with all of the others, but eventually he realized that he was laid out at his brother's mechanical feet.

Izuku had wasted no time the night before bringing his beleaguered brother to him, the unwavering smile large and pronounced on his face. It filled Sho with both loathing and pity for the one who was once his friend and ally. In Sho's youth, after he'd defeated Izuku and taken the Shi Kaze from him, Izuku had spent years further training his younger brother in many things, building a bond between them the young and foolish Sho thought would never be broken.

In time, as the more natural Izuku emerged and was eventually nothing more than the man smiling and leering before him, the bonds broke down and each resolved themselves to the fact that, although brothers, they were nothing alike. Their minds functioned differently and never saw things the same way. After the death of their father and his consequent actions, they were never close again. When Sho almost killed Izuku in their last encounter, it was a safe assumption that their relationship was beyond salvation.

Their history led irreparably to this moment, with Sho at last defeated and his elder brother right there to bask in the glory of it.

Sho remained quiet. His body was sore from the positions it had been twisted in to during his trip here.

"The silent treatment? Not terribly mature of you, is it," Izuku chided.

"What would you have me say, Izuku? Plead for my life? Ask you to stop? Try to run away? Continue listing things I will never do? We are both old, Izuku. Too old. Play your game. Inflict your pain. Save the clichés. I'm tired."

A smirk appeared on his brother's face, one that deferred the act of gloating to another day. "Fine. You never were any fun. I'll inflict pain, but all in good time. Tell me, as you sit there on the floor a beaten man, why did you come? Why join the phoenix and your mother, not to mention the young dragon-boy, to stand against me?"

"I saw what you were doing," Sho answered. "I knew you couldn't keep your hands off my land. I couldn't sit and wait for you to become more powerful. Besides, I allowed your Herald to enter mother's Haven. A part of me foolishly thought you were willing to talk."

"Yes, that wasn't smart. For my brother, you certainly are dense. A weakness from both of your parents, I suppose."

"Look," Sho began, standing to his full height in the cramped and cold quarters in the large transport Izuku called home. Once on his feet he looked at his brother, the top of Izuku's head barely at Sho's shoulders, and shuddered at what his brother had done to himself. Why did he not just die? Where was the failure in losing with dignity as their father had? Well, the first time, anyway. "Kill me. Hurt me. Torment me all you like. But don't look for reasons you can't understand in the things I do. As I see it, even when you beat me down and finish me off, the grand total will still be two to one in victories for me. Even in my death, you lose."

With a loss of the smile and a flick of the wrist, the sword forged from the Est Vacuus by his own mother was out and brought to within a hair's width of Sho's nose. Then, the true torture began.

Sho had never experienced the Est Vacuus and its infinite sprawl of crippling nothingness. Even with his full command of the Power, he doubted he could have done much to prevent the mental and physical rape of his psyche when he laid his eyes on the weapon for the first time.In an instant, he was both drawn into it and repulsed by it, losing his mind to the hint of something so terrible in its vast emptiness it would have brought tears to his eyes had he the command of his faculties to do so.

How could his mother withstand the forces he was being subjected to right now? Better question: how the hell did she *control* it to make this weapon? The short answer was that she couldn't, really, without the aid of the Echoes of the Omnis. It was a spiritual balance that put the user in a very precarious and at times unenviable position of seeing both the awesomeness and emptiness of the universe at the same time.

Then the blade was sheathed once more, and piece-by-piece Sho Tokugawa came back together. The memory! By Gods, the memory alone could drive someone mad. He understood completely the look in his mother's eyes when she lost herself to the memory and power of that which is the Est Vacuus. The 'Is Empty'.

"See, brother? Do you see the power I command now? Forget the army. Forget the Embracers and their worthless ideals. Forget this body you forced on me. Forget the Power entirely. *This* is my Power now. This sword. No one would dare stand against me now. Not you. Not the phoenix or your mother. Not even your false hero, the whelp who carries the Shi Kaze. What do you even know about Aryu, Sho? Where does he come from? Why does he have wings? These are questions I know the answer to, and I promise you the answers would only prove that I am not going to be defeated this time. He will be my key to everything."

He heard Izuku rant but understood little of it. What about Aryu? He couldn't make sense of it all yet, but he was certainly trying.

When he focused his eyes again and shook off what he could of the muddle that the sword had done to him, he found the strength to speak to the twisted shape of metal and flesh his brother had become. "I… I should have killed you…" His words sounded softer, weak and distant. The experience of the Est Vacuus gave everything a hue of un-reality that wouldn't shake free. Nothing seemed as real as it had just moments before. "I should have… should have let you rot in Hell."

Izuku leered gleefully over his little brother. "Hell? Hell is practically a day spa compared to where I can send you, Sho. Hell would seem welcoming. Hell is real. Where I can put you is most certainly not real at all. That's where you should have tried to send me. Hell is a retreat for murderers, rapists and thieves. The Est Vacuus is where you send someone like us.

"Besides, we both know you couldn't kill me. You possess the cliché traits of honor, goodness and hope. You tried, too. You tried with everything you had, and although you did beat me, twice, you couldn't kill me. Look at me!" He spread his mechanical wings and whirled his artificial limbs to prove the point. "You *tried* to kill me and here I am. You obliterated most of my body! You wrecked me, bound me to my bodily destruction and forgot about me and yet, here I am! No Sho, you couldn't kill me then, and I doubt you would kill me now."

The large body of Sho shifted on the ground with no small amount of effort in his current state. He needed to make sure Izuku knew his next words were the truth. "I... I promise you if I had the means, you would be dead. I'd... I'd make it so that not an atom of you remained."

"I believe you, Sho. I do. Or at least that you might try. Now you would see to it that no part of me had a chance to survive. Now, after all this time and all of our years together, you know what I am at last. Your hope shielded you from the truth for all these ages, but now, in your last few moments, you see free and clear what your big brother is capable of. And now, it's too late."

With another quick flick, the blade was out again, and just as Sho had grasped what he could of the reality he found himself in, once more was he lost to the void.

For hours this continued, the world passing the brothers by as Izuku tossed Sho to the Est Vacuus and dragged him kicking and screaming back again. Every venture into the void brought back a weaker and sicker man in Sho. Izuku persisted, waiting for the moment his brother's body would simply fail him, and then he would cast him into the abyss and be done with him.

Neither the victim nor the assaulter in this exchange believed in fate, but that was still the only reason left to explain why, just as the morning grew long, while somewhere to the north the first wave of Izuku's soldiers were clashing with the defenses of the United Peoples Military, and while in the city of Bankoor the available technicians had just successfully completed the needed steps to arm the famous spire into an giant EMP-producing weapon, that Izuku was torn away from his task with a feeling he'd not expected; a feeling that shook him to his core, pulling him from the gleeful torment of his brother to the full reality of the situation at hand.

Lights were flashing all around him, and it seemed there were multiple Heralds trying desperately to get his attention. All things he was blinded to so easily in his rapture. These weren't the things that pulled him away, though. No alarm or whistle or even tug of his arm would have done that. No. This thing was more than that. What it was pulled him away from his hapless brother like he wasn't even there, leaving him a broken mess on the floor as his Makashi armor rippled over his body like black mercury in small waves, was something more important than revenge. Something that in one instant warned Izuku that every one of his carefully arranged plans suddenly had a much stronger possibility of going up in smoke.

The Power called to him like a beacon through the fog of glory. Something south of here had full use of very large amounts of it. *Dangerous*amounts, and the reality of everything hit like an atom bomb.

Izuku went from glory to fear. He left his enfeebled brother on the floor of this dark, useless supply room, mentally crippled and so weak he couldn't even raise his head as his body had seized up and prevented him from even blinking for minutes at a time. Sho was slipping away at last, but Izuku didn't care in the slightest now.

The phoenix had risen! It was angry. It was more powerful than measure. And it was coming right for Izuku.

***

During the long and bumpy ride, Aryu and Nixon had discussed many times the plan of attack once they encountered a significant number of Izuku's forces. Nixon would lead the way, sword and wrath in hand, with Aryu doing his part behind him. Nixon would ensure he didn't lose his young charge, and Aryu would fight to keep up.

As the sun rose, so too did a tired-but-ready Aryu O'Lung'Singh.

He'd moved the Shi Kaze from his back to his hip for faster use when needed and easier stowing when not. Despite how the experts made it look, sheathing any weapon on your back was hard and unnecessary when quickness was required. One of the things he'd learned from Nixon over the time they'd spent together.

He was looking forward to the unleashing of Nixon's true power. He'd seen snippets and glimpses of it and heard stories of its wonders, but had yet to see it for himself. A deep part of him also feared it, as he'd been raised to. But wasn't there an even deeper part curious about what he himself could do with it? The more logical part of his mind wasn't even willing to entertain the idea, but the fact that a shred of the thought had appeared gave him just cause for worry. His being wrong would mean the end of him and the loss of Nixon as an ally to his cause. Simply not worth it.

They'd seen no signs of the enemy, and if they were followed (which of course they were, but Izuku by this point was so lost in his own perverse actions that the warnings his Herald attempted to give him about their proximity were falling on deaf ears) they didn't know it. They both suspected a trap to be sprung, but as of mid-morning, nothing had.

They came over the final rise and through a cluster of trees into the true Vein Valley, and suddenly all that mattered was what they saw.

Aryu was terrified, never having seen so much of anything, let alone something as horrifying as this. The ground below them and carrying off into the increasingly-sunny morning was a ripple of metallic bodies, strewn about and pressing northward as far as the eye could see. They stretched up the valley to Bankoor, which was now a small but visible spot on the horizon. Even Nixon with his superior sight couldn't see the other side. The Vein River split the land forces, but the water was black with warships of one kind or another, all heading upriver to the Blood Sea.

Trees were pushed over and crushed. Rolling hills disappeared under their massive form. Larger machines popped up between the ranks everywhere, some for cargo, some with armaments, others with towers made of steel. Even from here on the hilltop miles away the vibration of their constant march was becoming noticeable.

To the west and north they were everywhere. Hundreds of thousands of them. The Army of the Old, awake once more and off to conquer the world.

Nixon looked at Aryu as they stopped and took in what they were seeing. There was much more strength in Aryu now than there had been the day they met as he'd cowered in the rocks on the earthen plateau. This was a man. A young one, but most certainly a man.

"So where do we go from here?" Aryu asked, waiting for the next move, not wanting to sit here in the open on a hilltop for long.

Nixon looked at the masses, scanning for something specific, until he found it, far in the distance halfway between the river and the foothills. A jointed rolling structure, not dissimilar to the place called HOME in design. If there was a command module, that was almost certainly it.

He pointed in its direction and explained what it looked like while Aryu listened and grew tense. "Tha' is where we'll go. It's as good a place t' start as any. Of course, if Izuku was smart, considerin' what we did t'is last home, he won't be there."

"And we go by air?"

"Aye. Once we get close enough, you'd better be ready. They'll not let us just walk into their ranks. They'll release whate'er means they may 'ave t' stop us, especially if the time comes t'unleash the Power before we reach it."

"Were you this, Nix? An army so large?"

"No, honestly. I thought we'd crippled'em with the destruction of HOME but it seems we've underestimated the size of the enemy. Let's make sure we don't do tha' again."

"Agreed. Can I stop these attacks? With just this sword and shield?" Aryu had a mental image of the Ark 1 laser blasts and H.Y. bombs.

"Aryu, with those two weapons in yer' hands, there isn't a thing in the world tha' you should fear. The only fear is movin' fast enough t' not get a piece of ya' blown off."

"Thanks. Very reassuring."

"A spade is a spade, Aryu, but I'm certain yer' up fer' it." A nod of thanks but nothing else was said on the topic.

"What if we get separated? Do I help you or go for Sho?"

"Ya' go fer' Sho. Period," Nixon answered matter-of-factly. "E'en if he releases every Embracer he's got at me, ya' get t' Sho. If we 'ave the ability t' get 'im 'is command o'the Power back, after everythin' he's seen and been through lately, ye'd better belie'e 'e'll unleash fury so pure it'll turn yer' 'air white. Tha's if we're not too late."

"Don't say that."

"The truth is we may be, Aryu. Don't forget tha'. Reality is 'arsh and life is seldom fair. He's been 'ere fer' 'ours at Izuku's 'ands 'n tha' damnable blade of 'is. It's a fact we may /ave t' simply deal with."

"Are you and your kind always so pessimistic? It's not helping us at all, you know."

"It's not pessimism, Aryu. We'll do our best or die tryin'. We'll fight with the strength tha' God gave us, but God's plan may not be one we want t'ear today."

"Then we re-write God's plan."

"It's never tha' easy."

"You did. You are rewriting it every minute you're with me."

Nixon looked at him and smiled his relaxing smile. "Aryu, 'ave I taught yanothin'? The plan ne'er changes, only the interpretation. The will of God is flawless, 'Is creations 'owe'er..."

"Wasn't it your God's will to kill me?"

"Perhaps, but look at all we've done together. The good we've accomplished. Ya weren't misguided before ya met me, e'en by my strict standards, 'n I'd ne'er been sent t' anyone who didn't deserve it. No, 'Is message about ya' is still out there t' be found. Perhaps today I'll see the answer at last."

"I hope so, and I hope it's in my favor."

"It already is, my young friend." He drew his sword, letting Aryu *see* it at last. The message of hope and fear, love and hate, life and death and all its glory and shame in one mind-numbing moment. But for Aryu, it was as if it had always been there and he'd just been too foolish not to see it. Now he understood the Power on a level Crystal could never teach him. The truth was that everything was not black and white.

"Draw yer' sword, Aryu, 'n see wha' I see." He did as he was asked and looked at the mythical Shi Kaze. Much like Nixon's great broadsword, the voice in his head screamed of history and horror, pride, lust, truth, lies; all of the great and powerful realities of the world.And not just this world, but others as well, universes upon universes, realities atop realities and back again, all to the tip of this legendary weapon.

"Astonishin', isn't it?" Nixon asked. Aryu didn't respond. He simply nodded and tore his eyes away, looking into Nixon's frightening eyes of fire. "They are older than time itself. The feelin's I mean, not the weapons. If ya' learn nothin' more of the Power, learn this: it was 'ere since before time was time, 'n it'll be 'ere when we are all long dead. As much as we use it, it uses us. We're together in this. The Power battles the Est Vacuus. Today these things'll all come together. May we live t' tell the tale."

"We will, Nixon. We must. We can't have it any other way."

"God may not wish it."

"God's been wrong before." With a smile and a nod, the leathery wings of the young man were out and the sword stowed at his side, and with one simple push he was off, gliding away with fire in his eyes. The phoenix and his wings of flame followed behind him.

There would be no more hiding. Today, he would be who he was meant to be: Nixon of the Great Fire and Ash, God's keeper of the balance.

Aryu could feel the trail of heat come from the beast as Nixon passed him and was comforted. He knew that the time was at hand to stop the games and do what was required.

Aryu was optimistic about the day. Rescuing Sho.Defeating the army. Laying waste to Izuku. Making it to the city, which was the most logical place to meet up with his brother-in-arms.The thought that the remaining men of Tan Torna Qu-ay were surrounding this inhuman enemy on both sides like a vise made Aryu smile. Filled with the adrenalin rush of the battle to come, the sight of the fire-demon ahead of him, and knowledge that somewhere to the north his friend might be feeling the exact same thing, Aryu readied his shield, braced the sword against his hip and followed the phoenix as he arched over one last apogee and began the dive into the heart of the enemy.

The enemy noticed the intrusion at once. The sudden sight of a giant ball of fire rocketing over the rear of their ranks and tracing a straight path to their central command would alert anyone, including Izuku, who at that moment at last realized the mistake he'd made as Nixon allowed the Power to engulf him entirely, and the short-sighted Embracer pried himself away from his beleaguered brother as if he wasn't even there. Once this blatantly aggressive move was made and Izuku had regained his senses, the order was given to stop them at once by any means necessary, except for the use of the H.Y.s. Truthfully, this wouldn't have been needed if Izuku had seen them coming in time instead of being so distracted. If he'd even bothered to stop just once he'd have felt the phoenix power up his wings. But now, surrounded by thousands of his own troops and leery about the fight to come with the armies of the north, he didn't want the bombs to deplete his forces, and opted to just hit them as hard as he could with what he had.

Aryu held back once he realized he could no longer keep up with Nixon, drawing the Shi Kaze and preparing to mop up the aftermath. It was a good thing he had, as no sooner did he slow than the forces on the ground opened fire with any number of energy and exploding projectile weapon on the hapless dark spot in the sky behind the crashing fireball.

They'd began firing on Nixon as well, but all efforts to get anywhere near him were stopped by his shield of Power-driven fire, and soon with a crash and explosion that sent a pulse of energy along the ground consuming all it touched, large vehicle and cargo transports included, Nixon was in the fray.

Aryu had no time to marvel at the Power he'd just witnessed. Nixon's and Sho's weeks of lessons had paid great dividends and Aryu was able to maintain control as he fell, using his weapons to deflect any shots from Ark 1s. Like a man possessed he spun and twirled as he landed, surrounded on all sides by mechanical limbs and the weapons they carried. The haze of fear that had dominated him in Tan Torna Qu-ay, and after in the Haven of Crystal Kokuou, was nowhere to be found.

As he stabbed and slashed with his feet back on hard and trampled ground, while hoards of the heartless soldiers rushed him, only to each be sliced down and shredded in turn as the Shi Kaze and the spinning blades of the shield passed through anything within reach as if it wasn't even there. Aryu was no longer amazed at the sharpness and effectiveness of these weapons. He could *see* them now, knowing them for what they were. Nothing but something similar to them could stop them, and these weak and fragile bipedal robotic monsters weren't even speed bumps now.

Still they came, their numbers vast. Blocking the shots and slicing the limbs closest to him would only get him so far, and soon he began to push toward Nixon's epicenter of destruction, guided by the forbidding image of plumes of fire erupting skyward, as were multitudes of artificial bodies and even the occasional large vehicle. Nixon was enjoying himself, it seemed.

With a push of his wings when the proper hole opened, Aryu thrust himself along the ground, bladed weapons leading the charge, breaking any opposition they found as he went. Soon his feet began kicking at ash and singed pieces of the enemy, a sure sign he was getting closer. In the circle Nixon had created with his impact, he noticed the numbers attacking him begin to lessen. By the time the (fully powered and extremely angry) phoenix was in view, only a sparse few remained, though many still continued to open fire, hoping to hit anything that could stop these two new attackers.

Nixon saw Aryu coming and deflected as many as he could away from the exceptionally nimble young man. The anger subsided enough for Nixon to let Aryu in to his defensive circle.

"You missed the command vehicle!" Aryu shouted at Nixon, overtaken by adrenalin.

"Aye, I 'ad to!" Nixon called to him, the roar of popping Ark 1s and alike mixing with the static burn to the flames around them. "If there's a cure for Sho it's on board! I can't risk losin' it like we did t' HOME!"

"So now what?"

"Now we push t' its front door. A little of tha' speed ya' just showed would go a long way right now!"

Nixon bullied his way into the enemy numbers anew, bowling them all over as he moved like they were blades of dead grass. Once they were within sight of what they assumed was Izuku's command post they noticed the shots of any kind die away, until at last nothing but useless mechanical forms were in their way as they moved. Something knew what they were and was no longer wasting their time trying to stop them with such weak attacks. The rising image of the base ahead and the shadowed form above it with dark wings stretched to its side told them who it was who had given the order.

The form rose up under some unseen power as the wings on its back stayed stationary. Then, as if fired from a gun, Izuku was nose down and heading straight for them.Aryu saw the ground ripple when struck by the powerful landing until nothing was left but the phoenix and the attacker, both with weapons drawn and staring at each other.

Nixon and Izuku were face to face at last.

The masses ignored them now. Whatever command Izuku had given to attack them was clearly rescinded and Izuku had opted to take matters into his own hands.

Tempted at their inaction to take out as many as he could, Aryu instead had the weapons he carried drawn and went to Nixon's side, only to be halted by the beast. "Wait, Aryu! Ya' do as I told ya'! Find Sho and 'elp 'im. This monster is mine!"

The deep-rooted core of Aryu that wanted revenge for all the evil caused by this evil protested immediately, but after looking at the expression on the half-man's face, the smile gone and anger replacing it, something told Aryu that this was not a fight he'd win. Aryu brushed himself off and began to circle around behind the two and headed toward the base.

"You know it's no good, Nixon," Izuku said, his voice more irritating than frightening to Aryu now. "Do you think I'd have kept him alive this long?"

Nixon smirked, though it wasn't his easy-going smile. This was purely malevolent. "Aye, I do. Ya' likely spent every moment you've 'ad usin' tha' abomination of a sword t' do who knows wha' t' 'im, didn't ya'." Not a question.

Izuku wasn't fazed by the demonic nature of the fire-beast as he loomed over him. "Maybe, but no mortal man can withstand that much exposure to the Est Vacuus, even my brother. If he's not dead by now, I assure you he will be very shortly. It was impressive that he lasted as long as he had. A credit to his strength, if not his foolishness."

"E'eryone is always more foolish than ya', aren't they Izuku?" Nixon scowled, leaning closer to the enemy he faced. "Yet 'ere I am, the Sword of Light in my 'ands 'n the Power t' use it."

Izuku sneered while his hands, both real and mechanical, clenched tightly. "True, an unfortunate surprise, one I'd love to hear the details about some time, but not a surprise I'd neglected to cover. You are impressive, Nixon, but so am I." A slight 'ping' sound and a quick flash of light came from somewhere on Izuku's mechanical body. Nixon thought he'd waited long enough and rushed forward, only to have his great broadsword turned aside with a shower of sinister sparks in shades of deep blues and purples, and Izuku out beyond his reach.

Without hesitation, Nixon summoned his great Power and released waves of heated energy at Izuku like bolts, only to have them obliterated or turned aside with swipes from Izuku's ethereal blade. The void contained within the weapon seemed to simply disperse the Power it touched, if not eliminate it all together. Nixon would not be stopped, and he used Izuku's parrying to get closer to him once more, pushing him farther away from Aryu as the army marched ahead and Aryu's destination rolled on.

Aryu was torn now. He had the weapon to stop Izuku in his hand. Nixon clearly had his hands full as Izuku countered each attack, sending more sparks flying as the weapons met. Izuku's command of the Power may be less than Nixon's, but that weapon made all of Nixon's Power useless. Aryu became frozen with indecision, but once Izuku was hit by one of Nixon's attacks, sending him backwards into a mass of mechanical bodies, Aryu saw the resilience in Nixon and knew that there was still a considerable amount more to his hidden

Power, coupled with rage and the intelligence of the ages. Confident, Aryu turned and ran after the mobile monstrosity ahead.

He was distracted once more halfway there, with the sound of an explosion behind him. Not one created by the Power, but by what looked to be an impact. Something else had landed, but Aryu couldn't see what it was from here. He looked back, worried for his friend as clouds of dust and debris filled the air at the battle site. He rushed back and looked around furiously, trying to find Nixon in the chaos.

When at last the smoke had cleared enough to see him, Aryu did not like what he saw.

Nixon was on the ground and shaken, Izuku far away. There was something here, and it came into view like a dark specter.

With a sword that was almost a perfect replica of Nixon's own, a tall, black, and clearly powerful mechanical form stood between the fallen phoenix and Izuku. Red, glowing, freakishly normal eyes locked on the man-beast before him. It vaguely resembled one of those damned Heralds, only more complex and, dare he say, human? The features of its metal face and body were not as ridged or sharp as what Aryu had seen before.

Aryu couldn't believe Nixon was down, but what was even harder was the expression on his face.

As Nixon looked over this newcomer, confusion and fear swept over him, and that fact alone made Aryu believe he was right to return. Or so he thought. Then he *saw* the enemy, and then he had a hint at why Nixon looked as he did.

This enemy, this mechanical man standing like a statue on this fresh battlefield, was an item of focus. A weapon of the Power. Not just one, though. The message in Aryu's mind was confusing and disoriented. As if many voices were trying to speak at once like a crowd of people. They were speaking in images instead of words deep in Aryu's mind, many of which were not pleasant in the slightest. They were terrible images. Images of death and pain.Immeasurable suffering.

Then, with the evil smile retuning to Izuku's face, the truth dawned on Aryu: this thing wasn't an item of Focus; it was *many*, all crafted by some arcane power into a fully functioning and terrifying machine with an aged weapon of Power in its artificial hand. That was why Nixon was so shocked.

"Wha'... wha' manor of evil is this, Izuku?" Nixon asked, never taking his eyes off the thing as he stood once more, weapon out and prepared for attack or defense, whatever was warranted.

"Do you like it?" Izuku smiled, approaching the thing between them, mechanical wings tucked back and away as he moved. "It took a long time and a lot of personal sacrifice to construct. Do you know how much it can take out of a man to reshape and forge items of Focus?"

"Ya' can't. It's not possible!" The defiance in his voice was betrayed by the clear fact that there was no doubting what this thing was. "E'en one as powerful as yer' father couldn't begin t' attempt this."

"Well, judging by the looks of things, I'd say that means I'm not as weak as my father, doesn't it? Every part, every servo, every chip and wire, all forged piece by piece into what I wanted and needed. The world was scoured for anything that could help me build it. Do you think I spent all this time finding an army? Hardly. I spent decades finding the tools."

Aryu watched as this unreal scene unfolded, no longer prepared to just jump in now that the numbers were even and the situation suddenly favored the enemy in terms of power and brute strength.

Nixon could feel the Power emanating from the machine, leftovers from the parts it was made from. Sure they seemed weaker than his sword or the Shi Kaze, but one weaker focus item could be beaten. Hundreds, though? It was a situation Nixon had never encountered and he was unsure what might happen. And in the end, it carried *that* sword.

As Aryu noticed, it was a near-perfect copy of the sword Nixon carried in length, heft and even the ornate carvings that adorned it. Aryu would have thought it a dead ringer had he seen it on its own, but the voices in his mind told a different story: the story of peace, oddly enough. Of unification and respect. It was so counter to the machine that wielded it. "And how did ya' get tha' fuckin' sword?" The anger in Nixon's voice was frightening, but the beast still didn't move.

"You like it? Just a little something I picked up along the line. Once your beloved chorus of God-fearing helpers were gone, getting it wasn't so difficult. They tried so hard to hide it but alas, they faded away in time. It took a little hunting, but perseverance paid off." Aryu almost charged the cocky Izuku in that moment and would have if Nixon hadn't done it for him, thrusting out his flaming sword with lightning speed and releasing an inhuman screech as he moved.

The black monster was fast as well. It moved in unison, parrying the thrust and clashing the weapons together. The force of their mutual impact was enough to ripple the air around them, and the taste of the Power hung like an aftertaste as the two combatants drove into one another, neither giving way. The phoenix and the machine planted their feet and pushed, the flames of Nixon rising and soon engulfing his enemy, which pushed back almost effortlessly and held its ground.

Nixon screamed, and the heat became greater with each second as the fire climbed higher, backing Aryu and Izuku off, until at last he pushed with all of his considerable might and the implanted feet of the robot were nudged back a few inches, deep holes gouging as it moved. That was all it would give. The next second it pushed back, even taking a step toward the phoenix, and then it gracefully spun away from Nixon, throwing him clear with the fire still rising off his body in waves as he crashed into the ground near where Aryu was standing.

Aryu rushed to help him but couldn't get closer than a few feet while he was in this state. With flustered and surprised look on his face, Nixon stood again and turned to face the two across from him again.

"Let me help you, Nixon," Aryu said, his shield already up and the precious sword at the ready. "We know they can't beat this sword…"

"*Aryu!*" Nixon yelled with an anger that made Aryu jump. "I told ya' t' go! These monsters are mine!"

"No!" Aryu countered back, turning the hellacious eyes of the firebird to meet his, staggering him with the rage he saw there. He stood his ground as the amused Izuku watched the scene play out while he stood beside the battle-proven new toy he'd made. "I will not! Let me help you! Together we can take them both and end this!"

"I will end this! You help Sho, Gods damn you! Yer' no good t' anyone if yer' dead!!"

"Who says I'll be…"

"Damnit Aryu! This isn't some useless machine! Tha's not some headstrong Embracer! Save Sho! Get 'is Power back! Tha' will be more help t' me than dyin' 'ere 'n now, which I assure ya', if ya' stay, ya' will 'n there'll be nothin' I can do about it!"

"What makes you so…"

"He has my sword!"

Confusion on Aryu's face. How could it be Nixon's sword?

Nixon's eyes locked onto Izuku's smirking face as he spoke. "It's another version of it, the sister t' mine, 'n this twisted fucker stole it from the loyal and faithful tha' protected it 'n now I'm going t' take it back. The Shi Kaze may stand against it, but I'm not willing t' risk you t' find out. Go, Aryu. Save Sho. Let 'is wrath against 'is brother be released 'n then we will all fight together."

Aryu hesitated, confused by the statement, but the look in Nixon's eyes stopped him. Now was not the time to argue, so instead Aryu gave him a nod of understanding and turned to leave.

Nixon briefly watched him go, heartbroken at having to turn him away. He loved Aryu in his own way, and he wanted him here with him to get the revenge he deserved. He'd watched Aryu grow stronger and smarter every day he'd been with him, and although he had no doubt that Aryu would put up a valiant fight, the odds were simply too stacked against him. Maybe, if Sho could be saved, this would all end up all right.

"Aryu," he called, eyes back on the two across the clearing of mechanical soldiers which continued to march past them in waves oblivious to the goings on around them.

"Yeah?" came an answer from farther away.

"Good luck."

"Like I need it!" was the response. With the audible flutter of wings he knew the young man was off, likely cutting down every machine he saw on the way.

"Now, where were we?" Izuku said in mock-boredom. "You know he won't make it, don't you? Even if he did, he can't help a dead man. The only cure I know of isn't even there." He pulled back a wing and produced a vile from some unseen compartment on his robotic back. "It's here. Sho is going to die and there's nothing Aryu can do about it. Then, he will become exactly what I want him to be."

"Ha!" came a shrill voice from over the cacophony of marching soldiers. "If it's anything like you, I think the world could really do without, thanks!"

The voice seemed to come from all around them. A voice each of them knew and hated in equal measure. Like a cat, with speed no mortal could possibly possess without hundreds of years of training, a bleeding and battered Crystal Kokuou appeared from nowhere like a pale blur, her gossamer hair frayed and singed behind her. She broke from the mass of soldiers and caught Izuku, Nixon, and even the machine by surprise.

Before he'd grasped what was happening, the vile was in her hand and she was off again into the tangle of artificial limbs, only the hint of her wicked smile remaining. She'd waited patiently for this moment, and now that it was here she couldn't help but laugh as these two enemies were so wrapped up in their dispute that they missed her entirely. The command to ignore Nixon and Aryu that Izuku had given the army, a command to ignore the singular enemies that attacked from the rear and focus on the march forward, had the unwelcome effect of having them ignore her, too. If he weren't so shocked, Izuku would have laughed at his own mistake.

Stunned back to the here and now, he shouted in anger and was in the air at once, the sword in his hand wiping away all soldiers around him looking for her.

Nixon, flabbergasted by the turn of events, never took his eyes off the thing ahead of him. This thing took all of his attention. Once he was done with it, then he'd find them both and kill them.

"Alright my shiny new friend," Nixon spoke to himself more than the thing. "Let's see wha' you've got."

He needed to get that weapon back. Having it in the hands of Izuku or anyone with dark intent was simply something he couldn't allow, let alone a soulless machine. If someone with any *hint* of the Power got hold of it, much like the Shi Kaze, they would hold more power than he cared to imagine. Gods, how did it ever get here? Had Izuku killed all of Nixon's helpers and followers, or was it true that time had simply done that for him?

Stories for another time it seemed, as the thing moved toward him with ill intent in its red eyes. Nixon was doubtful. He had tried to use his considerable strength to topple this thing in their last exchange and had failed. He had far more in reserve, but perhaps it did too?

Wanting to help Aryu, especially now that it seemed Crystal was around with her own damned agenda, Nixon focused his mighty strength and came forward, shimmering hair alight and powerful arms flexed.

The clash of weapons rang out, and Nixon knew it wasn't going to be as easy as he'd hoped.

Chapter 9: Pulling the Trigger

Merrik Caspar had been in constant contact with the front lines, sending and receiving any and all information he could. He wished he could be there, joining his other Riders in battle. Not watching blips on a screen that were people he knew. People he respected and trusted. One second they were a blip, the next the blip was gone.

He'd have given just about anything to be one of those nameless, faceless blips.

When he unlocked and opened the door to retrieve the three guests at the base of the spire, they were already up and finishing the breakfast that had been brought to them. Each tired face looked up from their silent meal and regarded him in turn, but said nothing. He was here for a purpose and they simply wanted him to get to it.

"Morning," was his only greeting as he came into the room dressed in full Rider regalia. "Auron would like to speak with you. He'll meet you in the main chamber with the remaining members of the WGC."

"Remaining members?" Johan asked.

"Yes. It seems some of them weren't entirely comfortable with the way things have progressed and decided to disappear into the night."

"Lucky for them," Esgona replied. The others ignored him.

"Have things gone badly?" Seraphina asked. "Did we miss something last night?"

"All I'll say is yes. I'll let Auron fill you in on the details. If you'll please come with me." He indicated the exit and waited as they stood, grabbed a few scattered belongings, and left the featureless room to the hall that led back to the spire main chamber. He wasn't sure at what point he had become a lackey for Auron Bree, but he prayed it wasn't going to be for much longer. Soon, he'd either have to join his fellow Riders, or do something far more productive in the city. Why couldn't the great Auron Bree get them his own damn self!

The small party entered into the great hall with the echo of their footfalls bouncing around the room. They could see the WGC head table, and each noted that more than half of the chairs were empty. Not a promising sign of the faith they had in any plan Auron Bree had presented to them.

"Good morning all. Sleep well?" said Bree's voice from the far side of the room, his feet moving quickly and his appearance betraying his upbeat greeting. He looked much as Caspar did: men with very little sleep to their credit. His salt and pepper hair was unkempt and his clothing was far less formal than their last meeting. He continued after receiving no answer. This young group was not in the mood for any pleasantries. "Yes, well, if you would please join us, I'm sure you will find more than enough vacant seats." The loathing in his voice was clear. He was not a happy man, and it was likely only his political side that gave them a greeting at all.

They found seats around the opposite end of the table, with Johan and Seraphina on one side and Esgona at the other table head. "I feel that we must let you all know the goings-on that have occurred since last we spoke." He pressed a button at his side as he returned to his seat. Suddenly a gap opened in the center of the table, splitting it in two. The three watched in shocked amazement as thin rods rose up from either side of the table, standing like tiny towers on a child's playset. With another button, the gap between the towers seemed to fill with light and images floating in midair. The images eventually formed into photographs of various battle scenes.

"Last night," Auron began, "the enemy sent an invading brigade of troops and equipment ahead of its main offensive force, attacking our front lines in an effort to disrupt us and generally piss us off. The offensive lasted only a few hours, and our ranks outnumbering them in both men and firepower. Many good people didn't get much sleep last night, myself and Chief Rider Caspar included." He indicated Caspar who had taken an empty seat at his immediate left. "The enemy was defeated, many of which were destroyed, and the rest were sent back south in retreat.

"It was clearly a diversion. A way of disrupting us and exploiting our weaknesses as mortal men and women. It wasn't unexpected, but it was still annoying."

The images changed to blurry photos from a higher vantage point. The photos showed swarms of blackness against the ground in every direction. "The enemy," continued Bree, "is more numerous than expected. Not terribly, but still beyond our best conservative estimates." The three shifted uneasily in their chairs. There were a lot of machines in these photos, and the images were disturbing. "These images were captured with cameras mounted on the spire above us, unaffected by their jamming and blocking abilities due to their distance. They've begun launching aerial strikes in the form of small bombing runs." Eyes went wide. "Relax, there are still no reported H.Y. attacks, and what efforts they have launched have been repulsed by our own countermeasures. They can't even use their small surveillance drones without us knowing about it and shooting them down, but still, the offensive has continued for the majority of the night and continues even now.

"This, ladies and gentlemen, brings me to my main points. A sort of 'good news / bad news' situation. The bad news, since that's generally the best place to start, is that these images, as well as reports from the front line, lead us to believe that the Embracer offensive is coming sooner than expected, likely because they have given themselves the option of striking while the iron is hot."

The three had no idea what an 'iron' was, at least in these terms, but they didn't have to. The point was clear: the Embracers were likely to be on the move shortly. "The moment they do, we will have no choice but to pull our people back immediately and begin their evacuation north."

Silence in the large, hollow room. No one said a word, each person thinking about this information. The time to act was coming quickly.

"But," began Bree, startling everyone with the word, "as I said, there is good news. It's two-fold, actually. I doubt either will be enough to stop them as planned, but it's something. The first is that, as of about an hour ago, the work was completed on the spire above all of your heads." More than one set of eyes looked up. "Your weapon is finished, Johan."

Realization dawned on Johan's dark face. The spire had been converted. "It's ready to fire?" he asked, still looking up, marveling at the weapon he'd created sitting right above his head.

"It is. At least, we assume it is. Remember, it's still somewhat beyond us in some respects, but yes. The power to the rest of Bankoor has been ceased, and it is currently charging all batteries and capacitors, feeding all power it creates back on itself. It will still take time, roughly another hour, but at that time everything will be as charged as we can make it, thanks in part to the Gods gracing us with a beautiful day."

It was true. From what they'd seen, there wasn't a cloud in the sky, perfect weather for charging a solar battery.

"I still doubt it will succeed, Johan," Bree stressed, "but regardless, it is ready to go, as is the transportation for our little surprise."

Johan still shivered at the thought of the H.Y. bomb located in the same building as he was now. "It won't be affected by the blast? It is a machine, after all," he asked eventually.

"No," was the reply from Caspar. "We will move it shortly to a series of underground tunnels that will eventually lead to a bunker beneath Gracious Park, the main attraction of Bankoor for one entering from the south. It is a vast and beautiful public area just inside the southern entrance. The tunnels branch around the city at great depths for many purposes. Cargo, drainage, power lines, etc. They are deep enough that the transport, under its own power, will not be hit. The ground below us is dense and too hard for this to penetrate. It and the bomb it carries will be fine."

"You assume," Esgona added, snidely. "There's no way for you know that for certain. You all keep telling us how far advanced this all is to you, so let's not be so confident."

"Well, Esgona," Bree began with confidence, "we know more than you and your friends do, and that's going to have to be enough for you to believe us, isn't it. It will be moved. It will be in the proper location, and it will be fine. Trust me."

Esgona didn't reply. He just sat there in a huff doubting every word he was told, which was unsurprising to anyone who knew him.

"You said there were two items of good news?" Seraphina asked, anxious to get something a little more reassuring than a possible-yet-unlikely solution to the impending Embracer and army of the Old problem they were facing.

"So I did," smiled Bree. With a click, the picture changed to a blurry image of something distant: what appeared to be a very large and imposing vehicle surrounded on all sides by robotic soldiers. "This is what we assume is their current base of operations, an impressive mobile monstrosity many times larger than any others we've seen, and it's located to the rear of the centermost point of their ranks on our side of the Vein River, the logical place for such a base. What I have to show you has little to do with it now, though we're hoping that changes." Questioning looks met the statement, but Auron Bree and his flair for the over-dramatic would not be denied. Another click and the image moved to the left of the machine and focused on a field of never-ending soldiers. "I'd like you to watch here. I apologize for the quality, it not being up to our usual standards, but we'll have to make due." The image began to move, the mass of soldiers marching in perfect unison like waves rippling in water. The scene continued for almost a minute, each set of eyes riveted to it even though it was blurry and non-distinct. There was a noticeable air of anticipation in the three young viewers.

Then, from the upper left corner, seemingly out of the clear blue sky, came a bright red streak of fire hurtling towards the ground. In an instant it hit the mass of soulless bodies and a grainy, soundless explosion rocked their numbers. The camera image panned around to center on this new development more clearly, and soon the quality of the picture improved.

The better image followed as fire began erupting from the ground, taking more bodies and half-track vehicles out as it went. After a few moments of this, they could each clearly see a crowd of machines disperse, leaving a gap with this fire-plume in the center. Another moment passed and the fire died down, followed the flames rushing toward the base again.

"It would seem," Bree said, speaking over the video, "that we have some powerful allies."

Two of the three faces from the south looked somewhat confused. The third, however embittered it usually was, knew what it was seeing and what it meant, a truthful realization that made him sick to the core. "You son of a bitch."

Johan turned to Esgona like a shot. "What did you say?" he demanded. "What is it? Do you know who's doing that?"

"I, too, would like any information you may have on this, Esgona," Bree added, seeming to glare through the continuing images of fire-born destruction on the viewer.

Esgona relented, "It's Nixon. The fire-man I told you all about. The one who saved me back in Tan Torna Qu'ay."

Johan's eyes lit up at once. "The one Aryu went with?" His mind raced. Was his friend and brother back? Had they found him after all these weeks?

Esgona said nothing. He just looked sour, proof enough that it was indeed the same person.

"Well," said Bree, breaking the excited moment, "it's not over. Please keep watching." The faces went back to the viewer, which now showed a clear view of a large gap in the crowd. In the gap stood the suspected fire-beast, and a winged man standing across from him.

At first Johan was ecstatic, thinking this form was that of his friend. A moment later it dawned on him what they were really seeing. This person was smaller, black in color, and angular, almost…

…like a machine. It *was* a machine, or at least partly. "This is very interesting," Bree continued. "It appears to possibly be the leader of the enemy forces, a 'man', who we believe is also an Embracer, believe it or not." They could. Very easily. "He carries a powerful weapon, though what kind and the source of its power is still unknown. We are quite certain his name is Isuzu, or Izuka, something like that. He's seen giving orders and controlling some of the soldiers. This, however, is what I believe you are looking for."

The image froze and zoomed into the crowd at large, focusing on the fringes on the circle around these two combatants. There, plain as day even in a blurry image, was Aryu O'Lung'Singh. Battered. Better armed.Much angrier, but undoubtedly him. The wings and general look about him proved it. Johan was on his feet in an instant, hollering and shouting with joy at this development. It was him! He was here! He'd made it to them at last.All the weeks of hardship and trials and both of them made it. They followed the plan and they had a chance of being together. Johan was awash with a hundred different emotions and was on the verge of tears. So close! He was only a short distance away!

Unfortunately, that short distance was almost completely covered with a horrible and murderous army of the Old, but that was simply a matter of semantics now. If he was that close, there was no way they were going to let the chance to join up with him again slip by.

Esgona was simply Esgona. There was proof that Aryu was not the enemy.

"Johan, please, take a seat," Bree spoke over his happiness. "There's a bit more, and it's very important."

Smiling from ear to ear, Johan sat back down and watched. They watched as a new form appeared, a very large and black one. Soon, Aryu was gone, the other winged enemy giving chase, and only Nixon and this new form remained. "What's that?" Johan asked about the newcomer.

"We don't know, but in a moment it will engage in battle with the fire-thing on the ground, and after that we lose them as well as their leader and your winged friend, who are lost in the crowd surrounding the base. We assume they're in it, but we can't say that for certain. Their leader is very strong and very fast. If it is your friend though, I assure you we hope for the best." A weak sentiment that went without saying, but the politician in Auron Bree was never far beneath his surface.

"We know this: that large black newcomer came from here, the city itself. Other videos caught it lifting off and joining that little fray. Likely a spy, and a damn good one to make it past all of our security. We don't know where it was, what it learned or even how long it was here, but we must entertain the possibility that it knows a great deal more about us than we'd like."

Smiles faded. "Such as?" asked Seraphina.

"We have to consider that it knows our plans, my friends, and that is a chilling thought indeed. If it knows what we have and how to use it, it's already too late."

The somber tone of the room returned.

"However, we can't say for certain, so for now we must carry on as planned. The day is new, the battles are about to begin and it's time to get underway. Johan, it's time you gave me your knife and have you and your group evacuate, and I'm afraid I can no longer take 'no' for an answer."

Johan could only smile at him, still mentally high on all of this new information. "No," was all he could say before bursting out in laughter.

Johan started with a small chuckle and eventually let it roll into full-fledged hysterics.Seraphina smiled at him, having never seen this side of Johan before. Even Esgona seemed to have a glimpse of understanding about what had driven him to this point.

Auron Bree and Caspar were not smiling. Bree began scowling with anger at this bold defiance. After a few minutes of waiting, he pressed the issue. "Excuse me, Johan?"

Johan couldn't be stopped. The exhaustion, trials and shear dumb luck of the moment were too much, and Auron Bree wasn't helping matters at all. "No! No nonono! No, and no again!" The laughter continued, much to the ire of Bree and his militaristic companion.

"*Johan!*" he yelled over the noise as it rang through the massive room. "Damn it man, what the hell are you laughing at!"

No answer. Just laughing. Seraphina had even begun to start small giggles at the scene. It was simply infectious at a time when it seemed laughter was a precious commodity.

"Gods damn you, Johan Otan'co!" Bree screamed. "This isn't funny! There are people dying out there! Good people like your friend Stroan! Would it be funny if he died?" The laughter died down at the words, but the beaming smile remained, much to Bree's irritation.

"No, Auron, it wouldn't be funny at all. It isn't something I take lightly, but you have to see it from my point of view."

"Well why don't you stop laughing like an idiot and tell me?"

"Fine," began Johan, bracing himself on the table and looking right at Bree though the hazy ghost image, "we have fought our way here for weeks. Through fires, explosions, attacks on our lives, the crashing water of the great Thunder Run, the tragic loss of friends and family in the Paieleh River valley, and finally to here; a city ripped from all of our nightmares. We have seen Hell, Auron Bree, and it certainly isn't that army. The world is vast and full of unimaginable danger.

"Through all that, I have been driven forward with a quest, a task I gave myself to fight through to here, Bankoor. I followed my heart and it led us here because that's what I promised my friend that I would do.

"So here we are, right where I promised we'd be, and now what do we find out? That after all the hardships and pain we made it through, so did Aryu. That video you just showed us had an image of him, so close we could almost touch him. And do you know what I saw? Even in the blur of the picture I saw a man who was tired, broken, empowered, fearless, and ready to die for the cause, all things which are true about me. That was a man who has walked a lifetime of steps in only a few weeks. A man who, somewhere down the road, got his hands on a really badass looking shield! I mean, did you see that thing? It had fucking *spikes* on it! Where would someone even find something like that?"

Auron's patience for Johan to get to the point was fading quickly. Reading this, Johan summed his maddening glee up. "After all we've been through, do you think there's any possible chance in this world or the next that you could pull me away from here with my tail between my legs, running north and praying to see Aryu again knowing he's in the thick of it, putting his life on the line for the cause we all share?"

Bree relented. The strength of these young fools was undeniable, but so was that of many he'd met. The difference here was that these fools *knew* they were fools and fought on just as hard anyway. Bree couldn't decide if that was noble or pure insanity. Both, he supposed. "So, you won't give me the knife?"

"No Bree, I'll follow our deal as agreed on my honor, but that makes twice you've heard something I didn't say. I said you could use it, not take it. Where it goes, I go."

Curse this bastard and his damned semantics! With one button press Bree could command any security forces in the area to his location and just take the knife and be done with these nuisances! One button and he could do anything he wanted and not give another two shits about these three.

One simple truth stayed his hand preventing this. He didn't like Johan Otan'co at all. His fierceness and intelligence were completely overshadowed by his inability to see the big picture, but that was a flaw he could get over in time. When that time came and his childlike naiveté was washed away, may the Great Gods Above help anyone who stood against him, just as Auron Bree had done here and now.

Merrik Caspar was silent and watching the scene unfold around him. After only a few dealings with Johan he'd grown a tremendous amount of respect for him. Merrik Caspar didn't dole out respect every day. In fact, he was known to be terribly stingy with it whenever possible.

Now, it was Bree's' turn to laugh, once more catching all around him off guard as they all clearly expected the man to take the forceful security route and be done with it. The laugh wasn't as pronounced as Johan's had been, but it was no less infectious. Soon, Bree and the three from the south were all smiling and laughing. The screen retracted and they all saw each other clearly again.

"Alright, my foolish young friends. You stay with Chief Rider Caspar and myself from here on out. We do this together, as planned."

Bree reached down under the table and pulled out what looked like a metal picture frame. He held it up and the empty space within filled with abstract images, just as the one between the towers on the table had. "This is my master control. It has been programmed to remotely detonate the spire, as well as the High Yield bomb. We go, together, to our below ground command center, the place I showed you before that houses the bomb. From there, we plan the next step. Are you all coming?"

A good question. Johan couldn't speak for either of them and he turned to look at Esgona first, followed by Seraphina. When he looked into her dark eyes and saw tears there, he knew and understood at once, but she spoke anyway. "I can't, Johan. I can't go with you."Expecting the words, Johan was no less upset to hear them. "We've come so far together, but you have to know your path isn't mine. I still have others from my family and home out there, running north and worried about me. I can't go fighting some war on the back of that stupid bomb. You made a promise to do this, to make it to your friend Aryu, to finish this fight and avenge the loss of your home. I can't go with you because I want to help the people I love escape. I owe you my life, Johan, and nothing pains me more than thinking I may never get the chance to repay you, but not like this. I can't let my feelings stop you from doing what you must."

Johan was saddened to see the tears in her eyes, but he understood what she was saying. He took her soft hand in his and held it for a moment, brushing away her short hair from her wet eyes with his other. "I'll make it through this. I promise. You go, find your family and run until you can't run anymore. When I'm done, I'll find you." He looked at her, still stunned by her beauty and strength.

She smiled. "You have to Johan. You have no choice." He looked confused for a moment. "You made a promise to your friend, but you also made another promise. A promise to Skerd. You said you'd return, which isn't very likely if you're dead." He hadn't forgotten about Skerd and his threats against mankind. Although he'd acted hastily to stop the attack, he still intended to honor his words. It was, in fact, one of the main reasons he was so intent on keeping his knife close-at-hand. Skerd was still in the Paieleh Valley somewhere, waiting for Johan to return with his knife to whatever was left of Huan and that damned Thunder Run again. "On my honor," he had told the beast. At least now, with the clarity of vision he got from the precious knife, he at least had a slight inkling as to why. "It's that promise," Seraphina said, pulling him out of the memory of confusion and fear he'd been lost in from the meeting with the great Stalker, "that I will hold you to, because that one guarantees you will return, and when you do, I will go with you back to that monstrous thing that killed so many and see where fate takes us."

Johan was still amazed at her strength and forwardness, even in times of crisis. "Alright. I'll be sure to uphold my word to him, but I do it for you, not some mystic old Stalker."

Seraphina wrapped her arms around Johan just as she had the first time they'd met (outside of the Thunder Head waters, that is) and kissed him, deeply and passionately this time. After a few moments, her wet lips left his, and once more he was left feeling lost without her.

As they turned to see her out to the awaiting transport that now housed the other council members, something dawned on Johan: the three of them were all that was left.

Somewhere, in the middle of the kiss and the aversion of watching it, Esgona had at last slipped away from the others, just as he'd always wanted, and after so much together and even saving Johan's life at one point, he had finally had enough and parted company with the other survivor of the destruction of Tan Torna Qu-ay.

"There he is," said Caspar, pointing to a non-descript head of hair in the mass of people that were leaving the spire from a different exit. The scraggily dark tuft was clearly Esgona. The limping and uninterested way he moved proved as such. "He's getting onto a transport, by the looks of it."

Johan was still flustered from losing Seraphina and was barely paying attention as Caspar spoke. They'd only put a small amount of effort into finding Esgona above ground, and now, deep in the earth at the heart of the WGC command center, the eerie visage of the H.Y. bomb behind them, the three of them were scanning recorded video of the area around the spire, the only places they could see due to the rest of the city being without power now.

Once they'd seen him get onto the awaiting carrier with a crowd of others, some being fleeing members of the council itself, the truth of the situation was fully realized: Esgona had enough. With Aryu not being involved with the Army of the Old, and what looked like an imminent reunion between the two blood brothers, he seemed to pick his exit and left without a fuss. Not that Johan would have given him one.

"I guess that's it, then," Johan lamented, a part of him relieved, another almost saddened. Johan hated debts, and as much as was loathed to admit it, he owed Esgona a great one from his actions in the Paieleh Valley. He had reached as far as they were planning on going for this phase of the trip, and as such, their deal with Aryu was completed. Esgona, safe with others now, was able to leave without a word said on the matter.

They watched the image on the large screen in front of them. Not a transparent screen like the one in the council chambers, but an impressive one all the same. Soon, with no one left outside the transport, it pulled away and was lost off camera.

"Where's he going?" Caspar asked. "Those transports lead to the north of the city, the hub of our population evacuation. Is he really just leaving?"

"Yep," Johan said, explaining the deal they'd made with Aryu as well as an abbreviated version of the relationship they had with the troubled boy.

"Still," said Caspar after they were done, "one would think he'd still want to help. Find a way to defeat the enemy. Make sure we win!"

"One would be wrong, Chief Rider," Johan answered. "Esgona, even after all he's been through, still only looks out for himself."

Auron Bree shook off the scene and ushered the other two along to the awaiting bomb. He touched the flat panel in his hand and all of them watched as a tray containing a flat, metal box slid out from the perfectly formed side of the weapon. Johan stepped back as it did so, not trusting this thing at all. As the tray continued to slide out, seemingly being the entire width of the machine, Bree explained what they were seeing. "This is the 'Enhancement' tray. When the time comes, this is where you will place the knife, Johan. Once inside, the device will align it automatically, scan the knife, transfer the information about it that it collects, and modify itself accordingly."

Another button press and the tray slid back inside silently. However, the dark and blank screen now showed a soft, glowing single word that sent shivers down Johan's spine.

"SCANNING," flashed dimly in the top left corner in attractive blue letters, followed by it making a soft 'click click clickclick' not unlike the sounds a certain phoenix encountered a few weeks previous when faced with a flying black dot. Then, as the word faded away, a new message appeared. "NEGATIVE ENHANCEMENT FOUND" followed by the words disappearing and the screen looking as dead as it had before.

The unsettling truth was evident. The screen may seem to appear off, and the device itself may look unpowered and harmless, but this menace to humanity was still very much active and ready to go. It was just waiting for its time to shine.

Bree held up his control panel and addressed them. "The key controls to this devise, as well as other information this defense system collects," he indicated the room beyond with its screens and tracking systems, "are sent right to this for the time being. Then, with the bomb in place, we trigger the spire blast. Once we assess the situation from there we decide if we use your knife or not. My vote on the matter is fairly well documented."

It was: blow them all up. Do it twice. Do it with as much firepower as they possess and be done with them.

"So, how do we get to the location we're sending it?" Johan asked, eyes never leaving the bomb.

Another casual button press and off to their right a spiral door opened in the floor, forcing each of them back until it had stopped growing. "Right through there, my friend. The bomb is resting on a unit that can carry it and us to the blast site. There, below and beyond the force of the spire explosion, we can use the protected system below ground to see if we were successful. Then, with or without the knife, we set the bomb in place and use this carriage to take us to the other side of the city, where we will emerge with the remainder of the evacuees and watch the fireworks."

From somewhere behind them, something started beeping and glowing red, catching them all by surprise. Johan noticeably jumped. "Ah shit," Caspar said at once, rushing over to another screen that showed a series of words but no pictures. "Yep, as we thought. Word from the front-line scouts, sir. They're coming."

Bree looked upset but resolute. "Hmm, sooner than I'd have liked, but when is a good time to face Embracers. Alright Caspar, you know what to do."

Caspar smiled, an odd action considering the news they'd

just received that the Embracers were now approaching. "I do sir. Thank you." Caspar typed a serious of words and commands onto the display's flat keyboard and pressed a button, sending the orders away. Then, he returned to the other two, took each of their hands in turn with a vigorous shake and said goodbye and good luck. Auron Bree returned the sentiment, but Johan simply shook his hand and looked at him in confusion. Without another word, Chief Rider Merrik Caspar was gone, wheeling out the door, armor of the Riders banging as he left in a rush.

He looked at Bree for an explanation, still bewildered by what had just happened. Bree sighed, "He's off to the war, Johan. He's been itching to get back to the front lines since day-one at my side as head adviser. A tribute to his bravery, if not his stupidity. We agreed that once the Embracers began their advance and the order to retreat had been given, which by the way it just was in case you missed that, he could return to his Riders and our forces and assist in the fighting, what little there will be anyway, and help them fall back into the city and away. Those Inja Riders are something else, lad. Brave to a fault."

No argument here. "So, what now?" Johan asked.

"Now," replied Bree, his hard face cracking a faint smile, "we go for a little ride." And with one last button press on his control panel, the two of them, as well as the whole section of floor they were standing on, began retracting into the hole that had opened, beginning their trip to who-knew-where and the fate that awaited them below ground.

The sudden and baffling arrival of Aryu O'Lung'Singh was only part of the reason Esgona had felt the urge to at last be done with these idiots.

The other and greater reason was Johan and his heroic lunacy. Esgona had watched him dive into the sure death of the waters below the Thunder Run to save a pretty face, an act that would have been suicide if not for the magic knife he carried. He'd seen Johan do undeniably brave things, too, like the deal with the Dragon Stalker leader. However, he'd also seen some foolishness he couldn't believe, and today's was the last he would witness.

When Johan had again used his verbal wordplay to keep his knife from the hands of Auron Bree and the WGC, Esgona saw the truth behind the action. It wasn't just foolish bravery that had done it; it was also addiction.

Johan needed that weapon now. Deep down he likely didn't even know it, but he did. On some spiritual level he was connected to it and the things he'd been through with it, and that connection betrayed his common sense. For all the claims they'd made of seeking revenge and winning this war, withholding their ultimate weapon seemed completely illogical, but it seemed only Auron Bree and Esgona knew that for certain.

Bree was also a fool. A fool who had a thousand chances to just take it and be done with them all but never did. At first Esgona thought he was saving them from something bigger, but now he saw he was nothing more than a conniving politician who welcomed a chance to resist obliterating members of his populace for no more reason than the bad press it would create. It had nothing to do with nobility.

So, after everything, Johan had resisted that final time and Esgona had seen the truth: Johan Otan'co was never going to give up that knife unless he was forced to do so, and for all his talk and cunning, Auron Bree alone was not someone who could do that. Johan had proven himself a worthy foe to Bree and that misguided respect would be his downfall, and perhaps the downfall of all mankind.

Esgona's stomach lurched as the transport he'd boarded quickly in the crowd leaving the spire began to pull away, carrying the remnants of the WGC and their families to farther, safer ground north. He looked at no one, not wanting to strike up any unwanted conversations about why he was here and not with his 'friends' back at the spire. He simply watched his feet and prayed his instincts were correct.

Naturally, after having seen so much in his life, his instincts were potent and finely honed. Soon, after a few blocks had been traveled, another collection of the straggling population was seen beside a park, likely the one Esgona and the other two had spent so much time in the day before. The transport pulled alongside the group and began loading them all on.

It was time. Without a word, Esgona, from his strategically chosen location near a side door, slid like a viper off of the machine and with as much grace as he could manage in his current condition. He slipped into the park and a thick grove of trees. If anyone saw him do so, they never said a word. As the transport finished loading its weary travelers and pulled away, Esgona was off, south and away from his intended salvation. A salvation he knew wasn't real. South was where his *real* savior could be found. The same savior he'd come to worship like a God during hard times in his life. The only savior that had never let him down. The only person Esgona had ever truly trusted. Esgona's favorite person in the world, as anyone could tell you.

Himself.

Chapter 10: That One Special Moment

She ran like a fiend through the crowd of machines and abominations, none of which took any notice of the svelte pale wraith as she moved.

She clasped her prize tightly, shocked by how small and fragile it seemed. Here, after everything, was the key to ending it all. One move, one shot, and she would make them all suffer. Make them all pay for the pain they'd caused her.More to the point, they would pay for the pain they caused *him*, and that was far worse. No animal alive is as dangerous as a mother protecting her child. This was a fact throughout history, and now that fire raged inside her.

It was a hard road to get to here. She had waited in her dark hiding place in one of the smaller transports until at last the ride had stopped, and she could faintly hear the sound of many others around her: other machines and footsteps were audible even beyond the rumble of her own ride. She was here, and she was close.

She had waited until a time she thought it would be safe to move, a time she had believed was long enough to let her get as deep into their ranks as she was likely to get. She slid out to feel her way back again.

Then, unexpectedly, Nixon arrived, and Hell followed with him as it often did.

He was merciless in his destruction, casting aside any manor of device he saw like it was a child's toy, including sadly, her own.

Soon she was being rattled around inside hundreds of tons of twisted steel, bounced off of walls and into hard corners like a pebble in a crushed tin can. By the time she'd realized she had stopped, there wasn't a single part of her body that didn't ache or show some sign of damage. She climbed up the walls of the now sideways machine and out a hole that had been ripped into its side, shielding her eyes against the harsh sunlight after so many hours in perfect darkness. She was beaten and bleeding, but alive and able-bodied. That would be enough. With a quiet curse at her damned mortality and a deft hop, she was on the ground, off to the epicenter of the phoenix's arrival and the large and unmistakable rolling base beyond him.

Now, as she ran, she heard the thunderous crashing both ahead of her and behind. Ahead was her salvation. Indeed, the salvation of the world, as long as things kept progressing as she'd originally planned (which even she had to admit was unlikely). Behind was her damnation, the specter of death that would not stop until he had her. Her tentative truce with the demon seemed to be over after she grabbed the vile. It wasn't where she expected it, but she'd take it all the same.

Her destination was a cold, gray, three-story tall monster of a vehicle, bigger than most buildings she'd ever seen and twice as noisy. It rolled along on giant tracks like a tank, crushing any and all that were foolish enough to get in its way.

A scream of anger and horror bellowed behind her and Crystal knew Izuku was getting closer. He was in the process of destroying his own army just to get her, summoning vast levels of the Power to cut them down. She was all he wanted. Her and her clutched prize, the antidote to the infamous neural inhibitor drug.

At first, as she hid among the mass of twisted, walking steel around her, Crystal had prepared to just take the item and use it herself, eager to regain the abilities she'd lost. When she'd heard where Sho was and what had happened to him, her plan changed entirely. Anger boiled her blood as Izuku spoke, telling Nixon and Aryu about what he had been subjecting her son to for what appeared to be hours.She hated herself so much in that moment for not protecting him like she should have. She hated her deals with Izuku but could only chastise herself for not telling Izuku to leave his brother alone. She'd only spared a word for Aryu, who at the time she'd believed to be more important.What kind of mother thinks that of her own son versus a man she'd known for only a few days?

She needed Izuku, she reminded herself, but was it for the right reasons? Once she'd thought so. She'd thought that even the life of her son and so many innocents were worth the risks she was taking.

She ran after Aryu and the path he cut like a seasoned pro through the masses ahead of him using Ryu's sword and Sho's shield until he'd reached a locked outer door of the machine. She still believed Aryu to be the savior she'd been searching for, but now she knew she never should have involved Sho at all. The thought of him, weak and unprepared, at the mercy of Izuku and the Est Vacuus combined, brought tears to her eyes as she moved.

Any though of using it on herself was lost in the anger and pain she felt. She needed to get it to her son and give it to him. Once she did, he'd regain his use of the Power and get a reprieve from both death and the Est Vacuus, which she considered much worse. No one knew more about the physical and mental pain and suffering caused by the Est Vacuus than she did.

She ran on, watching as Aryu, with the quickness and skill of an Embracer, leapt onto the moving beast at the locked door, plunged the Shi Kaze into the hull, and cut apart the door locks much as he had to the fuselage of the plane on their way to HOME.

The door fell open as if made of paper, exposing the twisted blackness of the inside. However, before he had a chance to enter on his own, Crystal was at him, legs pumping as the heat and radiant energy of Izuku and his immense power made the hairs on the back of her neck vibrate. She reached out, grabbing the arm that held the Shi Kaze tightly, and heaved him into the space he'd created with unimaginable force, wrenching him in with a yelp of surprise, his wings fluttering behind him like a grotesque kite that had fallen too close to the ground.She pulled harder still, drawing him into the blackness that now was becoming softly illuminated as they moved, their motion seeming to trigger faint lighting around them, guiding them onward.

Before they reached the first turn, she felt his arm yank back powerfully toward him, eventually releasing her grip and halting her progress. "Crystal?" she heard him yell in surprise, but it was too late.

The silhouette in the mangled doorway beyond was eerily similar to that of Aryu, only more ridged. Izuku had stopped his frantic pursuit, seeming happy now that he had her trapped. He said nothing as he began to walk forward, the 'clang' of metal on metal as his feet walked across the floor. Even in the darkness he could see the terror and confusion on the young man's face.

"Aryu!" she called back hurriedly. "Please, stop him! I'll get Sho!" She held up the vile to show her meaning, but his face was still etched in fear. "Please Aryu, trust me! I can get to him! I can save him! But only you can slow Izuku down!"

A laugh rolled down the wide hallway as Izuku approached. "What?" Aryu called back, lost in the words she was speaking. "What the fuck do you mean, 'stop him'?"

"Only you can now, Aryu! Please!"

"Wait, what about back at…"

"Forget it, Aryu! Just *trust* me! I'll tell you everything! I'll explain anything you want! Where you came from! Why Nixon is chasing you! *Everything*! But you have to stop him!"She could hear Aryu's breathing get heavy as she spoke, as well as the sudden heady rush of the Est Vacuus getting closer. Soon, she'd be so lost in madness that she'd be no help to anyone.

"What about me?!" Aryu demanded. "Where do I…" but he never finished. Instinct trained into him over the last few weeks under the tutelage of Nixon and Sho had taken over, and he thrust out the Shi Kaze to block an incoming blow from Izuku with his own powerful blade. He had no choice but to fight now, the air around the collision of weapons a mix of a warm glow and a harsh ripple similar to heat off a paved road in the summer. Izuku would never recklessly try to pass Aryu's weapons in this tight hallway, both of which could easily kill him. Soon, Aryu was wheeling around, forcing Izuku back with the combination of the weapons he possessed and the things he'd learned, grunting and fighting for his life and the lives of so many others.

As the two battled, Crystal knew she wouldn't have another chance. With a soft wish of luck, she dashed off into the bowels of the machine while the sounds of a life-or-death battle filled the air. Somewhere ahead was her son, her beloved Sho, and in her hand was the thing that could save him.

If, and only if, she wasn't too late.

Startled didn't begin to describe what had just happened to Aryu. He was building pride and confidence in himself as he thrashed his way to the giant rolling base. With each stroke and slice that felled another machine, there was a deep and welcoming sense of satisfaction in him. Once he'd reached the machine and cut his way in, it was almost intoxicating.

It was short lived once he was pulled forcefully into the hole he'd made at the doorway and through to the dark hallway beyond. It took a moment to realize what happened, and another for him to realize who'd done it.Confusion came to him first, but anger was close behind. As he twisted and pulled his arm away and met Crystal face to face, he was surprised to find that her beauty and look of innocence only made him angrier, a reminder of what he'd been through lately and the possible role she'd played in it all.

"Trust me!" she pleaded, but he was so unsure what to do. He'd known she was manipulative, and that she could twist someone like himself, but he saw fear and urgency in her soft pale eyes. After Izuku had arrived and began his slow pace down the hall, as he looked back and forth between the two images, he remembered all of the times Sho and Nixon had told him that the first clear and unmistakable image of a situation a true warrior has is often (though not always) the correct one. There was pain in her eyes as she spoke, a pain that conveyed a need to save Sho. He'd seen what she had in her hand. He knew her plan at once: to get to Sho, inject him, and allow his command of the Power to heal his mental and physical wounds before it was too late.

All she needed to do was put that into herself, which she clearly hadn't done, and she would be back to normal. She hadn't. She'd wanted to get it to Sho, and with Izuku getting closer, he was an instant from simply letting her go.

Until she mentioned where he's from and why the phoenix was chasing him. Did she really know all of that? He'd tried to make her explain, instantly ignorant of his surroundings, but the small and alarming voice in his head that told him to turn and fight took over, and he thrust the Shi Kaze out. He blocked a downward swipe from

Izuku, letting the two opposing weapons clash together in a rush of energy and strength. By the time he'd began his counter attack, something he did strictly out of instinct, he heard Crystal run off. Only he and Izuku remained in the dimly lit hallway of the transport.

Izuku was enraged as he watched her go, but couldn't risk ignoring Aryu and his weapons. If either of them wanted to get to Crystal or Sho, first they had to deal with each other.

This realization caused them both to step away, guards up and reflexes, both human and mechanical, poised on the razor's edge of readiness.

Izuku smiled in the darkness, his eerie and unsettling appearance causing Aryu to shake in both anger and fear. "Lights please," Izuku spoke softly, followed by a sudden and jarring rush of light into Aryu's eyes.

Izuku took the moment of temporary blindness in Aryu to attack again, not with the Power but with the weapon. The Power was useless against these items and only a direct assault would do.

Aryu had Sho's shield up at once, deflecting the blow off with hardly a sound. The rush and pulse of the collision wasn't as forceful as it was when the two swords met, but it was still disorienting to each of them.

Partly blinded, Aryu dashed forward, anger driving him like a piston up the hallway, taking Izuku with him as he moved. Izuku let neither weapon near him, deflecting each with the Est Vacuus, and he stepped back as Aryu advanced.

Izuku was incensed. He couldn't risk losing it all now, so close to the end of this first grand step, but here was a whelp of a boy lashing out with cunning and rage in his eyes, gaining ground on him all the time. Why? Why was Aryu so brave when faced with such power?

Then it dawned on Izuku: Aryu wasn't afraid because he had no reason to be. He was guarded from the Power of Izuku by the need for revenge that drove him forward, past Izuku's frightening appearance and obvious combat superiority.

That just left the flooding void of the Est Vacuus. If he could get the Shi Kaze from Aryu's hand, or at least land a safe blow, one that would tell Aryu in no uncertain terms what he was up against, he would crumble before the awesomeness he was facing. The question was how to do it without Aryu himself landing a killing stoke in these tight quarters. After looking into the eyes of the determined youth in front of him, he had to concede that the prospects of doing so were grim. This boy, with his hard stare and clenched teeth, would fight him with anger and determination, not the deep thoughtfulness aged and wised Embracers were prone to. This one was still very young and hadn't been corrupted by these things yet. He would fight hard, desperate to plunge one of his many blades into Izuku any way he could, even at the cost of his life. Aryu would fight Izuku like a demon until death.

And of course, as they both knew, deeper still into the bowels of the machine ran Crystal. Another horrifying realization came to Izuku. If she was successful and reached Sho in time, she would use the antidote on him, restore his powers and unleash her son with all of his faculties on the world, a fate Izuku knew would cause him much more harm than good.Conversely, if she was too late and Sho was dead, as Izuku suspected, she would use it on herself, and that was no better than the other option. Although not as powerful as Sho, Crystal Kokuou was more than enough to put a sizeable dent into Izuku's plan.

The solution presented itself almost instantly, and as he stood motionless once more in a dead heat with the winged avenger before him, he knew only one solution would do. Do to them as they did to him. At least then he'd have the advantage of knowing how many, if any, of his enemy he faced.

Aryu only saw cowardice as he stepped forward, attempting to attack Izuku again, when Izuku gave an admonishing wave of his hand at the young man. Before either of them could say a word, Izuku was gone, using his large mechanical wings to thrust himself backwards, sending a wave of dry, smoke-filled air down the hall. Aryu had to squint despite his bodily urge to stay wide-eyed. Then, he was gone, off in to the sky and away.

Aryu ran to the door, recklessly thrusting his head out to see where Izuku had gone. He could give chase, but he was here for Sho. Izuku's time would come soon enough.

He rushed back into the body of the now-illuminated machine, looking desperately for some indication of where to go, at no point feeling uneasy or sick at the scene of screens and buttons, machines and contraptions that surrounded him in this corridor junction. Three seemingly-unfinished soldiers of the Old appeared around a corner, ignoring Aryu as they moved, but still he cut them each down, letting the smooth blades of the shield begin again with the gripping of his hand. Nothing was going to escape him now. Not until he found Sho.

A second later, the scream of pain from what sounded like a young girl was heard reverberating down a hallway to Aryu's right, and like a shot he was gone.

Aryu had become hardened in these past few weeks. Toughened in ways his year away from home with Johan could never accomplish. Even in the last few days, after learning of the Power within himself, so close and so ready to be used, or in the battle with the Embracers who took Sho where he had killed living men and women with the Shi Kaze, he unwittingly had grown exponentially. He so far beyond the boy that had left Tan Torna Qu-ay over a year ago that his parents would hardly know him.

After all of the thing he'd seen, nothing could shield him from this.

The first horrifying indication of what had happened was felt long before it had actually been confirmed. As Aryu ran he was hit with a sudden shockwave of invisible energy, one that seemed to flow everywhere, and eventually even seemed to bring the massive vehicle to a standstill.

It was a feeling Aryu had felt before, only this was far more intense and powerful. It was the same feeling he'd felt at his core as he dispatched the Embracers on the mountain side. There it had been violent and destructive. Here, it was almost peaceful and cleansing, like a great weight had been lifted from his shoulders.

He burst into a darkened supply room, far away from the chaos all around them. Crystal Kokuou was kneeling on the cold floor, crying heavily and gasping for air sharply between sobs. Her body was enwrapped in an astonishing ice-blue cocoon that looked as if it was made of glass; her infamous though seldom used Makashi armor. Her beautiful face was red and twisted in pain as she howled, blinded to anything and everything around her. She was ignorant to anything but the sight that now rested on her lap.

Tokugawa Sho, son and destroyer of the great Ryu, caretaker of the Eastlands and lover of all life he saw, lay lifeless. He who could be the greatest of all the Embracers, should he ever have chosen to be, was limp, eyes staring blankly at the ceiling above them. His face pale and wet with his mother's tears as his seemingly-massive head and shoulders lay propped up on her legs. On his chest, clenched in one of his massive hands, was the empty vile of the neural inhibitor antidote.

Aryu could no longer stop it, try as he might. The pain, the loss, the unimaginable feeling of helplessness devoured him, and he ran to their side, screaming Sho's name and trying to rouse him uselessly.

Tears welling up in his eyes; no amount of sadness could keep the anger at bay. In this place, at this moment, Aryu O'Lung'Singh knew that he was unstoppable. Izuku and all he commanded, every soldier, every machine, every Embracer, every single atom of existence that would dare stand against him was going to suffer today, because today, in this moment and until his revenge was complete, no one on earth could defeat him.

As the power of these things climbed within him, and as he knelt beside his large and trusted friend and teacher, he cried deeply, just as Crystal was. Her son's lifeless head stayed on her lap while her soft white hands caressed the sides of his older rugged face.

Aryu placed his hands onto the eyes of his friend and gently closed them, ignoring the sickening feeling of Sho's damp, clammy skin as he did so. It seemed Sho had been in a terrible state for some time, and the physical and mental toll Izuku had taken from him had been too much. Izuku had at last defeated his younger brother.

Minutes seemed to pass as they both cried on, not wanting to speak in fear words would fail them and only more crying would come. Then, without a word, Crystal took Aryu's hand, which had since dropped both shield and sword without a second thought, and held it firmly above Sho's unmoving chest, now bare save for the modest shirt he wore, his great Makashi armor nowhere to be found. After a moment of holding it there, she sniffled hard, fighting back her pain, and steadied herself as best she could.

"I need to tell you something, Aryu. I need you to know why I did what I did." Aryu watched her apprehensively. He wasn't sure now was the time and place for this conversation, but he let her carry on. "I did it for my father, Aryu. That may sound strange, but his message was so good and pure that I couldn't let it die. This world is so far from his vision that I was afraid it would never return. He was so close to bringing the peace and strength of the Power to the world in a way that wouldn't have ended up so destructive. Had he not died saving my life as a girl, he likely would have succeeded. Maybe not in his lifetime, but he would have. I live with the fact that I'm the reason he failed. His love for me was greater than his love of the world.

"When Ryu knocked on my family door years later, I saw in him that same vision, only this time with the Power to make that change happen quickly. Despite my best efforts, he never saw things the way my father did. I loved him so much, but you know how that ended up.

"Then, there was my son…" she looked at Sho, tears streaming down her face like steady rain, falling onto his lifeless body. "Once more, I had my champion, only this time I would work with him. He felt so guilty, though. Every day he'd walk around our home and hear the voices on the wind and he couldn't blame anyone but himself. Ryu may have destroyed all of the Embracers he could and cast their souls to the wind, but Sho had to listen to them. That much power doesn't just go away, and it ended up torturing him.

"But I still couldn't give up, so this time I put it on myself. Maybe I should have sooner, but I never thought I was ready. I had to try, though. My father was long dead, my eternal lover had gone mad and nearly destroyed the world, and my son was locked in a spiral of pain he had no true claim to. It was then that I began setting wheels in motion. Ryu would have been proud, honestly. He always had plans within plans that branched in a million directions. Choices he could make to keep things steady at any time, and this time so did I."

Aryu was still hazy and lost, but something inside him told him to keep listening, as if it was something he had to do because no one else would. "When Izuku resurfaced with another foolish plan to defeat Sho, I saw in him what I needed. He was still weak. Too weak. So I met with Izuku, told him what I wanted and agreed to give him a weapon so powerful only the Shi Kaze could stand against it. While he was digging up his precious army and slowly and methodically creating his master plan, I was creating his weapon with more personal sacrifice than I chose to admit, followed by tearing apart mountains in order to find the weapon you hold now. I did, and I prepared it to be found. I just needed the right bearer."

She was still unsteady, but the story was clearly giving her strength. "Tell me, do you remember why you climbed that mountain that day so long ago, the day you found the sword?"

Aryu looked at her with confusion. It wasn't even that long ago, really. Not in the grand scheme of things. It took him a moment to pry himself from this situation and remember. "Yeah. We were looking for a meadow to spend our last night of the Journey in. We were told there was one on the mountains near the village we were in at the time."

A faint smile from Crystal. "Right. Do you recall who told you?"

More confusion from Aryu, then sudden realization. "Johan told me a pretty young girl had told him about it. She said exactly where to go. We just figured we had climbed the wrong mountain or something. We didn't, did we."

"No, you didn't," she said, smile fading away. "You went right where I told you to. I told your friend where to go so you would find it."

Aryu was astonished. "Why? Why send us?"

"Not 'us', just you."

Confusion and anger on his face now. "Aryu," she continued quickly, "I'd watched you two for weeks in those mountains. I saw your friendship and brotherhood. I watched, making sure I was right. Once I saw how you treated your wings, I knew I was. They make you that much different. In you, I found my new champion. Someone who had led a hard life. A life with amazing highs and terrible lows. You weren't a fool like so many others, and the Power hadn't corrupted you. You were mortal. In you I saw the hard life of my father, the desire for great balance of Ryu, and the mortal respect for life of Sho. You were so perfect."

"Perfect for what?" Aryu asked, lost in her words. "To be your champion?

"Izuku is old, older than me, older than anyone I know. His power is amazing, but cruel. Once he had the Est Vacuus in his hands, he was nearly unstoppable. He was at last the symbol of unimaginable power the world had to see! The world needs balance, Aryu. In you, it can have it."

"No way!" Aryu yelled into the darkness. "He's an Embracer, I just have a sword and shield! He'd destroy me!"

"But he hasn't, has he? He's had more than one chance and he keeps failing. You must be that balance, Aryu, and in that, you must return the Power to the world. I knew it would be you to find the sword. It had to be. It's just the way the world works."

Aryu looked at the sword with a sudden feeling of disgust. "You were wrong, Crystal. All I want is to destroy Izuku for what he's done to me. For what he's still doing now. My home and family are gone and he needs to answer for that. When that's done, so am I."

Crystal said nothing but looked at him doubtfully. She knew as well as he did that it likely wouldn't stop there. Not with this sword, and now shield apparently, in his hands. "You will do what you feel is right, Aryu, and I believe it is to bring balance to the world. The earth once again sees what it can do and there will be Embracers living peacefully again. We can't stop that. Once they see it, it will happen. They'll watch one man destroy an army and they will want that power for themselves. I believe that in you lies the ability and vision to see that it's done right. For my father. For Ryu, even though he hardly deserves it. For me." She looked at Sho, her last attempt at creating this perfect champion. "And for him."

Aryu was awash in a million emotions. "Didn't you think this would happen?" he asked. "That you would start a chain reaction that would end like this?"

She shook her head. "No. Sho was so wrapped up in looking after the land I thought he'd stay there. I never expected the phoenix, which went a long way in convincing Sho to go. I... I never wanted this to happen, Aryu. He was too good. It wasn't fair." She sobbed heavily once more, her white hair falling around her face as she leaned over her son's body. Aryu saw the guilt and pain there. She didn't want this, and she was paying the price for her mistakes in blood now. That was her weakness, it seemed. She was still much too human to be a real champion, so she tried to make them instead. That was to be her role.

"I... I need you... I need you to do something, Aryu." Her hands trembled, but Aryu only looked at her eyes as she spoke, letting her say what she needed to. "I need you to... to take that which was his... take the rest of what he held so dear."

Aryu looked on in confusion but held firm. "What? What do you need?"

"The Embracers. They're coming. Some of them, anyway. To us. Right now. They're coming to stop you. To stop us."

"How... how do you know that?" Aryu asked, her words steeling him from the image of his lost friend who rest just a hair's width from the hand she held above him.

"Because I can feel them." And with a sudden movement, she thrust Aryu's hand onto her son's chest, slapping it firmly down as Aryu looked on in bewilderment.

Then, he felt as if he was being eaten by a thousand small snakes, each made of ice and with teeth like razors that ate his flesh as it moved, and he watched in horror as his hand became covered in a harsh black ooze, covering every inch of skin as it went, until it began rushing up his arm and eventually to his chest and neck.

The feeling was painful and disorientating. He fell to the ground beside Sho, shaking and crying all at once, trying to speak but finding no breath to make words. He just lay there, looking with confusion and fear at Crystal and whatever evil it was she was using on him, and the sickening rush overtook his head and body, wings included, like a wave of ice-cold water.

There, on the backside of Crystal's arm, was a red circle with a pinprick sized hole in the center. She had used it on herself and had now regained her command of the Power. That was how she knew the other Embracers were coming. That was why she said she could *feel* them. She was back to her old, infinitely powerful self once more.

Then, the icy blackness engulfed him, and the room around them exploded in a ball of white-hot fire, destroying everything.

Had this been a living person, Nixon would have been spilling over with honor and pride at the skills and tenacity of this opponent, humbled to have been in the presence of such a true master.

This was not alive. This was a machine, created with more power and twisted black magic than Nixon could have ever believed possible. He'd never seen such alchemy before. Had he the time to formulate thoughts beyond simply fighting, he would have certainly been looking for the answers to how and why.

E2-0901 was not so entrenched in such mysteries. True, it had wondered about its creation numerous times, but such thoughts were natural for such a well-made, deep-thinking machine. Besides, although devoid of emotion, it was still somewhat savoring this moment, when at last it had been called upon to battle its prime target, the one called Nixon of the Great Fire and Ash.

The battlefield was littered with the collateral damage. Robot bodies were tossed about and littered the ground all around them. A part of Elutherios' extremely advanced mind had even calculated that the odds of it succeeding with Izuku's mission strictly on its own, with no assistance from this worthless army or Embracers and sub-standard machines, was approximately 17.342%; astonishingly high for just one device.

Those odds were dropping quickly now that it was at last engaged with Nixon. The mythical fire-beast was amazingly strong and ruthless in his methods, not hindered by training and logic as the other Embracers it had faced were. In fact, as it fought tooth and nail against this formidable demon, it calculated higher and higher odds that Nixon wasn't an Embracer at all. He was too powerful and too well trained. He appeared to be a complete unknown, but with each counter attack and forceful use of the Power he employed, Elutherios Duo was more and more certain this assumption was correct.

It didn't matter now. The phoenix was slowing down. Only

slightly, but he certainly was losing speed and time.

Nixon, faced with this new development, didn't care in the slightest. Even if this thing outpaced him, Nixon would not stop. His very purpose defied that possibility. He was like a train with no conductor, pushing forward until he ran out of gas or hit something.

Nixon, encased in his shield of fire, swung the massive sword around, clashing it against the sister-sword the machine carried, causing them both to stagger backwards and begin the dance again. Tired or no, Nixon would battle on.

The big man leapt backwards, the ground around them clear now, except for the dismembered bodies. The massive bulk of the Army of the Old had moved on entirely. Only a trodden and lifeless landscape was left in their wake, covered with the footprints and wheel ruts of those that had passed.

"Do ya' speak?" Nixon asked the thing when he had a moment. "Do ya' understand me?"

Elutherios stopped, weapon still at the ready, its mechanical arms ridged and firm as if carved from solid stone.

"I do."

The voice was similar to Izuku's, but also different, as if modified to become something more. The underlying tone was the same, but above it were layers of what sounded like different voices, likely a sick joke by Izuku about the nature of this glorious thing he had made.

"Are ya' just a machine?" Nixon asked, not looking for a real answer as much as he was trying to simply sort out what this thing was and where its weaknesses may be. "Do ya' think for yer'self or simply follow orders?"

"Both." Short, simple answers. No more effort used than needed.

"Do ya' control your purpose? Doya' command yer' own movements in this world."

A soft click from inside the devise. A sound Nixon knew very well. "No."

Nixon didn't falter. He was still trying to learn. "A shame. Ya' fight well. Ye' would do better beyond these menial tasks Izuku gives ya.'"

"Menial?" A lilt of curiosity. Perhaps Nixon was making progress?

"Yes, like battlin' me, 'ere 'n now. Somethin' such as you could 'ave so much purpose in this world."

"You are my purpose, Nixon of the Great Fire and Ash."

What did it mean? That Nixon was its current order, or that he was its designed and intended purpose all along? How long had Izuku been making these plans if that was so?

Before he had a chance to answer a sudden pulse of energy rushed past them both. The force of the ripple brought them both to their knees, although no physical presence of its passing could be seen.

Elutherios was instantly confused about what had happened. Something beyond its opponent had staggered it; a force, a thought process…

A… a feeling?

Not feelings as humans were prone to, more like the message of a hint of a spark of one. Something that resonated with its very core, sending a confusing and scrambled message straight to its central processors.

The effect lasted just a microsecond, but it was still disorientating and sent every bit and byte it had available into a self-scanning mode, analyzing every iota of itself looking for some kind of malfunction.

It found none, but the core memory of the event was instantly logged, saved, and set aside for further analysis.

Nixon knew the feeling. He'd felt it years and years before, with the death of Crystal's father, Allan Kokuou. He had felt it in his sleep; the moment Allan had died saving her, and his considerable energy had been released into the world.

Just as this had.

Sho was gone.

There was no time to think on it. Before he had time to scream in rage, the machine was at him again, its body crashing down sword stroke after sword stroke.

Nixon, fueled by the short breather and sudden realization that Sho was dead, pushed back forcibly, driving the thing away enough for him to regain his footing and strike back, pushing with all of his strength until the thing called Elutherios Duo was forced to take steps away from the reinvigorated phoenix. The fire that had surrounded Nixon died away, all outward signs of his greatness fading. It poured back into him as he moved, his clear mind giving him more focus than he'd thought he could manage.

Elutherios felt it at once, the increase in the resistance Nixon battled with. It wasn't more than it could handle, but the brute-strength tactic it had worked with up until now risked having to change slightly. Nixon was still beatable. It would just take more time and planning.

With fiery eyes clear and shimmering reddish hair flowing behind him, the massive phoenix struck out again, this time making contact with the elusive body of the pearly black machine. The strike was clean, though not as damaging as Nixon would have liked. It was still enough to force Elutherios Duo back a few more steps in caution. What it needed was something to distract the fire-beast, something to give Elutherios a split-second to fall back farther and take a moment to change its battle tactics.

What it got was more than it could ever hope for.

From ahead of them, still in the mass of the Army of the Old beyond, the rolling base was suddenly consumed by a huge white fireball; one so perfectly round that it looked like a bright growing balloon. The explosion instantly caught Nixon's attention, giving Elutherios the moment he needed to fly backwards, putting fifty paces between the two.

Once it landed it was surprised and confused to find Nixon still standing there, watching the massive machine as it was destroyed, the ground and all remaining drones and vehicles around it vaporized along with it.

What surprised it the most was the illogical expression Nixon had on his face.

The phoenix was smiling widely. Almost laughing, really. As he turned back to the fight he was currently locked in, he pointed a menacing finger at the black machine.

"Now, my ridged 'n unfeelin' friend," he said as he smiled, the same peaceful and relaxing smile it had used many times before to ease the nerves of those it had met, "you and all of yer' kind are well 'n truly fucked." And before Elutherios Duo model 0901 could process the possible meaning of this statement, the phoenix was at it again, weapon out and ready to battle once more, the smile still firmly etched on his face.

Izuku knew that things had not gone as smoothly as he'd have liked. The appearance of the phoenix, the emergence of the Shi Kaze long thought lost to the ages, the sudden (though not entirely unexpected) betrayal of Crystal moments before, taking the vile he held and rushing off towards Sho.

Things had also gone well, though. The labor-intensive creation of Elutherios Duo model 0901 had been extremely taxing on Izuku's mind and body, but after he had succeeded he knew he'd done something more than his father could ever do, and by the look of concern on Nixon's face as he met the machine the first time, the experiment was a complete and rousing success. Even if the machine didn't defeat Nixon, it was doing an excellent job of tying him up for a while, more time than Izuku truly needed.

As he chased Crystal through the crowd until they reached the mobile base, it was only when she entered, taking Aryu with her, that the first true fear of something happening that was more than he'd bargained for. Something might actually happen now that could stop him completely, and he had to find a quick and easy way to deal with it.

After the brief and unsettling encounter with Aryu in the dark hallway (*How did he get so skilled so quickly?* Izuku had asked himself. *I didn't think that was possible.*) he decided to simply attempt to cut bait and run. With only a few strong swoops of his mechanical wings, Izuku was high in the air, looking down on the masses he'd uncovered so far north, buried deep beneath encroaching glacial ice and far beyond where any mortal man could have found them.

The slow-moving dark patch was clearly approaching the city of Bankoor in the distance. Things had changed and the plan needed to be sped up. With a few mental clicks, he made two things happen: he increased the speed of the masses, calling on all slower-moving supply vehicles to fall back and let the standing army through, and he sent a Power-based message to his loyal Embracers farther ahead, a message which very clearly gave them two distinct orders.

Half of you begin your push forward, the others come to me. There is no more time to waste. No one should be left alive. Failure will be met by the blade of the Est Vacuus!

When the energy rush of Sho's last breath hit, he was all the more certain that his problem was about to grow exponentially. He pondered a number of actions before coming on his imperfect solution.

Attempting to get ahead of matters, he focused the Power into his hands like an ethereal vacuum and let it suddenly pulse freely, sending a crashing white bolt into the heart of the massive rolling machine.

At first there was nothing, and then he saw the light grow and erupt from the core of the structure. A split-second later, the whole machine, as well as any stragglers of his own army, were obliterated as if they were never there, leaving nothing but a smoking crater outlining a perfect circle, not unlike the destruction left by the great H.Y. bombs Izuku was so fond of. The sound of the sudden and extremely powerful blast rumbled throughout the valley.

By the time the light of his destructive blast had started to grow, however, he knew the truth. He could feel it in his still-human core, the parts of him that were so well in tune with the Power.

When the dust cleared and the smoke dissipated, he saw what he expected.

Off to the side, slightly out of the center of the blast, was a faint icy glow. As he looked closer, he saw it clearer. The glow was a circle, shaped like a small dome. The shell of the barrier was opaque, giving him a muddled but no less unsettling view of the inside.

As the barrier fell away and faded into nothing, he grinned his malicious grin. *Now things get very interesting* he thought, as he felt the new arrival of nine Embracers rushing at him from the front lines, likely curious about what had caused the blast. Their instinct would tell them what it was, but not the why. They were all still so young in their mastery of the Power they might not be able to tell one Power source from another.

A good thing too, because if they could, they'd know more than he thought they'd want to. In the center of the now faded glowing shield was the great Sho Tokugawa, dead from over-exposure to the Est Vacuus; Aryu O'Lung'Singh, passed out on the ground with the sword and shield at his side; and of course Crystal Kokuou, fully restored to all of her frightening power, hands outstretched and pale eyes seething.

Izuku knew right away that her eyes were locked onto him like a laser sight, the pain and loss of her son compiled into one direct fury, her reddish eyes starring daggers at the man hundreds of feet above her.

Chapter 11: **Broken Toy Soldiers**

The trip from the control room at the base of the great spire had been extremely unnerving for the traveler from Tan Torna Quay. The soft lights in these tunnels deep below the city of Bankoor illuminated a tight and foreboding space.

Johan and Auron Bree were silently lost in thought. The ride was taking much longer than expected, an unforeseen oversight on Auron's part, and by now the forces of his amalgamated military should have been deep in the throes of getting out of the city far above them. The depth and constant movement made getting a signal on his wireless control panel, now firmly clenched in his right hand, practically impossible. All the panel did was show occasional signs of life, and then going blank again. Only the icons that controlled the H.Y. bomb remained. It was right beside them and was in constant and uninterrupted communication with the panel.

Bree had long since lost his bearings down here. At last the machine came to a rest, parked neatly at the base of what looked like a giant ladder. Lights higher above them illuminated the space, letting them each see the smooth dark walls and a small lit panel with two screens and numerous buttons at the opposite end of where they stood.

"Well Johan, we're here."

Johan looked around in the darkness. "About time, Auron. That ride took forever." He stretched his sore back and stepped off the transport device onto a solid steel floor. "So, where are we?"

Auron Bree didn't even look around. He was quite confident in his surrounds, clearly. "We're deep below Gracious Park. This shaft can carry the bomb right under their feet. First thing's first, though, so if you'll excuse me..."

Bree walked over to the panel on the wall across the space and pressed a few buttons. At once each screen came to life, glowing blue and filling the dark hole with an eerie light. Then, Auron Bree had his portable control panel up, bringing it to life and looking at what seemed to Johan to be various pictures and brief, soundless and blurry videos.

His face was unchanging, but his eyes told Johan more than words could. He put the panel down and deactivated the screens on the wall.

"It would seem..." he began, faltering slightly, "that you were correct, Johan. The Embracers never entered the city." He stopped short, concern in his eyes.

Johan pressed him on. "So what happened?" he asked, knowing at least parts of the answer.

"They... they are here," was all Bree answered at first. Then, he seemed to draw from his politician's ability to be strong on the outside during a crisis. "The enemy troops have entered the city. They seem to have used a strong backup from the Embracers to push harder and faster than we anticipated."

"Where are they?" Johan asked, wondering what was going on far above his head.

"They are everywhere." Auron's face shuddered for a moment. "They seem to have flooded into the city directly above us and are pushing to the spire."

Johan's face lit up slightly at the news. "That's good, isn't it? That's where we want them."

"It is. Actually, I doubt they could be in a better position."

His face grew brighter. "Really? That's great! Are our people making their way north now? Out of the city?"

With this question, Bree's political super powers failed him and his face saddened. "N... No, Johan, they're not."

Johan looked crestfallen suddenly. "Where are they, Auron?"

"I... I don't know."

"What do you mean 'I don't know'? Where are they? What did the video show? Where did they escape to?"

"The... the video never showed anyone from our side entering the city. I checked it three times. Just explosions, then the enemy."

Johan went white, the face of August Stroan a clear image in his mind. After a moment of silence, Johan steeled himself and looked at Auron Bree. "Don't blame yourself, Auron. It was a good plan. You never suspected they would strike so hard and fast."

"That doesn't make their losses any easier," Bree said, seeming to feel revulsion for Johan with his words, as if the pity was poison to his ears. "They were good men and women, every one of them."

"I know, Bree, but that doesn't change the plan. There are a lot more good men and women running at top speed north right now, and you have the power to help them. Hit the button, Auron. Blow the spire. Let's get the fuck out of here. Set the bomb and let's end this! For them! For…"

"Stop!" Bree yelled. "Don't fill me with worthless clichés, boy." The bile in his words rose to the surface. "You walked into this city, *my* city, just days ago. You don't know them. You don't know what it took to build this city. What it took to defend it. You don't get to tell me who to do it for."

"Fine, do it for yourself Gods damn it, but do it *now!*"

Johan hated the sudden weakness in Bree. It was uncharacteristic and unnerving to see. Bree seemed to agree, and with a quick flick of his wrist his control panel was airborne and coming at Johan, who deftly snagged it from the air. "It's your plan. You do it. Just get that knife of yours ready, Johan. If you saw their numbers and how far they reach like I just did, you'd know for a fact that we were going to need it."

Johan ignored the words, focusing only on the screen in his hands. It was time. Do or die, as they say.

As Bree glared at him from the other side of the small cavern, Johan met his eyes with all the strength he could muster. "For Tan Torna Qu-ay," he said with confidence as he pressed the floating icon marked 'SPIRE'.

***

Everything was a blur when Aryu opened his eyes. His head ached and his body tingled as if he'd just been electrocuted by a very mild voltage.

When he sat upright, he instantly felt somehow restrained, like he was being sat on or weighed down somehow. As the images in his eyes became clearer and his head de-fogged, he looked around him for a better idea of what was going on.

The dead body of a good friend beside him was more than enough to jog his memory. Sho's lifeless form still sat only a step away from where Aryu awoke, the expression on his face one of calm and peace, his arms neatly folded on his chest, clasping one another. He'd clearly been positioned this way, but not by Aryu. He remembered all that Crystal had told him; how she had been trying to turn him into some kind of global hero. He remembered closing his eyes, Crystal taking his hand… and then… and then…

He remembered the icy cold pain that shot through his arm and into his body. He was on his feet instantly, despite the resistance he felt, and once there he was all the more convinced that something was different.

He looked down, expecting to find his precious weapons were the culprits for holding him down, but no; they were still resting off to either side of him, undisturbed since he dropped them when he walked into the room with Sho.

He wasn't in the room now. He was clearly outdoors, the bright sun shining down on him warming his face and hands.

Instead of being inside of that dark, foreboding room he was now in a lush field. The horizon was still the same, with the faint line of the Vein River and Blood Sea to the west and the impressive rise of the Hymleah Mountains to the east. There was no sign of the Army of the Old, Nixon and the monster he was locked in combat with, Crystal, or Izuku. There were grasslands and trees peppered throughout the landscape, but that was all.

When his head was completely awake and the throbbing had all but disappeared, he looked back to his friend in his peaceful and eternal rest. His marvelous and imposing suit of mystical armor was gone.

The thought of the armor had triggered something in Aryu. Not a thought or memories; more like a repeat of the electric feeling he'd had a moment ago. It was then, as he concentrated on the feeling and what had caused it, that it happened.

In a rush, his body became awash in blackness, the metallic shimmer covering him from the neck down. He first tried to wipe it off in concern, but after it proved fruitless, he only took a second to figure out what was going on.

Once the pieces came together in his mind, the Makashi armor finished the metamorphosis over the young man.

At first he thought it would be heavy, as any armor must be, but it was deceptively light. He could move freely, with the armor moving with him and flowing almost like water. It still had hard edges and the illusion of individual plates, but its weight and range of movement indicated that this was simply how it looked and was not an indicator of how it functioned.

He looked at the impressive suit, holding his arms out before him, now wrapped in metal sleeves that hinged at the elbow and shoulder. His hands were encased in gauntlets with points on the fingertips, as if his young fingers had been replaced with the talons of a large bird. This was not the same style and shape of the armor Sho wore. This was smaller and less imposing. The Makashi armor had formed with Aryu in the image that best suited him, lightweight and extremely flexible.

The deep, soulful vibration still hummed in his mind. As he looked at his hands, he again focused on this strange new feeling, and just as one learned to move a muscle they didn't even know existed, so too did Aryu O'Lung'Singh learn to quell this new feeling until it was gone, taking the armor with it. It was a slow process, a few minutes at least, but he knew he'd get faster with more uses, just as it had been with Sho.

"I need you to take the rest of what he held so dear," Crystal had told him, and now he knew what it meant. She had her Power returned, and he now had the shield and armor Sho had worn and used so proudly. Slowly but surely, she had made him the ultimate weapon against Izuku and his forces. She'd even taught him how to use the Power, though that was still a trick Aryu had no intention of repeating.

In an instant he knew where he was. This was a Haven. Likely just a small one created by Crystal to protect him while he was knocked out. The calming and peaceful vista around him tipped him off at last. He'd been here before, although it had been somewhere much farther away.

With a thought the memory of the deep electrical feeling returned, and once more his body became covered in the liquid metal until it had completely reformed. He watched astounded as it covered even his dark, leathery wings, coating them with a kind of pearl shimmer. With a few test flaps he was confident that not only did they work fine, but somehow the metallic coating was an improvement. The wind resistance around them was lessened by the smooth covering.

A smirk came to his face, followed by a profound sadness from remembering what it had cost him. There was no luck here, only tragedy.

As he bent to retrieve the bladed shield and the great Shi Kaze, both bringing warm feelings of familiarity to his heart as he did so, he took a moment and knelt beside Sho and bowed deeply. "Thank you," he whispered before steeling himself, the pain and torment of what had happened returning, as well as the confidence in his victory over any and all he was going to face today. The unimaginable feeling that today, in this moment, he could take on the world and win. Not for Crystal and her insane vision of his great triumph, but for himself and his friend.

Truth be told, he was starting to believe that despite all of their great (or terrible) deeds, Embracers, and the Power itself, was simply too much for the world. Every time he looked at himself, he saw the results of a million tragedies the Power had caused.

With a last look at his friend and one or two more test-flaps of his gorgeous wings, he pulled up the shield while readying the sword, and rushed forward faster than he ever had before. Havens admitted and released people based on the whims of their creators. He had no doubt that Crystal had already set the wheels in motion to have him leave whenever he was ready. Just another of her many apparent paths she'd set him out on.

With a rush of anger suddenly washing over his body as he

moved, erasing the peace he'd felt a moment before, he grinned knowing he was right, and it was time to end this.

In his heart, along with his great confidence in his ability to win this day, there was also the undeniable truth that he was complete, and here and now he was ready not to be the Ryuujin of the People this world demanded him to be, but the champion of those he knew and loved.

He could feel the edge of the Haven approaching, and a small part of him smiled as he prepared to rejoin the fray.

"For Tan Torna Qu-ay!"

***

Had Izuku the time and energy to be angry at the way things were turning out, there was no doubt that he would be. More to the point, he would be absolutely furious!

As it was he was far too wrapped up in his current task, that of killing Crystal Kokuou and finding where on earth she'd hidden her son and Aryu. Havens were tricky things. With his great power he could likely find hers in relatively short order

He had no time. Crystal, from her fortified position on the ground, was still surrounded by the blast crater Izuku had created trying to kill all of them. She fended off all attacks and was currently doing an excellent job of both defending herself with a million and one tricks conjured by the Power, and putting up an excellent offensive against Izuku and Izuku alone. It was as if the other nine Embracers currently doing their best to break her defenses on all sides, including above and below ground, weren't even there.

Pulses of power energy struck out at her like knives, shattering over her natural protective shielding as if made of glass. He even attempted to get closer to her and use the Est Vacuus blade, but she was so fast.

As the battle wore on, it became obvious what she was doing, and that realization caused Izuku to fight even harder, trying desperately to either stop her or find the Haven.She was buying time for Aryu to arrive, and although Izuku thought he could beat the young boy very easily, he'd much prefer not to have to contest with the Shi Kaze or the shield to do so, be the user an Embracer of the Power or not. Too much could go wrong with that kind of wildcard in play.

As he flew above the scene below, with a legion of loyal Embracers throwing everything they could at her, from lifting massive objects and trying to crush her to opening the ground beneath her feet and attempting to swallow her whole, nothing seemed to be able to slow her down.He contributed what little assaults he could on her, but with her constant barrage of immense energy waves finding him almost every moment, he began to doubt he would be able to get to her in time.

With a sudden rush and a dark streak of light from his left, the time he needed had run out. He now had to debate what was worse: a fully powered Crystal or a fully armed Aryu. The devil-he-knew with the fire in her eyes was a formidable one, so he opted for the less-traveled course of the devil-he-didn't, turning to Aryu as he surged forth from wherever Crystal had hidden him and her son.Even still, the image was not one Izuku enjoyed. Intelligence and caution had gotten him this far, and both of those things were blaring very loud warnings about the enemy he now faced.

Aryu was practically hovering from moving so fast, his eyes glued to Izuku and the weapon he carried. There was no fear there. Was the choice to face Aryu the correct one? Too late to go back now, as Crystal had seen Aryu emerge and face Izuku, which let her turn her attention to the Embracers that were trying in vain to put a dent in her defenses.

Izuku and Aryu were alone as Izuku descended from the sky while keeping a safe distance. They faced each other with malice in each of their eyes, powerful swords at the ready and metallic inhuman wings stretched behind them.

He has the Makashi armor, Izuku thought. *He is truly complete.*

Although the Makashi armor was legendary for its durability, it still couldn't stand against the Est Vacuus. However, it could deflect most energy bursts if needed. There would be no help from his army anymore.

As Aryu charged, screaming in rage and anger as he went, bladed shield spinning and Shi Kaze pointed before him, Izuku at last realized the weapon he'd wanted to create in Aryu was possibly more than he'd bargained for. *Good*, he thought just before the weapons met. *I like surprises.*

Aryu was prepared for the scene to unfold around him as he drove forwards beyond the reach of the Haven, but it was no less impressive when he saw it.

The once lush and fertile ground was brown and trampled, covered in marching footprints and track lines that all drove north. The forces themselves were gone now, still clearly visible, with many transports lining up in the rear as their huge numbers surrounded the distant city.

The gut instinct that Johan was somewhere in that astonishing maze of impressive and strange buildings was undeniable. A part of him *felt* him there. Was it his bond with him? Was it a part of him subconsciously tapping the Power? He didn't know, but it was an instinct he trusted.

The ground directly below him was scorched and burnt, a reminder of what had happened. He looked around for Nixon, or possibly even Crystal, although he still wasn't certain what side she was on despite what had just happened. Nixon was simple to find, his glowing red presence off in the distance, his battle with the frightening beast of many voices that had confronted them still raging on.

Crystal appeared, her ghostly white hair trailing behind her like smoke as she moved like lightning above him, pulses of energy erupting both near her and from her. A second later he saw her attackers: a number of colored dots that surrounded her on all sides, seeming to be trying anything and everything to get to her, but even from here he could see she was easily holding her own.

He now turned and found Izuku, watching him with interest but not moving. He was waiting, and the Est Vacuus sword was as well. Aryu didn't know the Est Vacuus (and judging by what he'd seen it do to both Crystal and Sho, he didn't want to, either). He didn't know its power or its purpose. To him, it was just another strange and magical piece of all things, much like the Power itself. The truth was that the Est Vacuus was as far from the Power as anything could ever be away from something else. The Power was, at its heart, a living, flowing part of the Omnis. However, to the untrained eye they were seemingly cut from the same cloth.

Aryu had such eyes, thus he did not fear this sword any more than he feared his own.

Their eyes locked while the feeling of overwhelming personal power fed his rage. Aryu braced himself and attacked, screaming like a banshee as he dove the short distance to where Izuku waited. The Power didn't fuel him, only anger and the need for the revenge.

Izuku dodged the attack easily, but the avoidance was short lived. Aryu's most recent acquisition did something neither of them expected. Once Aryu realized Izuku had moved aside, the Makashi armor flowed outward, seemingly on the mental need form Aryu to stop moving so quickly and turn around. Like a living thing, it grew and thinned out around Aryu, creating more drag to aid his turning efforts. The result was a stop-and-return far faster than he'd ever have been able to manage before, and although it left his head somewhat flustered at the sudden deceleration, he instantly knew what had happened, found his amazed target, and attacked again.

The first strike came with the Shi Kaze, lashing out like a rapier intending to end this battle quickly. Izuku's senses returned just in time to parry the attack, folding in his wings as he moved to aid the speed of his spin away. Again he almost wasn't fast enough, the trailing shield and its spinning blades coming within fractions of an inch from his face. So close that he could feel the Power emanating from it as if it was on fire. Aryu may not command the Power, but his weapons certainly did.

Aryu was around once more. Izuku was not as surprised this time, and counter-attacked himself, looking in vain for a hole in Aryu's defenses. Finding none, he was content to simply slash the shimmering non-blade at him wildly, letting it strike his shield and blow him back, causing Aryu to temporarily lose control and fall well away from him until he regained his bearings.

Again, a pause as the two took each other in. Izuku smiled

his menacing smile and waited, knowing Aryu could not resist attempting to attack first.

Aryu was irate that his first two attempts were failures. Izuku was too old, though. Too powerful to have it end just like that.He attacked again, moving quickly, eyes remaining on Izuku as he spun like a twisted black ballet dancer in a pirouette. Izuku countered again, deflecting both the Shi Kaze and the shield, the Power pulsing off each blow as he did so, causing his head to suddenly fill with flashes of unimaginable Power and hollowing emptiness all at once.

Aryu felt it as well, but to a much lesser extent. His head was simply not equipped to understand what these feelings were. To him, it was more like a combination of being bloated with a feast and the aftereffects of throwing up for hours all at the same time, only all over his body.

Izuku backed off, dodging another skilled and surprising attack from Aryu as he moved. Aryu would have normally been shocked at his sudden ability to hold his own against someone such as this, but in his current mindset it was simply the way things had to be, the necessary talent that had to be tapped in order to win the day.

As he backed off, Izuku flew up with the Power pushing him as his wings folded behind him.

Amazingly, Aryu was right after him. Although he still couldn't fly, he could leap incredibly high and breathtakingly fast with the help of his wings. Izuku dodged another attack and was on the ground faster and landed with a staggering 'thud' that kicked up all the dirt and dust around him as he did so. Aryu, having lost him in the haze, slowed his descent instantly, not wanting this strong and wise Embracer to use his centuries of training to fool him.

It was a correct thought. From the dust and smoke of his landing came a number of fast and powerful bolts of energy, each being dark as midnight and fast as a bullet. The shield was up at once, but not before one of them ripped through his defenses and slammed into his body at his chest. The armor took the brunt of the hit, but even that seemed to almost dissolve with the blast. Aryu was tossed back instantly, the pain of the blow causing his mind to leave him briefly, his wings no longer holding him aloft. Down he fell, realizing what was happening moments before he hit the ground.

Even the Makashi armor couldn't save him once he hit the ground while sprawled sideways, shimmering wings trailing behind him and coming to a rest. His skin under the shot to the chest burned, and a faint smell of burning meat hit his nose.

It wasn't enough to stop him by far, and once Izuku emerged from his impromptu-smoke screen, Aryu was already on his feet again, battle-ready and still seething.

"Impressive," Izuku chided. "Not many like you could take a blast like that without being killed instantly. A credit to you."

"Cut your shit, Izuku," Aryu spit between clenched teeth. "I don't want your praise." He lashed out again, avoiding another series of blasts from Izuku, who then followed it up with arching sweeps from his sword, radiating powerful waves of energy as he did so in crescent-moons.

Aryu blocked the initial strikes with ease as the shield dispersed them on contact. The waves of energy, however, were not so easily blocked. Once one hit Aryu square on, the power of the blow lifted him like a paper bag in a breeze, throwing him backward with a grunt.

Wind rushed past Aryu as he fell, suffering another hard landing.

He sprang to his feet, feeling prone and vulnerable now that Izuku was holding back less and less. Again his mind screamed at him to end this as soon as possible, but Sho had taught him patience, and that was what he remembered now.

Izuku had disappeared while he was down, but Aryu did see Crystal, her battle with the multitudes of Embracers carrying him to within shouting distance. She was likely infuriated with everything, but her face showed that she was also very happy to be her old self again, and her toying and amusement with these much weaker Embracers was her own sick way of dealing with it.

Once he looked back, he was suddenly assaulted by a barrage of his own to avoid. Like meteors from Heaven, the sky before him was filled with items of all sizes and kinds that were propelled towards him. Broken transports, mangled robotic bodies, and various technological bric-a-brac pounded the ground, causing him to use every muscle he had available to avoid them all. When he couldn't avoid them, he blocked the larger chunks with his shield, the force of which would drive him backwards and send painful vibrations down his arm. Or he would slice them away with the Shi Kaze, the blade cutting through anything it touched as if it wasn't even there.

Soon, he was simply blocking everything, his breath leaving him faster with the extra work he was suddenly doing.Bursts of dark Power passed him, their hot vapor trails searing past his ears. Somewhere, beyond the debris that was attempting to crush him, Izuku was propelling these things forward, adding the extra twist of forcing him to dodge the painful blasts.

It was more than he could manage, and as he glanced away a broken hunk of tank tread another shot of Power slammed into his leg, forcing him to the ground in an instant. Without any protection to aid him, another hunk of twisted metal raked across his face, tearing his skin from his eye and nose to back past his ear and into his scalp as it moved. As he screamed in pain and fell backwards his eye flashed on the passing piece, sickening him as it did so.

Pieces of his skin were trailing behind it, bloodied and hanging from one of the sharp edges.

In an instant his face was on fire, the left side now hot from both the pain and gush of blood that began pouring down it. It seemed to miss his eye, but beyond that he had no idea.Frankly he didn't care about the pain, or if he lost an eye or that entire half of his face. What he did care about was not letting Izuku catch him while he was down, and he was on all fours as quick as his body let him. His leg that took the powerful blast from Izuku protested, but his mind overrode it with a mix of fear and adrenalin, getting himself into position to use his wings to propel himself along the ground out of Izuku's range.

More chunks of fodder landed around him, but once the opportunity arose he was airborne, jumping and gliding with a newfound ease. Soon he was beyond the things that attempted to destroy him.

His left eye filled with blood, burning as he tried to wipe it away. He could feel the warmth of it trickling down his neck. The amounts were not small.

Another searing bolt of black energy hit the back of his shoulder, spinning him around once more, sending him crashing back down for a third time. This time the force of the landing coupled with the already-battered state of Aryu's body caused Aryu to release the precious Shi Kaze, and it now spun away well beyond arms' reach as he sat up.

Terrified at what he'd done, he scrambled to get it at once, fearing what Izuku could do to him without it. He made it only half a staggered-step before he was instantly frozen into place. It wasn't an otherworldly power that held him; it was his own mind. Aryu was suddenly frozen by a horrifying sight; one he never believed could be as incapacitating and blindingly-strong as it was.

Izuku had appeared, the Shi Kaze resting perfectly between the two of them, and the Est Vacuus blade was in his hand. The sudden sight of the Is Empty in all of its unrelenting horror drained every ounce of fight Aryu had in his body as if it was raping his mind of all conscious thought. The nothingness that consumed him forced him to fall to his stomach once more. His eyes locked onto the thing in Izuku's hand, unable to look away. He wanted to. God how he wanted to. But the sword, or more specifically, this chunk of Est Vacuus *shaped* like a sword, refused to let Aryu do anything voluntary with his own body. It held him as if he were paralyzed from head to toe.

A soft whimper escaped Aryu's lips as Izuku stepped closer. Izuku relished every moment of pain he was now causing. It had been so simple putting Aryu into this state, but that didn't make this victory any less sweet.

"Now you know, don't you?" he said, at a volume just a hair above a whisper. "Now you know what it is you face. Are you scared now? Do you at last understand the enormity of the forces you stand so foolishly against?"

Aryu couldn't answer. The emptiness consumed him, his mind being nowhere near the level needed to form rational thought in the wake of such enormous power. Even Izuku's words seemed to echo from some distant place, as if reaching through fathoms of dark water to reach him.

"You were so sure you could do this," Izuku continued. "So certain your shield, armor and beloved Shi Kaze would be enough." He stepped forward more, his feet practically touching the sword on the ground now.

Aryu's eyes follow the blade Izuku held, now close enough to almost reach out and touch. The added benefit to this movement was that it now brought the Shi Kaze into view as well, and with a sudden flash in his mind, and possibly places deeper in his psyche, the eternal voices of the Four Winds were at war with the empty vacuum of the Est Vacuus. The end result was that although his mind was almost torn apart with the sudden eternal conflict (*Is this how Crystal lives now, with these two forces in constant battle?*), he had enough sense to understand what was happening.

Izuku followed his gaze and understood. "Hmm, I could just pick that up and have both of the ultimate weapons of this world in my hands, but since I'm holding the more recent and, should we say, persuasive one, I think I'll just leave that where it is. Once I'm done with you, maybe I'll use it again.

"It was once mine, you know. I was the greatest and most ruthless Adragon this world had ever seen, until my disrespectful younger brother took it from me. I knew then that there was more out there, more of the Power in the universe to tap. I was wrong, however. What I needed wasn't in this universe, or any other of the unfathomable number there are out there. What I needed was behind them all of the time."

With the words, he kicked away the Shi Kaze beyond Aryu's sight, sending him once more into the void. He was about to scream, the Makashi armor now flowing over his body uncontrollably, when something steadied him; an unnatural voice of calm in a place where there should be nothing at all.

The feeling was familiar, and while he was still incapacitated and unable to move, somehow the pain of the nothing in front of him was almost bearable. When the voice spoke, the source of the calming feeling came to him. "I'd get up, lad," it said, sounding almost out of breath. "We can't keep this up all day."

The soothing feeling was Nixon. It was the same calm one felt when looking at Nixon Ash's smile.

Nixon hand battled the machine to back within earshot, trying to help Aryu as he lay prone on the ground. Izuku saw the phoenix come closer, trying to get within range to help with more than his encouraging words. "Oh no, my devilish friend, he's mine, just like Sho was."

Nixon was battling Elutherios with everything he had, but the disturbance of the Est Vacuus being so close to him was too much to ignore. If Aryu didn't get up and do something about it quickly, the force of its power on one born of its antitheses would almost certainly be his downfall.

Izuku came forward again, almost touching Aryu, which would end his life in a way so agonizing Aryu didn't have the mental capacity to even begin to understand what it would do to him. He writhed on the dirt, his body not even listening to the smallest command he could give. Only with the deep elemental assistance of Nixon was he able to even grasp the basics of what was happening as emptiness and pain devoured him.

"I hope you're enjoying your little test, Nixon," Izuku yelled out to the embattled phoenix. "He was my crowning achievement." He flashed an evil and knowing smile at Aryu, who by now couldn't even see through the horror he was in. "Well, maybe second, if I ever let this one do what he was supposed to. Oh well.

"Sorry to keep you waiting, Elutherios," Izuku said passively as the black monster also approached to reengage Nixon. Unlike Nixon, E2-0901 was in no way slowed or in any way affected by the deep mystical powers swirling around it everywhere. It was just as fast and quick thinking as ever. "What news do you bring from my new city?"

A short, electronic transmission jumped from Elutherios to Izuku, and everything changed.

The world beyond the message he just received disappeared. There was no Aryu. No Crystal. No Nixon. Just the words.

Izuku sheathed the blade of the Est Vacuus and was in the air in a move so fast Aryu didn't even see it happen, leaving him gasping for breath and convulsing on the ground. Moments later Izuku was off like a shot towards the city.

Nixon, shocked at his sudden exit, could only watch in agony as Aryu twisted around. Elutherios was keeping him away, and he doubted he could get close enough in time.

Crystal saw him as well, and although she was entrenched with her own issues, she was still closer and more in control of her situation. Begrudgingly, Nixon called out to her, on the deep waves of the Power. "Crystal!" he shouted. "Get 'im the sword! Put the Shi Kaze in 'is 'ands!" He had no idea if she would listen, or just take the sword and do what she wanted with it, but he had no choice. Thankfully she picked up on it right away, and she led her attackers back, forced them away enough to give her room to reach down, take the sword, and hand it to Aryu.

The effect was instantaneous. Aryu's eyes shot open with perfect clarity, and suddenly he was up again as if nothing had happened.

Nixon breathed a sigh of relief and returned to his more-than-capable opponent. He'd deal with Crystal later.

Aryu was still confused about what had happened, and the memory of the Est Vacuus was still present, but diluted to a point of being a strange and distant memory, though no less potent in its horror. He looked at the sword in his hand, understanding dawning on his face. He quickly looked to Crystal, who simply winked at him, blew him a kiss, then continued on with her battle. Aryu noted that there were only six now.

He looked back to Nixon, tempted to help him and return the favor he'd been given, but Nixon waved him off instantly. "Go!" he called out loudly. "'E went to the city!"

The strength returned quickly to his body, more like he'd just woken up as opposed to being neck deep in the Est Vacuus. He started to leave, gaining speed as he went, when he heard that strong accented voice once more. "Aryu!" He looked back just as the huge man tossed Elutherios backwards with a giant swing of his sword, buying him time to complete his last message to Aryu. "Don't drop tha' sword!" Aryu nodded. As if he had to be told. "And win!" Not having to be told again, Aryu was off in his gliding dash along the ground, using his wings to propel him at unimaginable speed.

Then, leaving behind the two to whatever demons it was they

faced, Aryu headed out with full speed to the city, his grip on the Shi Kaze stronger than ever, his new Makashi armor fully reformed and ready for what lay next, and the pain from his injuries muted with the need for revenge.

Chapter 12: **Fools that Follow**

Everything went black the moment Johan pressed the button. The only source of light in the underground tunnel was from the faint glow of the control panel in his hands.

Auron Bree's clear and authoritative voice spoke out of the darkness, "Is the controller still working?"

"Yes," answered Johan, listening to the stillness and silence for any sign of something going wrong.

"Good, that means that if the pulse worked, it never made it this far. May I see it please?" Johan held it out in the direction of the voice, and after a soft shuffling sound, a ghostly hand appeared and slowly took it away.

They could each see the controller's transparent screen floating in front of them, and then the soft 'beeps' it made from Auron cycling through menus and various screens. "Like I thought. Every camera in the system is gone. I'd say for the most part it worked."

"For the most part?" Johan asked.

"Well, there are still two relative unknowns," Auron answered, his aged and stern face now glowing in the light as he looked closer. Before he could ask what those were, suddenly the bomb sprung to life, a soft whirring sound coming from inside the device.

Johan jumped instantly, and then he dashed blindly in the dark to where he thought he'd recalled the exit tunnel being. "Wait!" called Bree over their commotion. "Wait, it was me! I did that!"

He stopped. "What?" Johan called back from groping his way forward. "What the fuck, Bree?"

"I'm sorry, I had to see if it was still working."

"Well you could have fucking told me!" Johan said, yelling back at him in anger. Although he likely respected Johan, Bree wasn't his biggest fan. Because of Johan he was in a dank utility and transport tunnel instead of pushing northwards peacefully with the rest of the populace. Oh, the sacrifices of office.

Bree said nothing, continuing to press buttons and making the screen on the weapon come to life. He stepped over to it, looked at it appraisingly and nodded, a frightening scene in the dark.

Still irate, Johan spoke, "Well?"

"It's fine. No ill effects. Still primed and ready to go."

"Good. Was that one of your unknown factors?"

"Yes. Down to just one."

"Which is?"

"Isn't it obvious? Did it work above ground? That's the most important thing to know."

"Well, how do we find that out if every camera is out?"

As if on cue the faint lights returned, casting a hard yellow glow on their surroundings once more. "Ah, right on time," commented Bree as he walked over to a control panel on the side of the space. "Backup power for necessary below-ground systems. Lights, air ventilation," suddenly, as he pressed buttons, the on-rails transport the bomb sat on came back to life, lights dotting the outside in straight lines, "and transportation. We take this up to a larger holding room just below the park, use an emergency exit to assess the situation, and go from there. We leave the bomb and take this transport back to the tunnels, where we'll go to the far end of the city and escape with everyone else. If you were right and this idea of yours worked, we'll only need to set the bomb at its most basic and confined setting. We'll be well out of the way before it goes off. The ride may be rough if it came to that, but it beats the alternative."

"Barely. We'll die just as well buried far below the city, you know," Johan answered, not caring much for the option.

"If you couldn't take the responsibilities, Johan, you should have shut your mouth and let me do my job," answered Bree, his professional face warping slightly with the words, a reminder whose idea this had all been. Bree stepped back on to the bomb's platform and indicated Johan do the same. "Let's go. We've got a lot to do before we can start dragging our feet."

With another press to the controls, the machine gave a lurch, and then proceeded to climb straight up into the darkness above them.

The light from below faded quickly as they moved, and Johan was careful to avoid the open sides of their makeshift elevator. "Mind the drop," Bree chided. Even in the dark, Johan could hear his smile.

They climbed for some time. Johan couldn't make out what was coming, but he could feel the walls close around them as the upward tunnel narrowed. They couldn't see it, but each man could hear and almost feel the ceiling above them get closer, followed by a faint puff of air that swirled around them as the lift entered a new room once the ceiling opened and they came to a stop.

Johan could smell the fresher air here. The tunnels below were well ventilated, but still heavily recycled. Here, the smells of greenery were plentiful.

"No lights here. Looks like the EMP made it at least somewhat into the ground. One second…" Bree pressed another icon and soon the whole control panel was glowing in a soft white, illuminating a stretch of ground before them like a flashlight or torch.

Johan could see crates and boxes, none with names or writing he could make out. They were sporadic and many lacked any kind of definition, but they were obviously in some kind of warehouse or storage room. "These rooms are below every park in the city," Bree told him, speaking very softly now, careful not to attract the attention of any waiting mechanical armies that may or may not only be a few feet above the roof over their heads. "They're mostly used to store landscaping supplies." He pointed in the direction the light traveled. "Over there is a stairway leading to a shed in the park above. We'll see what we see when we get there."

Johan agreed. The room was larger than the space they'd come from, but not by much. They reached a door that hung slightly ajar, with Auron pushing it open slowly.

It creaked as it moved, causing Johan to tense up, but soon it was open and natural light filled their eyes in small doses. Johan could see a set of stairs going up at a slight angle, the light coming from the cracks in the doorframe he saw above them at the height of the stairs.As if it needed to be done, Bree placed a finger to his lips telling Johan to be quiet, an action met with what passed for a vulgar response from Johan. Then, they each began slowly climbing the hard stone stairs, slowly creeping up to the shed door that led to the sprawling Gracious Park.

Neither heard a thing from above. No heavy footsteps, marching, or weapon fire. As near as they could tell, it was a lovely and quiet sunny day in the park above. When the base of the door was at eye level, each of them strained to see outside, neither being successful. After so long in the dark, the harsh light only made things a blur.

Bree indicated to Johan to stay where he was, letting himself go on alone. It was either a noble gesture or his natural need to be a leader, but either way Johan welcomed it. Never before had the knife next to his chest felt so heavy, and soon it would either be weightless, or impossible to hold any longer.

He held his breath as Bree slowly grasped the handle, the moment of truth arriving at last. Bree seemed to be doing the same, as nothing but a soft wind from above could be heard. Then, the light above grew exponentially, and Auron Bree opened the door, blinding Johan (and likely himself) with the pure light that streamed in.

Still, there was only silence.

Moments later, when his eyes adjusted, Johan could see treetops above, and soon the blue sky and faint clouds appeared.

Still holding his breath, every muscle in his body ready to dive back down the stairs as quickly as he could go at the first sign of trouble, Johan waited for Auron Bree to look around.Auron was peeking out of the gap he'd created, taking the scene in. As the door opened more, the wind carried with it the familiar smell to Johan's nose. Something above them was burning.

Bree looked back to Johan, his face obscured by the brightness behind him. Johan couldn't read his expression, so he could only come closer, trying to see for himself.Beyond, once the park came into clear view, what Johan saw almost drove him to jump and yell, though he resisted.

Outside, spread far and wide like fallen statues, the mechanical soldiers of the Army of the Old were laid out on the ground. Some twitched or flailed slightly, but not in a threatening way. It was just the motions of broken toys.Beyond the fallen soldiers sat motionless tanks, as well as numerous other vehicles of various descriptions, frozen just as they had been for thousands of years in the far north until they were at last freed.

Bree then got Johan's attention, pointing silently over to their right. There, Johan was startled to see the spire, or what remained of it, twisted and hollow as if it were only a skeleton and not a massive gleaming spike. Smoke was pouring from it and it looked as though it would topple at any moment. Still, Johan thought it was the most beautiful thing he'd ever seen.

"Well," whispered Bree, still wary of speaking loudly when surrounded by so many machines, "it would seem you were successful."

Johan couldn't answer, but he also couldn't wipe the smile off his face if he tried.

They descended the stairs once more, much less cautious than before, each feeling much safer considering what they'd each witnessed. At the bottom, Auron Bree reactivated the all-white screen in his hands and began leading them back to the H.Y. bomb.

Not wanting to waste time, Bree immediately began pushing the weapon off the platform and onto a waiting stand. The machine rolled easily on its well-oiled wheels. When he finished and the platform was clear for them to board and leave the city, he turned again to Johan and looked at him. "Now we wait. When the Embracers arrive, we pull the trigger and run." He spoke in a normal tone, confidence in what he'd just seen above them causing him to forget the possible need for silence temporarily.

Johan, still overcome with rapture, took the lead to the platform, ready to leave the instant he was told. "Hey Auron, how will we know when..."

A 'thud' and a rattle from behind him shook Johan as the faint light of the controller skipped and fluttered away into the room as if thrown, leaving Johan in the darkness temporarily. Johan looked back quickly, angry with Auron Bree for being so clumsy, but the feeling left at once when he saw Bree face down on the platform, the thin controller on the ground in front of him, white light shining upwards.

Johan's knife was unsheathed and ready in the blink of an eye.

It wasn't enough. The danger moved quicker than he could, and before he could react, a ghostly figure sped across the beam of light to his left, followed by a sudden jarring pain in Johan's head.

In an instant he was down, blood dripping across his face, colors flashing before his eyes, and a limping set of legs now standing before him. As the realization dawned on him what had happened, another blow landed cleanly on the side of his head, and Johan Otan'co was out. The knife he'd protected until now dropped neatly to the ground beside him.

The pain in Esgona's body was considerable. From the time he'd left the transport and slipped into the park greenery, he'd been moving as quickly as his body could carry him. His legs were weak and extremely tired by the time he'd reached the border of Gracious Park.

The park was still mostly empty as he entered, but by the time he'd found the entrance to the underground storage room, the first wave of troops had already begun filing into the city. Doubting this course of action, he had no other choice but to find a hiding place and wait. The next few minutes were a blur. He could hear the marching overhead and the rumble of vehicles as they passed, but nothing entered the doorway and came down the stairs. Only the rumble of the march above his head could be heard, and it stayed that way for some time.

As the rumble carried on, he eventually heard something else. Voices?

There were gaps in the floor, with cracks of light pouring in from below. After putting his tired head to the space and listening, he could do nothing but smile at his luck. It was them, and they were right below him.

The next action was unexpected. While he listened, he was startled back by the loudest sound he'd heard since the bombs dropped on the shores of the southern ocean when the Army of the Old first attacked. In an instant the small storage room filled with what sounded like an avalanche. A deep rumble that grew until it shook the walls all around him, and when he thought the whole room was about to collapse, he was suddenly filled with a feeling of nausea, coupled with all the hairs on the back of his neck standing at once as if he was outside in a lightning storm.

It was Johan's magical electric wave, he realized, just as the sound changed from the low rumble to loud crashes. Then, wave after wave of bangs and explosions echoed all around him, smashing into the ceiling above him and reverberating like a drum around his ears. Large things crashed into the ground with great force. Minutes of this sound continued, as well as the air filling with electrical smoke.

Esgona knew everything that had happened right away. Johan's plan had worked, judging by the perfect silence that now filled the air. And if his plan worked, that meant only one thing, and all the pain in Esgona's body suddenly evaporated. His purpose for coming here would be justified.

Johan would now refuse to use the knife, as well as the bomb's full potential. Esgona was here to stop that.

True, it was blissfully dumb luck that had put him right on top of them. He knew there was going to be a drop-off point somewhere below Gracious Park. Where he was now described that place. Fate drove him onward, it would seem.

By the time he'd hidden himself away, letting his eyes adjust as best he could to the darkness, the space in the floor had already began opening. He waited as they rose up from the ground, watching them fumble in the dark to find the door and see what had happened, then disappeared up the stairway he'd come in. It was simply too easy. Esgona had found a simple piece of piping used in the park's irrigation system. He watched from the shadows as they returned, faces beaming with victory as they came in. Now they were prepared to set the bomb to its lowest setting and be done with this city.

As Johan returned to the platform, Bree set the bomb in place, making him the best target. With a strong swipe Bree was down just as he'd turned to assist Johan with more light.

His trademark smile, the bane of any child he'd once bullied, returned to Esgona's face, and he relished the moment as Johan turned around and ran back, leaving himself wide open to attack. There was more than a feeling of sick pleasure as he struck the first time, sending Johan to the ground in a heap, but not surprisingly Johan wasn't so easily dispatched. He took his second swing, sure to land it cleanly, and Johan was down without another word.

He took the knife in his hand. He had a brief moment of fear as he looked at both the controller, now in his hand, and the bomb before him, afraid that he wouldn't find the place to put the weapon, or even how to arm the bomb at all.Once more, damnable fate intervened and Esgona saw instantly that Auron Bree had made this a very simple task. The controller, he now saw, clearly read "Bomb Access" over one icon, and with a quick press the bomb's on-board screen lit up a faint grayish-blue, and below the screen the access drawer slowly slid open. A cursor flashed on the screen now, a lone flashing light that told Esgona the weapon was ready and waiting.

Not needing to be asked twice, Esgona placed the knife on the tray, which then closed and locked tightly.

A series of 'clicks' sounded form the core of the machine, followed by the hum of tiny motors. After a moment, the screen flashed "SCANNING" once more. Esgona sat watching, curious what might happen next.Anticlimactically, the screen only flashed the words "ENHANCEMENT ACCEPTED. SYSTEM READY" and sat there silently as if nothing had happened.

Esgona had seen enough. He'd have simply walked out the door were it not for his foolish new nature not to want people to die. Another look at the controller in his hands and he located the controls for the lift. However, it also revealed two new icons.One simply read "10 Minute Countdown." Not terribly handy. The other was the more important one. It was a red button that Esgona noticed to his twisted amusement was a frowning face, likely a joke made by Auron Bree. That sentiment was all but confirmed by the text below it.

"30 Sec. Non-Stop BOOM Clock!"

"Cute."

With another bout of pain coupled with hidden strength, he dragged them both over to the lift. Locating the "Lower" button on the lift controls, he pressed the switch.

Nothing happened.

He tried again.

Same result.

He looked over the controls, wondering if there was something he missed. The panel was laid out so that even a child would know what to do. It wasn't hiding any secrets he could see. He pressed it a third time, this time seeing the message that flashed on the screen for only a brief second.

"Power system failure.Attempting backup power transfer. System will retry shortly."

Damn it! Whatever power that was left down below that had gotten them here didn't look like it was going to take them back. The three were suddenly stuck here it seemed, at least temporarily.

He looked at the exit across the room and pondered it for a moment. Could he do it? Could he leave them here to die? He wanted revenge on the machines and the ones that controlled them, not these two. But if he stayed, he'd never get them out in time, and once they were up the stairs, what then?

He never had a chance to get these thoughts any farther, as the room sudden flooded with natural light coming from the doorway that led to the stairs.

With a rush of hurried steps echoing down the hallway, Esgona realized they were no longer alone, and they were very, very trapped.

***

Izuku had used every ounce of strength he had, mechanical, flesh, and Power-aided, to reach the city beyond. The speed he'd traveled blinded him to the truth of what was going on below him. As of yet, he still didn't see what had really happened.

He arrived at the twisted and destroyed spire in a heartbeat, eager to see if what Elutherios Duo reported had been true: they had an *adaptive* H.Y. bomb, and the fucking dagger he himself put into play was somewhere in the city as well. Those two things together were a mix he wanted nothing to do with.

Once discovering and freeing the massive army and all its accoutrements in the glacial ice in the far north, Izuku had set out to learn as much as he could about everything he saw. Soon, he realized that everything was perfect for what he'd intended. Everything, except for the Adaptive High Yield Bomb.He discovered a treasure trove of H.Y. bombs, but once he'd learned what the adaptive variant was designed for, he made certain to destroy every single one of them he found. Not so much for himself, but for the loyal legion of Embracers that followed him.

If done properly, one of these special weapons could destroy every one of them.

The adaptive model and its ability to absorb and use the characteristics of whatever was placed inside of it made it too risky. Just one Embracer item of focus inside this weapon and suddenly you had something that could defeat even Embracers, unless they were as powerful as himself. Unless a weapon that could destroy *him* arrived and was placed inside it. Mortals and their need for power had unknowingly created a weapon that handled the Power and its infinite resources with more carelessness than he liked to consider. Alas, after so many eons, he could still be both pleasantly and horribly surprised. This was one of the latter.

Adaptive H.Y. weapons were designed to kill Embracers. A weapon humanity had created to give them a fighting chance.

During his amusing and gratifying battle with Aryu, he had at last tapped the dormant information stored by E2-0901, flooding his mechanical brain instantly with a multitude of useful information. Maps, population specs, building blueprints, and, of course, learning of the existence of their adaptive H.Y. bomb. That sudden influx of information had taken only microseconds, but the result was an instantaneous desire to abandon this weak fool on the ground in front of him writhing at the power of the Est Vacuus and get to the city as quickly as possible.

The twisted steel of the spire and the mountains of glass on the ground still didn't distract him from his goal. He forced his way into the belowground control center easily, but learned at once that the weapon was gone.

A fraction of a second later he was scanning the computer records of the city Elutherios had sent him. There were tunnels here. Then, after considering a multitude of possibilities, Izuku realized the most likely location they were going to put it was at the heart of their forces, and the closest place to that was going to be the place called Gracious Park. If they invaded by means of the path of least resistance, that park was exactly where they would end up.

Humans! Why did they come up with a brilliant plan *now* of all times! Then, just as quickly as he'd arrived, he was gone again.

***

The faint memory of the Est Vacuus and its emptiness was still strong in Aryu's head as he flew towards the city as quickly as he could. Why? Why would anyone even want to know such a powerful and destructive force? He still had no experience with the Omnis, but he was convinced that it couldn't fully counter this kind of deep-rooted feeling. Just look at Crystal. She went mad when she lost her command of the Power. Even though she could remember the Est Vacuus and the Omnis, only one of them pushed itself forward and made her crazy, and it sure as hell wasn't the good one.

Never before had Aryu been so certain that the Power eventually ended up nowhere good, and that realization was a powerful one. It was a sudden culmination of all the stories he'd heard as a child about the great Ryu and the inhabitance of the East. The thought that any one of them, with enough time, patience and mental fortitude would be able to not only feel the Est Vacuus, but even go so far as Crystal apparently had and pull a part of it into this world was simply overwhelming. No one needed that kind of power anymore. Ryu Tokugawa had proven that centuries ago and no one listened. Only his son Sho seemed to know it was too much for one person, and now Sho was dead.

Aryu could feel the power of the Shi Kaze, the closest thing this world had to a piece of the Omnis, and although its voice was both glorious and terrible, it was still only marginally able to stop the Est Vacuus. In essence, this sword was the best hope the world had at balance. Had he the time, he thought he might try to destroy them both if he could, but he would have to be content with just one.

And, of course, the man who controlled it.

Aryu was traveling too fast and with too much rage-fueled purpose to notice the pulse pass around him, but as he came to the rear guard of the Army of the Old as they started falling like dominos, he thought it was an attack. His weapons were up, but he didn't need them. Suddenly, it was dead still.

He stood dumfounded as the spire in the distance erupted into a black plume. Something had happened. Something big.

Convinced after a few moments that he wasn't in any immediate threat, he pushed himself forward again as the soldiers toppled around him mysteriously.

He needed to find Izuku. Someone like that wasn't one who took to hiding. Except, perhaps, for the purposes of surprise attacks, but even that didn't worry Aryu. Izuku had Aryu beat, face to the ground and the Est Vacuus destroying his will to exist. Something had pulled him away, and whatever it was seemed to be very important. Possibly losing his entire army seemed to qualify, if that was indeed what had happened.

As the city's outskirts passed by him, the ground was littered with black metal bodies as far as he could see. There wasn't a human in sight.

Well, that wasn't entirely true. Far in front of him, entering into the center of the mass of broken weapons, were nine flesh and blood humans at the edge of some kind of greenspace where the buildings around him fell away. He was in no way shocked to find one of their numbers were getting closer by some nefarious means, and the distant tingle in the recesses of his head told him very clearly that those means were the Power.

Although prepared for an attack, one never came. He simply stopped there as this new enemy approached, quickly at first, then cautiously. Aryu knew instantly they'd seen the weapons they faced and the visage of the man who carried them, and had taken a steadier pace.

Embracers. His own small army of Embracers he had to deal with

Ahead, a man with ice-blue hair and beard levitated mystically into his path, a short sword that whispered with the voice of the Power in his hands in a defensive position before him.

"So it's true," he said, eying Aryu top to bottom. "The Shi Kaze has returned, and it's in the hands of a Power-less whelp, no less."

Aryu simply wasn't in the mood to entertain a conversation with this man. Instead, he flapped his metallic wings into a ready position and stepped forward, the point of the holy sword getting closer to this odd-looking man. The intention was clear.

"Now, now," he said, "no need for that. I was simply curious. Truth be told, if one of the younger of my kind were to be standing here, I believe they would be terrified and would simply run. I am not young, however, and I will not run. I believe you and I can find some kind of compromise, yes? Perhaps one that would aid you?"

Aryu stopped but never lowered a weapon. "Such as?"

"Well sir, as you likely are aware, we Embracers don't live long siding with the least powerful. You seem to be holding not one but two very persuasive cards there, not to mention the legendary Makashi armor. That's a strong hand against one like Izuku. Strong enough to persuade me and my friends back there to change our current course of action."

The words weren't meant to sound cowardly, and indeed to Aryu they sounded more professional than anything else. In days past, Aryu may have considered these words, and then would have lowered his guard just enough to give this smooth-talking blue man a brief second to strike with whatever abilities he had and get the best of Aryu. He still held disdain for Embracers, no matter what side they claimed to be on. Although ones like Sho were kindhearted and strong, Crystal's confusing actions and Izuku's treatment of his brother reinforced that they thought themselves beyond morality. With his burgeoning hatred, he instead opted to drop the Shi Kaze only slightly less than he would have in the past when he was more naïve, giving the illusion of one willing to talk.

The blink-of-an-eye attack came just as Aryu had assumed it would, and instead of Aryu being crippled by a pierced defense, he instead pulled around the shield in one fluid motion, deflecting the burst of hot blue light. Then he leapt upward like a shot and thrust out the Shi Kaze.

His opponent was not fazed, and any fear of this sword he had was well hidden. He blocked the attack with his own sword with ease and was in the process of attempting to use his considerable use of the Power to gain control of the boy in front of him, just as he had Edgar Taft and his precious trailer when this battle had begun, when the *feeling* of the Shi Kaze and its contact with his beloved sword struck his brain. By Gods! The *Power*! How could he have thought they could stand against is? He'd been such a fool!

The realization came fast and distracted him just long enough to allow Aryu to land on the far side, twist with astonishing grace for a non-Embracer, and leap again while gripping the specialized handle of the shield with a force akin to trying to crush rocks. Then, with no hesitation and a reasonable-sized chunk of self-satisfaction, the arm with the shield stretched out, smashing into the man's hand that held the sword.

There was no hand left. Just a sliced and bloody stump, the sword that had been his best friend and reliable sidekick for hundreds of years was tossed away and fell like a stone to the ground below.

The pain of the blow, both physically and mentally, left his mind suddenly devoid of his command of the Power. He had long ago mastered the ability to focus without the sword, but the blow from the shield, a weapon of focus much stronger than himself, had sent a weakness through his body. Mentally crippled, he felt the Power leave him as he began to fall with a look of loss and shock on his face.

By the time he'd thought he might have a faint hope of focusing in time to save himself, the hard-packed ground was already there to meet him.

The other Embracers watched in horror and fear as he landed, not as an Embracer would with safety, but as a human: painfully.

Aryu's eyes burned with anger as he landed and charged at the stunned form on the ground, and as he approached the remaining Embracers, he sliced with an incredibly deft hand across the neck of the blue man, and that was the messy end of him as his body slumped down in pieces. Was this what meeting one more powerful than themselves could do? Doubt was suddenly everywhere in the eyes of the other eight.

Once the moment of his true death came, they were all overtaken with the sudden rush of the Power as it exploded out and floored them all. He was old, many times older than them, and his Power was great. The sudden blast was blinding, and they all fell backwards as it came and then receded.

Then, moments later, more Power.

From the south, waves of it were getting closer, coupled with feelings they knew to be that of their comrades. The other Embracers, the one's Izuku had called south, were returning very quickly, though there were much less of them. Behind them all was a source of Power that rivaled even Izuku. A moment later, they saw what it was.

Now only four remained from the group sent south, and they all were running as quickly as they could at them across the lifeless battlefield, with the unstoppable Crystal Kokuou charging in behind them. Fear overtook each of them, overriding the fact that as a collective they could likely beat her. As it was, they only saw a death they didn't want, and were soon pushing north themselves. Within minutes the remains of Izuku's mighty legion of loyal Embracers were running like cowards into the fallen city of Bankoor.

The man Aryu was now was so much more than the one that had emerged from the Great Range weeks before. Since then, he'd suffered deep losses, tragic frights, and unthinkable betrayal. What had started as a quest to help Nixon and get these mysterious answers had become a battle for his life and the lives of millions of others. Some could say even the world, but Aryu wasn't so certain. Izuku's army had been strong, but they'd seemed to hit a wall when they met the combined forces of the North. Even now their supply lines were cut, and it would seem that their forward progress was once more halted in this funnel of land. Did Izuku really believe he'd be successful against whatever lay beyond this city? Whether he did or not, Aryu doubted it was possible, even with Embracers.

As he chased the monster he'd been hunting deeper into the park, the shadowy form of Izuku emerged, apparently livid with what he was surrounded by. Every one of the machines he commanded was broken and on the ground, twitching and smelling like acrid smoke. Something had stopped them all, and whatever it was it looked like the broken tower that now leant dangerously to one side at the center of this place was the cause of it.

Aryu stopped. The park itself was amazing, had it not been littered with such unsightly debris. Whoever these people were, they had clearly been very advanced to be able to build and maintain places like this. Yet another reminder that he, his village, and all of the lands around them were seriously out of touch with what was going on in the world. A self-imposed exile they'd all been forcibly removed from.

Aryu approached Izuku as his back was turned, anger obvious in his movements even from here. Aryu would not be taken by surprise again.

He stepped over a fallen Herald, remembering how he'd feared them so much not long before. He remembered the attack on the Haven, when Crystal went mad while Sho seemed more at peace, the state he remained in until Izuku ripped him out of it. Aryu passed over it without another thought and carried on to Izuku as he approached what looked to be a small shed with door on its side, then opened the door and entered.

Perfect, thought Aryu. *He's trapped.*

As he got closer, he saw the stairs leading down to who knew where. Undeterred, he folded back his wings to fit the space ahead, his tall frame slipping into the abyss.

Halfway down he heard a 'thud' and grunting followed by laughter. Someone was down there with Izuku, and they certainly weren't winning.

Aryu silently stepped to the doorway, careful not to tip Izuku off to his presence. Once his eyes adjusted enough, he set his weapons in a ready position before him and entered the room swiftly, but also cautiously.

His caution wasn't needed. When Aryu turned, he could see only the back of Izuku and the form of someone else at his feet, a metal pipe between them both. "Tell me, you young brave fool, you wouldn't happen to know what happened to my precious army, would you?"

Silence at first, causing Aryu to stop moving. A few more feet and he would be within striking range and end this whole mess forever. "I do," they said.

Aryu froze. He knew that voice, even in its hushed tone. "It was some kind of electrical pulse created by the spire at the city center."

Esgona! By the *gods*! And if that was Esgona, that meant…

He looked around, needing to know if he was alone. Looking past a stack of wooden boxes, he saw that he wasn't. The new icy demeanor of Aryu O'Lung'Singh was broken in an instant. There was Johan, as well as an older man, slumped on some kind of platform. It was difficult to make out their exact circumstances in this poor light, but he could see each of them breathing faintly.

His mind steeled once more. *Celebrate later, Aryu,* he told himself. *Deal with this maniac and then look after your friend.*

"An electric pulse, you say. How wickedly clever," Izuku continued, seething through clenched teeth while inching closer to Esgona. "I should never have underestimated your kind." There was venom in his voice now, and Aryu watched as his sickening robotic fingers clasped the handle of his sword.

Once Aryu came into Esgona's view, his eyes went wide at what he was seeing. Suddenly tipped off, Izuku moved away with a quick side-step just as the Shi Kaze rushed past him.

It wasn't a complete miss. The aged and powerful blade connected with his wing as it traveled, slicing through it like a newborn tree branch. Even without a strong stroke, the power of the weapon itself was more than enough to shear off the wing's end effortlessly, causing a large chunk to fall to the ground and making Izuku howl in anger with a volume that was deafening in the tight quarters.

Shocked by the sudden noise, Aryu flinched as Izuku rushed him, ignoring Esgona completely and unsheathing the Est Vacuus sword as he moved.

Aryu countered at once, his grip on the Shi Kaze akin to a hydraulic vise. Once more, the glistening sparks and ethereal shimmer flew out of the two weapons' point of contact. Although immune to the debilitating power of the Est Vacuus, the pulse sent a stern and powerful reminder to his brain just what it was he faced. The fear of it was still alive and well.

Queasy and unsettled by the feeling of the weapons clashing, Esgona was thankfully spared the full view of Izuku's sword and used their sudden skirmish to slip away.

Aryu attacked and countered strike after strike from Izuku, watching Esgona move while he had the chance. Izuku was extremely skilled, but the events of the past hour were catching up to him and anger began to overtake his moves. His strikes, although superhumanly strong, were well-telegraphed and easy for weapons such as Aryu's to fight back against. Had it not been for Esgona's sudden act of bold and stupefying self-sacrifice, an action that no one would have believed him capable of just a short time ago, Aryu was certain that he would have won this fight. Esgona didn't believe Aryu O'Lung'Singh could even compare to this monster's amazing powers. He was going to die here fumbling in the dark and he knew it. At last, he found what he was looking for, and his hands wrapped around the handheld control panel.

In a panicked rush, he scanned the strange icons until he found what he was looking for. With a sudden boldness, he reached out and pressed the ghostly red frowning face.

At first, he simply expected it to begin counting down and that was that. What he got were two new icons, one on the left and right of the screen. One of them was in the shape of an old dial and read "Blast Effectiveness and Circumference." The other, much more ominously, simply read in bold letters "MAX."

Remembering what Auron Bree had told them, he realized he had to choose the power and range of the explosion.

He looked up at the two battling winged monsters above him and sighed. This was it, and after everything, it was still completely worth it. Johan hadn't had the balls to do it. That was why he needed to be 'convinced' that it was the best course of action. Esgona wished he'd have been able to gloat about this to the fool, but it looked like he'd never get the chance.

He pressed the "MAX" icon, and watched as the lights on the

H.Y. bomb only steps away from him lit up, forcing his heart into his throat at a thousand beats a minute. Here at last he could die in peace, a hero to millions. The silent screen on the weapon glowed with its faint, haunting light, with only the number "30" shown on it. Then, "29," and Esgona knew the task was complete.

So too did Izuku. His head flew around and looked at the bomb across the room. Taking the chance, Aryu struck again, this time missing Izuku's body but hitting the undamaged wing cleanly. As if plucked like a feather, the wing fell off and landed with a crash on the floor echoing into the darkness.

Enraged at what was going on around him, Izuku needed to take desperate action. Eager to rid himself of Aryu and this weapon, Izuku focused his mind and tapped the Power around him, causing a sudden forceful pulse that threw Aryu aside and against a far wall, as well as all the boxes, bags and miscellaneous equipment. In an ever–expanding wave he tossed aside everything not nailed down or immensely heavy (i.e.: the H.Y. bomb) to the outer ring of the room. Aryu was instantly winded but otherwise unaffected by this new attack, and was back on his feet once more, as was Esgona across the room, covered in splinters from boxes. The damaged side of Aryu's face screamed in protest.

It had bought Izuku enough time, though. He had reached his destination and he stood before the silent weapon that would in thirteen seconds spell his demise, and that of every other person in the city. With a soft touch on the screen, while Aryu and Esgona looked on (Aryu in confusion and Esgona in horror) the machine beeped and the countdown stopped. With his wicked smile back firmly in place, Izuku looked at Esgona. "My dear boy, this thing and I are cut from the same cloth. Do you think I don't know how to speak its language?" He removed his hand, the screen flashing the number "7", then going dark.

Esgona desperately looked at the control panel, but the impact of Izuku's attack had shattered the casing around it, rendering it useless. Esgona looked crestfallen, his hero's death lost to this mechanical man.

Aryu renewed his attack in the confusion, leaping over the fallen wing on the floor. He knew he could damage Izuku very easily and he was eager to do so once more.

Izuku turned to Aryu in anger. One problem was solved, but the greater and more pressing issue of a fool with the Shi Kaze was still here.

"I can always get more wings, Aryu. Yours, however, don't tend to grow back!" He faced Aryu and attacked with fresh confidence of his own. They continued their battle as Esgona looked on in shock and wonder at just what it was Aryu had become and what he was doing. Their movements were much too quick and skilled to allow him to see the true nature of both weapons, but with each clash he felt the Power course through the room. It was this sense of astonishment that blinded him.

Eyes fixed on the epic battle in front of him in this dark, damp room, he never saw the attack from behind coming. With nothing but a fist that felt like iron on the end of his arm, Johan blindsided Esgona with as much force (and pleasure) as he could muster. With a hard, fleshy 'thud' Esgona was tossed to the ground in a heap, his leg audibly snapping as he fell awkwardly. Whether it was his good leg or bad one Johan didn't care. All he knew was that his head was bleeding, Auron was still out and something that looked vaguely like his best friend was battling a half-robot/half-human thing across the room.

Esgona's legs were the last things on his mind after what he'd tried to do. Checking for his knife and finding it missing, he realized what had happened and just how close he had been.

Letting the two others in the room have their battle, he knelt down to check on Auron. After a moment, and more than a fair share of shaking and slapping, Auron came to. "What… what happened?" he slurred out, eyes refusing to focus on any one thing at a time with all the activity in the room.

"Esgona did," Johan answered. "He tried to take us out and set the bomb himself."

"Then why are we on the lift?"

"Who cares? I guess he had some stupid idea of honor in his head. We can talk later, but Aryu's in a big fucking fight over there and it looks like this lift isn't working, so we need to get out of here before we get ourselves killed!"

Auron looked as though he was about to pass out again but Johan heaved him to a sitting position. "Oh no you don't. You need to get up and help me."

"I'll... I'll try, but I feeling like I'm drowning and... did you say Aryu? Your friend with the wings?"

Johan nodded. "That's him over there." He pointed to Aryu, who currently had the shield blades spinning at top speed and was attempting to pin Izuku against a wall. Izuku was desperate to channel any of the Power once more, but every time the weapons collided it rippled through his mind and forcefully broke his concentration. The Power wasn't just there and ready to use at all time. Even the oldest and most powerful Embracers needed a meditative-like mental focus, even for a fraction of a second, to tap into its vastness. Aryu simply wasn't giving him that chance, either knowingly or not, and Izuku was stuck battling with him like a common mortal.

Aryu saw Johan yank the man up. This was no place for them and he wanted them gone. He hated to think that after all this time he'd lose Johan here, moments after finding him.

In the end, it was Izuku who gave him the chance. Sick of being baited into a fight he despised, Izuku swallowed a fair bit of courage and allowed himself an extra microsecond during an attack to use the Power once more, heaving the solid ground beneath Aryu's feet towards him like pulling out a carpet, causing Aryu to stagger back and almost lose his footing.

Being so close to both winning and losing, and as opposed to simply using the Power to blow this room and all who were in it up (an attack that would simply dissipate once it hit the Shi Kaze, just like the bursts he'd attacked with before), Izuku opted instead to fall back to the higher ground. In a wide-open area, he had a hundred times more options on what to do next. He could not be careless now. Even if he had lost his army, he still had his Embracers and Elutherios Duo (provided Nixon hadn't destroyed him. Unlikely, but possible). That would likely be enough. The bomb was no longer a threat now. He'd overwritten Auron's simple commands and deactivated it completely, so he simply left it where it was, lifeless and still. Then he retreated up the stairs and outside, eager to send a call out to all remaining Embracers to join him and continue the assault on Bankoor. They would pay for what they'd done to his army. That done, he would wait for Aryu to battle him once more, this time in the open where the advantage was his.

His blood was running hot like molten lava, but still Aryu couldn't give chase. Not now, while his friend was so close. Instantly, he turned to him, joy overtaking him as he approached. Johan was helping the man into a sitting position. "Can I lend a hand?" Aryu asked.

They both turned, and their looks of worry and uncertainty were erased at once as they took Aryu's face in fully, Auron for the first time and Johan for the first time since the rooftop of the mountain village inn. At last, they were back together.

Practically dropping Auron as he moved, Johan rushed over to Aryu and embraced his brother. Although each still had a tremendous hill to climb before this day was over, for the moment they were together again against life's challenges. Two beaten and bloody faces smiled at each other. The sons of Tan Torna Qu'ay united once more.

Chapter 13: The Last Hurrah

The two of them were almost in tears as they stood in the darkness, but they simply were each too overwhelmed to cry.

When they pulled apart, Johan tried to fight the darkness to see just what had become of his friend. By now, Aryu was bleeding badly from his facial wound, his hands were dirty and beaten, and he was clad in the most astonishing suit of armor Johan had ever seen. It even stretched over his wings. "What happened to you?" Johan asked, speech improving. If he was referring to why they never met up earlier, the state he was in or about the weapons and armor he now wore, Aryu wasn't sure. It was really just a blanket question.

"It's a very long story, like I'm sure yours is. I'm just glad to see you."

"Oh man, me too, Aryu," said Johan. "A long story doesn't even begin to describe it."

"Well, we'll catch up when this is done. I need to go after Izuku, can you guys get out of here safely?"

"What's an Izuku?"

"The man I was just fighting, he was the one behind everything: the army, the Embracers, everything. He even knows about me it seems. About where I come from and why, but I need to go after him. I can't let him get away again."

Johan saw the pleading seriousness in his voice and knew this wasn't their long-awaited reunion full of catching up and harrowing stories. "Alright, but we haven't got many options to leave, and it's a safe bet he's waiting for you up there. He'll likely kill us all when we get out in the open."

That was true. Izuku wasn't about to give up so easily. "How did you get here?" Aryu asked.

Johan indicated the platform with Auron on it. "That brought us up from below," Johan answered, then he indicated the smashed control panel next to the crippled Esgona, "and it was controlled by that, which doesn't look like much help now."

As if on cue, the lights on the side of platform illuminated. Astonished, they both looked over to where a slumping Auron Bree had reached around to an unseen control panel on the side of the lift.

"What?" Bree said, incredulously. "Did you think there was only one way up or down? You two and that Esgona kid are pretty damn backwards."

The mention of his name brought a scowl to each of their faces. "Why did he have that?" Aryu asked.

"It controls a lot of things. This lift, the blast that shut the Army of the Old down, and that…" Johan pointed the bomb. "He was trying to set it off, destroying the city and everything in it, Embracers and all."

"What? How?" Aryu had no idea what exactly it was he was looking at, but the picture was getting clearer all the time.

"Aryu, I'd really like to explain it, I promise I would, but we're running out of time to escape. You may be ready to face off against him and his Embracers, but we're not. We need to get out of here."

Aryu was saddened at the thought of losing his friend again, but he also understood. The time for stories was almost here, but it wasn't now. "Alright, how do we get you out?"

"I can get us down from here, but we need to hurry," Auron said, still a slur in his words from the blow to the head.

Aryu indicated the mysterious man with the plan. "And he is?"

"Auron Bree," Auron answered, not extending a hand. "The head of the War and Glory Council." Aryu looked at him confused. Auron just waved him off. Now wasn't the time for explanations.

Johan was looking over the bomb intently. Aryu came to him, trying to hurry their escape. "My knife." Johan told him. "I'm pretty sure Esgona put it inside, and since that Izuku person shut it down, I can't get it out."

"Why would Esgona do that?" Aryu asked, trying to help him look but having no idea what he was searching for. His fingers ran over the smooth surface looking for anything other than polished metal.

"Because it's a weapon of the Embracers.An item of Focus. And this is an H.Y. bomb designed to use it."

Aryu instantly took his hand away in horror from the weapon and looked at Johan like he was mad. "Again, not the time, Aryu. I was just hoping I could get it before we had to go." Crestfallen, he gave up. Whatever Izuku had done to it, it seemed to be permanent. He put on a strong face and returned to where Esgona was laying awkwardly on the floor. "And as for this useless bastard... I'd be just as happy to leave him to the wolves, but I guess that's not in our nature, is it?"

Aryu still wasn't certain what had transpired between these three in the last hour, but it seemed to be coming to a head right here. "No. Whatever he did, he did it with a greater purpose in mind."

"Ha! Maybe in his own, but no one else's." With one last hard kick to ensure he was truly out cold, Aryu and Johan lifted him and none-too-gently placed him on the lift beside Auron Bree.

"He'll get his, Johan," Aryu assured him. "He always does."

Johan looked uneasy. "Well, let's hope he doesn't kill us before then. I feel obliged to be there to witness that."

They looked at one another, just as they had on the roof of the mountain inn weeks ago. So much had changed, both in the world and inside each of them. "Be safe, Aryu. That thing meant business."

"So do I, Johan. For all of us, I promise he won't live to see another day."

"Don't take long, Aryu. My story alone will take days to tell. It looks like yours may be even longer." That was an understatement on each side.

"I won't. Soon, it will be the two of us off again." Johan was about to mention Seraphina, then thought better of it. That was a surprise for another time. "Get out of here. Do what you have to do. Go north with all the others. I'll find you, just like I did this time."

"Next time, don't take so long," Johan told him, extending his hand, which Aryu took warmly and shook.

"I wouldn't dream of it," Aryu answered. They were each so much more than the young men from the mountains, and today they had proven it.

Johan stepped to the platform next to Auron and found the soft green light that said 'LOWER' on it. "Fight hard, Aryu. And make sure nothing happens to that bomb. The way it's set up now, if it goes off it will destroy everything, and I mean everything! The Army, the Embracers, the city, innocent people trying to escape north of here, you, us, everything, you got it?" A part of him knew Aryu would win this day, but another part was also terrified that this may be their last meeting together, as Aryu was about to face an inhumanly powerful enemy while they were about to descend into who-knew-where, possibly trapping themselves. Between them would be a version of the weapon that separated them in the first place.

"I've got it. You fight hard too," Aryu answered. With a nod, Johan pressed the button and the room filled with noise as the lift began falling away.

Aryu looked at the weapon, the one that was apparently completely offline, and yelled back, "I thought it didn't work anymore?"

"You know our luck. Nothing is ever that easy," Johan called, descending farther. Aryu could no longer see them and could only hear the lift as it lowered. A pause, and then from the depths came a call.

"For Tan Torna Qu'ay, Aryu!"

Aryu hardened himself. "For Tan Torna Qu'ay, Johan."

Without another word, the sound of the lift died away, and soon there was only black stillness.

With one last look at the silent weapon across the room, Aryu solidified his nerves once more and headed for the door, shield and Shi Kaze firmly in hand.

He climbed the stairs very slowly, waiting for the first sign of an attack from Izuku. The shield was raised above his head, blocking the light (and point of attack) ahead.

The attack never came. The tension in each step was almost unbearable to Aryu, but he came to the door without incident. With one last push the door flung open and the harsh sunlight poured down the stairway like fire.

Aryu was out in a flash, his wings tucked back and weapons raised to fight.

Again, nothing.

Aryu, his eyes flying back and forth across the sky like a hawk, moved out into the open and tensed his muscles. Izuku was somewhere nearby, Aryu could almost taste it

"Looking for me?" the same maddening voice called. Aryu whipped his head back and forth madly, searching all around him for Izuku. "I'm here, Aryu. I have no desire to hide from you."

Looking around, Aryu saw Izuku sitting patiently on a park bench like an old man who fed birds and told rambling stories to passers-by. Izuku was also in the open, the Est Vacuus sword swinging back and forth beside him like a pendulum between black metal fingers.

Izuku didn't move. He simply watched Aryu, one robotic leg crossed over the other. Any issues he'd suffered from the loss of one wing and the severe damaging of the other seemed all but gone. His long chunk of metallic flying appendage was tucked tightly against his back. Aryu approached cautiously, his eyes never leaving the sword Izuku carried.

"There's no point in running, for either of us," Izuku said. "Our paths would just cross again somewhere else along the line. I'm not much into fate, believe it or not, but that's a truth I know is real."

Aryu barely listened, his heart racing as he moved slowly to where Izuku sat. "I hope you had a nice goodbye with your friend," Izuku continued. "I doubt you'll be seeing him for some time, if ever again. Not if you do what you're supposed to, anyway."

"And what am I supposed to be doing?" Aryu asked, still moving but slower now, trying to keep a safe distance from the sitting Izuku.

"Well, not this, for one thing. You and your kind were never supposed to be brought here to oppose me. You were brought here to aid me. To be my key to everything. Sadly, like so many things in my life lately, it didn't turn out as it was supposed to."

Aryu stopped. The bodies of Izuku's fallen army were all around the park, but nothing but grass was between them. "You've been going on about this for some time, Izuku, so why not just spit it out. What am I? Where do I come from?"

The irritating, maddening smile came to Izuku's face, so out of place in the beauty of the daylight. "Well, that would be a long story, but let's just say you're not quite of this world."

Aryu grinned while he listened to the foolishness Izuku was spouting. "Really, are you saying I'm an alien of some kind?"

"Of some kind, yes, but not from another planet. Alien does not have to mean from space. The word 'alien' is just another way of saying 'different.'"

Aryu wasn't sure letting Izuku speak was a wise course of action, but it seemed that of all people, Izuku seemed to know more about Aryu than anyone. That curiosity had plagued him all of his life, and now it seemed to have a hold over him when he should be attacking.

"You see, Aryu, to explain where you come from would ages, and although I have that kind of time, you do not. It's disappointing that you came to me as you did; with fire in your eyes and blood on your hands. You and your kind were meant for so much more."

"What 'kind'? There are more like me? With wings? They look like me?"

"Yes. Many more. You just haven't found them yet. If this confrontation went another way, I'd say you would find them eventually, considering all of the enhancements you seem to have come across lately." He slowly lifted himself up, walking away from the bench and circling around Aryu. "Having felt the power of the Est Vacuus, do you really believe you can defeat me? Here and now? Do you believe that you, with no command of the Power, no more fighting skill than what could be taught in a matter of weeks, no more friends to aid you, no more than that ridiculous sense of honor, loyalty and revenge, can defeat me, the oldest and most Powerful creature alive? I've seen it all, Aryu. Do you really think there's something you can do that I haven't seen before?"

Aryu was tense. These were things he'd considered more than once, but he still felt that he could bring something more. Something Izuku couldn't win against. Why else would Izuku be talking to him now if he didn't believe there was some threat from Aryu? "I do. If your father can be killed by a mortal man, so can you."

Izuku stopped walking, considering the words. "True. An

excellent point, but Sho was destined for Power and greatness from birth. What about you? What is your point in being here other than that I destroyed your home? Guess what, Aryu; I destroyed *a lot* of homes. I destroyed a million lives before you've finished breakfast! What makes you different from any of them?"

Aryu smiled slightly. That was a question he had an answer for. "Because I'm here," he answered. "Where they couldn't be. I'm here and they're not. I'm the one that made it this far. All I'll ever know is my story, and so far that story has brought me here."

Izuku's smile left. Interesting. That was a very wise answer. One he hadn't expected. "Perhaps," he replied. "And a very tragic story it is, but like all of the others, it doesn't end well, Aryu. Just because yours was longer and marginally more successful won't make it end any differently."

Izuku faced Aryu, still nothing but open greenery between them. "I wish I could tell you everything, Aryu. The why's and where's of you and those like you I assure you is both interesting and tragic, but as your little story has brought you to the here and now, I suppose you'll never know. A shame, really. So much potential lost. So many doors closed for the both of us." He raised the Est Vacuus and held it out menacingly. Reality seemed to twist around it in every direction as if it repelled away while also wanting desperately to fill it. *Not as if,* thought Aryu, the memory of the sickening and encompassing nothingness it contained still fresh in his memory. *It is being repulsed, pushed away like opposite sides of a magnet. There isn't anything there; it's just a hole in the world in the shape of a sword.*

"Come Aryu O'Lung'Singh. I'm grounded now thanks to you, but I am no less powerful. Let's see what your merry little trio of trinkets and teachers could cram into your head in such a short period of time."

Needing no more provocation, Aryu braced himself and charged, sick of the talk. He no longer cared about where he came from. At least, not enough to prevent this fight. If Izuku knew, so did someone else. Crystal, or perhaps even Nixon. If he really wanted to know, he would find a way to learn.

Aryu closed the gap between himself and his enemy. The battle cry of a true warrior pulsed from his lungs, and the memory of his family and home remained strong and finely detailed in his head.

At times in history Izuku had fought for the betterment of mankind. At others it was just for fun and enjoyment. He'd fought beside his father for centuries, against him for countless more. He'd even fought with his brother for a long time. He now considered those his defining years, the years that made him who and what he was today (especially considering that it was his most recent battle with Sho that had crippled and destroyed him to the point he was at now). So many times he'd put his life in the hands of his mastery of the Power and the skills he had learned.

So many times, and never before had he had the rush of exhilaration he had now fighting this unskilled mortal child and the insanely powerful toys he tossed around so recklessly. He couldn't quite place why that was. Perhaps it was because of the weapons themselves? No, that wasn't it; he'd battled these before. This wasn't even the first time he'd faced them at the same time, though they had been split between two people last time, Sho with the shield and armor, his father with the Shi Kaze. That time had been simple sparring. This time was serious. Was that it?

Maybe it was the fact that this moment was the culmination of everything that had happened up until now? Perhaps, but even then there had been huge moments Izuku had lived through. Moments with years and years of buildup that boiled down to one final fight between two hungry opponents. After a brief second to think about it, he decided that no, this was even bigger than that, which was why it felt so much different.

Whether Aryu knew it or not, he had suddenly become the complete culmination of almost every major plan that Izuku had ever done or been witness to. He was a combination of universal fates that had strung together an epic weaving of forces, circumstances and actions. He had become everything Izuku now sought to destroy in order to move on and take this world to begin things anew. Hundreds of thousands of years had bonded together to make this exact moment. After defeating Aryu, and with Sho now dead, only Nixon and Crystal would be left to defeat him. And with every Embracer he commanded now doing their best to stop Crystal and the terrible-yet-amazing thing that was Elutherios Duo 0901 pushing Nixon to limits the great phoenix didn't know he had, the only real enemy left to defeat was this helpless, desperate child. Izuku could feel in his soul, or what passed for a soul, that the tide would turn considerably once Aryu was destroyed. Perhaps his army lay in ruin around him, but did anyone truly believe that this was all he had? The people of the Old were as prosperous as they were paranoid. This was only a fraction of the mass of soldiers and weapons he'd found in the far north buried beneath the ice. He could always return with more, or find other Embracers on farther reaches of the Earth. He simply had to get past this boy and it would all be in his hands. He didn't want to start from scratch, but if he controlled everything just as he had this time, as well as being the holder of the Shi Kaze and Sho's shield, who alive could hope to stop him then. He just had to beat Aryu and the world was his.

So why the fuck can't I do it!

It was more than anger that forced him into this outburst of the mind. After only a few minutes of this confrontation, Izuku was beginning to know just how Nixon Ash must be feeling right this second. Frustration, pain, and perhaps even panic. Here in the open and with the hot sun beating down of them both, Aryu O'Lung'Singh was a man possessed. Powerful and frightening bursts of the Power were being deflected off sword and shield as if made of nothing at all. Every aggressive move Izuku could make, moves that had aided him and beaten hundreds of those opponents he'd faced in the past, were simply not getting the job done here and now. Something about Aryu seemed to be able to move and counter attacks almost as if he knew they were coming.

When he tried to make the ground cave under his feet, Aryu took to the air. When he formed fast and straight bursts of the Power to cut him down while aloft, he always had the shield in the proper place to block. Even though he'd only inherited it a few hours prior to this meeting, it was an extension of himself already. When he used his considerable abilities to encase Aryu in a cocoon of Power devoid of any atmosphere in an attempt to suffocate or simply weaken him, the damnable Shi Kaze would just cut through the casing and absorb the Power around him, and then he'd follow up with another barrage. If Aryu got a decent hit in like the ones that had taken the wings off Izuku's back, then it was the end for certain. If luck favored the bold, who could be bolder than a mortal boy who challenged a god to a fight to the death?

Still, he was running out of options. His considerable power simply was outclassed by his father's sword, his brother's shield, and the demon-child of Tan Torna Qu'ay.

In Aryu's eyes things were going exactly as they should be. His body hurt, his face was still bleeding considerably, but he was also flying on emotions and experiences he'd never imagined. He had Izuku right where he wanted him. Given the time, Izuku could simply have waited him out. Tossed attack after useless attack at him for hours until Aryu's body, which was nowhere near as well versed in this kind of confrontation as Izuku's was, gave out. A twisted ankle? Sprained wrist? Even something as harmless as plain exhaustion would do, but Izuku simply didn't have that kind of time. His forces were on their heels and he needed to end this quickly and regain the momentum he'd lost. Aryu couldn't feel the grandeur of the moment quite as palpably as Izuku could, but he was also not immune to the moment either. If he lost, Izuku was free to continue his push north and chase after the countless innocents and whatever worlds there were beyond that to conquer. At no point did Aryu see himself as Izuku did: the combined actions of history given flesh. Aryu simply lacked that kind of mental scope.

So it was as they battled on fiercely. Izuku tried tossing Aryu around (not unlike the blue man he'd encountered could), which was an attack easily foiled. It felt as if Aryu was simply being moved by a paper wall he just had to cut through. Izuku then encased Aryu is white-hot flames, which were doused with one simple wave of the Shi Kaze.

At last, with anger and frustration in his eyes, Izuku charged Aryu while he blocked another barrage of Power-based attacks, and the Est Vacuus and the Shi Kaze met once more.

Izuku was still aided by both the Power and the mechanical enhancements he possessed. Although most effects of the Power were useless on Aryu, the pure natural strength and speed Izuku had short work of proving his instincts: Aryu as a hand-to-hand fighter simply paled in comparison to Izuku, and soon the mighty blows that struck his shield, the lightning-quick punches that breached his defenses, and the nimble and unnatural kicks and thrusts of Izuku's mechanical legs had Aryu falling back in leaps and bounds. Cuts, welts and bruises began forming with alarming frequency, and after more time was spent embattled with this horror of man and machine, the roles were deftly reversed.

Izuku didn't let up. Soon the Power wasn't even a part of the equation for him. He realized that he only needed his hardened and mastered skills to win this fight, with a healthy dose of fear that the Est Vacuus emanated whenever it came within Aryu's view. He could remember the terror and hopelessness of the void very well, and it was that memory that helped Izuku's cause more than anything else.

"Come Aryu!" he taunted. "Take a look at my little toy!" He'd wave the sword he carried in front of Aryu's eyes before continuing to attack. "Drop your weapons! I give you my word of honor that I can beat you without raising a finger. Just take a look at this marvelous weapon!"

Aryu fought desperately to force the memory of the Est Vacuus out of his head. With every clash of weapons or clear view of the curved empty space in Izuku's hand came a sudden flash of its haunting visage. The mental picture of exactly what true nothingness looks like.

The Shi Kaze in his hands fought bravely against the void, and although it couldn't completely eclipse the feeling the Est Vacuus created, it was more than enough to keep it at bay. Aryu could deal with the memory later. For now only victory mattered.

The world beyond their own had still been spinning very quickly, and so it was that both of them were suddenly taken aback by what happened next. As Izuku stuck hard and fast, twisting and spinning like a bladed top, Aryu blocked and countered with all of his might, putting up more of a fight than either of them believed possible. They were so locked into their own struggle that neither were prepared for the sudden crushing impact that erupted beside them. It was an impact so powerful that it tore a hole in the ground and tossed them both away with ease.

With the aid of the Power by Izuku and the dark pearly wings of Aryu, both landed deftly away from this new attack. Before either had a chance to look skyward to see where it had come from, a sudden nauseating pulse exploded from the crater, powerful enough to bring them both to their knees as the shockwave blew out like a gunshot.

Once gone, they both realized it was a familiar feeling. One Izuku had felt many times in his life, and Aryu had felt a grand total of four. It was the obvious and off-putting feeling one gets with the death of an Embracer.

Aryu was terrified at once that it was Crystal, though if you asked him why he would have had no idea. He still wasn't sure what to feel about her and the things she'd done to him and his friends. Still, there was something about her that told him to trust her, even if her cause wasn't exactly his own. He just didn't want anything else to happen to someone he cared so much about anymore. He had just found that his friend was alive (for the moment) but he had no desire to lose one of his new ones.

Izuku was far more experienced in these matters. He knew right away that it wasn't her; the after-death burst was far too small. That was one of his own Embracers, though he had a hard time telling who it was. They were all so young and fresh to him it was difficult telling one from another.

He looked around quickly, eager to find Aryu and continue this fight now that he was beginning to feel some kind of upper hand in it. When he did find him a third of the way around the new hole, he found him peering down into the gap as the dust settled. It was a perfect opportunity to strike while he was distracted. Before he had the chance, he too found himself taking a quick look into the hole, and was suddenly taken aback at what he saw there.

The hole was far larger than in should have been, and instead of hard rock and dirt, there were boxes and man-made objects. It took them both a moment, and then almost simultaneously they realized the hapless Embracer had been blown through the ground and into the warehouse-space below. Aryu then saw it at once for the room he was just in. He could recall the room having a very solid surrounding, with heavy bricks and metal lining the roof. Now, with the body of the Embracer dissolved into thin air (*Why didn't Sho do that?* he thought) all that was let was the twisted wreckage of the roof collapsing, making the hole below them fall away almost twenty feet down, like a vortex of dirt and broken cement.

Izuku saw in the distance the floating form of Crystal across the park with a carnival of colors dancing around her, lighting her up on all sides in a vain attempt to break through her defenses. She had made it to the city, and she had brought all of the remaining Embracers with her. Izuku made another quick glance into the hole at his feet, making sure the Adaptive H.Y. was still very much off-line. He saw it knocked off its platform and covered in debris, intact and inoperative in the failing shadows of the side of the room.

Well, now he had them both to deal with, as she was apparently not having many issues with his unstoppable E-Force.

The sudden image of Crystal and her current predicament distracted him just enough to let Aryu get in a sneak attack of his own now, with the winged avenger dashing across the gap with an amazing push from his wings. Izuku blocked just in time, dodging away from the blades of the shield as he moved. Damn it! He had to get back into the rhythm quickly or it was all for nothing.

He ran to the far side of the hole, heading straight for the collection of remaining Embracers. With his keen ears he could hear the strong wings of Aryu beat as he moved to follow, but even aided by those awesome appendages he couldn't keep up with the inhuman robotic speed of Izuku. Izuku's newest plan, one hatched only moments before, was suddenly in full swing.

All Aryu knew was that he had Izuku on the run, and he was apparently trying to regroup with his cronies.

Had Aryu trained as long as Izuku had, he'd know that wasn't the truth. Izuku was far more likely to just write off his Embracers and let them fight their own battles. It was a trap that Aryu fell right into.

Just as Crystal came into better focus, Izuku waited until her back was turned to him, and then launched a huge pulse of Power at her like a giant bullet. As near as Aryu could tell, his intention was to take her out himself. Blinded with panic he watched as the pulse rose and sped towards her. He had a sudden idea to throw the Shi Kaze or the shield to destroy it, but even now he could see that it was too fast. He would never catch it in time.

He watched as it got closer to her, her back still turned to them both. He tried to scream, but before he could even make a noise, the pulse hit Crystal square in the back.

Nothing happened. The shot simply broke over her like water over a bell jar.

Fear hit as he put it together, but a moment too late. Izuku never wanted to hit her with a full blast! He just wanted to scare Aryu and use his feelings towards Crystal to distract him.

The blow came fast. Izuku opted for the far more physically painful strike to the side of Aryu's face with his hard metal fist.

Aryu was airborne in an instant, flailing away like a rag doll before he even knew what was going on. He was in a new world of pain as he felt the good side of his face cave in like pudding with the hit. By the time he stopped twirling away and crashed into the twisted fallen body of a Herald, Izuku was on him again.

But once more he turned down the obvious chance to finish Aryu for the far more torturous attack of a forceful kick with his artificial foot. Aryu was blown backwards as his ribs cracked and broke like popcorn. He could taste blood very clearly by the time he stopped, and it became very hard to breathe.In just two simple moves he had gone from champion to fool. He had been foolish once more in thinking he understood what kind of thing it was he faced.

He still held his precious weapons tightly. That was something. Not that he thought he could even raise either of them in his current state, and both of his eyes were going blurry with either tears or blood, he couldn't tell which. Neither would have surprised him.

Now he felt Izuku standing over him like a vulture about to devour a carcass, and a new wave of anger and strength filled Aryu from places he didn't know he had. He was amazingly up on his feet again, looking around through the haze for the dark shadow of his enemy, but he was too late. "Oh no you don't, boy," he heard from behind him. "How you're even standing is a miracle to me, but also not surprising, knowing what I know about you and your kind."

He turned quickly, dizzying himself with the action, but before the blade of the Shi Kaze made contact, his arm was stopped dead by the cold tight fist of Izuku clamping around his wrist. He could almost hear the smile on Izuku's face as he squeezed, crushing his bones, forcing many of them to shatter and suddenly jut horribly from his broken skin, and then before he knew what was happening, a sharp knee thrust into the back of his arm, bending it around in a blaze of pain. No matter how hard he tried now, despite all of the effort in his considerably brave body, he could simply no longer hold the Shi Kaze with a crushed wrist and broken arm, and he was flooded with sadness as he felt it slip from his fingers. When he heard it hit the ground with a soft thud, all hope was suddenly in a rush to leave him. Without the Shi Kaze, how was he to stand against the Est Vacuus?

He never had a chance to think about it. As he felt the dark wind rush around him, he knew it was Izuku going in to end it all for him now that he had dropped the sword and could no longer see well enough to attack with the shield.

A sudden sigh left his lips as he abandoned all hope and waited for the Est Vacuus to take him.

It didn't. Before he could understand why, Izuku gave a heavy grunt and Aryu heard the gears, servos and hydraulics that made up the inhuman parts of his body fire to life in one movement.

That movement was as clean and powerful an upward punch to Aryu's gut as Izuku could manage. Aryu's body folded over the motion like paper, and for one brief moment the two of them were frozen, with Izuku's dark robotic arm buried in the depths of Aryu's caved-over body. Then, as if shot from a cannon and with the loud 'clang' of metal meeting metal, Aryu was airborne, spraying a vapor trail of blood and vomit behind him as he went and the last good breath of air was forced from his lungs.

Crystal turned and watched in horror as a twisted and broken

Aryu was catapulted into the air, his wings trailing behind him and the Shi Kaze nowhere to be seen. He arched upwards in a sick ballet, his face red and body limp. He flew across the sky like a perfect rainbow and finally peaked, giving him the appearance of almost floating. It was a moment in time that almost froze for every living thing watching this shocking and sickening display.

Then time rushed forwards as it should, almost needing to catch up with the moments it had somehow realized it had just lost. Aryu, barely conscious, felt the familiar rush of air past his ears, and he was suddenly back home in the Valley of Smoke, falling away like a rock from the heights of Tortria Den as if this whole ordeal had never happened.

The blissful dream vanished instantly as the baffling image of a broken ring surrounded him as he fell. Then, with a crash not unlike the one that had proceeded him into this space, Aryu slammed into the floor of the warehouse space beneath Gracious Park, having been sent flying up, over, and then into its waiting maw.

Pain wracked his body like a blanket as every part of him was likely broken. He forced open his eyes and took one last look at the sky above. "Please let my brother escape," he said to no one but himself, and even then it was just a garble of sounds through the blood. At last, blissfully, he was out. All while Crystal screamed at the top of her lungs as if the Est Vacuus had taken her once more, before she continued her fresh and renewed onslaught against the Embracers.

Izuku stood at the top of the broken circle looking down at the glorious thing he'd done, the blades of the Est Vacuus and now the Shi Kaze clenched firmly in his hands.

Crystal could only watch as a wingless Izuku leapt into the hole after him, both weapons pointing downward as he moved. The memory of Sho consumed her anew, but this was not the time or place to lose her cool. She prayed secretly to the Heavens, to her lover, to her father, to her son, and even to her long-forgotten mother, as well as anyone else that would listen to her. She couldn't lose Aryu as well. She just couldn't. So much was riding on him. So much work for nothing if he died.

It had been far too long since this weapon had been in his hand for purposes of a malicious nature, and it saddened him to realize that it simply no longer felt as right as it once had. The Shi Kaze had no more place in the hands of Tokugawa Izuku.Compounding this fact was the war raging in his mind at the very moment he picked it up. A war between the Everything and the Nothing, using his body and spirit as a conduit to wage their battle. Were it not for his considerable power, it likely would have torn him in two.

He paused over the unconscious body of Aryu. The young man's limbs and wings were spread out around him. His red and beaten face swelled around the eyes that were staring at the blue sky above them. Little remained of the room except slivers of boxes and bags that were torn apart.The only indicator that Aryu was even alive was his breathing, but that was raspy and extremely shallow. He was certainly not long for this world.

It was a shame considering how much he liked Aryu. It was weird to say that now, but Aryu represented a time from the past that likely would never come again. A time when Izuku believed Aryu's kind were destined to be the true saviors of this world if they ever came out of hiding. This was the main reason Izuku, when finding himself in need of a new body thanks to his brother, chose one so similar to Aryu's. Partly tribute, and partly because he believed that *he* was going to be the savior the world needed, so he may as well look the part. It was that form that would allow him access to the world's secrets.

Now, as Aryu lay dying at his feet, his youthful and strong body a twisted wreck, Izuku was only filled with loathing and shame at himself for not stopping him sooner. He was angry at his fear of the Shi Kaze for helping Aryu get this far.He watched as Aryu's eyelids began to flutter, a common occurrence when the electrical impulses that ruled the body went into a state of chaotic flux once they were overloaded. Izuku knew that it was Aryu's body being overrun with pain on levels he'd never felt before.

Izuku also knew it was something the brain did just before it stopped working. "Oh no, Aryu," he said in a soft whisper. "Not yet.

Soon, but not yet."

Izuku knew what to do, and although his command of the Power likely could save Aryu, he didn't want waste a drop on him. Truthfully he didn't want to save him at all. What he wanted was to know just how powerful both the Shi Kaze and a spirit like Aryu's could be. If he got to look into the defiant eyes of this infuriating child before he cast him into the endless void of the Est Vacuus, then all the better. Izuku was an intellectual. He prided himself on always learning.

With a strong thrust he pulled the Shi Kaze above his head. Sunlight danced off its perfect edge for just a moment, before bringing it down and driving it straight through the quivering Makashi armor and directly through the chest of Aryu. It slid right below his heart, out his back, and into the hard concrete floor beyond until only a hands-width of blade remained jutting from Aryu's chest.

Now all he had to do was wait. Death was nearby, and his curiosity was about to be absolved.

Evil in Ways Evil Should Never Be

Death is an odd thing. That is to say, the *entity* of death, not the action. The action is straightforward: life is terminated, life is dead. 'Death' was really more of a title for that who is also known as The Grim Reaper, The Taker of Souls, The Man at the End of the Path, etc. A title that had changed hands many times. With each new iteration there is a thousand lifetimes of knowledge that flows from one titleholder, hosts called 'Deathmores', to the next. In essence, Death is not the thing that holds the title as much as it is the accumulation of the memories that the bearer of the title has acquired and passed on to the next. Different situations call for different ways for the bearer to act, hence the constant change in the ones employed to do it, but the tasks and duties of the post tend to fall on these memories as a collective. For a very long time, a new Deathmore was selected every few days, depending on what was required.

This Death, however, had held the title for centuries. It was his and his alone, now. No new Deathmores followed. Deep within him was the amalgamation of thousands of previous Deaths. He was Death's end-all/be-all.

It is in these accumulated memories that Death found himself digging for any point of reference with what to do about the situation it's found itself in during the last few days. This Death was once human, one of a very select few Deaths that had been, and it had a particular emotional connection to everything humans do.

In these memories, it at last found itself a point of reference to aid it, but it didn't like what it found. The last time it was so difficult was *that* time. A time it had first-hand knowledge about. Had it truly been Death during the worst catastrophe the universe and the balance he serves had ever seen?

It recalled the time when Tokugawa Ryu, the False God, was

resurrected, and went on a one-man rampage against Death's logical solution to a galactic problem. Death couldn't let him die! But Ryu didn't see it that way, and then mistakes were made. Death wasn't eager to make those mistakes again.

The last few days had seen an abnormal amount of Embracers of the Power find their end. One, maybe two could be handled, but the last three days had numbers quickly approaching double digits, one of which was the awesome power of Tokugawa Sho, a figure who could keep Death busy for a very long time just on his own. As it was, Death had to put the reclamation of his body on hold, praying a more suitable time to take it would come up.

Death's primary role was to take the accumulated life force of a dying creature and redistribute it accordingly throughout the universe. Death was no more than a maintainer of the balance of all things within the Omnis. Although "civilized" societies through history had feared it and canonized it as dark and sinister being, the truth was that it was little more than a caretaker, created by the Omnis out of necessity to keep the worlds at an even keel.

Once an Embracer died, their life-forces were so far beyond normal that they required special attention in redistribution, or else all of that collective Power would scatter erratically, sending this world and millions of others into states of uneven disarray. Just like *that* time.

Anything that even came close in similarity always made Death think back to that time. In these memories it found the two best ways Death as an entity had discovered to cope with the added workload: complain endlessly and just do its job.

***

At first Aryu thought he was dead, although the feelings he was wrapped in seemed to negate every theory he'd ever heard about the afterlife. There certainly was pain, and it was everywhere.

As his mind began putting the pieces together, he realized it wasn't death he was feeling but life, horrible, painful and unwelcoming life. By some divine joke, he had lived through Izuku's attacks and was now awake once more, forced to feel the life slip out from his body.

His face was crushed. His jaw was pulverized beyond usefulness. He couldn't move his arms. His right one was broken at the wrist and elbow by Izuku and the other was apparently crushed with his landing, still strapped to the bladed shield and unable to move. His legs were bent at grotesque angles, crossing over each other with fractured bones straining to escape from beneath his skin.

His wings, now pinned below him, seemed to be the only parts of his body that came through this all right. Of course. The one part of him he hated the most was the one that was hardest to destroy.But now he realized that his eyes were clear; the blood gone. The sunlight blinded him temporarily until he could focus anew. What he saw simply caused more panic.

There jutting from his chest was what little remained of the great Shi Kaze. Although unable to move, he could only assume where the rest of it was.

Laugher from his left side. A soft sound he knew at once. He found himself not caring, though. Not after all of this. Let him laugh. For Aryu it was over.

"Confused?" the irritating voice asked. *Not really,* thought Aryu. "I admit I was curious how this would go. Would you die, or would you live by some stupid joke just by having my father's sword run through you. Since you're alive, I wouldn't take it as a sign of your strength. It appears that the power within the Shi Kaze has given you this ever-so-brief reprieve. You will still die, but slower than you'd like. I promise."

Izuku stepped into Aryu's field of view, blocking out the sun above him. "That is, of course, if you *were* going to die. You're not, though. Not the way you'd wish, anyway. My experiment is over."

He pulled around the vacant space in his hands that resembled a sword and held it out for Aryu to see. As if cutting through the pain, the Est Vacuus and its great emptiness poured into his memory again, though not as it had before. It was a steady echo, not a screaming invitation to oblivion. "The Shi Kaze again, my young friend," Izuku told him, reading his mind like a book. "Just because it's impaled through your chest and not clenched in your hand doesn't make it any less powerful. As long as you're touching it, you are given this temporary salvation from the Est Vacuus. That is, until I yank that weapon from your chest to cast you directly into the void. I want you to think about what it will be like inside the great emptiness. Whatever you think it will be, it will be infinitely worse."

The realization that Izuku was telling the truth sent a panic through Aryu. He had no desire to remain in this crippled state, but he'd take it for a thousand years before having to spend one second in that place. The worst things he could imagine and remember about the Est Vacuus paled to the truth of what it was.

Aryu knew that even when Izuku pulled the Shi Kaze out, he could never move away. He was too broken. Izuku had him and there was nothing he could do about it.

His body shook with horrible anticipation, and in doing so he felt his least damaged arm quiver with life, not as broken and fractured as he'd have believed. With a modicum of assistance and a lot of inner strength, he could likely move it.

That was it. It hit him.

In just that one moment the world became clear. He embraced this clarity. A sudden, terrifying flare of an idea lit his brain. If his spark of an idea worked, he may be able to go out doing something good. With no options left, he embraced the idea.

Aryu knew what he had to do.

The consequences of succeeding were almost as bad as failing. No matter what, Aryu, and likely everyone left in the world worth caring about, was going to die. Was that really the best option?

The best option, he realized, was doing what he was trying to do all along. If he succeeded in this at all, he prayed that his friend would see that. If there was an afterlife he could meet him in, he hoped the option of dying by his hand and getting revenge was better than dying somewhere else down the line by Izuku's hand and losing everything for nothing.

Izuku saw the quaking in Aryu's body, and then saw Aryu's eyes as he braced himself. "I see your pain and panic, Aryu, and I admit although I'm generally above such feelings, I love it all the same. Enjoy your brief stay in the glory and majesty that is the Est

Vacuus. Rot in the Hell you deserve for daring stand against my will. I am Tokugawa Izuku, and this reality is mine." With his beloved otherworldly sword poised to strike above his head, Izuku reached down and grasped the handle of the Shi Kaze.

Then he pulled, and the moment he saw that it was in motion, Aryu tried his final card.

The loving memory of Johan, Sho, Crystal, his parents, and others he could recall from his village, for good or ill, etched themselves into his mind. All smiling. All laughing. All happy. Just as Aryu hoped they would be when this was all over, in this life or the next.

He never thought of Nixon, though. If (and what a big 'if' that was) this went according to plan, that was a face he may see again very soon.

As Izuku continued to pull back, Aryu took as deep and ragged a breath as his crushed torso could muster, and heaved his pained and shattered arm up to meet it, actually clasping the blade as it came free from his body, startling Izuku with his foolish tenacity while meeting his/ Aryu painfully squeezed the beyond-razor-sharp edge. For a brief moment, the air hung still around them as Izuku stared at Aryu's bloodied and swollen eyes, shocked at the movement, and was terrified of what he saw there.

"For Tan Torna Qu'ay," Aryu said, as clear and as powerfully as he could muster. In his thousands of years of life, on any side of what was perceived to be right and wrong, Izuku had never heard or felt such power and conviction in spoken words.

It was dooming himself to death, but a noble death as far as he was concerned. A noble death was far more appetizing than a moment spent in the Est Vacuus. The pain of this death having to take the lives of so many innocent people, his best friend included, was the only thing that clouded Aryu's mind before the clarity hit him. The undeniable peace of mind one got when they tapped the Power and its majesty.

Just like the time before on the plane with the robotic soldier gripping his wing and threatening to haul him into the vast expanse of the ocean below, Aryu saw the truth of what the Power was, and that realization shielded him from even the horror of the Est Vacuus. In an instant, his mind was clear and his actions solidified.

Unlike then, this time it was not an ever-moving spiral of air particles that he was channeling, but the constant field of moving protons and electrons that made up the huge field of the electromagnetic spectrum around them all. He had no idea exactly what it was, but he knew that in these base elements were the means to do what it was he was attempting.

In an un-measurable period of time he was channeling his focus back through the blade in his hand, the pain gone from every part of him but his heart, and that wasn't enough to stop him. He could feel every moving iota of life around him, and he found he could manipulate it all just as if he was still in his body and pouring a glass of milk. Just reach, tip and pour. It was so simple.

He reached. Mentally he found what he sought: the terrifying orb across the room.

He tipped. Finding the sub-atomic base matter of the thing's advanced control system, looking for the machine itself to tell him what it was Izuku had done and reverse it. Success

He poured. His new-found focus hit the non-existent switches within the bomb's controls, finding the right one every time as if guided by fate. The positives and negatives.The ones and zeroes.

Then, he poured again, this time hitting another.

And again.

And again.

Repeating these steps and connecting that which Izuku had disconnected, until at last, after what had to be millions of tiny electronic switches were thrown, he felt the Power start to flow away on its own, and a chill calm fell over him as he realized that he had succeeded in his task. The Power had guided his hand as he knew it would. The Omnis wanted the balance. The Power was its tool to that end. Damnable fate would win the day.

With one last pull, he focused himself through the Shi Kaze once more and pulled his mind home again. He returned to the battered and crippled form which was now no longer pinned to the floor. During his ride along the infinitesimal, a trip that in his mind could have taken seconds or centuries, Izuku had only now finished pulling out the blade, trying to determine why it was that Aryu had grabbed it so foolishly.

As Aryu moved, Izuku felt it surround him, raw and untamed but unmistakable.

The Power! Not from Crystal of Nixon or any one of his own loyal Embracers. This was fresh and new.Gods be damned, it was Aryu! Why? How? What had Aryu done? When had he learned to do this?

Then, he heard the 'beep' from his right and realized what it was. What foolish thing Aryu had done with that brief and barely controlled use of the Power.

"Resuming Countdown," the screen said, now tilted more toward the ground after it had rolled off the platform. "7."

Confusion exploded in Izuku's mind. How had he done that? When had he learned? So flabbergasted by this new development was Izuku that he never finished his downward stroke with the Est Vacuus. He only stared at the bomb in disbelief. The immortal had actually been surprised.

Aryu had found himself focusing the Power inward as if it was first nature, using its soft and all-encompassing hands to cradle him from the pain that was everywhere. He rose up, broken legs protesting but muffled to silence and held in place behind a buffer of the Power like a cosmic bandage. Aryu rode it like a wave, using his inexperience to just throw giant plumes of Power around himself as opposed to focusing it to do what he wanted. It could very easily flow through his body and fix his wounds in an instant, but that was a level of control he didn't have. The bomb activation was simple. The human body was not. For now, using the Power to pull him around like a marionette was enough to get the job done.

Izuku was still watching the bomb, trying to focus himself to undo whatever it was Aryu had done. The panic of what had just happened clouded his perfectly trained mind until he had no hope of grasping the Power around him and reversing the process. He could only watch as the screen showed "6." He didn't see Aryu rise up like a grotesque puppet in front of him, his brother's shield still strapped to a mangled left arm, making Aryu tilt slightly.

Using the Power to push his limb, Aryu traced his hand up the blade of the Shi Kaze, careful not to let his contact slip, and retook his weapon, catching Izuku completely off-guard as he did so. Izuku had just begun turning his head to Aryu when Aryu reached out again with his shielded arm and snatched the handle of the Est Vacuus sword, pulling the weapon around and wrenching it from Izuku's flesh hand like a parent taking a dangerous toy from a child.

"5"

Aryu's clarity faltered, as if his hands were gripping two live wires and were shooting volts of pure energy through him, neither of them relenting.

At last he thrust out the arm with the non-existent blade and drove it through Izuku's confused and terrified face. It was the greatest feeling he'd ever known; that of releasing the handle, knowing he never had to touch it or feel that Gods-forsaken emptiness again. Only the memory remained, and that was something he could cope with.

"4"

Izuku fell backwards with this new action as the screen read "3" and out of Aryu's way. Knowing it was time to try his best to escape, he focused the Power through his regained sword and watched as the world below him suddenly fell away at speeds he'd never dreamed possible. He refused to die at the hands of a technological nightmare. He may have doomed his best friend to that fate, but that was his burden. They weren't both going to die that way. Someone from Tan Torna Qu'ay was going to die by the hand of something far more honorable, even if he didn't deserve it.

Away he traveled, faster and faster, using the Power to push and pull him away from Bankoor like a rocket. Some Embracers of the Power lived for thousands of years and never came close to mastering the kind of travel Aryu was zipping away in, but where they were aged and experienced, Aryu was raw and ignorant. That was how the Power worked. Aryu needed it to ride on and carry him away from the coming destruction as fast as he possibly could, so that's exactly what the Power did.

Far behind him Aryu felt the power of destruction rise up. He refused to look back. His soul could feel it, amplified by the Power itself. The feeling of helpless sadness encased him as the fireball grew behind him, illuminating the clouds in all directions. Tears filled his bloodied eyes, and it hurt to cry.

Behind him, the great city of Bankoor erupted in a wall of fire and devastation the world had not seen in centuries. In a pillar of controlled flames everything it touched, Embracers and all, were wiped out without a second thought.

Despite the sadness, in the back of his mind, Aryu also felt the exhilarating mix of a million emotions, and it was the positive ones he chose to latch on to. Those of a successful revenge, of great satisfaction at what Izuku was likely going through this very moment encased in a combination of the power of the blast and the void of the Est Vacuus, the pride in what it was he had done, and indeed was still doing, and at last and certainly the strongest, the pleasure in knowing that even though one of them was his friend once, he had just wiped out every hint of the unnatural technology as well as every Embracer of the Power in this part of the world. All of their kind was not welcome here anymore. Not to Aryu, at least. Embracers and machines were now lost to the fire.

After all that had happened, Aryu had at last succeeded. Now, all he had to do was wait for the phoenix to come and finish the job as he promised he would. *After all of this,* Aryu thought, *I welcome it.*

***

The blast that consumed the city of Bankoor and the surrounding area was unfathomably large. Fueled by the knife at its core and the setting that had it reach out as far as possible in every direction, the Adaptive H.Y. bomb fulfilled its purpose perfectly, sparing nothing in its wake.

Unlike standard H.Y. explosions, this one spread along the ground first as an infinitesimally small, chaotic event that shot out like a ring only micrometers from the ground, cutting through everything on an even path with the weapon. Solid ground, buildings, trees, anything it could reach was instantly encompassed and affected. Vehicle tires popped, buildings teetering on the edge gave way for a brief instant, even some of the people attempting to escape in the north of the city were overcome with a sudden sharp pain wherever it was this sub-atomic particle ring reached out.

There was a brief moment when the world went silent, almost exactly one full second after the bomb's timer reached '0'. Then, it started.

The explosion erupted up from the ground in a red and orange rush. It pushed out all air around it, creating a pressure wave many times more powerful than the ones the Army of the Old had been creating with their weaker devises in places like Tan Torna Qu'ay.

People who were far enough away, including the very wounded and very lucky August Stroan, who had made his escape and fled north before the pincers of the enemy closed tightly behind him, saw the blast and were shocked and terrified at the scene they were witness to. Even as far away as most of them were, the ripple of the air around them and the heavy winds that followed when the concussion wave blew past was enough to bring many to their knees and snap strong limbs off of the old trees that surrounded them. Carts and transports flew like paper. Buildings in feeder cities not far from Bankoor fell apart or were blown inwards. This wave of sound and air alone was the cause of almost seven thousand deaths.

They were still the lucky ones.

Within the city or traveling the roads north were the last remaining transports, with thousands aboard moving away as quickly as they could. Had the blast been contained as the original plan stated, then the majority of them would have lived.

But the fire rose up from their feet, devouring every inch of them as it moved. The action happened so quickly that they each had the terrible and shocking sensation of being consumed by fire until nothing but their heads remained. It was a quick and painful death that none of them expected or deserved. Many of them were left only because they had remained behind to help all of the others. Their heroism was only met with the loss of their life.

Far to the eastern outskirts of the city, a small cart was upended and thrown through the sky into a collection of trees in the distance moments before the trees themselves were uprooted and thrown away. The cart, containing two young men and one old politician, was swallowed up in the chaos. Still, each of them was still lucky they'd made out of the blast radius in time.

The Heaven-bound blast hit the closest shores of the Blood Sea as well, vaporizing the water instantly. More water rushed toward the blast, trying in vain to quench what fire it could, but it failed and was repulsed by the power of the blast. Only after the eventual dispersal of the flames when the explosion had run its course did the water rush in once more, steam and dirt flying around the sky as it did so, causing a hazy fog to settle over the scorched land and massive waves to travel across the sea. Yet more lives were lost to the tsunami created.

The last vestige of mankind's vain glory was the peak of the Spire of Bankoor, which fell just as easily as a snowflake in a raging campfire.

After thirty seconds of uncontrolled fury, the pillar of fire dispersed, leaving only a black glass circle where once had been the great city of Bankoor.

***

Unlike Death, who worked in shadows and arrived late to every party, Nixon of the Great Fire and Ash was at the forefront of every major struggle the world had ever seen since the idea of the Power had become something more than an abstract concept of ancient philosophers.

He was born from the Omnis much like Death, though by the hand of one specific entity who represented it. Nixon took his role of maintainer of the balance very seriously. Nixon came in when things had gone too far, and Death cleaned up the aftermath. They were two simple cogs in the gears of the Omnis.

Now these two cogs were wrapped up in their own baffling struggles. While Death was busy trying to sort out the damage caused recently, Nixon was trying his damnedest to rid the world of one Elutherios Duo. Like Death, he was having little luck and making no discernible headway, and was swearing considerably. A part of him was still completely enthralled to have such an amazing and worthwhile challenge set before him. As the fight carried on, he realized more and more that he would never have a fight like this again, and although he knew he needed to win and carry on, he also was saddened by the thought that it would never be better than this.

He also knew that stopping this thing wasn't enough. He had to destroy it.

It was such an unnatural thing that leaving it was simply not an option. If a typical human with an open mind and closed heart were to look at it the voices alone would likely drive them mad. 'Elutherios' indeed. The liberation of the mind and body through madness.

He knew Crystal had led the other Embracers toward the city, leaving only Nixon and the machine to finish their epic battle. How long had she been gone? Or Aryu for that matter? Damn it, why couldn't he just get an upper hand! Elutherios had matched him move for move. When Nixon flew backwards to create space, it was there with him as he went. When Nixon charged and attacked with all of the power he could muster, it either blocked him or moved and began an attack of its own to counter him. The strength of each of them was perfectly matched, Nixon by his God-given might and Elutherios by the advanced techniques and materials that crafted it, as unnatural as they were.

Nixon was growing tired once more, and had more than one physical wound to show for this battle. The sword the machine used could deal its fair share of damage to Nixon, and although Elutherios hadn't escaped Nixon's advances either, Nixon had to judge that he was the worse for wear of the two. Not a promising thought.

So wrapped up in this battle was Nixon that all thoughts of his purpose were wiped away. No longer did he feel the hunger to follow Aryu and kill him. No longer did he drive himself to find the answers he sought. No longer did he yearn for his rest. All there was in his heart was this fight, and what a fight it was. It was a fight that gave a warrior purpose.

So when at last all the answers he was looking for all this time came to him in a rush, it nearly knocked Nixon out with shock.

Elutherios was on the offensive, using its powerful sword and manufactured strength to push Nixon backwards into a pocket of overturned transports and non-functioning leftover robotic soldiers. The machine was attempting to cut off his routes of escape. This was a common practice for it, having tried it two or three times before. Although the technique wasn't likely to end up killing Nixon, it did give Elutherios a distinct advantage and likely a chance at another hard and damaging hit. The machine wasn't running a sprint to finish off the phoenix, but a marathon. Soon, with its limitless power, it would simply wear him down.

As it moved Nixon backwards, everything changed for the fire-demon.

Even during attack after attack, a deep and unmoving part of his mind stayed forever linked, knowingly or not, to his Divine and ultimate purpose. He thrust back at the machine, taking it back a half step, when this innocuous and forever vibrating part of his being erupted with a force so deep it startled the phoenix with its intensity. In an instant it all came together, and the fear of all the truths hitting him at once threw his mind into a haze. Even a creature such as Nixon couldn't handle this kind of sensory overload.

His eyes erupted crimson like fireworks and his wings formed as if from nowhere. Elutherios could only watch as Nixon was aloft with a speed it had not seen yet, and an ethereal-power output that gave Elutherios only the briefest of pauses before it decided to give chase as it attempted to evaluate what it was just witness to. That pause would end up saving its non-life.

Nixon was in the air, flaming sword at the ready, rocketing towards the city with a speed he'd never known he possessed. He felt the Power clear as day now. He felt it push him forward to his target with noble purpose, a target he never would have believed until this very moment. His wings weren't even flapping; only the Power drove him forward, just as it was apparently driving his target away.

This time he would not hesitate. This time he had to finish the job.

Elutherios, RAMjets and all, was airborne behind him but had no chance at keeping up. Confusion about many things overtook it. How did Nixon get so fast? Where did this newfound power come from? Why was he running? It was so uncharacteristic.

Having been built for close-quarters combat, Elutherios Duo possessed none of the advanced weapons his distant military cousins did. Not that they'd have done much good anyway. Bullets traveled too slowly at this speed and energy weapons would be useless breaking through the renewed outer shield of fire Nixon now wore, brighter and hotter than it had ever been. For now, E2-0901 could only give chase.

With the southern edge of the city approaching quickly, Nixon was nothing more than a red lightning streak across the sky, followed by a slightly slower black missile.

Elutherios detected the coming storm almost instantly, or at least, as quickly as a device like it could process the electronic signal it had just received. Were it not for the brief pause in surprise when Nixon lifted off, it never would have seen it coming in time and would have been wiped away like everything else. It stopped as if it hit a brick wall and fell back as fast as it possibly could.

Nixon was given no such warning. Only the hunt mattered, and that was all he knew. That, and unbelievable anger and rage, both at the target and himself. God, why did he have to do it? And why was Nixon so *blind*!

It was this distraction that stole away his attention from what was going on below him, and by the time his eyes saw it, it was too late.

The wave of fire erupted all around him in a perfect circle. He was right in the heart of it, and even at top speed he had no chance of escape once he realized the blast was coming at him. He could barely slow down before the first of the plumes of fire reached him, searing his wings like brittle paper and tossing him backwards in pain.

Once before, when he laughed at the foolishness of his enemy only to be taken by surprise at their power, had he felt something like this.

This one overtook him right down to his soul, more intense and volatile then he'd have thought possible. He fell backwards, unable to maintain his bodily shield or wings as the upward force of this new blast enveloped him. He felt his skin burn as the flames wiped away his paltry onyx armor.His hair was vaporized, as well as his eyes which were burned out of his skull. Soon the great and powerful muscle tissue was exposed to the heat and charred itself away.Nixon tried to scream, both in anger and defeat, but the fire only swarmed his mouth, pouring down his throat, and roasted his innards without mercy.

Being a phoenix, Nixon had never known what being truly burned was. His faith in God and His creation never gave him reason to believe it was possible. Who could create a more powerful and incendiary fire than God? Then he had met the small drone that had brought the first explosion with it, vaporizing him, but not so badly that he couldn't reform himself. This was much worse, though. This was terrifying.

His iron grip released his sword into the sky as he hurled it with every bit of strength he had left in a desperate attempt to save the weapon from the fate he was suffering, and he could only reflect on the moments that had brought him to this end. How blind he'd been. How hypocritical. How stupid.

As the waves of flames overtook the last particles of his being, Nixon had time for a single thought: the steeled and toothless face of the old man at the bar who had begun this whole thing, and the futile and worthless final prayer that followed.

God.Please, forgive me.

***

Crystal would have never believed it was possible to get hurt in her current state, but pain was exactly what she was feeling now. The physical pain was tolerable, though. It was the emotional pain that hurt the most.

She had been deep in the battle with the Embracers when she felt the new arrival of Aryu's Power. Then, she realized what he'd done.

She rushed away, taking more than one blast from the Embracers below as she went. Ignorant to why she was running, they simply thought they had scared her off and were about to celebrate their victory and find Izuku when the explosion hit, instantly and permanently ending any other thoughts they were ever to have.Like popping light bulbs, each of them was instantly destroyed, their built-up Power exploding outward in sudden rushes while their bodies were obliterated.

Crystal was still only a hair's-width from that fate herself, and as she moved out over the expanse of the Blood Sea the tail end of the blast hit her, filling her with an unexpected rush of familiarity before the outer edge of the explosion reached out and broke down her Power-fueled escape.Having missed the heart of the blast, she was still hit with sudden feeling of pain, followed by the pressure blast tossing her away into the sea, knocking her into the distance with a splash. It took all of her considerable Power to stop the blast from simply liquefying her.

She crashed into the water like a bullet, and by the time she had made it back to the surface the salty water around her was dark with blood. Her body covered in painful burns and wounds. Still, she was alive, and once the shock of what had just happened wore off she had all the faith in the world that she could fix these ailments. Her heart wasn't likely to be fixed any time soon. She realized what had happened. As much as it pained her to admit it, what had just occurred was so much worse than just losing her only remaining child.

She knew what Aryu had done, and it was so unexpected that she had no words.

Her white and damaged skin burned as she floated on the surface, watching the huge wall of fire beyond climb higher and higher until it was past her vision. It took on the appearance of the finger of the Devil himself bursting from the ground below to strike at the Heavens. If she was right about what fueled that blast, the Devil may just succeed.

As the fire licked at her heels and blew her backwards, she could taste the Power that aided it. It was a Power she knew very well. It was a Power she feared more than any other.

The Power she felt was her own, though how that could be was still a mystery.

She pondered that and many other things as she floated. Soon, a massive rush of waves tossed her around as the untouched parts of the Blood Sea rushed forward to refill the void left by the parts that had been blasted away once the explosion ceased.

Crystal simply recovered and resumed her floating. Once the air became still again and the clouds returned after being so forcefully pushed away, Crystal took a brief moment to gaze up at the hazy blue sky before collecting herself, stopping her seemingly-endless tears and beginning the process of trying to heal.

Only herself, though. Healing the world now, after all of this, was impossible.

Swimming in a sea of both water and guilt, she once more rose up, mended her extremely painful wounds like a surgeon with the Power, and set out back to where the city of Bankoor once stood.

What good was causing this much unbridled chaos if you never took the time to look over your own handiwork?

***

There was suffering aplenty when the explosion peaked. Bodies were vaporized. Lives were snuffed out instantly. The world changed in an instant. And although this was not to be the fifth (or final) Fall of Man Izuku intended it to be, it was still devastating on more levels than many grasped.

But this was all just useless noise to Izuku Tokugawa. The words have not been written that could describe the torment he was suffering as his head reeled in the depths of the Est Vacuus, pulled inwards instantly when Aryu had driven his beloved weapon into his face so mercilessly, all while what remained of his body, both flesh and robotic, were vaporized within the power of the blast he sat in the epicenter of.

There was no rational thought. There was only crippling incineration, coupled with hollow nothingness.

The two sensations were incapacitating. Only briefly, when the moments before he lost his rational thought occurred, did Izuku instantly believe he'd been wrong. He never should have fooled with the Omnis and the Est Vacuus as he did. His father, Gods damn him, was right. Any man, even an Embracer as powerful as himself, simply paled in comparison to each of these levels of the universe and beyond that he was now privy to.

Then, half in one world and half in no world at all, Izuku lost all control, all Power, all hope.

The Nothing and the Everything fought one last battle inside of him, and then, along with the ethereal blade that had started it all, Izuku was gone, with both a soft whimper of nothing, and an ear-shattering 'pop', depending on what plane of existence you were on to see it.

***

Death sighed. Another rush of Embracers and now Izuku Tokugawa as well? It seemed it was going to be one of those days. This may be more than it could handle, and now all it wanted was a decent cup of coffee.

Chapter 14: Faith

They had left Aryu's company and once more descended back into the darkness. When they had reached the bottom, Johan was beside himself with all that had just happened, and even in their rush to escape he grinned happily. Aryu was alive. Aryu was fighting a robotic monster. And apparently, Aryu had become a complete badass.

That was still all secondary to getting them out of here. At the bottom of the lift Auron pressed the buttons on a screen against the wall. The controls had remained silent, but soon there was a flicker of life, followed by the screen illuminating completely. The surface of it was an almost exact duplicate of the portable version that was now smashed above them.

It still had the stupid '30 Second Non-Stop BOOM Clock' icon, but that now had a red cross through it. Johan knew that meant little in this world. Anything can and likely would happen very quickly.

As he scanned the other icons, Auron found the one marked 'TRANSPORT CONTROLS'. Pressing it brought up a list of options. Most of them were useless commands that were supposed to take them to various parts of the city.One of them, highlighted in green, read 'ESCAPE ACTIVATION'. "You son of a bitch," said Johan over his shoulder. "You had a fucking plan all along." Auron Bree only smirked and said nothing.It didn't surprise Johan. At no point did he ever suspect Auron Bree had plans to be a martyr. It simply wasn't in his nature.

Auron pressed the option and watched as the screen went from deep blue to a large white number '5'.

"Johan, grab hold of the lift and your companion. This is going to be a lot faster than our arrival." Auron rushed back to the lift while Johan did as he was asked.

Johan held his breath and made sure Esgona was secured. Then he hit the deck as the counter reached "0" and beeped softly. The lift lurched forward, shaking them all and threatening to throw them off were they not pinned down and huddled together. Then, with none of the sluggishness from their trip here, the cart began speeding forward, gaining in momentum with every inch it covered.Wind rushed at their faces and even in the pitch-blackness they could feel the tight walls only an arm's-reach from their heads. The cart snapped back and forth, heading for the mysteries that lay ahead.

The ride was confusing and terribly fast. The cart lurched up and down like a thrill-ride, tossing them from side to side as it whipped back and forth. Johan and Auron held the handles and sides with death-grips, neither wanting to risk falling backwards.

Minutes later the narrow tunnel filled with a hard screeching noise, and the two who remained conscious now shifted to the front of the lift as the breaks kicked in. Soon, as if nothing was amiss and this was just another leisurely trip beneath the city, the tunnel opened into another large room and the transport came to a stop.

Exhilarated by the ride, Johan looked around the dimly lit room. It was similar to the one they'd just left only nowhere did there seem to be a way for them to rise up as they had before. Just a black ceiling above faint hanging lights.

"Johan, over there," said Auron, pointing into the darkness.

Johan followed his eyes and saw it. A grin appeared on his face at once. "You *double* son of a bitch," he said.

Sitting on a flat surface near the other side of the room sat a small, streamlined and obviously fast power cart. Once Johan had inspected it as best he could, he determined that it was a fuel-powered vehicle, likely chosen specifically by Auron because in the event of the electronic EMP getting down this far, the engine of this thing wouldn't be affected.

It was silver and the outside was smooth. A vehicle made for speed and little else. It had a high rigid frame that arched over the driver's and passengers' heads. The back was boxy and the front was low to the ground. Behind the only two seats was an open compartment that looked as if it was made to carry cargo.

Johan chuckled as they quickly loaded the dead weight of Esgona into the rear of the machine.

"What's so funny?" Auron asked as they moved him.

"Only two seats," Johan replied.

"So?"

"So it appears the bunch of us making an escape was never part of your plan."

"Johan, I can safely say that absolutely nothing today other than *your* part of things has gone to plan. Frankly, not a Gods damned thing about this situation was part of my plan."

Auron took the driver's seat as Johan hopped in beside him. After a 'click', the engine sprung to life with a soft rumble, and as Auron fumbled with the other switches the way ahead became instantly illuminated. A tunnel stretched out ahead of them, and a door opened on the far end.

Auron eased the throttle forward and the little cart pushed away with a jolt. Soon, they were breaking out into blinding daylight and onto a service path that connected to a major paved road beyond the eastern Bankoor city limits.

As they drove, Johan looked back to the walls of the city now shrinking in the distance and wondered how Aryu was doing. Auron paid the city no more heed. No matter what, this was the end of Bankoor. It would take years to rebuild the spire again, and without power, there could be no city. He was a politician before anything though, and that part of him said that this was the way it had to be. Oddly, things had turned out better than expected.

Over the shaking of the cart and the louder noise of the engine, Johan shouted to Auron, "Where are you going? We want to go north!"

"Not until we get far enough from Bankoor in case the bomb goes off."

"But it wasn't working!" Johan caught himself the moment he said it. That little fact wasn't enough to stop his string of luck lately.

They drove as far and as fast as they could when Johan looked back after Auron had turned them even harder east towards a forest that lined the foothills of the mountains, and then he saw the first light of the explosion behind them, followed by the sudden feeling of being kicked by a folm, and at last the sickening sensation of uncontrolled flight.

Even at speeds so fast that Johan was positive he'd never moved so quickly in his life, the outward pressure wave that burst from the city overtook them. It seemed that escape tunnel had already stretched them out a considerable distance. As the ripple swept over them, Johan could feel the breath get sucked from his lungs. Auron reached up and grabbed a handle above his left arm and simply braced himself.

The cart drifted through the air like a leaf on a breeze, floating away from the blast center. Johan caught his breath and watched as the world tumbled past them in all directions. Johan was certain they were dead once they landed. The area here was heavily forested, and if the trees didn't smash them, then the debris certainly would. They were so close. They'd almost made it.

Moments before they crashed, a series of large airbags burst out from all around the cart's body, wrapping the occupants in a cushioned balloon. It wasn't enough to make the impact painless, but it certainly saved all of their lives. They crashed and bounced away, ricocheting off unseen obstacles until their protective barriers popped or tore away in the chaos.

Once the flames of the bomb died away, the rumble echoed around Johan's world. It may have just been in his head, but he was afraid he'd never get rid of it. He unclipped himself and looked around. Auron was gone but he couldn't have been far. Johan's face was cut and bleeding.It was fortunate that they'd hit a thatch of trees that likely saved his life. They cushioned his fall even more and brought him to a relatively gentle stop. Now, to find the others.

Esgona was a crumpled body in the back of the cart. Although completely destroyed and likely never to work again, it was still in considerably better condition than Johan felt.Inside, cocooned within the roll cage and padding of the seats ahead was the twisted body of the boy who had tried to kill him, damaged more than when they started, but also alive, according to his breathing. It was more luck than he deserved, but at least Johan hadn't left them for dead.

Ignoring him, Johan tried to call out for Auron, only to have his voice break and crack with pain. He couldn't remember screaming when they were lifted, but it appeared he'd shouted himself hoarse. With a stagger not unlike Esgona's, Johan Otan'co slogged forward over fallen trees and twisted debris until he finally found the slumped form of his gracious host against a tree stump.

At once, he thought the worst, but when the older man inhaled sharply with a stuttering lip, he knew he was fine.

That left only the emotional pain for Johan to cope with now, and in the first few moments of trying he realized the whole truth. It was too much for him. Too overwhelming to really believe. Too amazing and horrible to grasp.

It was over. No more army. No more Bankoor. No more Embracers. No more battles and useless war. No more running to (or from) the next challenge.

No more Aryu. He never could have escaped the blast without killing that demon first and running or flying faster than he believed possible.

It was the simplest thought, but the one that hit him the hardest. Growing up, they each saw something in each other that connected them. A friendship of outsiders who found strength in each other. Strength against people like Esgona, who Johan happily realized he no longer owed his life to. Now they were even. Small victories in the face of such painful defeats.

So he sat as Auron shook loose his own cobwebs and looked back at the destruction and the plume of smoke that had been his city. Johan, covered from head to toe in wounds, cried. He cried until his face hurt from the contortions and a series of streaks from his tears lined his dark face. The glimmer of humanity not corrupted by politics understood, and Auron stepped away to test his legs and let Johan have his moment. He had much more to deal with now.

How long passed? Minutes? Hours? The sun said only a short time, but by the time he'd gotten past the worst of it, Johan felt as if it had been years. If there was ever doubt about any of his childhood remaining, now there could be no questioning that it was long gone. Johan felt sick with the loss.

Then he had another horrible thought, one Auron had considered immediately and was in the throes of dealing with.

What about the others? The innocent people? The ones who were running north? 'What about' were useless words. Everything had been reset for them now. Although Johan was hoping Seraphina had made it far enough away, there was always the possibility she had stayed to help others, or had been hurt in the shockwave. There was no way to know.

Johan never did finish his train of thought. He couldn't. They no longer had answers, so they did what he and Aryu did best: he set off to find some. New ones. Ones he wanted to hear. He was sick of only learning things they hated knowing.

Returning to the wrecked cart, they pulled Esgona from the gap he was lodged in and assessed the damage. Auron had a broken nose, that was certain, and Esgona's 'good' leg was twisted and likely snapped in more than one place. Other than some nasty cuts and strains, Johan seemed fine, but inside his body where the straps had tugged at him so forcefully he could feel the bruising already start to form. He feared he may have some more serious internal damage.

As the day became evening, the two had fashioned dollies from the parts of the cart they could scavenge, and then began the arduous task of fighting through the mess in front of them. As they moved, taking turns hauling Esgona out, Johan stopped and looked at the smoldering flat horizon where only hours before had stood the most amazing city he'd ever seen. After all the time to ponder the day's events, there was only one question on his mind. He seriously doubted a man like Auron Bree could answer it, but it was a question that demanded his voice.

"Do you think he died well?" Johan asked at last, without the hint of a quiver in his voice or tear in his eye. Auron was the only one to ask the question to, and the truth was that Auron likely didn't care one way or another.

The shred of uninfected humanity popped up again. "From what we saw, albeit briefly, I'd say so. But what I think is irrelevant. What do you think, Johan? He was your friend."

Johan smiled. "I know he did. Did you see him? He never looked so great. And the way he so willingly fought that thing! How else could he have gone?"

Auron nodded. It was truly a brave thing to face those odds so willingly. It seemed the men from Tan Torna Qu'ay were cut from some strong cloth.

Johan faltered, needing a moment before continuing. "I loved him. He was my brother, Auron. My brother and my best friend."

"I know. And he always will be. But you're not finished yet. There are still two remaining sons of Tan Torna Qu'ay."

"Fuck two! Two tried to kill us. Two can go to hell." Still, he was the one carrying Esgona, and as such felt the bitter pang of irony as they began to move forward again until the going became easier on the open road they'd come in on.

As they went, the sun fell and silence was replaced by the sounds of the coming darkness. Night birds and chirping bugs began to spring up as they moved.

"What do you do now, Johan? Where will you go?"

The last thing Johan wanted to think about was the future, but it had to happen at some point. The sinister thoughts of what to do about a certain elder Dragon Stalker up a frightening valley occurred to him. He'd made a promise, but the key element to that promise was now long gone. "I'm not sure, Auron. Try to find Seraphina. Hope Stroan made it out alright. My advice though, don't make any trips to the Thunder Run for the time being."

Auron wasn't sure what the meaning of that was, but guessed it had something to do with Johan's harrowing trip to get to Bankoor and left it at that.

Johan thought of the beast. Skerd said he wouldn't wait forever and he believed him. A creature like that didn't lie. Johan, however, took no pride in betraying his word to the monster. Trouble for another time, though. For now, only fighting to find others while they dragged the battered Esgona away mattered, with the youthful Johan doing the majority of the hauling.

Is this the life of the hero? Doing the brave things the rest of us never could, even if it meant losing everything you loved?

Night fell, and as the smell of smoke filled the Vein Valley, they walked on. One thing at a time. Always and forever, one thing at a time. Right now, just take another step forward.

***

Resting in a rolling green field far from the now-destroyed city, north of the people who had run from it, and well beyond the friend he now believed whole-heartedly was dead, and farther north still from anything he'd ever dreamed he'd see in his life just a few weeks ago, Aryu O'Lung'Singh rested. His body was a thousand shades of purple and reds from the bruises and blood. His arms were twisted, broken, and unmoving. His legs were the same. His chest oozed from where the Shi Kaze had been rammed through him and the mythical Makashi armor was now firm and stiff against his back; his mind no longer able to fully sustain it.

He was a broken man who had no more life to give and no more tears to cry. Only the pain was left, a pain he loathed and welcomed all at one time. True, with his new mastery of the Power he could likely cast away the pain, similar to what he'd done when he escaped the explosion and killing Izuku in the process, but he couldn't. He'd done enough damage with the Power and he deserved this pain. How many had died today by his hand? How many good people who did nothing wrong but try to help others before they helped themselves? How many innocent lives?

Now more than ever he despised the Power and everything it had done to this world.

How many died, including his very best friend, just because Aryu believed he was right? Was he really? Had he done what he had out of fear or bravery? What was the difference?

It was a last-second decision that even here, broken and in terrible pain, he knew he'd make again. They had promised themselves this revenge, and he had the only means to deliver it. An open and worthwhile chance to make things right again after everything had gone wrong.

Still, the heartache was enormous. Was his revenge really worth it?

Yes. To him, and he had to believe to his friend it was as well. It was more than the lives of the people of Tan Torna Qu'ay. More than the lives the enemy ruined all along the southern sea and northward. It was for everyone they were about to destroy beyond here. Izuku never would have stopped. He would have continued until he had succeeded. It was in his eyes: the madness that had consumed him. And now that Sho was gone, who could have stopped him?

Well, Aryu apparently, but even now he just considered that dumb luck.

Birds sang around him, oblivious to the perils of what had transpired so far south of here. How far had the Power taken him if he had traveled by foot? Days? Weeks? He had no idea. Even now, the moment the Power overtook him and whisked him away was nothing but a blur. The memory of the clarity it created was all that remained, a clarity he could grasp once more in an instant if he chose to. A clarity that successfully battled the frightening memory of the Est Vacuus, at least for the time being. No matter what, that was a memory that would never fully fade.

Now, he just waited. Waited for the image of the great phoenix to block out the sun, speak some kind words and do what he knew he must: destroy Aryu for willingly becoming an Embracer, and on top of that, using his grasp of the Power to destroy a multitude of other Embracers, including Crystal Kokuou. The great Nixon may not have had his answer before (an answer Aryu was still curious about) but he had it beyond a doubt now. Aryu had gone against him, and in doing so he had both doomed his soul and saved the world.

Aryu had all the faith in the world that he was only moments away from being destroyed by Nixon's flaming sword. What would happen to the shield and Shi Kaze then? The two items were sitting in the long grass next to him, silent and resting, save for the constant murmurs of their pasts calling out in voiceless whispers. Whispers Aryu O'Lung'Singh heard very clearly now. Whispers of joy and pain, life and death, glory and defeat. He heard the voice of Sho and Crystal, even Izuku. He heard the solid and deep voice of Allan Kokuou, Crystal's father. He heard the thousands of voices of the various users who had taken up this weapon for good and ill. What would happen to this now? Would Nix leave them here to be found or take them away, seeking his peaceful sleep at last?

Behind every voice was the one constant; a voice so far above each of them that Aryu had never noticed it before. A binding voice that was more of a gentle background wind than words. It was the voice of Tokugawa Ryu.

It wasn't as powerful and overwhelming as he'd thought it would be when he first heard it and knew it for what it was. His mental image of this false God among men was one of a Power-mad warriors who had lived a thousand lifetimes worth of pain and pleasure. What he got was an even, repetitive tone. A soft voice that only spoke of unification. The need to keep the conflicting forces within the sword together forever.

Balance, it whispered of. Forever keeping the balance.

Aryu waited. Since he was unsure where he was he was uncertain how long this would take. He took the time now to listen to that overarching voice, to better understand the man behind it. He was a young man who started even younger than Aryu down the path of the powerful. He was forced into a hard life, one filled with loss and love, only to rise up and become the most powerful entity the world had ever seen. There was a lesson there. A lesson Aryu wished to learn more of, were it not his time to die.

However, that time never came.

He waited there, fading in and out of consciousness, waiting for the great fire demon to arrive and finish him off. When the minutes turned to hours, Aryu began to worry that his wounds, specifically the one that ran right through him, would be what it was that did him in. This realization made him very scared. That was not how he was supposed to die. He knew that. He could feel it. He had to die at Nixon's hand. That was why he had done what he'd done so willingly. He knew that Nixon would understand, even if he still had to do what he must. Death by another means, even one caused in what he considered an extremely brave act, simply wouldn't do. It was for the honor of dying by Nix's hand that he did what he did, and that was the only way he wanted it.

So as the day began turning to night and the sun went down on this longest of days, Aryu made another decision. He would not die like this, alone and frightened in some alien valley so far from home, bleeding out from a list of wounds. He would die as he wanted to. As he was meant to. So, in an effort to both summon Nixon once more and keep himself alive until he arrived, Aryu focused his mind, his hand only lightly grazing the Shi Kaze's woven ray-skinned handle, and found himself within the glory of the Power once more.

As he channeled his mind and tapped the infinite expanse of the Power, he slowly, cell by cell, repaired the worst of his wounds. Now that he had time to actually focus on it, it didn't seem that hard. It was more difficult than navigating the electrical impulses of the bomb controls, but in actuality is was very similar. Soon, the hole that had been just below his heart began to close, until at last it was nothing more than flawless skin and strong muscles being fed rich youthful blood by a willing heart.

He opened his eyes in the dimly lit field once more, and a deep feeling of relief overtook him. That should buy him a few more hours, and there was no doubt Nixon would come now.

Once more, Nixon never arrived.

By now Aryu was certain something was up. Had Nixon been trapped in the blast? It was a possibility, but was that enough to stop him? Aryu had no way of knowing, but he knew Nixon had encountered a blast like this before and survived. Couldn't he do that again? All he knew was that Nixon wasn't here, and he had to ponder what to do next.

Darkness of the night was rich now and Aryu was very tired. Fearing sleep might bring death from his remaining wounds, Aryu once more tapped the Power to fix more of his ailments until he was confident enough he could either sleep or die by Nixon's hand when he at last came to him. He could feel the soothing feelings inside himself as he mended the damage he couldn't see from Izuku's attacks. Eventually he was sure he'd be able to rest without consequence.

Aryu slept, wrapped in his wings to fight off the chill. It was a harsh, dreamless sleep. It was the sleep of a man with a heavy conscience.

The sun came up once more to the east, and although Aryu

couldn't see it yet, he knew it was likely going to be another beautiful day. Still no Nixon. No wrath of God.

"Where are you, my friend?" he asked himself quietly. "I'm ready to go now. I've done too much to continue on alone."

Only the wind responded and it held no answers; just warm wishes.

After thinking about what could have gone wrong, Aryu decided two things were the most likely, though neither of them made much sense.

The first thought was that Nixon was still battling that machine he seemed so worried about, or perhaps the machine had done the impossible and beaten him, or at least incapacitated him. That wasn't likely. The Nixon he knew would have moved mountains to defeat an enemy, especially once he'd gotten the call to Aryu to finish his job. A possibility, but an unlikely one.

Not as unlikely as option two, however. That he was back asleep in the Lion's Den, or otherwise no longer drawn to Aryu. Both of these options were unlikely, but Aryu truly believed that nothing short of obliteration could call him off (an ironic thought, though he didn't know that). So, if that was what had happened, what did it mean? After everything Nixon had told him, the end was always the same. Aryu believed Nixon was correct, and Nixon did as he had to. As God had created him to.

After destroying so many Embracers, with the Power in the Shi Kaze no less, what possible way could Aryu escape retribution?

"If I did the right thing," Aryu began, beginning a terrible thought process, "then he would either go back to sleep or otherwise no longer be hunting me. So now, he wouldn't know where I am."

It made logical sense, even if he didn't believe it. He had killed so many, and even though his cause was noble, weren't a multitude of others Nixon had told him about? Fighting for what they *knew* was right, only to find out they were so terribly wrong?

It was hurting his head pondering these possibilities. Soon, he stopped and resumed his waiting. Nixon would come. He would defeat his enemy and arrive at last. He just had to wait. Sadly, that brought no new insights. What it did bring, however, was hunger.

Aryu hadn't eaten a square meal in a day and a half, and his aching body was telling him so.

Unable to move quickly due to his still partially-broken appendages, Aryu decided to once more test the waters of the Power, only this time, he did so confidently and without hesitation.

His logic was simple enough. He was dead. He was a dead man walking. He had sacrificed everyone and everything left that he had cared for and now he was alone, with no home or family remaining. He still fully expected Nixon to swoop in and finish things, just as he knew he was meant to. Until he overcame whatever it was that was delaying him, Aryu opted to continue on as best he could. How far or long would he make it? An hour? A day? A week? Nixon would come eventually. He had to. If he knew nothing else, he knew that.

And if he doesn't? he thought to himself after he'd mended his wounds and slowly came to his feet, body tense and protesting. He had no answer at first, but as he picked up the shield and the great Shi Kaze, placing it in the smooth sheath at his side and then moving it around his shoulders to his back once more, a reasonable one came to him.

"Then I live every day for them," he said aloud, shielding his eyes from the rising sun and looking for a direction of travel. "Every breath, every meal, every new memory made, I do for them. For all of them."

It was a moot point and he knew it. Nixon would come. Aryu didn't even believe death could stop that creature.

Seeing a collection of trees in the distance, he noticed beyond them what appeared to be a small lake with some houses on its banks. People. People unaffected by the Army of the Old, the explosion of Bankoor, and the wrath of Izuku or his Embracers. All because of him and his friends. "As good a place as any to start."

As healed as he needed to be, though still in pain (his conscience not allowing him any more salvation than he believed he needed or deserved) he set off for the distant town, sloping southwest from where he currently was. Where was he? How far had he really gone? How long did he have before Nixon took him at last?

No point in dwelling now, he realized. Having never been a

believer in fate, he didn't even care. It would be what it would be and nothing more.

Warm breezes blew through his tattered old clothes, the same dirty and torn collection he'd had on since this madness began. He didn't mind. Every strand and stitch could tell the story of where he'd been and what he'd seen, reminders he insisted stay with him. He scanned the sky, looking for a flaming ball of red anger, but found none. An oddity he wished he could explain.

His wings stretched out behind him, glad to be off the ground and compressed. The Makashi armor still lay dormant along his back, coating the skin above his spine like a tattoo. It could stay there, he thought. It had no place being out anymore. He hoped he could find a willing and worthwhile recipient of it before Nixon found him (not that he knew how to get rid of it, but he was certain he could figure it out when the time came).

Of course, people would see him and call him a freak, but after everything that had happened he didn't care. Eventually he may find someone who could see past his bloodied and mutated form and help him. Hell, according to Izuku, there was a whole collection of people like him.

Aryu stopped and remembered what it was Izuku had told him. *"You're not quite of this world,"* he had said. *"You just haven't found them yet."*

Aryu doubted it was lies or deceit. Likely it was just a stall tactic, but he still believed it was the truth. What had he meant?

"Bah! Fuck him!" Aryu said, pushing it aside. "Fuck him and his bullshit! He's dead, I'm alive, and that's all that matters!"

His words echoed through the open air, surrounding him. "To hell with him, and every one like him," he finished, remembering anew his hatred of Embracers of the Power. Considering he was alive, standing, and actually walking somewhere, it was a hypocritical thought, but he wasn't like them. He wanted no Power, no immortality, and no domination over the land and its people. He wanted no vast understanding of the Omnis and he certainly never wanted another encounter with the terror of the Est Vacuus. He only wanted to die in peace as he knew he was meant to. That couldn't be said for every

Embracer that may be left, or could possibly come from here on out. A sobering thought, but some of them might actually *want* to reach into those all-encompassing primeval forces.

With a smirk and a renewed pace for the lake and the people who lived by it, he had to laugh at the pleasing way the next thing that occurred to him entered his head, although he knew it wasn't likely to happen with the phoenix soon to be bringing him to Death's door. *Well, perhaps if I have the good fortune to see another day, I'll also live to try and stop those fools who don't know what they're getting into. No one is left alive who has seen what I've seen. I'll gladly steer them away.*

Insanity to be certain, but there in that moment, the seeds of what was to come were sewn. He had said it to himself in jest, but as one step became two—and two, four— and still Nixon never came, bit by horrifying bit, the fear of the phoenix subsided. Aryu wished for him to come. He wished for him to end this painful and lonely life. He wished for him to just arrive and tell Aryu he was wrong (or right, since that was a possibility too).Frankly, Nixon was the best friend Aryu had left in this world and he just wanted to see a familiar face, even if it was there to kill him.

In the meantime, Aryu walked on, sword on his back and shield at his side. While he waited, he would do as he promised. He would eat, sleep, live and breathe every moment for his fallen friends, and when the phoenix arrived at last, he would know that he would be the first Ryuujin of the People to die by Nixon's hand, thanks to this strange and unstoppable series of events.

That's something, he thought, taking what little pride he could in such a silly idea. *That is certainly something.*

Epilogue: In the Lion's Den

Time passed agonizingly slow from the moment the consciousness formed to the time the mind had the ability to piece together what had happened.

That was just for cognitive thought. The rest would likely take forever at this rate, and even then, just what state would the body be in? Would it even form together? These were all new paths to walk down, and it found itself scared at the possibilities. It wasn't accustomed to anything so new.

Bit by bit it came together until it felt mass and weight surrounding it once more. It knew then that this was not death, if indeed it could die. No, this was the same routine it had been through before, only, it was also very different.

Before, it had just reformed and continued on from where it started, but that wasn't happening here. Even though it was a long way from reforming its natural, God-given senses, it could tell right away that it was not where it was supposed to be. For reasons it couldn't begin to explain, it actually thought it was home. A place, if its memory was correct, it had no place being now.

It had a job to do. A very important one. This was the last place it wanted to be.

Still, as more and more of its core particles came back together, it was more and more certain that the place surrounding this rebirth was indeed its home.

How could tha' be? it thought once thought was possible. *How am I not back there, or at least destroyed? How'd I live?*

Vain questions until it could reform and see what had happened. Although it was curious, it was also upset. Reforming and starting again would mean hunting once more. Hunting one it had no desire to hunt. Hunting the one they should have killed in the first place.

For now, it could only wait, using what little ability it had to pull itself together.

Hours later?Days later?Years later? It had no way of knowing how much time had passed, but eventually the job was complete, and it took a moment in its newly-reformed body to assess its situation.

In the distance was the sound of ocean waves crashing on rocks. The smells were that of thick air and old wood. It rested on a hard rock platform.It was home. It was back where it had begun. But why? What had happened?It opened its fresh new eyes and sat up to find out.

It was on a harsh green plateau on high rolling hills, with the sun lost behind thick clouds giving the impression of it being almost dark when really it was the early afternoon. This was a feeling it generally loved; the beginning of a new day and a new hunt. Now, though, it was just confused and depressed at what these things meant.

Then it saw its body, and nothing made sense anymore.

Instead of the tall and strong body of a hardy warrior it had awoken with last time, Nixon of the Great Fire and Ash was shocked to find he (wait, he double checked. Yes, he's a man) was much smaller. He had a thin and lithe body with the same fiery red hair on his arms. He assumed his head was as well, only now instead of the falling reverse fire, his hair was short and well-trimmed with no trace of facial hair to be found.

He thought about this for a moment, and although awaking in a new body was nothing new to him, he wondered how on Earth he was supposed to catch and defeat Aryu O'Lung'Singh in this form. It just didn't seem possible.

He swung his naked legs over the side of the dark, cold pedestal he always awoke on when the time had come for the world to need him again. Looking over himself, he could surmise that he was in a younger form; likely resembling a man in his early twenties. He was toned and strong, but not as he was before. Where once he was large and imposing, now he was hard, like a well-trained athlete. His arms and legs were all well-defined and his stomach was tight. He was fast and light, or at least, he assumed he was. It was hard to say without a mirror.

Instinctually, he attempted to call upon the great armor he wore, always dark and fit to form. They were comforting coverings for one such as him.

This time, nothing happened.

He tried again, with the same results. This was a new development. Every time before he had simply formed his great armor and taken up his sword, followed by creating the great wings of fire and beginning his hunt. Once that meant finding a member of his devoted chorus, but he knew that wasn't going to happen this time. They were all gone.

Which was why when a voice came from behind him he was so startled. Without even processing what it had said, he turned and grabbed for his trusted sword, always resting in a mounted holster at his side.

Again there was nothing. Then he remembered losing it, throwing it away from fire from below that had consumed him in a desperate attempt to save it from his doomed fate.

But he was here, and it would seem he wasn't doomed at all. That simply meant he'd foolishly tossed away his greatest and most valued prize.

"I said," came the voice again, near one of the many other resting places similar to his that dotted the grassy wet hills of this land, "you'll need these. You can't go around with nothing on. It's unsightly, even in today's mixed up world."

He spun around looking for the source of the voice, still angered by all of the things that were going wrong here in the place he felt the safest and most at home. God, why had he thrown away his sword!

"Not bad though," said the voice. "You paint a fine-looking picture."

Now he saw her, her impish voice registering on a thousand levels. The anger grew. It was not a person who had any right to be here, and certainly no right to mock him this way.

Crystal Kokuou sat, legs crossed and dangling from an empty stone tomb that had once housed one of the many heroes of this land. Now it just lay in ruins. Only Nixon's remained in perfect form.

Nixon's, and one other, but that one would hopefully never

tarnish, even after Nixon was long gone. Indeed, when the world crumbled and the stars collided, *that* one would likely look as it did now, pristine and gleaming as if it had been freshly polished. However, thanks to a certain encounter he'd had with an extremely impressive mechanical man not long before, he knew that particular monument was missing a sword right now; a sword that looked just like his.

The cairn Crystal sat on was not gleaming. Indeed, it was dark and almost black, making her white skin and lacey, short dress stand out like a beacon. Her once long hair was cut to above her shoulders, giving her the look of a child in this light.

In her hand was a bag which she threw to his feet effortlessly. He ignored it, simply staring at her waiting for her to make some kind of move. She had to know that if she was to boldly step in front of him as she was doing now, she was going to have to fight to save her life. She had gone too far, and Nixon was primed and ready to end her and be done with it.

"It's clothes," she said, still half-smiling her perfect smile. "While you were, um, coming together, I found some I assumed were your size. I think I was right, but I'm sorry if I misjudged."

Still no movement from either of them. Nixon was ready for the fight, but also questioning every one of her motives in being here now. The fact that she'd even made it in was a very unsettling mystery. He never would have given her access, that was for sure.

Slowly, careful not to make any sudden moves, Crystal stepped down, her bare white feet being lost in the wet green grass of the highlands. "Frankly, you can run around like that all you want, but I just thought…"

"Wha' d'ya want?" he asked, scowling at her as he moved down from the flat rock, his voice noticeably higher than before.

"I want to apologize. Nothing more. I owe you that."

"Ya' owe me nothin'. Nothin' but a quick death, by my hand."

Her smile never faded. "I'd say I'm at the advantage, even on your home turf. Without your sword I'm more than a match for you."

It was true, but not an impossible task. He'd enjoy finding out. He wanted whatever shred of satisfaction he could muster out of this terrible and heartbreaking turn of events.

"I won't fight you, though. I just can't. Not anymore."

"Then this'll be a very brief encounter, I'd say," Nixon sneered back at her, taking a quick step forward. Thankfully, the welcoming feeling of the rising fire returned. At least *that* hadn't abandoned him.

She never moved, even as he closed the gap with murderous intent on his mind. She stood firm and watched as he got closer. When he was almost within striking distance, the fire of his existence rushed to the surface of his skin and his terrifying eyes glowed brightly. He was about to summon the flames when she stepped quickly aside and gracefully motioned to the platform she had just been sitting on.

Confused and distracted, he foolishly looked. She didn't attack. Instead saw what she wanted to show him.

It was his beautiful and trusted sword, resting peacefully and awaiting his hand, the familiar voice of its history instantly whispering into his mind.

Unthinking and eager like an addict needing their fix, he rushed at it, snatching it up in his hands and relishing the surging power it gave him. Then he turned, sword ready, and faced her again.

Even with the now-flaming sword only inches away from her face, Crystal didn't move. It was almost comically large in the hands of this new-formed, more compact Nixon Ash, but he still wielded it as if it was made of feathers and wind. She could tell it was no less dangerous in his hands now as it was when last they had seen each other.

"I will not fight you, Nixon. I wanted you to have that back so I brought it. Nice move, throwing it away to avoid the blast. I found it on the outskirts of the explosion's ring, near the Blood Sea shore. It was a hell of a throw, really. You're just lucky it was me who found it and not someone less trustworthy."

He inched closer, enraged at her taunting. She still stood firm, red eyes locked on his while the heat of the sword enveloped her. "Strike me down, Nixon," she said, smile fading to nothing. "Strike me down and kill me. I know you want to. I want you to. I did what I had to: returned your sword and saw you safely returned to this world. Strike me down and end this forever. You and I both know I have nothing left."

She didn't cry as she said this. It was more a matter of fact. This realization stayed his hand for the moment. She had truly lost it all.

Just like him.

With a heavy sigh, he lowered the sword to their feet. "I can'nah strike ya' down," he said. "Not yet. I think tha' would be too much, e'enfer me. One day, maybe, when all this is over and ya' cross the line, but right now there's much worse things in the world than you."

"Ha," she smiled back, "I killed six Embracers in that last battle before everything went to shit. If not for your need to hunt Aryu, you'd have been on my doorstep in a heartbeat."

It was true. Only Nixon's pull toward Aryu saved her. A pull he still felt now, stronger than ever. Aryu was east of here. Far east. He knew that for certain. "You feel him now, don't you?" she asked. "Feel the pull again?"

"Aye, I do. Strong and fierce it is. To the east. That's where I'll find 'im and end this." He returned to the bag that she had thrown him and pulled some basic cotton clothes from it. Until he could figure out what to do about his armor, these would have to do.

Crystal only watched as he dressed himself and placed his giant sword on his back, giving him a look that was more laughable than fierce. "You still want to kill him? Even after what he did? Didn't he save the world? Save it from Izuku?"

"No Crystal. He saved 'imself and followed 'is own path. I've no idea wha' went on, but I know there was another way. He opted t'use the Power on the bomb t'destroyeverythin' instead of jus' usin' it t'surprise Izuku. Had he just killed Izuku, this wouldn't'a be an issue, but he knew it would destroy all of the machines, working or no, and he also knew it would destroy the Embracers. Where he could've simply shocked Izuku and defeated him, Aryu opted t'take 'em all out, willingly and with the help of the Power."

"So he used the Power to kill a bunch of Embracers?"

"Yes, which is why I have a need t'hunt 'im now. It's why I always had to…"

Sadness and understanding came to each of their faces. "You know now, don't you," Crystal asked, knowing the answer. "You know why it was you were sent after him."

"I do. Is it why ya' thought? I assume ya' know too?"

She nodded. "I do. You hunted him because he *had* to be hunted. He was supposed to be killed all along, just as your God demanded of you. To let him live would make him the most unstoppable and dangerous force since Ryu. The Omnis couldn't have that kind of shift again, so it spun its damn wheels and wove its fibers through space and time and sent you to stop it before it could happen. Uncharacteristic of it, but not impossible.

"But now we just have an unstable child with three deadly weapons, a mild understanding of the Power and a serious hate for Embracers *and* anything mechanical. He's a seething young pool of conflicting emotions."

"Yes," Nixon said, eyes trailing off to the distant horizon where the ocean continued to pound away. "I was a fool. I ne'er should 'ave doubted it. I ne'er should 'ave doubted my purpose. Doing so doomed thousands t'death at the hands of a young man who simply didn't'na understand."

He looked back at her, longing suddenly for the days when he towered over her impressively. Now they were almost eye to eye. A reminder of how things had changed. "There'll always be Embracers, and it's not 'is place or anyone else's but mine t'tell 'em when they've gone too far, and it certainly isn't anyone's place, myself included, t'punish people 'fer what they *could* become. Only wha' they are. People, even Embracers of the Power, always 'ave free will; a right t'choose how they live and who they'll be. All they need is a taste of the balance of the world t'set 'em right…"

He looked at her deeply, a cold realization coming to him. "Which was why ya' did wha' ya' did, isn't it? Why ya' tapped the Est Vacuus 'fer Izuku? Why ya played both sides? T'provide that needed balance t' the world. If ya' made the ultimate evil, the worl' would naturally create the ultimate good. You'd push the powers of the universe t'unstable levels. Embracers would then rally t'their causes, battles 'wud be fought, and in the end there'd be balance. All ya' needed was a hero. But instead of creatin' the strongest Ryuujin of the People, all ya' did was create an unstoppable Adragon of the Rage!"

She looked away ashamed as the words filled the air. "This was jus' another attempt t'bring about the balance yer' father believed was needed, wasn't it. Another chance t'finish his long-forgotten work. God help us, Crystal, Wha' did ya do?"

"*I did what I had to!*" she lashed out, her considerable power rushing to the call of her emotions. "You have the power to do it, but all you do is sleep until your long-dead God needs you! Well guess what! The world needs you too, Nixon! With you passed out on a rock in Scotland, the world was rocketing backwards, casting off the Power for the hammer and nail again! Remember the last two times that happened! Everyone on the planet suffered for centuries! I did what I know needed to be done! I made my enemy, and then I made my hero, and I was so *close*! One mistake!" Her raised voice began to fade as her eyes became wet. "He just made one mistake and now we all have to suffer for it."

"Which was why ya' ne'er told me why it was I had t'kill him." Nixon surmised. "If ya' did, you'd lose yer' chance." She looked at him through teary eyes, acknowledging this as the truth without saying a word. "Well, now look wha' you've done. Ya' chose yer' champion poorly, Crystal. Now he needs t'be stopped before he throws the balance so far out of whack it canna' be recovered." He steadied himself under the size of his sword and turned his back to her. "So now I 'avet'go end this just like I was supposed t' from the beginnin'."

He began walking away, in no way looking forward to what it was he had to do, when Crystal called to him again. Softly, but direct and unmistakable. "You can't," she said. "It's impossible."

He stopped, turning to her again. "Ya' doubt I can defeat 'im? It won't be easy, physically or emotionally, but I assure ya' I can."

"No, Nixon. You can't."

He smirked defiantly. He most certainly could. "Wha' makes ya' so certain?"

She stood fully upright, letting the wind push her soft dress in any direction it could, with her red eyes holding his so she could truly convey the seriousness of what she had to say. "You can't defeat him, because you can't catch him."

Ridiculousness, he thought. He'd caught him before, he could do it again.

Suddenly the reality of what she said hit home. "You can't catch him, because you promised not to. The second you realized why it was you had to hunt him, you had your answer, the answer you had been looking for all along. Once you had that, your deal was fulfilled. From then on, you can no longer hunt him because as you promised: you and Aryu will never meet again."

Nixon was shaken at once. Bullshit! This was so much bigger than that stupid deal! This was his duty! That was just a deal he made to a weak young man who was scared and confused. Now he was a dangerous threat to the world, a threat that *had* to be dealt with.

But it wasn't that simple, and he knew it. '*Never to be bothered by you and your threats of death ever again*' was what Aryu had said. A deal Nixon had agreed to. A simple, harmless deal. "God will let me…" Nixon faltered. "God made me fer' this purpose."

"God will not allow you to go back on that deal, Nixon. God made you with free will, but your purpose is always His. And what's the one thing we learned about your God in all of this, Nixon?"

Nixon looked crushed, as if he'd just been beaten senseless. "That God is truly infallible," he said quietly.

"A deal is a deal, especially in God's eyes. To find him is to break that promise and prove that your God has faults, something even you yourself do not believe. You can hunt him all you want, Nixon. I almost insist you do, but I'm quite certain you will never catch him. A new enemy.An old friend.An exploding city. Something will always stop you."

"I… I have t'try. I can't live with this pull fore'er. I need rest. I can't go on so endlessly, chasin' someone I can ne'er catch."

"As I said, go for it, if only to learn that I'm right. When that happens, maybe together we can find another way."

He looked at her curiously. "Together?"

"I'm as guilty as you. More so, actually. You promised not to hunt him. I didn't, but I suspect I'll need the help of an expert. Perhaps we can help each other?"

"Unlikely," he scowled. He still wasn't terribly fond of her and what she had done, considering what the consequences had become.

He may not have killed her now, but a large part of him still wanted to.

"I understand. The offer is always there. Besides, I've got other matters to attend to in the time being."

Nixon understood. "Sho."

Crystal nodded, her short white hair bobbing. "Yes. Death spared me his body when he came to claim it. One last gesture from the Dark Stranger as penance for the crime that specter committed with his father. I took Sho home. Back to the place he tried so hard to keep alive. Now without me it will just die out, if it hasn't already while I've been waiting for you."

Nixon looked sadly at the surroundings. He knew that behind this dank-yet-beautiful countryside was a smoky ruin devoid of life. As painful on the eyes as it was the heart. He didn't want that to be true of someplace else in the world. Not if he could help it. "Very good. I should like t'return there one day, t'pay my respects."

"You are always welcome, Nixon. My door is always open to you."

"And mine t'you I see."

"Well, with no one but you to keep the door locked, Avalon mostly stays in a state of flux. With the right key, one can get in."

"That would require the right key," he said. "Do ya' have it?"

She walked back to the stone she had been sitting on, reached behind it, and produced a knife. Actually a dagger. One Nixon knew very well. "Well now, where did ya' e'er find tha'?"

"Truthfully I wasn't looking for your sword when I found it. I was looking for this. I realized that the blast was fueled by a very familiar source of the Power, and there are only two places to find it."

Nixon realized that she spoke the truth. The blast did have the mark of an Embracer. He hadn't noticed it in the fear and pain of the explosion, but he saw it clearly now. How else could such a weapon have destroyed him so utterly? "It's been a long time since I saw tha'. I assume it wasn't yer' doin' bringing it back t' this world?"

She shook her head. "No, I wouldn't have dared. Only the Shi Kaze and Izuku's damned weapon were my doing. I suspect Izuku did this as a way to keep me in line once we met the first time. What better way to counter me than using my own item of Focus."

"The great Yayoki dagger. I ne'er thought I'd see it again."

"Trust me, if I had my way you wouldn't, but here it is, only not in as great of shape as I'd like." She walked over to him, eventually handing him the weapon she had once used to focus her Power as a child. It was a true sign of her submission to this whole situation that she even dared handing it to him in the first place. As he took it, he saw at once what she meant. On the blade, halfway between hilt and tip, was a small hole no bigger than a pinprick.

"Impressive is the device tha' can damage an item of Focus," he said, handing it back to her.

"Scary, you mean. I never knew mankind had come so far."

"So wha' now? Cast it back into some unknown abyss?"

"I wish. No, I can't. When I found it, I learned it had a new purpose." She held it up before him, letting him 'see' it for the first time in centuries. At once the glory of its history flooded his mind, reminding him of times long passed when they had fought the same enemies and thwarted countless evils.

But then, the voices shifted, and the ones he heard spoke of the darkness where it had been lost (*Oh Crystal, just where did ya' hide this?*). Eventually it told him of being found by Izuku, handed around, and then falling into the care of another young man; a man who had made a deal with a very powerful enemy. Nixon understood.

"Ya' need t'find tha' young man and return it t'him," he said. It was a statement, not a question.

"I do. If the Dragon Stalkers of the world turn on mankind, I can't count the number of lives that would be lost. Besides, I figure I've helped doom enough people for one lifetime."

He agreed, but said nothing. "And wha' of the Est Vacuus? Did yer' search determine anything about tha'?"

"Yes," she answered, "I can't feel it anywhere. It, like Izuku, is long gone. I don't know what Aryu did with it, if it was even him at all, but it's not anywhere I can find it, and there aren't many places in this universe that I can't look." She took the dagger back and placed it in a concealed sheath on her back. "Where will you go?" she asked him.

He shrugged. "I need t'find Aryu. I need t'know the truth. Can I catch him? Can I orchestrate his death from afar? Can I be involved in any way? Just how literal is my God?"

"Very, Nixon, we know that all too well." Very true, he thought. "But I wouldn't be so rush-rush to get out there if I were you."

He gave her a confused look that needed an answer. "You still have a follower." At first Nixon didn't understand, but then he remembered Elutherios Duo. The machine that had stopped him and almost destroyed him the first time. It might be still out there, with its prime purpose in life being the destruction of the phoenix. Izuku's last cursed gift to the world.

"You're right," he said. "I need to find a way t'follow without bein' followed." The thought of a creation like that still roaming the Earth made his head ache. Izuku likely had no idea just what it was he had created.

Eventually, he simply agreed to himself that what had to be would be. If that Power-fueled bomb hadn't stopped him, perhaps Elutherios couldn't either? He didn't have a lot of desire to find out, and planned on avoiding the man-made demon whenever possible. Every adventure to come had to start with a single step. "How far behind am I?" he asked. "How much time has passed?"

Crystal straightened herself, also preparing to venture out of the safety of ancient Avalon. "Seven months. I've been watching over you. Waiting. You and I are the last of a dying line, Nixon Ash. Like it or not, we're in this together."

He looked at Crystal again, understanding what she meant. They were the last vestiges of a time of honor and Power that would likely never come again. They were as close to mortal enemies as they were to good friends. He couldn't waste time with her now, though. He had a job to do. He looked at her with seriousness in his eyes.

"Crystal Kokuou, daughter of Allan. You were a friend and ally t'me. Thank yer' father one last time, because not killin' ya' 'ere with the holy Cliamh Solais is my last favor t'his memory. Ya' acted in his interests, but much too foolishly. I pray ya' remember 'is true message: tha' keepin' the balance is ne'er easy and tha' one must be always willin' t'accept tha' it may be impossible. I bid ya' well. Find 'yer peace and think on 'yer mistakes, because they're so numerous tha' they may crush 'yer soul. One day, when 'ya finally realize the truth, and if I'm around, we'll drink t'gether one last time."

With a bow and wave, Nixon turned to go, leaving her behind as the winds picked up and a misty rain began to fall. Soon, he was gone beyond the borders of the Haven known as Avalon and back into the world as it truly was, and Crystal was left alone.

40422196R00154

Made in the USA
Middletown, DE
26 March 2019